Lord of the Dance

Stories by Andrew M. Greeley

The Cardinal Sins
THE PASSOVER TRILOGY
Thy Brother's Wife
Ascent into Hell
Lord of the Dance

Lord of the Dance

Andrew M. Greeley

W.H. ALLEN · LONDON
1984
A BERNARD GEIS ASSOCIATES BOOK

Copyright © Andrew Greeley Enterprises Ltd 1984

First published in the USA by Warner Books, Inc.
First British edition 1984

A Bernard Geis Associates Book

Typeset by Phoenix Photosetting, Chatham
Printed and bound in Great Britain by
Mackays of Chatham Ltd, Kent
for the Publishers W H Allen & Co Ltd,
44 Hill Street, London W1X 8LB

ISBN 0 491 03223 4

Grateful acknowledgement is made to Sydney Carter,
author of 'Lord of the Dance' for permission to reprint
selections of his poem. Copyright © 1963 by Galliard Ltd.
All rights reserved. Used by permission of Galaxy Music
Corp., NY, sole US agent.

For the Brennans – friends in need

WIPEOUT

Skilled ballerina spinning on the spray
She slices through the wake with disdainful ease
A mature woman, elegant at play
Aloof, discreet in her capacity to please
Then the tizzy teenage trickster topples from her skis
Cartwheels through the air, dancing on her face
A carnival comic choreography
A somersaulting epiphany of grace

Devised by God to guarantee the race
Who gifted them with smiles to incandesce the day
Sculpted summer sunbursts to celebrate in space
And with Technicolor splash our humdrum gray
A designer impeccable in taste
Such sacraments crafted to delight us on our way

The only God worth believing in is a dancing God.

Friedrich Nietzsche

Resurrection isn't easy.

Noele Farrell

I danced on Friday when the sky turned black
Oh, it's hard to dance with the devil on your back
They buried My body and they thought I'd gone
But I am the dance and the dance goes on
Dance, dance, wherever you may be
I am the Lord of the dance, said He
And I will lead you all wherever you may be
I'll lead you all in the dance, said He.

'Lord of the Dance'
Sydney Carter

There is a universal belief that the dance,
in so far as it is a rhythmic art-form,
is a symbol of the act of creation.

A Dictionary of Symbols,
page 76

Now
there was only the morning
and the dancing man of the broken tomb.
The story says
he dances still.
That is why
down to this day
we lean over the beds of our babies
and in the seconds before sleep
tell the story of the undying dancing man
so the dream of Jesus will carry them to dawn.

'The Storyteller of God'
John Shea

Disclaimer

It would appear that some readers are the victims of an incurable if not altogether harmless affliction of knowing better than the author who his characters 'really' are. Since nothing can dissuade them from this obsession, it is useless for me to try to tell them that the Farrell clan and all the other characters that inhabit this story are totally fictional and products of my own imagination. Nevertheless, I do assert and warn such readers that a search for resemblances between my characters and actual persons is pursued at the considerable risk of deepening their own obsession.

The portraits in my gallery of minor characters – priests and provosts, politicians and publicists, padrinos and political scientists, punks and prelates, publishers and professors – are drawn from recognizable Chicago types but are based on no one in particular. Nor are the incidents involving the members of the gallery, not all of whom are rogues, by the way, replays of specific incidents or events.

As for the major characters, I know of no priest/TV personality like John Farrell, no professor/politician like Roger Farrell, no naval officer like Daniel Farrell, no secret storyteller like Irene Farrell, no businesswoman like Brigid Farrell. I have known a couple of score of young women like Noele Farrell, but she is all of them and none of them.

I do not necessarily approve of the moral behaviour of my creatures. Nor do any of the characters speak with my voice, save occasionally Father Ace.

I wish to thank Sydney Carter for writing 'Lord of the Dance' and Mary O'Hara for singing it.

The Passover

The Easter Eve ceremony of fire and water, anticipated somewhat vaguely in the Jewish Passover's memory of the pillar of fire over the waters of the Red Sea, is the high point of the Christian Passover Triduum. The fire and water service was adapted from Roman pagan spring rites in the fourth century. The union between the male (fire) and the female (water) was interpreted by the early Christians to mean that when Jesus rose from the dead, his marriage to his spouse, the church, was consummated, and that those who are baptized in the waters of Easter are the first fruits of this union. It is therefore the Christian conviction that the fire and water ceremony of Easter Eve tells the story of human love that is a correlation and continuation of divine love.

FARRELL FAMILY TREE

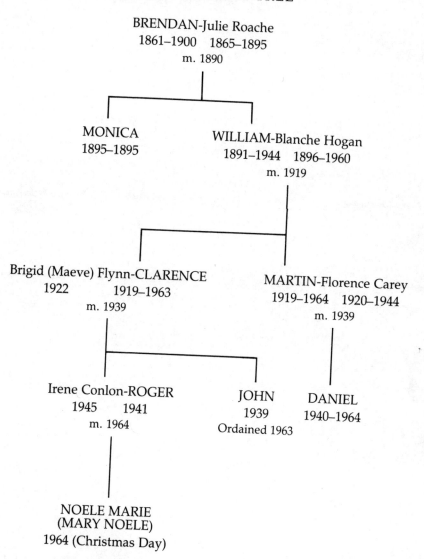

BRENDAN-Julie Roache
1861–1900   1865–1895
m. 1890

MONICA
1895–1895

WILLIAM-Blanche Hogan
1891–1944   1896–1960
m. 1919

Brigid (Maeve) Flynn-CLARENCE
1922   1919–1963
m. 1939

MARTIN-Florence Carey
1919–1964   1920–1944
m. 1939

Irene Conlon-ROGER
1945   1941
m. 1964

JOHN
1939
Ordained 1963

DANIEL
1940–1964

NOELE MARIE
(MARY NOELE)
1964 (Christmas Day)

M. N. Farrell
Class 3-A
Social Studies

FIRST
DANCE

Valse Triste

Tomorrow shall be my dancing day,
I would my true love did so chance
To see the legend of my play,
To call my true love to my dance
Sing, oh! my love, oh! my love, my love, my love,
This have I done for my true love

'My Dancing Day'
A Medieval Good Friday Carol

Glowing in the distance, cool, firm, confident, the Hima-layas reminded him of Irene. Irish male breast fixation, she would say with an amused little smile. He would reply that at least he had good taste in his fixations. And she would blush with delight, limitless in her capacity to absorb compliments.

He had made the prescribed sweeping turn over the Sinkiang plateau at a point a hundred miles short of the Russian border. At least his sextant, a dubious instrument at best, assured him that Russia was still a hundred miles away.

Halfway home. The sun now at his back. The prevailing winds, too. May the wind be at your back. A long way from the old neighbourhood, where that was a wedding toast.

And may you be in heaven a half hour before the devil knows you're dead. . . .

He grinned. No toast yet for him. Jackie would have to give it when he got back. . . . No, not the ruggedly handsome young priest, better the intellectual – Roger. Something more elaborate than an old Irish American cliché. . . . Damn. He missed them both. Too much of their father, Clancy, in them. Still, they were mostly Bri-gid's kids. . . .

Six more hours. The station chief had told him it was the less important half of the trip, not that you could believe anything they said there. He was stiff and uncomfortable in his pressure suit. This giant blackbird, for all its soaring grace, was more cranky than the others. It needed careful nursing every mile.

You flew over the Himalayas because they were there – and on the way to his destination in northern Thailand. They made him think of Irene again.

Was her ability to forgive as great as her passion? He thought it might be. Lord knows she would have to forgive him for the rest of their lives.

The sun turned the mountains red, reminding him of another haunting image: his uncle Clancy at the foot of the stairs, blood pouring from his head, all that anger snuffed out, looking like a broken Christmas toy.

And then more blood: a young woman's face. Not Irene. Someone else. His mother, probably. She and Irene were often confused in his dreams.

What had really happened to his mother on that day? Did he remember it? Or did he merely remember the stories he had heard when he was older?

A beautiful young face, smashed bloody like Uncle Clancy's. And he was responsible both times.

He would not let it happen to Irene.

Another year and a half on his contract. What could the Chinese be doing down there that was so interesting? In a year they would have spy satellites and they wouldn't need the great blackbirds, half jet and half sailplane.

They would find some use for them, though. And for the kooks who flew them.

They traded the Russians for Gary Powers. No trades with the Chinese.

God, I need Irene. Okay, God, since I brought you up, you know how much I need her.

And she needs me. She'll never survive them without me.

Irene leaning over him on the beach, her long hair touching his motionless body, tantalizing him until he thought he would lose his mind; then the edge of her fingernails . . .

And her blunt warning that he would have to grow up. Their last day together and their last fight.

He hardly noticed the flameout; there was only a change in the sound and an ever so slight downward tilt of the bird. It had happened before. Let her float a few thousand feet and start it over.

—4—

He tried at 60,000, 55,000, 50,000. No dice. The Chinese MIGs could make it no higher than 45,000 – that's what they told him.

The bird floated lower. 30,000 and still no MIGs. 25,000. Time to jettison, destroy the plane, walk out of Sinkiang.

Where to? Russia?

He pushed the eject button. No reaction. Sixty seconds and the plane would blow up. He pushed the button again. Still no ejection.

Something was beginning to smell. He watched the second hand sweep on his watch: thirty, twenty, ten . . .

Forgive me, I love –

No explosion. Something badly wrong.

Then the MIGs, dancing up to him like angry mosquitoes. The little puffs of light from their tracers. Shoot first, little Chinese friends, ask questions later.

Put the plane into a dive, evade them, try the motor again. It wouldn't start. A MIG following him down. More tracers.

A kaleidoscope of faces. His mother, eyes open and staring; Brigid, her white lace gown torn and covered with blood; Clancy, blood pouring from his head; John, the self-satisfied young priest; Roger, the faintly supercilious intellectual; Irene . . .

Dear God.

Irene.

DANCE
TWO

Pavane

Pour
une Infante Défunte

'A slow, processional type of dance, often combined with a galliard, and later with the saraband and the gigue, and occasionally a hornpipe, into the classical suite.'

John

'What was Uncle Danny REALLY like?' Noele Farrell handed her uncle an old newspaper clipping, her green eyes flashing dangerously.

Monsignor John Farrell regretted that he had scheduled this interview with his niece on Saturday morning. Jim Mortimer would be along shortly, and he should be planning a strategy for dealing with the cardinal's emissary instead of dodging questions about the Farrell family past. And there was a month of parish records to catch up on before confessions this afternoon. In the old days curates had done that sort of work.

'He really wasn't your uncle, Noele,' he said wearily, 'even though he and your father and I were raised together. He was our cousin and not our younger brother.'

Noele made an impatient face, a princess displeased. 'I know *that*,' she said, dismissing his passion for precision. 'It's easier for me to think of him as an uncle than a cousin. Right?' CHICAGO PILOT REPORTED MISSING OVER CHINA, said the black headline from the *Chicago Tribune* of seventeen years ago. John Farrell did not need to reread the story: The Chinese government reported that People's Liberation Army jets had shot down an American spy plane over Sinkiang, the vast and unpopulated steppe in western China, and that a CIA spy, Daniel X. Farrell of Chicago, was killed in the crash. The American government denied any knowledge of the plane or of Daniel X. Farrell. The Farrell family said through a spokesman that Daniel Farrell, a graduate of Annapolis, had left the United States Navy the previous year after three years of active service and was understood to be working in a secret government job. 'The son of the late Commander and Mrs Martin Farrell and the nephew of the late Clarence 'Clancy' Farrell, president of Farrell & Sons Construction Company, Daniel Farrell was a member of one of Chicago's most politically powerful families, a family that has been dogged by tragedy. . . .'

'Why is it necessary to understand Danny?' John asked. 'As a matter of fact, why is it necessary to write a term paper about our family history?'

Noele smiled, flashing two rows of flawless white teeth. 'It is necessary to do the term paper, Uncle Monsignor, because S'ter Amanda assigned it, and it's necessary to understand Uncle Danny because he is part of my heritage.'

'Don't try to glamourize him, Noele.' He placed the newspaper clipping on the carefully polished oak of the rectory office desk and straightened the edges of the red leather blotter. 'Danny was a charming, witty, gifted child on his way to wasting his life. He was thrown out of the Navy for telling off a commanding officer. Then he took a crazy job with the CIA because he wanted to make a lot of money in a hurry. He thought he was going to be a writer or something of that sort. And he drank too much. If he hadn't died in that plane crash, he would probably be an incurable alcoholic by now. I think God did all of us a favour, including Danny, when he called him home early in life.

'Let the dead bury their dead,' he continued heavily. 'You're almost seventeen now, Noele. Soon you'll be an adult with adult responsibilities. It's time for you to discover what life is all about, to become serious and mature. . . .'

'Yuksville.' Noele's lips dismissed maturity with quick contempt.

Trying to tame Noele, John realized, was like riding a spring storm. Yet she had to be tamed if she was to be prevented from doing herself great harm.

—10—

And everyone else in the family too.

'It's true,' he continued, trying to sound relentless. 'And wasting your time daydreaming about Dan Farrell, dead for all these years, is simply not mature behaviour.'

A cloud seemed to appear in Noele's glowing green eyes, a cloud, perhaps, of shrewd suspicion. John stirred uneasily and wished the phone at his elbow would ring. One moment she was a giggly, gum-chewing sixteen-year-old, talking the strange teenage version of English, and the next moment an all-knowing, ageless witch.

'You sound like you didn't like him very much, Uncle,' she said softly. 'And why don't you want me poking around in the family past?'

John tried not to gasp in surprise. Once again Noele, without apparently noticing what she was doing, had responded not to what he'd said but to what he'd thought.

She was not a lush, full-bodied Venus like her mother, but rather a lithe, slender Diana, a dancer and a gymnast with the graceful movements of a ballerina or an Italian policeman directing traffic or a hypnotist conjuring up miracles. You almost did not notice her trim body and finely curved facial features because you were so startled by the colours of her beauty. She was a Celtic goddess in the nineteenth-century illustrations of Irish folklore books, strange, unreal, almost unearthly. Her long, bright red hair, contrasting sharply with her pale, buttermilk skin, swept across the room after her like moving fire. Her green eyes absorbed you as if you were a glass of iced tea on a hot summer evening; they were neither soft green nor cat green, but shamrock green, kelly green. She seemed a pre-Christian deity, a visitor from the many-coloured lands of Irish antiquity.

'On the contrary, Noele, I liked him enormously; so did everyone.' He hoped he sounded sincere. The words were at least partially true. 'Danny was one of the most charming and delightful men I have ever known, with a fantastic sense of humour. . . . You never knew what crazy trick Danny would do next.'

'It must have been hard on you and Dad and Grams when he was killed so soon after Grandpa Clancy died.'

John wet his lips nervously. How much did she know about Clancy's death?

'It was very hard on your grandmother, Noele. She loved Danny like a son. In fact, your father and I, we used to kid her that he was her favourite son.' They never would have dared say that. Brigid's fury was often much greater than her husband's because she could be angry cold sober. Only Danny dared defy her. John occasionally wondered if Brigid had had a love affair with Martin, her brother-in-law and Danny's father, long ago. She was capable of it, God knows. That might explain her delight in Danny and her grief when Danny died.

Damn him. And damn Brigid, too. A notorious and public sinner.

'And she was only a few years older than your mother is now,' John continued. 'Awfully young to lose a husband. And especially because he was, well, moderately drunk, something that didn't happen to Dad very often. But you know Grams. She pulled herself together and took charge of everything.'

Noele was looking at a photograph of Danny in his white naval aviator's uniform that she had taken for a folder full of clippings, notes, and family pictures. 'I wonder what he would have been like if he had lived. Maybe he would have surprised us all. He sure was cute. . . . Is the CIA certain he was killed?'

'The CIA never admitted to us that he was working for them. But Congressman Burns, the father of our present Congressman Burns . . .'

'I know all about the Burns family, Uncle,' Noele said complacently. 'I mean, like totally, right?'

'Oh, yes, I forgot that our next Congressman Burns is a special friend of yours.'

'Jaimie is going to be a senator,' Noele announced with the timeless confidence of an Irish woman who has planned her man's life for him. 'At least if he listens to me he is. ANYWAY, what did his grandfather find out from the CIA?'

'The man who came to visit him in Washington wouldn't admit he was with the CIA but said that the Chinese didn't have the anti-aircraft guns to shoot down a U-2. They had learned the plane had crashed because of some mechanical failure, and Danny survived the crash but died later, either because of injuries or because the Chinese executed him. That's all we were told.'

Noele shook her head sadly. 'Poor Danny. . . . Well, Uncle Monsignor, you've looked at your watch five times in the last two minutes, so I'd better gather up my notes and go home and start to write the paper – after I watch Jaimie beat Miami on TV.' Noele bounded up from her chair, scattering the folder of family photographs on the plush carpet of the rectory office. With pantherlike grace she was on the floor scooping them up before John Farrell could move from his custom-made executive's chair.

'Hey, this relative is totally gorgeous. Notre Dame sweat shirt, too; they haven't changed much, have they? Which one is she, Uncle?'

'That's a picture of Flossie Carey, Danny's mother, before she married my Uncle Martin.'

'Did they ever have funny hairstyles in those days.'

Poor Flossie. She had been gorgeous. Should have stayed away from the Farrells.

How many bitter fights with her son, Daniel. And good times, too. Great fun ditching Roger. John had hated Danny Farrell's guts, and at the same time adored him. When he thought he was in love that summer at Grand Beach, it was Danny who persuaded him to return to the seminary. Said the girl was worthless. Then fell for her himself. . . .

All the Farrells in Noele's dossier are dead. . . .

'I know they're dead,' Noele said, responding to his thought again, 'but they're part of me. And I have to know who I am.'

The rectory door bell chimed as he opened the office door for her, an office carefully designed to create an atmosphere of solid, dark brown warmth. He checked his reflection in a mirror in the hallway to make sure his razor-cut, stylishly long hair was properly arranged and his clerical suit as trimly fitting as it ought to be.

The housekeeper, somewhat awed, was admitting Monsignor James Mortimer.

John introduced Noele to Monsignor Mortimer with a touch of pride. Balloonhead would not have a niece like her. She favoured the cardinal's errand boy with a smile and her warmest 'Hi, Monsignor.' Balloonhead hardly acknowledged her existence, save for a vague grimace of disapproval at Noele's green Notre Dame warm-up suit. . . . Emissaries of the cardinal had no time for teenagers, especially when they were dressed inappropriately for a rectory office.

'Thank you, Uncle John. Do you have skeletons in your family closet, Monsignor Mortimer?'

'Only the rich Irish can afford to have skeletons, Miss Farrell,' Balloonhead replied solemnly.

'I opened a closet the other day and five skeletons fell on me.' Noele pecked at her uncle's cheek and then bounded down the stairs into the golden October sunlight, turning to wave merrily at him just as he closed the rectory door.

She's not going to let go of it, John Farrell decided. When I get rid of Mortimer I will have to call Irene and warn her. There are too many things that could go wrong, especially if her father is dumb enough to decide to run for governor.

'Come on upstairs, Jim,' he said to Mortimer. 'Mix you a drink?'

Balloonhead blundered up the staircase like a hippo coming out of a tropical river, his idea of the way a man weighed down with the problems of the church would walk. 'I never drink before lunch,' he announced at the top of his voice.

Even sounded like a bull hippo.

Noele

Noele wore her new green and gold Notre Dame warm-up suit, which matched her eyes, when she went to the rectory neither to impress her uncle nor Father Ace, whom she knew she would see at the Courts after she left the rectory.

Noele wore her warm-up suite and tied a green ribbon around her hair because there might be boys at the Courts. Though she was in love with Jaimie Burns, she was certainly not about to forget her image when there was a possibility that there might be cute boys around.

The trees on the curving streets of the Neighbourhood, which Noele thought was the most totally cool place in the world, were turning red, reminding her of the vestments the priests wore at Mass on Pentecost. And the big oaks around the Courts were pure gold, making the sun-drenched asphalt look like a grove. Noele, who loved Latin and was upset that the nuns didn't teach Greek anymore, insisted that the Courts were sacred. They were the centre of the parish. When the kids said, 'Let's go over to Saint Prax's,' they meant not the church but the Courts.

Sacred grove or not, the Courts were devoid not only of cute boys but all boys. Only Father Ace was there, still trying to dunk, and at his age. . . .

He was real old, over forty-five, but definitely kind of cool, with curly brown hair and dancing blue eyes, and a thin, handsome Irish face that was always in motion, usually smiling or laughing – not exactly Paul Newman, but nice just the same. And he could still run on the Courts with any of the boys.

A long time ago, when Moms and Roger and Uncle Monsignor were teenagers, he had been a young priest at St Praxides. Then he became a marine chaplain and a doctor in psychology and taught at Loyola and came back on weekends, and all the kids liked him, especially since Father Miller wasn't in to teenagers, for sure.

Not teenage girls, anyway.

'N.D. going to take the Hurricanes?' he said, bouncing the basketball at her.

'And Jaimie is going to score the winning touchdown on an interception,' she blurted as she sank a jump shot and began the inevitable game of horse with Father Ace.

Shit, Noele thought, permitting herself language she

never used even mentally except when she was really bummed. Well, I didn't mention that the poor black boy is going to be hurt, though not real bad, thank God.

'So he's going to play?' Father Ace watched her intently just before he missed his jump shot. 'They'll let the sleepy-eyed freshman in the game?'

Which is what the newspapers called Jaimie.

'How should I know?' Noele tried to brush it off, realizing that rarely did she fool Father Ace. 'And he's not sleepy, either. He just totally looks that way.'

Everyone thought that Jaimie was a dreamy young man who did what Noele told him to and then went back to sleep till the next time she gave an order.

But then they had not seen him the night in the bar in South Bend, where they shouldn't have been, when the two flakes had tried to paw her.

Jaimie had flattened them both.

'What was Danny Farrell like, Father Ace?' she asked, trying to sound innocent.

'Still on the term paper?' the priest said, making an expert left-handed hook shot. 'And you have to shoot it right-handed.'

Noele, who was left-handed, ordinarily would have protested loudly. Now she was more interested in Danny Farrell than in winning the game of horse.

'I mean, you were here when they were young. . . .' She missed the shot.

'I didn't know him very well. He stayed away from the rectory. Nice guy, though afraid to be serious. Was sweet on your mother once – that was after I left the parish. And why are you interested in him?'

Noele held the basketball in her hands and studied the faded label on it, the game forgotten. 'I have to know who I am, Father Ace. How can I know what I'm going to do with my life unless I know who I am?'

'I think you have a better idea of who you are than most teenagers do.'

'I do not!' she retorted hotly. 'I pray and pray and pray.' She bounced the basketball fiercely with each *pray*. 'And God, like, kind of doesn't say anything much back, and that makes me soooo bummed.'

Father Ace laughed, which he did a lot. 'You are some-one very special, MN, you know that.'

'Just because I sometimes know what people are think-ing before they say it?'

He laughed again. 'No, just because you can persuade almost everyone to do what you want them to do and to enjoy it.'

'A bossy little bitch,' she said disconsolately.

'Only sometimes,' he agreed.

'Nerd.' She threw the basketball at him.

'But also because you love people so much, and they know you do.'

'So I'm president of the High Club and vice president of the student council and captain of the volleyball team and director of the folk music group. . . . I mean, I can't spend the rest of my life doing those things, can I? So I have to figure out who I am. I know there's something I simply have to find out, right?'

'At least you don't deny you're special.' He rolled the basketball toward the edge of the court.

'Like Moms did. . . .'

'There you go again.' He laughed very loudly this time.

'I'm sorry.' She felt her face turn hot. 'I can't help it . . . but that's what you were thinking about Moms, wasn't it?'

Father Ace became very serious. 'A young priest thinks he can save people from their families. Your mother was bright and happy and graceful. She entertained us all with wonderful stories.' He shrugged his shoulders. 'I thought if I told her she was special she wouldn't listen to her family. They won.'

'And she thinks she let you down,' Noele said, reading his thoughts again. 'She still writes stories, but she won't show them to anyone, not even me. Well, I won't do that.'

'And what will you do, MN?' His eyes were not dan-cing at all now.

'Maybe I should be a nurse or a teacher or even a nun . . . something in which I can help people. Or maybe a politician like Mr Burns . . . or Roger, if he really runs for governor. Do you think I'd make a good nun, Father Ace?'

'No way I'll answer that, except to say that you should

not become anything because you must. Our God doesn't work that way.'

'That's why I have to find out . . . I mean, I keep hearing this kind of voice telling me that there's something I have to find out.'

'And it has to do with your family?'

She nodded solemnly.

'Is it bad or good?'

'I don't know,' she said miserably. 'It's just, like, there. All the time. Like somebody or maybe everybody needs my help. I have to find out what it is.'

And when you find out, Father Ace thought to himself, you may wish you never knew it.

'I don't care if someday I wish I never knew it,' Noele said stubbornly. 'If I don't find out, I'll never be anybody.'

John

John Farrell tried to calculate how much damage he had done by losing his temper with Monsignor Mortimer. Every rectory in the archdiocese would know about it by tomorrow morning.

The son of two aggressively respectable employees of the Chicago Board of Education – his mother a school-teacher, his father an engineer – Mortimer had been a few years ahead of John in the seminary, distinguished only by his lack of intelligence and his obvious penchant for culti-vating superiors. No one took him seriously in those days. Indeed no one took him seriously after ordination until the cardinal sought a docile errand boy to preside over his expensive and useless television channel, a plaything in which his eminence took great delight. Mortimer promptly adopted a style of speech, dress, and behaviour appropri-ate for a senior official in the Roman imperium, striving for the impression that he was a confidant of the cardinal, indeed one of his principal policymakers. No one paid much heed to these pretenses. The cardinal had no confidants; he was the sole policymaker in the archdiocese. Nevertheless, Mortimer, bald, overweight, and ponderous of speech, had become something of an important personage, if only because in the group of juvenile delinquents with which the cardinal had surrounded himself, Mortimer looked and acted more like a successful, ecclesiastical bureaucrat than any of the others.

Disregarding the fact that it was half an hour before lunchtime, John Farrell mixed himself another J & B and soda, his imagination drifting to the warm nights at the beach with Irene almost twenty years ago. Mild affection by today's standards. Enough to persuade himself that he didn't have a vocation in those days. He banished the soft and insidious images and willed himself to concentrate on the cardinal's emissary. He stretched out on the luxurious red couch he had inherited from his predecessor. The smooth leather of the couch linked temporarily with the fading memory of the feel of her belly.

'Your health, Jim,' John toasted his visitor. 'And more success with the television.'

'I notice your ratings are down,' Mortimer said sombrely. Balloonhead was about as subtle as a 747 landing in the fog.

'Not really,' John replied lightly. 'A little higher actually than last week and substantially ahead of a year ago last week.'

'The cardinal is wondering how long your series will last,' Mortimer added, blundering ahead. 'You and I know these shows don't run forever.'

John Farrell put down his drink, doffed his jacket, and removed his rabat and Roman collar. Noele often needled him for the vanity of his dress. 'And a tailor-made shirt with French cuffs. . . . Really, Uncle Monsignor, sometimes you dress like a geek.'

'Even Sheen suffered from overexposure,' he said cheerfully. 'Heaven knows, I'm no Fulton J. But I've just signed a new contract, so I suppose that you can tell the cardinal he can see me on Channel Three once a week for the next twelve months.'

'I see,' Mortimer said in a tone of voice appropriate for a police captain who had just heard a murder confession. Everyone in Chicago television had heard of the new contract – everyone, that is, but Jim Mortimer.

'I've got to be frank with you,' Mortimer continued, his deep voice falling several notes below normal. 'The cardinal is embarrassed by the programme, John. He goes to meetings around the country and other bishops ask him about the monsignor in his diocese who has a talk show and interviews actresses and feminists and homosexuals and radicals and even heretics like Hans Küng. They wonder why he lets a priest of his own diocese do such harm to the church.'

Harm to the church. So that was the new line about his programme. '. . . and saints like Mother Teresa.'

'The cardinal thinks Mother Teresa is a faker.'

The issue, John knew, was not Mother Teresa's authenticity. The issue was, rather, whether anyone in the archdiocese would long be tolerated if he seemed to attract more public attention than the cardinal did. For a number of years John had directed the diocese's hand-to-mouth mass-media office, filling up public-service space on Sunday mornings as best he could on a virtually nonexistent budget supplemented by Farrell family money. Then the cardinal purchased his own personal television channel (on which he spoke to 'all the priests and laity' of the archdiocese for an hour every Monday night, in competition with Howard Cosell) and John's job was abolished. He was rewarded with St Praxides, his home parish, and, although the cardinal didn't know it, a neighbourhood with which he had always been hopelessly in love.

And there he stayed, happily anonymous, until the general manager of Channel 3, more to spite the cardinal for messing in the TV industry than for any other reason, offered John his own half-hour interview programme after the news at ten-thirty on Saturday night. Astonishingly, the programme was a huge success. John's crisp wit, husky black-Irish good looks, and gentle but probing questions won the fancy of Saturday night television viewers. But if *The Monsignor Farrell Show* routed *M*A*S*H* and *Star Trek* replays on the other channels, it also earned for its host the criticism and the envy of many of his fellow priests and the animosity of his cardinal archbishop.

As the pastor of an exciting and prosperous parish, and only a couple of years past his fortieth birthday, John had no desire to break ranks with the ecclesiastical establishment or clerical culture. His identity as a priest who was accepted and respected by his fellow priests was as important to him as a rare painting would be to an art collector. He had 'gone along with the guys' through all his years in the priesthood and was unnerved by the acid comments that his classmates and friends were making about the diocese's 'TV personality.'

He had enough other problems: an effeminate curate and an angry Mother Superior, racial integration, an unstable parish council, a huge school budget. But even though almost half of his classmates had left the priesthood, John Farrell could not imagine himself forsaking the active priesthood. Yet there was a part of his soul that seemed incurably weary, depressed, and lonely.

And angry. A chain reaction about to start. Damn his temper.

'You know how the guys feel about the programme,' Mortimer said, striking at the weak link in his armour. 'A lot of them think you are on an ego trip, John, promoting yourself and not caring about the good of the church. They say you want to be another Sheen.'

'My hair is white at the temples, but it's curly, and Sheen's was straight.'

'That's not the point, John.'

'Well, what is the point?' John's temper was rising, despite his best efforts to control it. 'If the cardinal orders me to give up the programme, I will do so. If he doesn't, I will continue for at least another year.'

'The cardinal can't order you to give up the programme.' Mortimer had now adopted a tone he thought smooth and diplomatic. 'You know what kind of an outcry there would be in the media if he did that. He's not going to make you a martyr, John.'

There was a model airplane on John's coffee table, a remnant of a boyhood collection he had shared with Danny. He picked it up, trying to restrain the rage building up inside him. 'You know this plane, Jim? It's a Mustang, a P-51. A great plane in the Second World War, looked a little bit like a German Messerschmitt. It was good for about a year and a half, and then the war was over and along came the jets. You tell the cardinal that I'm going to be as obsolete as a P-51 in another year or two at the most.'

Mortimer relit his cigar as if it were a solemn liturgical function. 'It's not good for morale among the guys for one of us to get all that attention,' he warned.

A few years ago, even a year ago, such a threat to impose the sanctions of clerical caste would have devastated John Farrell. But that was before he had tasted success in something that did not depend merely on his being a priest.

'God damn the guys!' he shouted, suddenly abandoning his efforts to keep his anger under restraint, and astonishing himself with his own vehemence. 'I'm not very good at what I do, but there's nobody else doing anything like it. And if the guys are so small-minded that they can't support one priest on television, then I say screw what they think.'

A startled and obsequious Mortimer had left, and now John Farrell wondered uneasily what had happened to him. He was not a fighter, not a hero, surely not somebody who would courageously take on a psychopathic cardinal and an envious presbyterate. Male menopause, he told himself, thinking of the psychologist he had interviewed on his programme a few weeks before. And, God, how I love being recognized when I walk down Michigan Avenue or buy something in a shop. Male menopause and vanity.

'I will be right down,' he yelled impatiently at the housekeeper, who was ringing the lunch bell for the third time. Jerry Miller, his associate pastor, would not be in until supper. He was attending an interior decorators' convention at the Marriott Hotel. And the Ace would be on the basketball courts, as always. Lunch alone again.

Reviewing his conversation with Mortimer, John realized that he had acted like a damn fool. He ran his fingers through his thick black hair. *Maybe I ought to go away for a week's retreat, straighten myself out. I have too much to lose if I leave the priesthood.*

But his fight with Mortimer was not the only thing that troubled him. He must call Irene about his interview with Noele. Momentarily he anticipated the pleasure of hearing her voice, pictured in his imagination her spectacular figure, which looked as it always did – as if her clothes had been thrown on hastily and would blow away if you turned your head for a split second.

Desire for Irene lurked in that same secret corner of his soul where lurked the desire to fight the cardinal and all the balloonheads in the archdiocese, a longing that had begun when she had been in eighth grade, a blossoming brown-haired wonder, and he a senior at Quigley, the prep seminary. And thinking he was in love with her that summer in Grand Beach, he had been ready to give up the priesthood, everything, to possess her. It was Danny who had persuaded him to return to the seminary – said that the Conlon girl was worthless, then fell for her himself. . . .

Was that why he had resented Danny all these years? They had been rivals for his mother's love, and for Irene's. And as clever as he was in concealing his emotions, perhaps Noele, with her damned fey sensitivity, had guessed that. But in the end neither he nor Danny had claimed Irene. She belonged to his brother, Roger. Noele was their child. And Danny was dead.

John drummed his fingers on the telephone. What would he say to Irene: that Noele was rattling the skeletons in the family closet and she must be careful what she said to her? Irene was not a Farrell; she had nothing to hide. She knew nothing. . . .

She was a beautiful but rather dull woman. Still, she was an overwhelming physical presence who challenged him to the limits of his manhood. And even if he had built a concrete fortress around his desire for her, inside the bunker it was still fierce, implacable.

—23—

Why couldn't he forget her? Why couldn't he erase the memory of Danny from his mind? John Farrell had the common sense, he told himself, to ignore these ghosts of the past. But as he dialed the phone number of his brother's house – on the portable wireless phone that enabled him to answer anywhere on parish property – he thought wistfully that there were many things in life that defied common sense. Vanity, jealousy, lust . . .

Not, however, if you were a priest.

Irene

She was sipping a vodka martini in her bathtub when the phone rang. Stumbling out of the tub, she spilled most of the drink, and then slipped on the bathroom floor, barely regaining her balance before she bumped her head on the wash basin. With a towel clutched protectively to her throat, even though there was no one else in the house, and trying not to drip water on the newly shampooed powder-blue rug, she rushed to the phone in the bedroom to answer it before the ringing stopped.

Roger would not permit a telephone in the bathroom. 'You'd lie in the tub and talk all day,' he had insisted, laughing genially when she suggested it.

'Irene, it's John.' The usual mysterious enthusiasm was in her brother-in-law's voice, as it always was when he began a conversation with her. It would fade quickly. 'I hope I haven't disturbed you.'

'Just climbing out of the tub,' she lied. 'Roger is over at his office at the University, and Noele is off doing research for a term paper. She was interviewing you, wasn't she?'

'That's what I want to talk about. She's working on some family history thing. She was asking a lot of questions about Danny. The skeletons in the Farrell closet ought to stay locked up, Irene, especially now.'

One summer, long ago, she had thought John Farrell terribly sweet, and the touch of his strong hands unbearably gentle. She had just graduated from high school and wanted to fall in love. He was supposed to be on leave from the seminary, 'trying to make up his mind.' She thought he had made it up. Otherwise she would have avoided him. She did not want to fight God.

Their romance had ended as swiftly as it had begun; now he was a self-important ass, charming the women of the parish with his smile and his Irish Republican Army good looks, and winning over the men with brisk, locker-room camaraderie. She supposed that he was a good pastor, although she found his pose as an open-minded, liberal priest unpersuasive. And his success on television made him even more pompous.

How could she, in a stupid teenage crush, have once dreamed of going to bed with him?

The mirrors in the bedroom were beginning to steam from the moisture that had escaped from the bathroom. The fifteen pounds whose loss she was celebrating with the martini clutched in the same hand holding the towel didn't make much difference. Irene turned away from the mirror, embarrassed as she always was by the image of her swelling breasts and full hips.

'Are you still there?' John demanded. 'The less said about the past, the better for all of us. . . . You know Noele.'

'Yes, I know Noele.' Irene was intensely envious of her daughter's confidence, popularity, and grace. She hated herself for her envy, fought against it, and yet could not exorcise it. If only she were sixteen again and had a chance to live her life over.

'I think the child should be steered off the subject.' John, like her husband, had a tone of special officiousness when he was giving her orders about Noele, a child they tried to spoil at every opportunity. To Noele's credit, she was immune to their indulgence. Irene supposed that she indulged her too. For in addition to envy, she felt enormous love for her Christmas child – and had no idea how to show it.

'I'll do what I can, although, as you know, she is at a very difficult age.' She yearned for the comfort and the warmth of the tub, so like the beach that summer she'd been frightened by *The Birds* and revelled in 'Those Lazy, Hazy, Crazy Days of Summer.' As she sang for everyone, she was 'Irresponsible' eighteen. Her crowd that glorious, wonderful summer thought that John Kennedy on his sailboat was the most handsome man in the world. In a few months he would be dead, and then the next weekend Clancy Farrell would join him in the land of the dead. Her last happy summer. . . .

'You ought to alert Roger, too, don't you think?'

'I'll tell him. He has a much better relationship with Noele than I do.'

'Thank you, Irene. Are you going to watch the game this afternoon? It's a big one.'

'Wouldn't miss it for the world,' she said. The Farrells always watched Notre Dame games when they were on national television, if they were not sitting in the seats the family had owned for thirty years at South Bend.

But in fact, she had no intention of watching the game. She would use the precious moments of Saturday afternoon's peace to draw her stories out of the dark blue Florentine leather file case in which she kept them and continue the delightful task of refining and perfecting them.

'All right,' John said. 'Give my regards to Roger. I'll see you at Brigid's for dinner tomorrow night.'

Irene sighed as she hung up the phone. Second Sunday at Brigid's, as much a part of life as the sun rising in the morning. Part of the comfortable but iron-bound coffin that the Neighbourhood had become for her.

She wrapped the towel tightly around herself for the brief journey back to the tub and took a quick gulp from her martini glass. Then, shielded from the bathroom mirror by the heavy humidity radiating from the tub, she folded the towel neatly over the towel bar and slipped back into the water. Her body, a sponge for sensual pleasure, soaked up the reassuring warmth. She had not needed to lose all of the fifteen pounds; her large frame and solid flesh carried weight well. The diet had been for her own morale. It was designed to make her feel less ungainly and assure herself again that she could stop drinking if she wanted to.

Roger had not noticed the weight loss. When he had been informed about it the previous night, after they had made love as routinely as they went to church on Sunday, he said characteristically, 'You look fine to me, but then you always look fine. Maybe a little thin now. Why don't you put back about five pounds?'

Everything she did, or was, seemed just a little bit off to Roger. He was almost successful in hiding his embarrassment at faculty parties. His wife led an idle and unproductive existence, mothering their only child, who scarcely needed mothering, and presiding over their elegantly furnished house in the woods at the north end of Jefferson Avenue with the help of two part-time maids. She was an amusement to the older faculty wives and an affront to the younger ones, many of whom tried to raise her consciousness at government department gatherings. But Irene had learned, after making both herself and her husband look ridiculous when they had first returned to Chicago from Berkeley, to remain mysteriously silent at such gatherings. And Roger had paid her the highest compliment of which he was capable when he had said, in his usual half jesting way, that she was at least not an obstacle to his promotion, as were some of the more outspoken faculty wives.

She sank deeper into the waters of the tub and reached for her drink. Unfortunately she had left it on the wash basin, just out of reach, and had to stand halfway up in the tub to claim the glass. It was an act typical of her, she thought – forgetful, awkward, and not very intelligent. At least that was the way everyone saw her – her brother-in-law, her mother-in-law, her husband, even her own parents – and that was the way she sometimes thought of herself.

Noele had a different view: 'As a mother, Moms, you can be a trial, but as a woman I think you're, like, kind of interesting. Not just sexy, but sort of deep and knowing and totally awesome. A real woman.'

Irene had turned away to hide her pleasure. 'You should think of me as your mother and not another woman.'

'Mo-*ther*, you should be flattered. Most of the other kids don't have mothers they can think of as women.'

So it went with Noele. One never had the last word.

And Roger was fond of her, Irene knew; admired her durable good looks, enjoyed her in their low-key sex life, encouraged her volunteer work, and almost never raised his voice to her. She had learned long ago, when he was a doctoral student at Berkeley and she was typing his papers and working at a stenographic job in the administration building, that Roger was a good and generous man. But in his repertory of emotions sustained passionate love with one woman no longer existed. It wasn't his fault. It was merely the way he was.

He had tried to help her when she strove to finish her undergraduate work after Noele was in school. But his criticisms of her papers, in the form of gentle, lighthearted ridicule, as if she were just a child learning to walk, ended her final academic efforts. And he had encouraged her in creative writing courses she had taken five years ago. He insisted on reading the novella she had written at the end of the programme. When he was through rewriting it, correcting her punctuation, grammar, style, and story line (always in the most gentle of words), she had made up her mind never to show him or anyone else any of her other stories.

She was not a child, Irene thought, sinking deeper into the protective waters of the tub. She was almost thirty-seven years old. And she was not dumb. Her IQ when she was in the Academy of Our Lady high school was between 150 and 160, and the stories and poems she had written in the year and a half she was a student at St Mary's of Notre Dame received virtually automatic A's. She was smarter than most of the faculty wives and probably smarter than many of the faculty members, including her husband. She was not stupid; she was afraid.

Afraid of the Farrells, just as she had been afraid of her own family. Her father, Isaiah Conlon, was hailed as the most honest state's attorney of his generation; and he and his wife, Marybelle, had believed stern discipline essential to raise children to be equally honest. For their daughters that meant strict rules, harsh criticism of even minor 'unladylike' behaviour, and ridicule of all 'pretensions.' The harshest sanctions were contained in two questions: 'What do you think you are?' and 'What will people say?'

People said that Irene Marie, their youngest daughter, was the loveliest and most vivacious of their children. Isaiah and Marybelle took that acclaim as confirmation of their own darkest fears and began their campaign of ridicule – aided enthusiastically by her brothers and sisters. Irene, even as a little girl, could do nothing right. Her clothes, her hair, her friends, her grades in school, and, as she grew older, her spectacularly blooming body were the targets for their merciless fun.

When she married Roger she moved from a world of nasty ridicule to a world of gentle and amused dismay, a much more pleasant and amiable environment, where John's eyes reduced her to an attractive decoration, Brigid's smile hinted that she was fragile and weak, and Roger's patronizing words suggested that she needed protection like a harmless child.

Of course, she had her own secret, one that she treasured as though it were a priceless jewel, a secret that none of the Farrells would ever be given a chance to profane.

The martini glass was almost empty. Should she turn the hot water on in the tub and mix herself another drink? Or should she open the precious file box and rework the stories that no one would ever read? It was always difficult to begin, like plunging into a cold swimming pool, a scary entrance but then exhilaration the instant after.

It did not finally matter whether she had been born afraid or made fearful through a life of cruel Irish ridicule. The results were the same. Whatever chances she might have had when she was a young woman had been lost long ago. Only with one person had she ever been free, unafraid to be herself.

Irene sighed, drained the martini glass, and then climbed out of the bathtub. In the bedroom she put on her underwear, opened a bedroom window halfway to let in the Indian summer warmth, and reclined on the chaise longue next to her dressing table. Then, picking up the thin leather file case, which she had earlier removed from the secret compartment of the Sheraton desk in her scrupulously neat little office down the hall, she unlocked it and removed a carefully typed manuscript.

'I have a confession.' He leaned heavily on the windowsill, watching the black sky over the lake turn its first pale grey.

'My penances are light,' she said sleepily, hoping he would want to make love again.

'All I wanted last night was to score. God forgive me for it. I wanted to brag in the locker room at the golf club today that I had made you last night.'

'I know,' she said softly.

'I'm really a vicious bastard.'

'I know that, too.' She laughed.

He turned slowly away from the window. 'In God's name, then, why did you let me do it?'

'Because I knew that by this time, the morning after, you would have fallen in love with me.'

He came over to the bed, sat down next to her, and removed the sheet that covered her naked body. 'You're a scheming little bitch!'

'I know that, too.' She jabbed at his stomach, tickling him.

'I'm a victim of witchcraft!' he protested, twisting helplessly at her loving torture.

'Absolutely. And how long do you think I've been casting my spell?'

'Two years?' he said tentatively.

'More like four, darling.' She embraced him. 'And now that I've got you thoroughly enchanted, I don't propose ever to let you get away.'

Yes, it set the right tone for the middle of the story, Irene thought. The first part would be the young man's harsh lust, followed by his guilt and dismay at having ravaged an innocent virgin. In the second part he would discover that the virgin was not all that innocent, and that he was the one who was trapped. Then in the third part, the tragic ending, he would lose her to an accident in the lake, a propeller on a big lake cruiser cutting her in half.

'Hi, Moms,' Noele called, exploding into the room. 'Still working on those stories of yours? When are you going to let me read one of them?'

Startled, Irene angrily clutched the manila folder against her chest, protecting it as though it were a helpless babe. 'How many times do I have to tell you, young woman, you should not come through a closed door without knocking?'

'Mo-*ther*, I know Daddy isn't home, and I know you don't have a lover, and' – she whistled appreciatively – 'and you're totally beautiful in that pale grey teddy. Like, I wish I had the figure for things like that. Lucky Roger! Where did you buy it? Bonwit's? I'm really mad that I'm not your size. And you look awesomely cool with all the weight you've lost. You ought to start jogging, too. That'll keep your muscles firm. I want you to be the prettiest mother in the parish!'

It was Noele's firm conviction, Irene knew, that she could convert any situation into one that pleased her if she simply pretended long enough and strongly enough that what she wanted actually existed. In the will of Noele, red-haired, green-eyed, enthusiastic Christmas child that she was, she and her mother were friends, buddies, confidantes; maternal impatience was dismissed as irrelevant, and maternal envy was ignored.

As always, Irene was both flattered and disconcerted by her daughter's frank, almost clinical admiration, linked as it usually was with direct instructions about what she should do to remain attractive. 'What if I hadn't been decent?' She sniffed, trying to be indignant.

'Oh, Mo-*ther*, you're always decent. And always pretty, too. As a matter of fact, I'm getting tired of Jaimie Burns staring at you whenever I bring him into the house. I'm afraid we're just going to have to lock you up in a room when the boys come over.'

Irene carefully replaced the manuscript in its leather file and locked it, as though she were storing a priceless pearl necklace. Then she donned a robe that matched the colour of her lingerie. 'Which reminds me, young woman, if you want to go out with that Jaimie Burns tonight, your room is going to have to be immaculate by suppertime. As neat as every other room in the house.'

'Uh-huh.' Noele was unimpressed by the sternness of her mother's command. 'What was Danny Farrell like, anyway?'

Irene felt her throat tighten, her heartbeat increase, her gut wrench. *After all these years he can still do that to me.*

'He was the sweetest, kindest man who ever lived,' she blurted without thinking. 'A funny, crazy, Peter Pan kind of man.'

'Oh,' Noele said, surprised by her mother's intensity.

'You're asking because of the term paper?' Irene said, trying to recapture her composure.

'Kind of. Did he drink a lot?'

Damn you, John Farrell, for suggesting that.

'Not really. More than Jaimie Burns, I guess. Not as much as a lot of boys then or now.'

The quick little computer underneath Noele's red hair was churning away, trying to reconcile John's picture of Danny with Irene's. 'Was he running away from something, Moms?'

God, yes, child. More than you can imagine.

'I suppose you could say that.' She paused, wondering how to tell the truth and yet not the whole truth. 'He was really a casualty of the success of the South Side Irish. If we'd still been poor, Danny would never have left us.'

'How come?' Noele fingered the end of a strand of her bright red hair.

My God, thought Irene, *I sound like a social studies teacher.*

'We came too far too quickly. We tried to stop being Irish. We gave up poetry, laughter, and dreaming. We held on to our religion and our drink. And we clung to our property as if it were as important as our religion. For people of your grandmother Brigid's generation, property and respectability became a substitute for poetry. They locked themselves in a prison with broken glass and barbed wire on the walls and tried to lock their children up with them. Danny Farrell wanted the poetry – and the laughter, too. But they wouldn't let him have either.'

Noele, sitting now on the edge of the bed, was un-characteristically puzzled. 'I don't understand, Moms.'

'If he had been a naval aviator like his father or a busi-nessman like his uncle or even a priest like Monsignor John or a teacher like your father, no one would have minded. But he wanted to be a storyteller, a writer, even when he was four or five years younger than you are. The family, especially Grandma Brigid, and everyone else in the Neighbourhood said there was no money in that, and he was too gentle a man to fight them. So he acted out some of his stories, used laughter and drink to kill the pain, and died a young man.'

'Was that for the best? That's what Uncle Monsignor said this morning.'

Irene hesitated. God damn John Farrell's arrogant right-eousness. 'I don't know, hon; he might have been a great writer or a great drunk. He never had a chance to become either.' She waited, her head bowed as if she were a pris-oner in the dock, for Noele to ask her whether she had loved Daniel Xavier Farrell. How could she answer that question?

Noele did not ask.

'Another way to think about him,' Irene rushed on, 'is that he was a grown-up teenager. I know that sounds like a contradiction, but when he was twenty-four, right before he died, he hung around with kids my age. If he were alive today, you and your friends Jenny McCabe and Eileen Kelly and Michele Carmody would have a big teenage crush on him.'

Noele brightened, 'Oh! Now I understand. That makes a lot more sense than what Uncle Monsignor told me.'

'We all have to grow up sometime, honey,' Irene said, regretting her candor. 'And part of growing up and acting like an adult is learning that dreams don't come true. You're almost grown-up now, Noele, and you have to learn to give up girlish dreams about romantic heroes who died a long time ago. Don't think about Danny too much. Think about the future, not the past.'

'Dreams do too come true,' Noele said, her pretty little jaw set in a line of grim determination. 'If you want them badly enough. And how can I think about the future if I don't know about the past?'

The hard lines of her jaw vanished as quickly as they had appeared, and Noele rose from the edge of the bed to kiss her mother lightly on the forehead. 'You smell pretty, too.'

Irene felt, as she often did, that she was the child and Noele the mother.

Noele paused at the doorway. 'Did Grandpa Clancy drink a lot too?'

'He was a terrible drinker,' Irene said without thinking. 'That's why he fell down the stairs and killed himself. He was dead drunk that night.'

Images of that terrible evening, and Danny's cold fury when Clancy had insulted her and her family, rushed through her mind. Dear God in heaven, I should not have said that to her. I am so stupidly impulsive.

'You should never regret being impulsive, Moms. And you're not stupid, either,' Noele said, considering her mother critically, head cocked slightly to one side like a thoughtful robin. 'I'll never look good in pale grey because I'll never look regal. You should let your hair grow long.'

After Noele had left, Irene returned the file box to the drawer at the bottom of her dressing table, locked it, and put the key in her purse. While Noele was watching the football game, she would work on one of the other stories and then return the file to the desk in her office. Noele had told her not to regret her impulsiveness, as if replying to something Irene had said instead of something she had thought. She and Roger were so used to such fey behaviour that they paid little attention to it.

What if Noele heard her thoughts about . . . about . . . the past. Then the Christmas child would no longer pretend that she and her mother were friends. She would hate her mother for the rest of her life.

Irene hestitated. Roger did not like to be bothered at the University. Nevertheless, this was important. He ought to be warned before Noele caught him by surprise.

Then suddenly she was very angry at Roger, angrier than she had been in a long time. Damn him!

A thought to which she'd never had courage to give shape before exploded, jarring her brain as if someone had hit her jaw. She would never be herself as long as she remained married to Roger. He and his brother and his mother would keep her the dull, stupid woman they insisted she was. Other women her age were getting divorces and beginning life again. Why couldn't she?

As she pushed the 753 exchange on her Princess phone she laughed to herself. What a ridiculous idea! How could she possibly survive on her own? And what would happen to Noele.

Roger

Roger had become bored with the young interviewer even before the telephone rang. Joe Kramer of *The Republic* was tall, thin, blond, apple-cheeked, and painfully uneducated, the kind of naïf who took it for granted that everyone shared his left-wing Catholic ideology and vocabulary. The interview would drag on at least twenty more minutes. There would be no time between Kramer and Martha Clay to open his mail.

'Mr Farrell,' Roger said discreetly to the telephone. At the University faculty members were never doctor or professor.

'I know you don't like to be disturbed, and I wouldn't call unless I thought it might be important.' Irene was both anxious and guilty.

'I'm sure it is,' he said mildly, hinting faintly at his annoyance.

'It's about Noele. She's doing a term paper in family history and asking questions about Danny. Monsignor John was concerned. You know how Noele is; sometimes she senses and feels things without anyone actually telling her. John is afraid this might be one of those times.'

'Couldn't it have waited until I got home?' He raised the pitch of his voice.

'John wanted me to call you,' Irene said defensively. 'I thought I'd better warn you before Noele corners you.'

'I think I know Noele well enough to be able to cope,' he said patiently. 'You're quite right, however, about her intuition. I appreciate the warning. We don't want her to get hurt. See you tonight.'

He hung up before Irene could apologize again for disturbing him.

'Excuse me, Mr Kramer,' Roger said, smiling at the interviewer with the campaign smile he had been practising. 'Sometimes I think it would be easier to have five teenage daughters than just one. Now, we were discussing, let's see, the questions of the relationship between morality and politics?'

'Catholics my age' – Kramer talked with a faint lisp – 'find it very hard to understand how you could justify studying a man like Machiavelli.'

Oh, God, Roger thought. If I have to be interviewed by idiots like this, I may drop out of the gubernatorial race even before it begins.

'Niccolò Machiavelli was neither a moralist nor an ethicist, Mr Kramer; he was an empiricist, describing the reality of politics as he knew it. He observed that the Prince – any political leader, really – operated on a set of moral principles that were quite different from the ordinary canons of morality. For the Prince to lie, to steal, to deceive, to cheat, to corrupt, to bribe, was perfectly legitimate so long as the act increased the welfare of the state. Rather like Karl Marx.'

'But Marx was correct about morality,' protested the young man.

'Let me ask you a question, Mr Kramer.' Roger rested his chin on interlaced fingers, one of his favourite poses in the classroom. 'I'm sure that you, as a young journalist, are an admirer of men like Woodward, Bernstein, Hersh, and other investigative reporters, aren't you?'

Kramer nodded earnestly.

'I see. But, of course, they accepted stolen property,

they persuaded men to be disloyal and violate their oaths of office, they asked tricky questions and deceived many of the people they interviewed. Are not investigative reporters rather similar to Machiavelli's Prince?'

'They did those things to expose dishonesty in government and to end the war.' The young man's apple cheeks turned even rosier. 'Investigative reporters fight against corruption. They don't engage in it.'

'Well, I certainly don't subscribe to Machiavelli's pragmatism – and would not take him as a model in the event I should ever become governor,' Roger said smoothly. 'I'm sure if Niccolò Machiavelli were here in this room, in fact, he would say if the end justifies the means for somebody, it does for everybody.'

'You wouldn't be a disciple of Machiavelli as governor?' the young man persisted.

'Of course not,' Roger said crisply. 'Machiavelli is a theorist, someone who helps you to understand the way things are. As governor, I would strive for things to become the way they should be.'

Kramer jotted down that remark vigorously. It would certainly appear in the article.

Finally the young man left, promising that he would be back early the next week to interview students and other faculty members and read the manuscripts of Roger's published articles and books. He wanted to compare the manuscripts with the published works to see how Roger's 'creative mind' worked. All this for a thirty-five-hundred-word article for a college magazine.

There were a few minutes left before Martha would appear, all breathless and glowing and filled with intelligence and sexual energy. Roger opened one letter and then put it aside. He was so eager to possess her that he could not think straight. He had fallen in love with her – the first time that had happened in a career of judicious shopping in the academic slave markets. A sweet high school prom queen, with an overlay of feminist ideology and deep sexual hungers, which he had taught her to acknowledge.

I'm coming apart, he told himself with a sigh. Running

for governor is so much fun that my personality is disinte-
grating. I might as well enjoy it while I can.

He was a fully accepted member of the faculty community,
a little too witty and irreverent, but that was excused because
he was an Irish Catholic. And a little too modish in his dress,
light brown and light blue sport jackets and coordinated
slacks – not the dull grey three-piece suits or the jeans and
flannel shirts, the alternative-approved uniforms at the University. But that was excused because of his wealth.

He could spend, Roger knew, the next thirty years of his
life delivering witty epigrams at the round lunch table in the
Faculty Club dining room, and never do another honest
day's work. Or he could choose to write an article every year
and a slender monograph every two years – any more would
be judged excessive by his colleagues and proof that he was
not serious. But both choices struck him as profoundly de-
pressing, as did the prospect of more easy conquests in the
University's flesh market. The time had come to try the world
of active politics, returning, as it were, to the womb, but with
a very useful credential taken from the academy.

He would, of course, be known as Dr Farrell. After all,
Henry Kissinger was Dr Kissinger.

Nonetheless, he should not have permitted himself to fall
in love with his doll-like little WASP. Most imprudent.

Not so odd that Clancy and Brigid Farrell should produce
two incomplete sons, one a vain realist who was unrealistic
about his own vanity and the other an intensely ambitious
idealist who spent most of his time pretending to be indiffer-
ent to both ideals and success. For a moment Roger considered the elegance of his self-description. It could stand a little
polish and did not mention his delight in the female slaves on
the trading block. Yet it would do as a single-sentence sum-
mary.

He glanced at his watch. The annual woman was a routine
part of life for many academics, not all, by any means, but
enough so that he was hardly alone in his amusements. Brief
amusements. In the long run they became almost as boring
as the faculty lunch table. You returned them to the trading
block as quickly as possible.

Martha came into his office, eyes glowing with the enthusiastic zeal of a fundamentalist missionary going into the jungles of Latin America to bring salvation to a native tribe. Something remained of her grandparents' years in China, a pious and lovely young Protestant matron rushing to embrace the lions. No, he did not want to return her to the trading block. She was becoming more interesting rather than less. Her toughly worded ideology was only skin-deep. Beneath it she was a mixture of sweetness and passive passion.

'I think I have it this time, Roger,' she said cheerfully. 'If we look at the strongest relationships these women develop with the important men in their lives, we will find an alienating variable, a contradiction between their own middle-class self-definition and the realities in which they find themselves. This would account for their radicalization.'

'Let's see your numbers,' Roger said, sounding, he hoped, like a brisk and businesslike political science professional and not like a lecherous pagan hoping to seduce a Salvation Army volunteer.

Numbers were not Roger's thing. But Martha's gibberish was such a mishmash of Marxism and shallow feminism that the only hope for her book was some arresting statistics.

Alas, as he suspected, the statistics were a mishmash too.

Her book was a ponderously dull study of oppression in middle-class family life. It would be published, of course, if he could force her to let go of it and send it off to the press. Anything written about women political activists was published these days, especially when it was submitted to a woman editor at an academic press. Martha's chances of tenure at the University, however, would remain thin. As a rule of thumb a woman scholar must be one and one-half times better than the men with whom she was theoretically competing. Martha was not that much better than her male competition.

A neatly turned out, sweet-faced little honey blonde, she surely had been a sweetheart in high school before being radicalized at Stanford. And if radicalism was supreme in her head, she was still a prom queen in her heart and her body, captivated by the captain of the basketball team, whom she had married and then divorced after both had been caught up in the turbulence of graduate school in the early seventies.

The dope hadn't known how lucky he was. Probably couldn't cope with her feminist consciousness and didn't see the possibilities in her delightfully feminine little body.

An assistant professor could either be feminine or a feminist. Unfortunately Martha was an unstable compound of the two. She was thus an interesting sexual conquest but an unpromising candidate for a lifetime appointment – and you had to use the word *lifetime* often when you were probably going to reject a promotion in the social science division of the University.

Roger was committed in principle to her promotion. To reject her and accept a man not as good as she would be disgraceful. He would vote for her because she deserved tenure, because he would enjoy his colleagues twisting and turning as they explained that their decision to reject was really not sexist, and now because he loved her.

'I'm still troubled by the weakness of some of your correlations,' Roger said, looking up from her manuscript. 'They simply are not statistically significant, you know.'

'That's because you're a man,' she snapped. Then, changing quickly from an angry feminist to a helplessly feminine woman, she asked, 'Do you think I ought to rework it again?'

'I don't think so,' he said, weighing his words carefully and trying to concentrate on her text instead of fantasizing about her exquisite legs. 'The best way to cope is to acknowledge candidly in your introduction the weaknesses of the data and assert that your analytic models are presented for speculative and illustrative purposes, pending more elaborately designed research. If you do that, you can fend off both critics and reviewers nicely.'

'That's an excellent idea!' she exclaimed, shifting in her chair to a pose not quite unself-conscious in its sexual appeal. Sometimes Roger thought her recently awakened appetites were more intense than his. She did not want to talk research this Indian summer Saturday afternoon any more than he did.

'The important thing, Martha, is to send the manuscript off to your publishers. You already have a tentative agreement to publish. We know they have favourable reports from their readers, and we should be able to say to your review committee in January that the book has impressed a distinguished academic publisher.'

'How much do you think that's going to help?' Martha's hand darted quickly to his arm.

I really don't deserve a morsel as tasty and as eager as you. But, since I have you, I will certainly consume you.

'As I told you before, this case is not going to be decided finally in the department; it will be a weak vote either way. The decision will be passed on to the dean and the provost. A book in press will make them think twice about turning you down.' His hand moved to her adorable little ass, so small that he could cover much of it with his palm and extended fingers. He loved her with the romantic affection a teenage boy has for his first girl friend – and made love to her with the exuberant fantasies of an adolescent. Today she would be the missionary captured by a pagan monarch and introduced to the pleasures of sin for the first time.

'And maybe win over some votes in the department?' she asked breathlessly, her hand now moving lightly to his chest.

'It's always difficult to estimate the probability of the reaction of any given member of our department on any issue, but on the whole,' Roger said, trying to sound like a professor when he was about to be a sexual conqueror, 'the chance of a favourable vote in your case goes up considerably when you have a book in press.'

The critical ploy in edging Martha off the block and out of her clothes was that she must take the initiative herself. Otherwise he might be accused before the high court of ideological feminism of being an exploitive male and she of selling herself to an exploitive male to promote her career.

'Sometimes I wonder whether all the academic politics is worth it,' she said vaguely as she caressed his cheek, to her a signal of invitation, to him of surrender.

'It's unreal, I admit, and that's what tempts me about the other kind of politics; they're less unreal. Nonetheless, we must not permit academic politics to destroy your career.'

Her fingers, reassured by his hollow piety, travelled from his cheek to his chin and then to his throat. Irene never did anything like that. The trouble with her was that she did not have to be pursued and offered no inducements to the chase. She had long since been conquered and never required taming. She was attractive and mildly diverting, but not nearly so challenging and exciting as this passionate mixture of femininity and feminism he was about to take off the trading block and brand as his own.

Roger's head throbbed with the sweet taste of conquest. You could not stop now, my dear little slave, even if you wanted to. I can do with you what I wish.

Leisurely, as if he were sipping lemonade, he pushed up her sweater and unfastened the front hook on her sheer pink-lace bra, a convenient concession to femininity. He squeezed one small breast rather hard. She winced and exclaimed, although they both knew that she wanted to feel the torment of his fingers as much as he wanted to sink them into her flesh.

Then his amusements began in earnest. Soon her delicately lush little body was spread-eagled on his desk, and she was begging him to end the delights of her torment.

An easy conquest, my Salvation Army matron and right here in the corridors of the government department. Then he was flooded with a sweet torrent of affection for her. She was a sister or a daughter, not an amusing little slave girl. He would protect her and take care of her.

For a few moments after they were finished, she nestled naked in his arms, content and happy, sweetly affectionate and submissive. 'I love you, Roger,' she said simply, cuddling even closer to him.

'And I love you, too,' he said, realizing that he was swimming in deep waters. And heading away from shore.

Noele

'They are for sure going to lose, MN,' said Eileen Kelly, a tall and pretty blonde from whom the last traces of baby fat had yet to disappear.

In school Noele was known as Mary Noele because the nuns had decided long ago that she needed a Christian name. And to her contemporaries, she was often 'MN,' which she liked even more, but only from teenagers.

'Really,' she replied, using her generation's favourite all-purpose word. She knew that they were for sure not going to lose. She was not about to repeat her mistake with Father Ace, however.

She could not anticipate what would happen to Notre Dame every Saturday. And sometimes her feelings about the outcome of the weekly battle in defence of Catholicism – as Roger called it with his amused little smile – were wrong. But she was not wrong when Jaimie Burns was involved. He was going to intercept a pass in the last few minutes of the game and run it back for a touchdown.

And that was for sure. Just as her feeling that the first-string free safety would pull a muscle in the second quarter so Jaimie would play the rest of the game and not just on kickoffs had already been confirmed.

'I don't know what's the matter with them,' moaned Eileen, Noele's best friend since as long as either could remember, despite theatrical quarrels every couple of weeks. 'Like, they score two touchdowns in the first quarter every week and then fall apart. My dad says they used to be unbeaten.'

'And the Mass used to be in Latin,' said Noele.

'But a real long time ago,' Eileen replied. 'My dad says that Notre Dame is the best university in the country.'

'Really,' Noele said. According to Roger it was a passable undergraduate institution but did not begin to exist as a University. And Roger was an alumnus, just like Doctor Kelly. It ought to be better, Roger would add, given all the money they have taken out of the pockets of rich Catholics.

Noele did not care about such matters. She would go to Notre Dame because her father went there. And because Brigid wanted her to go there. And because Marty Farrell went there.

And because Jaimie Burns went there.

Mostly because of Jaimie Burns.

Besides, if you were a girl, you had to be at the very top of your class to be admitted, and that was the kind of challenge Noele loved.

'Jaimie's playing real good,' Eileen said as Congressman Burns's son batted a pass out of the hands of a Hurricane in the end zone.

'Really,' Noele replied.

'Are you two coming to the play tomorrow night?' Eileen asked.

'Dinner at Grams's,' Noele said. 'They won't need the head of crew anyway. We'll make the party afterward.'

Miami broke through a collapsing Notre Dame line for another touchdown, going ahead 17–14.

'Really!' the two of them exclaimed together.

Dr Finnbar Kelly, Eileen's father, was known as the only Democratic surgeon on the South Side. His political principles did not interfere with his life-style, however. The big-screen TV in his gadget-filled family room was as large as Grams's.

All the better to see Jaimie Burns.

He ran the kickoff back to the Miami thirty-five.

'One more block and the sleepy-eyed graduate of Saint Ignatius High School in Chicago,' said the announcer, 'might have gone all the way.'

'Really!' Noele exclaimed, more in anger at the suggestion that Jaimie was sleepy-eyed than at the absence of a block.

'Jaimie Burns go all the way,' Eileen repeated, giggling.

'No way, José,' Noele said firmly. Like many of her generation, Noele's sexual ethics had more in common with the 1940s than the 1960s. But with Jaimie Burns there was no need to draw any lines.

Notre Dame ran the ball up the middle on the first down, around the end the second down, and, with a third and seven, missed a forward pass by half the state of Indiana.

Suddenly Noele felt uneasy. Something was wrong. Something terrible. Someone was hurting. . . .

Miami ran the short punt back to midfield. Now was the time for the interception. Noele hardly noticed because the vibes of terrible loneliness were getting worse. Her loneliness. She was the one who was hurting. She was in a desert, all by herself. Cut off.

'I'm not lonely,' she murmured to herself. 'Why should I feel lonely?'

'Huh?' Eileen said.

Before Noele could answer, the poor kid who was the Miami quarterback threw a bomb in the general direction of the Notre Dame end zone.

'He has a receiver open!' screamed the Notre Dame announcer, as though the barbarians were at the gate.

No way, José.

Jaimie appeared out of nowhere, grabbed the ball from the hands of the Miami receiver, and tore down the sidelines.

There was pandemonium in the Orange Bowl – and in Finnbar Kelly's basement. Noele shouted as loudly as Eileen, not because she was surprised, but because she felt she had to cover up her advance knowledge.

But the bad vibes were still there. Total isolation from everyone. Floating on a raft in an empty ocean.

Was Jaimie going to be hurt before the game was over?

No, it was not Jaimie. She was the one who was cut off, completely alone, like some of the older nuns said the people in hell would be.

Slowly the hell feeling faded away.

Notre Dame won. The TV people couldn't find Jaimie after the game for an interview.

Really. By which she meant that of course they couldn't find him.

On her way home in Flame, her red Chevette, Noele gave little thought to the triumph of her Jaimie Burns. Someone needed her help. It was the third time in the last month she had experienced those terrible vibes.

She had to find out why.
Someone buried in loneliness.
And that someone was her.

Roger

Later that afternoon Roger drove home in his Seville – an affront to the University's culture, which virtually demanded that the younger full professor drive a foreign car, preferably Swedish. His wife's Datsun sports car and his own antique Mercedes never appeared in the University parking lots. The Neighbourhood, snuggled in the hills and the woods of the Chicago Ridge, once the dunes of an ice-age Lake Michigan but now the southwest fringe of the city, was also an affront to his colleagues. He chose to live there not so much to offend them as to enjoy a peaceful haven from the frantic University environment, intense both in its academic seriousness and in its pursuit of sexual pleasure.

And also because he thought his women were safer there.

Roger was in a thoughtful mood, not about the life that lay ahead of him if he chose to run for governor – surely the most important decision he would ever make – but about the life he would leave behind. After he had been rewarded with his 'lifetime appointment,' he had casually suggested to a couple of his colleagues that the Slave Market model of the higher academy was as useful to explain the behaviour of the professorate as was the Pursuit of Truth model. The campus, he had said, was a sorting mechanism by which the powerful men allotted themselves privileges over the most desirable women – such as these might be. Feminism, he contended, merely changed the rules a bit but also gave the powerful men an ideological support, Sexual Liberation, for asserting their privileges. Horrified, they had begged him not to publish such nonsense.

It was not nonsense. Many, probably most, of the faculty did not engage in the slave trade. And not all the available young women offered themselves on the block. But many came seeking wisdom and sex in equal amounts. And sex as a hidden agenda permeated the dingy gothic corridors of the University building like a pervasive if barely visible mist. Martha Clay wanted to become his slave for the current academic year at least as much as he wanted her. She wanted to take off her clothes for him as much as he wanted to strip her.

That they fell in love with each other was pure accident.

And that made him uneasy. It would mean more guilt. And with that thought, as surely as a winter cold comes, even though one pretends that its symptoms are not real, self-revulsion and disgust assaulted him. Why could he never remember before the fact how he would hate himself after the fact?

He pulled his Seville to the kerb of a side street next to the Woods, the northern boundary of the Neighbourhood, and slumped over the wheel. Dedicated Catholic idealist indeed.

Women were an obsession. Since high school days there had always been a woman to pursue and dominate. He was programmed in his flesh to do so, even though he achieved little permanent satisfaction from his conquests. None of the slim, small-breasted women he had mastered had meant anything to him before Martha. He had never felt as close to any woman as he had to Danny Farrell. Not even to Irene or Martha.

What would Danny have said of Martha Clay's piquant and intense sexual antics this afternoon, of her pleas that he release her from the cliff of sexual frustration on which he had kept her suspended until she cried out in need?

Would Danny have admired his technique?

More likely he would have laughed at the whole absurd business.

The waves of self-contempt ebbed, and he started the car. He had not forgotten Irene's phone call. Nor could he ever forget Danny, and in a way that was just as well. The memories were too sweet to give up. There was, for example, the glorious Holy Thursday evening when they'd been in their early years of high school. In those days Catholics went from church to church praying to the blessed sacrament 'exposed' outside of the tabernacle on the altar in preparation for a Good Friday service, which was not, strictly speaking, a Mass. Visiting churches had been a social event – a date for adolescents and young adults, a festive occasion for older men and women, a serious moral, religious, and social responsibility for parents, and a pre-Easter fashion show for upper-middle-class matrons.

St Praxides had been a much smaller parish then, and the church was in the basement of the school. The pastor, a solemn and pompous personage immensely impressed with his own importance, stood outside the school door in good weather and at the head of the stairs leading to the basement in bad, clad in all the purple his monsignoral dignity could muster, greeting visitors from other parishes and frowning slightly at the occasional Negro Catholic who dared to invade St Praxides on Holy Thursday.

Stationed at the entrance of the church on a soft spring evening in the 1950s, the monsignor was the last to know that St Joseph had lost his purple Latin veil and was now dressed in a Notre Dame sweat shirt. And on the other side of the church Blessed Mother had replaced her purple veil with a St Ignatius High School basketball warm-up jacket. Most of the people in the parish suspected that Danny Farrell was behind the prank, but only Roger, a frightened guard at a distance in the sacristy, knew for certain that his cousin had struck again.

Roger laughed aloud. A damnable shame Danny was dead. Good times died with him – and laughter and hope and a lot of other things.

Noele cornered him in his study as he was watching the news before supper. For a moment she made him think of Martha. No, he would not tolerate those fantasies, no matter how much the heady wine of political attention was dissolving his other inhibitions. Roger expected a descrip-

tion in her marvellous teen dialect of the awesome interception by which Jaimie Burns, the prayers of the Catholic
nation riding with him, had smashed the last-minute
expectations of the Miami Hurricanes.

Instead, she dismissed the victorious Fighting Irish as
unimportant. 'Roger, can I interview you about the family
history I have to do for Sister Kung Fu?'

'That's not her name, Snowflake.'

'No, it's Sister Amanda; we, like, kind of call her Sister
Kung Fu.'

Roger knew better than to seek an explanation for an
adolescent nickname. 'Interview away.'

Noele, in jeans and a Purdue University T-shirt, curled
up on the maroon-leather ottoman next to the TV set.

What would I do to a man who made love to her the way
I did to Martha Clay, he wondered. The guilt pangs for his
conquest that afternoon would last several days. He would
pay the full price for his pleasure, and then enjoy his new
slave again. That was the way it had to be. Maybe he
would fall out of love with her.

Noele flipped open a legal-size notebook. 'A lot of sudden deaths in your family, weren't there, Roger?'

For a fraction of a second, Roger Farrell panicked. My
God, how much did she know? He had been prepared for
a question about Danny X. Farrell, not for . . .

'Whom do you mean?' he asked, hoping his voice did
not betray his panic.

'Well, I mean, in 1944 Uncle Danny's father and Great
Gramps, who was Danny's grandfather – and Danny's
mother, too – all in the same year. And then Danny and
Gramps within a few months of each other. Aren't those
unusual coincidences?'

Roger marshalled his facts very carefully. 'Danny and
his father, my uncle Martin, were naval officers, indeed,
flyers, at a time when our country was either formally or
informally at war. Casualty rates for naval aviators, Snowflake, are high. Danny and his father knew the risks.'

Noele said nothing, but she made a couple of quick and
decisive notes on her yellow pad.

'And your great-grandfather, William Farrell, was in his

early fifties when he died. I know that seems younger now than it did then, but he had a tough life, and everyone in the family knew he worked so hard he would eventually kill himself. The only death that was unusual was that of your grandfather Clancy, as everyone called him. But that was a tragic accident, Snowflake.'

'Was he drunk when he fell down the stairs?' Noele said without looking up from her pad.

'Of course not! Who told you that?' Roger shook his head disconsolately. 'He simply tripped on the new carpet. I still can't quite get over it. It was so quick and so sudden and so . . . well unnecessary.'

Noele considered her grandfather's death thoughtfully. 'You haven't said anything about the death of Danny's mother, Florence Carey. Doesn't she count?'

'That was another tragic accident. The breaks failed on a delivery truck, and it ran her down while she was waiting for a bus. One of those terrible things. . . . The miracle was that Danny wasn't killed, too. She must have seen the truck coming and pushed him out of the way.'

'How old was Danny?'

'Let's see, he was born in 1940, so he was four, a very little boy.'

'What was he like, Roger? I can't quite get a picture of him.'

'If he had become a priest, he would not be a monsignor like your uncle John; he would be a bishop, probably a cardinal. If he had become an academic like me, he would be a university president. Danny Farrell could do anything he wanted and do it spectacularly, even fly a U-2, I suppose. And if his plane crashed in China, you can bet that it wasn't because of pilot error.' Roger, despite himself, was moved by his own description of Danny. 'Sometimes I dream at night he's still alive, and then I wake up half persuaded the dream is true, and all the fun, excitement, and all the good times and the craziness is still with us. Even when I was well on my way to being a stuffy academic . . .'

'You're not stuffy, Roger, well, not very often. . . .'

Roger laughed. 'Let's hope not too often. Anyway,

when Danny found out what I was doing and what I was interested in, he asked me the right questions about Niccolò Machiavelli without ever having read my Florentine friend, and without ever knowing anything of the history of fifteenth-century Italy. He was magic, Snowflake, magic.'

'You know, it's a funny thing, Roger: I've talked to you and Moms and Uncle Monsignor today about Danny, and it's almost as if all of you remember three different people.'

'That's the way he was, Snowflake.'

'And I sort of have the impression that there was something wrong about the way he died. Was there?' Her affectionate green eyes were momentarily as old as sin.

'Something terribly wrong, Snowflake. He shouldn't have died. He shouldn't have been in the CIA flying a U-2 on some crazy mission over China. He shouldn't have gone to Annapolis. He shouldn't have been pushed into something he wasn't.'

'Moms said that too. Who pushed him, anyway?'

'No one was guilty because everyone was guilty, Snowflake, even Danny. But talking about guilt won't bring him back. You're not Dana Andrews, and this is not that late-night movie you like so much. . . .'

'Laura.'

'Life is a serious business, Noele. You're at an age when you have to realize that it's not all fun and games. Danny is dead. Don't go falling in love with him.'

Noele laughed. 'I have enough trouble with Jaimie Burns, Roger, without taking on a ghost.' And she bounced out of the room, a vibrant mix of innocent child and glorious woman.

Her father paid no attention to the NBC Saturday night news. Rather, he searched through a cabinet next to his desk and dug out a stack of old pictures, looking for one in particular, Danny at thirteen in Grand Beach in the summertime. They were hiding from John during a Saturday afternoon matinee at the musty little movie theatre in Michigan City, closed now because of the big mall on the outskirts of the city. Roger suddenly found himself overwhelmed by an unfamiliar yet irresistible emotion, the same one he had felt that day when he'd reached out in the flickering darkness to touch his cousin. . . .

Danny had calmly repulsed him. It was never mentioned again. Yet . . .

Yes, they were always playing tricks on John, Roger thought. But damn him, Danny cared more for John than for me, even though he was the most important person in my life. John was jealous of him because he resented Brigid's affection for him. I loved him.

Roger put the picture away with a sigh. A foolish adolescent crush. But he felt his eyes sting with tears. He smiled to himself. He was the one who was in love with a ghost, not Noele.

If Noele found out the truth about Danny, it could mean disaster for the whole family, particularly with the election coming up. He hesitated to alarm his mother unnecessarily, but he reached for the telephone. Then he glanced at his wristwatch. Brigid and Burke were having supper at the club. He would have to wait until ten o'clock to call her.

Later that evening Irene came to his study just as he was about to phone the old house on Glenwood Drive. Roger withdrew his hand from the telephone. 'Did you talk to Noele?' she asked.

Irene was wearing a silver-grey short gown and matching peignoir. Bonwit's eroticism, he thought contemptuously.

'We had a little talk before supper. But I don't think there's anything to worry about. You know how kids are at her age. They jump from enthusiasm to enthusiasm. Today it's the family history. Tomorrow it'll be the junior play again.'

'You know best, I'm sure.' Irene leaned over to kiss him good night. Roger felt a faint touch of aversion and something else – terror, perhaps, a not altogether unsweet terror, that contact with his wife sometimes occasioned. Aesthetically, she was doubtless impressive. But by his standards she was too much, a Sears Tower kind of woman for a man who preferred the Prairie School.

'Expensive lingerie,' he murmured in faint disapproval.

'Not too expensive,' she said defensively.

'You look wonderful,' he said soothingly, now that his point had been made. He brushed the back of his hand down her cheek and across her throat with his thumb trailing on her chest. It was a promise of later affection that he would not have to keep. Irene would wait for him for perhaps half an hour and then fall soundly to sleep. Nothing ever interfered with the woman's sleep.

'Don't stay up too late,' she said, kissing him again.

Why did she think that if she looked like an overdressed mannequin in Bonwit's window she was automatically sexy? What is it about her that repels me? I wonder if Brigid breast-fed us? Might that have something to do . . .

He sighed in dismay at himself – a goddamned academic who had to analyze everything. Then he punched his mother's number on his private telephone with the touch of unease that marked all his dealings with that formidable woman.

Brigid

Brigid was hanging up her dress when the phone rang. She picked up the brandy snifter on her dressing table as she answered it, noting with approval that the woman in the mirror looked a decade, perhaps a decade and a half, younger than her fifty-nine years, even if tonight she was terribly tired.

It was Roger, sounding like the pompous professor that he was. Both of her sons were a bit of a trial to her, Monsignor John with his paralyzing concern for clerical respectability and Professor Roger with his everlasting pose of effete intellectualism.

Not, mind you, that she wouldn't willingly die for either of them – or tear the eyes out of anyone who dared to criticize them.

'No, Roger, I don't think I'm going to watch John tonight on his programme. He's interviewing one of those "actresses for Christ" people . . . not quite up to that. . . . Oh, dinner at the club is like dinner at the club always is. Too many people getting old there.'

Her husband, Burke, entered the bedroom and smiled appreciatively at his half-clothed wife. She winked at him.

'Yes, I had a phone call from Noele this afternoon. I know all about the term paper. What's the problem in that? . . . Asking about Danny?' An ever so slight increase in the beat of her heart. Not really a son, and yet her favourite of the three boys she had raised. 'Well, of course she'd ask about Danny. What do you and John expect? . . . Oh, come now. Children Noele's age aren't fey. That's an Irish American myth. I never met a single witch in Ireland. . . . Yes, of course she's quick. . . . Roger, it was seventeen years ago. . . .'

Nervously she put a cigarette in her mouth and tried to light it while holding the phone. Burke flicked the cigarette lighter with a single motion and patted her thick red hair, most of the colour of which was still natural.

Burke's hand was smudged, as it always was, with auto grease. His only hobby, other than making love, was fiddling with his collection of four moribund Alfa-Romeos in the vast garage behind their house.

An Alfa is something like a woman, he once remarked.

Brigid had flown at him with mostly mock rage. 'And an old Alfa is as good as an old woman.'

'I'm well aware,' she said impatiently into the phone while deftly dodging Burke's efforts to further undress her, 'that we all have much to lose if the closet door is opened and the skeletons come tumbling out. But, Roger, the child is only writing a term paper. . . . Yes, of course I'll be careful. Believe me, nothing will go wrong. . . .' She drew a quick breath as Burke eased off her slip. Then she winked at him again and playfully shoved his hand away from her. She had to concentrate on poor Roger. It wasn't like him to be so concerned. John was the worrier.

'Well, it's only natural that she should be asking questions about Danny. I'll tell her that your father's death was an accident. I know exactly how to handle the child.'

'Damn!' she exploded, hanging up the phone.

'What is it, Bridie?' Burke asked, his haggard, handsome face expressing mild concern, the most he ever displayed.

'Noele is poking around in the past for some term paper about family history. The child has always been too curious for her own good.'

She turned to look at herself again in the mirror, mostly undressed now. Would her skin be as smooth if she had stayed in Ireland? Probably not. And she would not have a lover like Burke to caress that skin. Her hair would still be red though, the colour of blood. And for an instant she remembered the blood on her hair the night Danny had found her almost unconscious and sworn revenge on her husband.

Roger

Roger and his brother were the only ones left in the shower room, where Roger felt inferior, as he always did when his body and that of his brothers' were naked and inviting comparison.

Both had given up the Chicago Bears game for an Indian summer golf round before dinner at their mother's. They had played in different foursomes, of course; they never played golf together.

'How did you hit them?' asked John, rubbing soap over his firm, masculine body.

'High eighties. I suppose you made your handicap?'

'Two over it,' John said, and sighed. 'A seventy-eight.'

John's strength and good looks had intimidated Roger all his life. John was a better athlete and could consume large amounts of food and drink with no ill effects on his trim waistline and solid stomach. Small wonder that the women of the parish found him attractive.

The physical resemblance between the two men was

strong, but Roger was wiry rather than muscular, and he prided himself on having a much better brain. His brother was the blunt-spoken ruggedly handsome Irish country-man, with a big, solid, hairy body, a face that stopped just a little short of being crude, and thick, black curly hair, dus-ted lightly now with silver, which hung over his forehead in permanently unruly tangles. In an earlier day he would have strode into the field with the men of his parish and swung the hoe with more strength than any of them.

Roger was the local poet or schoolteacher, with a narrow scholar's face, high forehead, inquisitive eyes, and a faint, self-mocking smile always on his thin lips. If women found his slight, smooth body attractive – and there was evidence to believe that they did – it was the intensity of the emotions hiding behind his smile that they admired, and not his phy-sical strength.

I am a feast for a woman of discernment, he thought, quoting some drunken Irish poet or politician whose name he could not remember. And my brother is a feast for a woman of the land.

Still, he envied John's gruff, forceful manliness almost as much as he'd envied Danny Farrell's explosive speed and coordination. Never satisfied.

Danny, blast him, was a feast for any woman.

Still, Danny was dead, and if John was stronger, Roger was smarter, and that was some consolation. They had cho-sen not to compete overtly, even as boys, mostly because Brigid would not tolerate either intellectual or athletic com-petition between them.

For her two natural sons, she was an absolutely fair and dispassionate mother, avoiding at whatever cost a repeat of the devastating sibling rivalry in the previous generation. Unfortunately for her sons, fairness was not a substitute for the affection she felt but would have had a hard time expres-sing even if she were not obsessed by the duty to be fair.

So the emotional temperature between them was low. They did not fight, but they were not close friends, either. Their only rivalry was over Danny, who soaked up all of Brigid's considerable excess warmth because he needed it, 'poor, orphan boy.'

And John had won that competition.

But Roger had won Irene, for whatever that was worth.

Did John resent the victory, the way he himself resented John's physical attractiveness and athletic ability?

Sometimes Roger thought that he should have been the priest and John the married man. John was good with women in a casual and superficial way. No woman could fail to find that rock-hard body appealing, even if his facial features were somewhat rougher than Roger's.

Poor Brigid. They were both probably a bit of a disappointment to her. She wanted one of them to run the company for her. Roger had turned to the professorate and John, the more manly of the two by a long shot, to the priesthood. Still, Brigid hadn't complained. 'God's holy will in a vocation to the priesthood is a great blessing on us,' she remarked, 'and, sure, aren't the Irish a race of saints and scholars anyway?'

Roger was not altogether certain she believed what she said, but it didn't matter, because she supported both of their vocations with all her very considerable strength. It might have been more generous of the Almighty, nonetheless, to have left John in the lay state. He would have done very well as president of the firm, and if he had married, he undoubtedly would have been faithful to his wife.

Roger was mildly amused by John's fascination with Irene, a fascination that she did not notice and that John thought he hid well. It dated back to that confused summer of 1963 in Grand Beach, when it seemed that the old rector would never be replaced at the seminary and John turned down the subdeaconate and almost abandoned his plans for the priesthood. They would have made an excellent match. Obviously he found her Bonwit's eroticism hard to resist. But there was no need to worry about them.

'Irene told me about your call yesterday,' Roger said to his brother, who had just turned off his shower. 'I had a talk with the child. I believe it was successful.'

John was drying himself briskly with a big towel. 'It frightens me every time she seems to be able to read my thoughts. I thought the doctors said it would stop with the advent of puberty.'

Roger shrugged as he turned off his own shower. 'Irene and I are used to it. As you doubtless remember, I have my doubts about the medical profession. Still, I am not troubled by these, ah, manifestations. It doesn't seem to have had any ill effects on her.'

Roger couldn't help himself. With John he always became the dry analytic college professor. Just as John doubtless became the concerned cleric.

John wrapped the wet towel around his waist. 'What did you tell her about Danny?'

'I was discreet.'

John tried again. 'You and Irene should do something to bring the child into line. It's time she started behaving like a mature woman.'

'Harness the cyclone?'

'So many of the children in this neighbourhood are spoiled.'

What a pompous ass you are, dear brother.

'We are not spoiling her, Monsignor,' Roger said stiffly. 'I don't notice your restraining her power as director of the folk group at the ten o'clock Mass.'

John shook his head solemnly. 'I'm worried about what the people in the parish think about that. I'm afraid that a lot of the old-timers must think she's dreadfully bold.'

'And the pastor's niece, too,' Roger commented with heavy irony.

'Precisely.' As usual, the pastor did not notice the irony.

The two brothers walked into the locker room together.

'We must all take our chances, I guess,' Roger said, and sighed as he turned toward his locker at the other end of the room from John's. 'See you later at Mother's.'

'Of course. Noele and Irene coming?'

'I assume so.'

'Are you really going to get messed up in a race for governor?' John asked, implying that only a fool would do that.

'I might. Are you really going to sign a new contract for that damn fool programme, and play the part of a clerical Phil Donahue for another year?'

'I might.'

Ah, thought Roger as he dressed, such great brotherly affection.

Ace

Captain Richard McNamara, USN (retired), PhD, professor of clinical psychology, was, as one of his friends remarked, crazier than most people thought he was. It was an epigram in which the Ace delighted.

Not very many chaplains would have dared to challenge the Cardinal Archbishop of New York, when that worthy was visiting his base, on the grounds that there had been a ghastly mistake in Rome and that he, rather than the cardinal, should have been presiding over New York.

At first the cardinal had seemed outraged. Then, good County Mayo man that he was, he realized his leg was being pulled and pulled back.

'That's corruption for you, Captain,' he had said solemnly.

Then they'd both laughed, the cardinal a bit uneasily.

Nor was the outrageous wit and the merry laughter a mask. McNamara did indeed have leprechaun blood in him.

And his father was reputed to have been the shrewdest police captain on the South Side, a shrewdness Chaplain McNamara had inherited.

So when he saw Noele Farrell flouncing toward the Courts, dressed in her Sunday best, he knew there was trouble.

Of course, he whistled with the other teenagers.

''Scuse me, guys,' he said in a loud voice. 'I have to get my weekly orders from Mother Superior.'

'Geeks!' said Noele in mock displeasure.

'You came by to distract us,' he said.

How had the Farrells, dull upper crust of the Irish

middle class that they were, produced someone like her, a dazzling mixture of fragility and strength, of naiveté and wisdom.

'I came to find out about Danny Farrell and about my grandfather's death.' The flattered teenager had instantly become the deadly serious young woman.

Was her intuition a throwback to an earlier phase of the evolutionary process? Or perhaps it was an anticipation of something yet to come, a mixture of shrewd hunches, keen powers of observation, and a remarkable sensitivity to the feelings of others. Whatever it was, she could be hurt so easily.

'I was in chaplain's school learning to be a lean, mean praying machine.'

'Keen, too,' she said, hearing his unspoken word.

'Anyway . . . anyway, what makes you think he was involved in your grandfather's death?'

'There is something about him, you know, that nobody wants to tell me. They all have different stories about him, okay? Uncle says he was kind of a bum, and Moms says that he was sweet and kind, and Roger says he was brilliant and fun. And they tell me different things about Gramps's death: Uncle says he was a little drunk and Roger says he wasn't. And Moms says he had really, like, bonged a load.'

'Bonged a load?' he parried.

'Don't gag me.' She would not be put off. 'I mean, like, totally soused.'

'He did drink a lot.'

'See? What did I tell you?'

McNamara flipped the basketball from one hand to the other. The boys waited silently, not daring to risk the red-haired goddess's wrath.

'I really don't know what happened, Noele. I think Clancy simply fell down the stairs, like everyone said he did. Why should you suspect differently?'

You didn't have to be fey to guess that the Farrell clan was loaded with guilty secrets, like a caravan of smugglers crossing the desert at night. If Noele was on to something . . .

'They're hiding the truth, and I'm going to find out what it is.'

'Be careful,' he said cautiously.

'Yes, sir, Captain, sir.' In another dizzy change of mood, she saluted him. 'Whatever you say, Captain, sir.'

The red car peeled away. Male catcalls followed, and Flame responded with a derisive bleat of its horn.

The captain did not enjoy the rest of the game.

Irene

After she had dressed for dinner, she watched the leaves falling on Jefferson Avenue, cascading like a multicoloured waterfall in the brisk autumn wind. Rain tonight and the end of Indian summer.

Multicoloured waterfall . . . not a bad metaphor. She reached in her purse and withdrew a small spiral notebook, in which she made a notation.

One must always record metaphors, even if no one else would ever read them.

Had Roger found a new mistress at the University? Probably. He found one every year. And to protect his ego she had to pretend not to know.

Why did a man with so little passion need a mistress?

She closed her purse thoughtfully.

Probably something to do with his relationship to his mother. That might make an interesting story. . . .

She took out her notebook again and made another note. She considered the note thoughtfully and then shrugged.

She closed the notebook, remembered something, and opened it.

Return manuscripts to secret drawer, she wrote.

She had a bad habit of not putting them away after she worked on them. They were still in her vanity.

Maybe she should do it now. No, Roger was waiting for her downstairs, the keys to the Mercedes in hand. After he had chided her mildly for being late, they would drive to Brigid's house over on the drive for second Sunday supper. Solemn high event.

She looked at herself in a mirror. Everything in order. Makeup restrained and skilfully applied. Beige dress not too tight and hanging neatly. A presentably attractive if somewhat full-blown matron.

Noele's teenage entourage, sweaty furniture in the house, covertly ogled her as if she were a naked statue in a museum they were touring under the watchful eyes of a nun. But there was nothing covert in Jaimie Burns's frank admiration. She should be flattered that the eyes of healthy young male animals deemed her worth measuring for a centrefold. Instead she was flustered.

Mysterious and sexy, as Noele claimed? Irene couldn't quite see that.

Her mother-in-law would compliment her on her dress, her hair, or some piece of new jewellery, but behind her soft brogue there would be an edge of ridicule for a woman who had nothing better to do with her time. And if, God help her, she ever ventured an opinion of her own, Brigid would smile condescendingly and change the subject. The unspoken assumption would be, as always, that she had nothing to contribute to the conversation.

And Noele, spunky Christmas child, would drag her into the conversation regardless.

They all underestimated Noele.

Why were they so upset with the child's questions about the past? What were they hiding?

Irene felt guilty. Some secrets belonged only to those who knew them.

Again she was angry at the Farrells, twice now in two days. Perhaps because the autumn leaves made her feel both mortal and cheated. Perhaps she should fight back before it was too late.

Roger

He sat in his study drumming his fingers on the corner of the desk, waiting for his wife. Why did she always take so long to dress? And why, when she finally appeared, did she always look so apprehensive, as if she were wearing someone else's three-hundred-dollar dress? Roger did not particularly enjoy these command performances at his mother's every second Sunday, continuing an alleged custom of Julie Farrell's, an earlier immigrant woman. But he was always amused by the way Brigid's eyes swept quickly and critically over Irene when they arrived. She could never find anything wrong, of course. Irene always looked like a model, if a hesitant and uneasy one.

And then John would follow her every movement, devouring her – stripping her, one might even say – with avid eyes. Small wonder that she often had a bit too much to drink.

Roger took a certain pride in his wife's beauty, if only because other men envied him. Until she opened her mouth, at any rate. But even if he was bored with her, he could not permit himself to be captured by one of his slaves the way some of his colleagues had, some of whom even wrote novels about such reversals. If the slave could dispossess the wife in a process as old as mankind's exploitation of womankind, then the new wife or the new 'relevant other' could as easily be dispossessed by one of her successors. . . .

Roger shuddered. As Noele would say, it was gross.

He might have fallen in love with his sweet, sexy little slave creature. He might stay in love with her, although he doubted that. But he would never leave Irene for her or for anyone else.

He believed in marriage commitments as a matter of principle, one of the many convictions from his Catholic Action days that still dominated his life, even though he would admit them only to himself. Moreover, he was quite content with Irene as a wife. Sex with intense, slightly masculine academic women was a pleasant enough obsession despite the self-hatred that came afterward. Living with one of them, however, would be quite impossible. Irene was shy and unobtrusively decorative. She was no particular asset to his academic or political career, but neither was she a liability. She kept the house neat and created for him an ambience of well-ordered tranquility to which he was happy to return. So he remained married for reasons not unlike those which supported his decision to live in the Neighbourhood: he preferred the atmosphere of an Irish political and professional neighbourhood to that of a mostly Jewish academic neighbourhood. And his daughter, as he told one of his colleagues, would not grow up being hassled to sign a petition every time she went shopping in the co-op.

Moreover, Roger felt genuinely sorry for Irene. She worshipped him and was completely dependent upon him. He had never really loved her; but then he had never really disliked her, either. Her constant need for affection was no more troublesome, really, than that of an affectionate Irish setter.

He would have, in principle, preferred being faithful to her. But fidelity, he had decided regretfully long ago, was quite beyond his powers. So he had remained married to Irene and continued to be a frequent and guilt-ridden sinner.

And, of course, there was Noele. The amazing and miraculous young woman adored her father and bickered with her mother – Irene's envy was all too pathetically open. Noele was, nevertheless, fiercely loyal to her mother. And with a temper as hair-triggered as her grandmother's and her clerical uncle's, she became bitterly angry at Roger whenever he seemed to slight Irene. It would be relatively easy to get along without his wife, but curiously enough, Roger would not want to have to face life without his bright, responsive, witty, faintly mocking daughter.

Noele had left no doubt on the subject of divorce. 'Have you ever thought of divorcing Moms?' she had asked him bluntly one night during the summer when he was several hours late in joining them at their summer home in Michiana, accusation and anger darting at him from her dangerous green eyes.

'Of course not, Snowflake,' he had said uneasily. 'Whatever would make you think that?'

'All teenagers worry about it, and besides, sometimes you don't take Moms very seriously.'

'Married people develop codes and protocols.'

'Stop talking like a political scientist,' she had said. 'And just remember, Roger' – she had called him by his first name since she had been a child – 'Moms and I may fight a lot, but if you walk out on her, you lose me, too. Is that clear?'

Roger had put up his arms in mock self-defence. 'God, I wouldn't want to have you angry at me.'

'Really,' Noele agreed.

Danny X. Farrell, Roger thought, if you were still alive, you would appreciate Noele; she would probably be the only woman in the neighbourhood who would be a match for you.

Noele

'Come on in.' Grams hugged her vigorously. 'I've put on the tea kettle, and we'll brew you a pot of tea. We'll have a wee drop before the others come.' They both laughed, because it was Grams's standard greeting. She was self-conscious about her brogue and tried to hide it usually, but not with Noele, because Noele had told her a brogue was cute. ''Tis a wondrous dress you're wearing there, if an old woman's judgement means anything.'

''Course it does,' Noele said, almost as pleased as she had been by Jaimie's touchdown run.

Noele had figured out long ago the reactions of all her relatives to a red-haired, green-eyed sixteen-year-old. She made Uncle Monsignor nervous and uneasy, as did all teenagers; she enchanted her father with a mixture of wide-eyed adoration and emerging intelligence; she frightened her mother, poor dear, who wanted to be like her and who didn't think much of herself. Noele accepted all of these transparent reactions as a matter of course. That's the way adults acted. It was a shame, maybe, but there was nothing she could do about it.

Grams, on the other hand, was a deep one, sometimes as soft as Irish rain, sometimes as hard as flint; sometimes a gentle angel, and other times, well, a raging devil. Noele often thought that she was more like her grandmother than like anyone else in the family. They both had red hair, though Noele thought that it was ridiculous to say she got her red hair from Grams. It wasn't the same kind of red hair at all.

'Grams's red hair,' she had pointed out sadly to Jaimie Burns, 'is beautiful; mine is only striking.'

Grams warmed the teapot, carefully deposited the tea leaves in it, after measuring them in a teaspoon first, then poured a precise amount of hot water over the leaves.

Unlike others of her age, who were acutely embarrassed at the suggestion of sex between people over thirty, particularly their parents, Noele was fascinated by 'old' sex. Probably, she told herself, because she was fascinated by sex. Period.

The coolness between her parents troubled her deeply. And she was delighted and a little frightened by the aura of physical affection between her grandmother and Burke Kennedy. They were like two pirates, saved from ugliness only by their attraction for each other. And the attraction itself, Noele sensed, could be dangerous and deadly.

Small wonder, she decided, that Burke was jazzed by Grams. She was erect and graceful, even though she had never been to modelling school, and had a really excellent build. The lines on her face merely added character. And she smoked too much, and ate and drank as much as she wanted, and it didn't affect her figure at all. Noele was totally bummed. I should be that way when I'm really that old.

'Well, I gather you've been poking around in the family closet looking for skeletons?' said Brigid, lifting the teapot as though to pour it, and then, as part of the ritual, deciding that it needed perhaps another half minute of steeping. 'I suppose we will have to put up with that until you are ready to settle down and run the firm for me.'

Unlike the other adults of the family Grams did not really expect a reply to her call for maturity and responsibility.

And she totally didn't get one.

'That's what I like about you, Grams. You don't beat around the bush. . . . Hey, look what I've done! I've made a family tree. Isn't it excellent?'

'I never was very good at figuring these things out.' Grams tilted the chart in a number of different directions and then put it back on the coffee table. Now the thick, black tea was ready to be poured – the tea before the milk, the Irish way, not the English way of the milk before the tea.

Noele picked up the chart. 'First of all, there was Brendan John Farrell, born in Tralee, County Kerry, in 1861. At the age of twenty-nine he married Julie Roache of Castle Island in the same County Kerry, and they migrated to Chicago, where Brendan John Farrell became a day labourer in the sewers they were constructing on South Parkway – that's Martin Luther King Drive now, Grams.'

'I'm not without knowledge of that street name change, young woman.'

'Good. Then, in 1891, they had a son who was called William Farrell, and four years later a daughter, Monica Farrell, and both Monica and her mother – the poor thing was only thirty, Grams – died in the cholera epidemic that same year. And Brendan Farrell died five years later in an accident in the sewers – and probably of a broken heart, too, or is that being too romantic?'

'People had broken hearts in 1900, child,' Grams said sadly.

'So that left Bill Farrell an orphan at the age of nine. He lived at a place called Feehanville – after some archbishop – which later became St Mary's Training School and then, even later, Mayville Academy, until he was fifteen, which would be around 1906, I guess. Then he went to work driving a garbage truck, with horses. Can you imagine that, Grams? Horses?'

'Just barely,' her grandmother said ironically. 'I can just barely imagine a horse-drawn truck.'

'Silly. Well, anyway, in 1911, only twenty years old, just three years and a few months older than me, he founded Farrell Construction Company with the money he'd saved from his job. And by 1917 he had enough money to buy an apartment building in Washington Park and to be rich. What was rich then, Grams?'

'About a half-million dollars, I think. But that wasn't all he had, child. Bill Farrell had lots of political clout.'

'Doesn't everyone?' asked Noele. 'Anyway, he was in the Illinois National Guard, 131st Infantry, and went into the war – that's the First World War, right? – and won a medal in a battle called Belleau Wood, means beautiful place. And then right after the war he married a young woman from Garfield Boulevard named Blanche Hogan. Let me see, she was twenty-three, and he was twenty-eight. Both her parents died in the flu epidemic right after the marriage. I don't remember Great Grams very well. What was she like?'

'Small wonder, child, that you don't remember her well; she was dead eleven years before you were born, as you'd notice if you looked closely at that chart of yours. Blanche Farrell was very pretty, and terribly dependent on her husband, a nervous, flighty little thing, who always got her way by weeping and sniffling. By the time I knew her she was as filled with hate as anyone I've ever known, and all of it hiding behind a sweet smile and a wet handkerchief. Poor woman – went crazy altogether after your great-grandfather died.'

'They had twin sons,' Noele continued. 'Clarence and Martin, both born at the same time, since they were twins, in 1919. But in 1944, just a month before his son, Lieutenant Martin Farrell, died in the first battle of the Philippine Sea, when his Avenger torpedo bomber ran out of gas, Bill Farrell died of a massive stroke.' Noele traced the lines on her neatly drawn chart. 'Martin Farrell had married Florence Carey in 1939, a girl from this neighbourhood. Gosh, the twins were born in 1919, so that meant that Martin was twenty and his first wife was eighteen. That's awfully young to get married!'

'He left Notre Dame after his sophomore year to go into naval flight training,' Grams said, her head turned away as if she were trying to remember, or maybe trying to forget. 'Those were reckless times, child. People thought very romantic things about not coming back; they didn't seem to realize that would mean they were dead. Your uncle Martin was very romantic, as was his wife, poor woman.'

Brigid poured them both a second cup of tea with solemn ceremony, permitting the tea to rise no higher than a half inch from the top of the cup. Noele waited respectfully till the ritual was completed.

'And then Florence was run over by a truck the year her husband's plane crashed. So their son, Daniel Farrell, born in 1944, was the second orphan in the family in this century. Fortunately he had someone to take care of him.'

'Fortunately.'

'Because here's where the story gets *really* interesting. Clarence Farrell, Martin's twin brother, had married just a week after Martin a certain Brigid Flynn, an immigrant from Ireland who was – and is – absolutely gorgeous and whose passport said she was eighteen, but she was really just sixteen, no older than me.'

''Tis the truth, I'm afraid. I wasn't even Brigid. I was baptized Mary Maeve, Maeve for short. My father didn't like me all that much. He said my red hair and freckles were evidence that I was a changeling – a gypsy child. So at the last minute he sent me to the United States to work as a maid and kept my sister, who really was Brigid and was two years older than me, home in Ireland.'

'And you've never gone back to see her?'

'You know the story, child, as well as I do. No, I've never sent a word back to them, much less gone to see them. And I never will. It was a cold winter morning with the water frozen. Da woke me up and pulled me out of bed and told me I was going to America instead of Brigid. I wept, I pleaded, I fell on my knees and begged him. All he did was box my ears and order me out of the house.'

Deep inside Noele there was a memory of the horrible morning, as though it had happened to her and not Grams, a vague and undefined, but terribly painful, memory, like smoke pouring from a burning room.

'But it was all for the best, wasn't it?' she asked anxiously.

'In a manner of speaking,' her grandmother said softly.

Noele rushed on to finish the story, not wanting to expose her grandmother to more pain.

'Well, you and Gramps had two sons: John, who is now a big important monsignor, pastor of this parish, and a famous television personality; and Roger, a college professor and future governor. In 1964 he married Irene Conlon, also from this neighbourhood . . . who in turn produced a nosy little girl whose name I don't remember.'

'Did she ever!'

'And you and Gramps took over the family business when Bill Farrell died, and Martin Farrell was killed, and Blanche Hogan Farrell went mad. You made heaps of money and bought miles of real estate and gasoline stations and shopping plazas and other neat things. And then, when your poor husband . . .' Noele trailed off.

'When in a fit of anger he slipped and fell down the stairs . . .'

Another explanation, thought Noele, not drunk, but angry.

'How did it happen, Grams?' she asked softly.

'It seemed as natural as though he were sitting down in the TV room after dinner. . . . We'd had drinks here: Father John, as he was then; Roger, home for Christmas from that awful pagan school in Berkeley; Danny, who was about to leave for his new job with the CIA; and your mother, of course. . . .'

'Uh-huh.' It was the first she had heard about Moms's presence.

'Well, Danny was in one of his black moods, what with him being thrown out of the Navy and all and sorrowing for President Kennedy, whom he worshipped – God be good to the poor man. And he and Clancy had a fierce argument, nothing that was new; they were fighting all the time. Clancy blamed the Kennedy family for an investigation of the firm. And he said some nasty words about the poor president. That made Danny furious. Then Clancy took out after Irene because her father had dragged him before a grand jury, and that made your mother cry. She cried too much, if you ask me. Anyway, Danny came as close to striking your grandfather as I'd ever seen him. He didn't, thank God, but he walked out of the club with your mother and took her home. So the party was spoiled. Father John went back to his rectory on the North Side. Your father went down to the basement to play cards. He used to like to play gin rummy at the club in those days – 'twas before he became a professor and too great a man to be wasting his time at cards. And your grandfather and I went home. . . .

'We were both tired and went right up the stairs, those stairs over there. Your grandfather was still angry at poor Danny – God be good to him, too. He raved and ranted about what an ungrateful child he was after all we had done for him. I watched him storm up the stairs, cursing and pounding the banister with his fist every step of the way. Then at the head of the stairs, he turned to shout something back at me. Dear God in heaven, he lost his balance, grabbed for the banister, and missed it.'

'Oh, Grams,' Noele breathed softly, 'I didn't mean to . . .'

'That's all right, child. It happened a long time ago, and I can talk about it now. Your grandfather fell all the way down the stairs, and when I rushed to help him, blood was pouring from his head. I looked down at my new white-lace party dress, and it was covered with blood. I didn't know what to do or where the boys were. So I called Burke. He called the police because poor Clancy was dead, even though I didn't want to admit it. He was still crumpled up at the foot of the stairs when the boys got here. Danny was the last to come home. He'd been driving around to cool off after the fight at the club, and you can imagine how he felt when he saw his uncle lying there in a pool of blood.'

'How terrible,' Noele said softly, wondering how her grandmother could continue to climb those stairs every day.

'That was all there was to it, child. Another inch and he would probably still be alive today.'

And where would you and Burkie be then? Noele thought to herself. 'God be good to him, too,' she said aloud.

'Aye,' her grandmother agreed.

'Then,' Noele went on quickly, hoping to blot out the memories of that terrible night, 'you became the president of the company – I suspect you were running it all along – and made even more tons of money, so that I can drive around in my brand new red Chevette.'

'And yourself probably wanting a BMW at that.' Brigid lighted a cigarette, even though she knew her grand-daughter disapproved.

'Which leads to the second most fascinating person of the Farrell family – after this beautiful granddaughter of yours – Daniel X. Farrell, born in 1940, graduated from Annapolis in 1961, resigned from the United States Navy 1963, missing, presumed dead, in 1964. Is he really dead, Grams?'

'Aye, child, he's really dead. Poor man.'

'I know that's what everybody says, but something seems weird about it.'

'Weird? He was flying a plane, one of them U-2 things, for the CIA, and it stopped working over China. That's not weird, Noele; it's tragic, but it's not mysterious. Besides, if he had lived, they would have released him when Mr Nixon went to China and all the other prisoners were released.'

'Hmmm. . . . What was he like, Grams?'

Brigid's face brightened, and her brogue grew thicker. 'Ah, he'd break your heart. He was a rascal, like his father, only worse. Smooth talker, witty, unpredictable – sure you'd think he'd swallowed the whole Blarney stone. But he was smart, God knows. He could have been a great man. But he wanted to be a writer, which was a crazy idea. What kind of good would come from something like that? And he was as lazy as sin. A fast-talking gombeen man who couldn't keep his mouth shut, which is why he got himself thrown out of the Navy, himself defending a lazy black seaman. That was your cousin, Daniel Xavier Farrell.'

'And you loved him a lot?'

'Everyone did.'

'What would he be like today if he had lived?'

'Ah, child, what's the use of asking a question like that. There's no answer to be had at all, at all.'

'Monsignor John said that he would have been an alcoholic, like Great Gramma Blanche. And Moms said that maybe he would have been a great writer. What do you think, Grams?'

Brigid Farrell frowned thoughtfully. 'Ah, could have been both of those things and a lot more, too. But we'll never know, will we?'

At that moment Burke Kennedy, who had been watching the Chicago Bears, came into the parlour and asked if he might have a cup of tea.

Noele thought Burkie was cute. And he didn't like to be called Burkie. So naturally she called him Burkie kind of all the time.

She hadn't told either of them that she didn't mind their life-long love affair. They would both be forgiven much because of their devotion to each other.

And, Noele supposed, as cute as they were with each other, there probably was a lot to be forgiven.

She shivered slightly and poured the tea for Burkie with the same elaborate ceremony that Grams used.

'You've been watching another redheaded woman pour tea,' he said. He smiled, like an old Roman general coming into his wife's villa, but it was an uneasy smile.

'If you're going to do something, you should do it right,' Noele said, mimicking her grandmother. 'Really!'

And you are as nervous about this conversation as she is, Noele thought. Look at the way your fingers are twitching. They're covered with yucky automobile grease, but they're frightened. I wonder why.

Brigid

The second Sunday dinner was over, a not particularly sparkling event. The child had everyone worried, Brigid thought, as she removed her earrings.

She had cleaned up some of the mess and come upstairs to find Burke waiting for her in his vast shaggy brown robe. He was a big man, and solid, with long white hair and a square red face, and looked like a Celtic warrior preparing to ravage a captive woman. He watched her with obvious admiration as she leaned against the dressing table. Her own body began its subtle cycle of response to both his tough masculine attractiveness and his admiration for her.

Burke Kennedy was a hard, ruthless man. She was a hard, ruthless woman. That's why they loved each other, though in their love there was breathtaking softness as well as harsh passion.

In 1944, at the time of the deaths of Bill Farrell and his son, Lieutenant Martin Farrell of the United States Navy, Burke Kennedy, who had inherited from his own father responsibility for the Farrell family's complex legal problems, had hinted that some of the legal problems the Farrells faced would be resolved if she would give herself to him. Brigid was flattered and attracted to him, but indignantly refused and reported the proposition to her husband. To her humiliation, Clancy Farrell ordered her to yield.

It was, he argued, essential to keep the firm out of the hands of a court-appointed trustee. If a careful audit was made, he might have to go to jail, though it was his father who had manipulated the funds and bribed the politicians and paid off the racketeers. Besides, they might end up without a penny. Did she want that to happen?

Brigid's feeling of degradation was made worse because she knew that her husband's orders were in fact her mother-in-law's orders. Blanche Hogan Farrell had told her son to give his wife to a man to win a favour for the family, and he had obeyed her.

Brigid had little respect for her husband. A parlour maid

in a rich friend's house to whom it was hinted that a much better life was possible if she responded to a young man's interest, she had more or less been purchased by Bill Farrell to assure that there would be grandchildren and heirs if Marty was killed in the war.

Why she had ever interested Clancy was beyond her comprehension. . . .

Brigid had wished that she had been purchased for Martin instead of his twin brother, Clancy. But Marty was quite capable of finding a wife on his own, poor, dear, innocent kid that Flossie was.

The first night with Burke Kennedy began in shame, fury, and terror and ended in mind-numbing pleasure. Both had insisted ever since that the other had been the conqueror.

With Burke's help Brigid had taken de facto control of the firm and made huge profits. Together they carefully covered up Clancy's inept plot to defraud his brother and his brother's son. Together they kept Clancy from doing any more harm to the firm. And together they regularly, if discreetly, made love till Clancy's death. In 1964, with Clancy at last blessedly out of the way, they became, in Father John's lovely phrase, 'notorious and public sinners' until Burke's mad wife, Eloise, died of chronic alcoholism and cirrhosis of the liver.

That was six years ago, and Brigid had said, 'half fun, in full earnest,' that marriage could be a mistake: 'Respectability might destroy the excitement.'

For thirty years she and Burke had loved each other with a need that grew more demanding each time it was temporarily sated, regardless of what anyone, God himself included, might have thought. She was wary of change, but Burke insisted that it was necessary to marry for the sake of their children, who found their relationship difficult to explain to their friends. Moreover, he said, 'I want you as my wife at long last.'

Her fears were groundless. She was as good a wife as she had been a mistress. The glow of approval and want in Burke's cynical brown eyes was the same now as on that first emotional, ecstatic night in the Palmer House.

'What can a sixteen-year-old child, admittedly an intelligent and perceptive child, possibly do to cause such concern?' Burke asked.

Brigid ground out her cigarette and leaned against the vanity table. She should brush her hair but was too tired. Instead, she reached for the brandy glass. 'The only thing that worries me is that Protestant missionary who claimed he'd been with him in the prison camp.'

Burke rose from the bed and placed his hands around Brigid's still presentably slender waist. 'Noele is not going to try to interview the director of the Central Intelligence Agency.'

She felt the thrill of excitement that always accompanied Burke's touch.

'I'm tired of having to pretend, Burke; all my life . . .' Much to her surprise she was weeping. She leaned her head against her husband's shoulder.

'I wish everybody else knew you, Bridie,' he said reassuringly, using the nickname no one else dared to call her as his strong fingers moved up her body, 'the way I know you, the frail, immigrant girl, not the tough, successful businesswoman.'

The firm, familiar pressure of his fingers made the tears flow more abundantly.

'We're old, Burke,' she sobbed. 'We don't look as old as our friends at the club, but death is drawing near for us, just as it is for them. And I'm so tired . . .'

Burke encircled her with his arms, soothing and caressing her. The weeping diminished. 'I'm an hysterical old woman.'

'Merely a tired and beautiful woman,' he said. 'A woman I love.'

Brigid knew she was damned. From the day of her arrival in America in 1934, her life had been nothing but sinful – lust, deceit, adultery, even murder. She was beyond forgiveness. Death would mean an eternity of blackness, not the hell fire of the catechism class of the west of Ireland, not the hell of frustrated self-fulfilment – about which her son the monsignor was probably talking with the pious young actress on Channel 3 at this very moment – but the hell of black nothingness reserved for those who are so profoundly evil, they can be put nowhere else by divine justice but in a dark and bottomless abyss.

A few more years, and the shadows would close in forever. Please God, though I know you don't listen to me, protect us for those next few years. Don't let the evil come out of the grave to destroy us.

'Love me, Burke,' she pleaded.

'I have every intention of doing that, Bridie,' he said. 'That's why I'm here.'

They were elaborately skilled in loving each other, knowing the motions and movements, the touches and the kisses that endeared, tantalized, surprised, and rewarded. As she slipped easily into the never monotonous routine, Brigid remembered the first night in the Palmer House suite, where Burke had been staying for a bar association convention. Tossing aside her clothes, she had stood before him, her face flaming as brightly as her hair, and screamed that she was there on her husband's orders.

Burke was surprised and stunned; he stammered that his proposition was not seriously meant and tried not to look at her.

'It's too late now to pretend that you didn't mean it,' she raged. 'And God damn you, look at me!'

And it was much too late. They both knew they were trapped. Neither wanted not to be trapped. Their embrace was violent and angry, then somehow – Brigid never understood how – it changed.

They had cheated damnation for thirty years. Time was running out. A few more years and the cheating would be over.

Clancy had beaten her often, though always privately and silently, without visible effects, so that no one would know what he had done – no one but Burke, who was furious at the big bruises on her body. Brigid accepted the beatings as punishment she deserved and forbade Burke to do anything about them.

Burke's body pressed down upon hers the way she liked it to, making her helpless beneath him, able only to respond to his implacable rhythms. She gave herself totally to those rhythms, arching up to meet him and revelling in her total dependence on him. Her world became a single point of pleasure that glowed with a bright red flame, then a fierce white fire that finally exploded and sent her spiralling into space. From a great distance she heard her wild animal cry of pleasure.

Oceans of sweetness washed over her, wiping out the memory of Clancy Farrell's blood turning the new blue carpet crimson.

Dear God, she prayed, as she sailed helplessly through the heavens, give us a little more time.

Burke

Still breathing rapidly, he turned off the dim light by which they made love and with his lips and his hands soothed his wife back to peacefulness.

'We'll civilize you Danes yet,' she said sleepily. 'Good enough for you.'

'Then you'll be the sorry one,' he replied.

Preliminaries of sex with Brigid were brisk and business-like. The actual encounter was normally violent, even savage – the way Burke liked it to be with a woman. But when it was over she was pathetically vulnerable. Even on that first screaming, clawing night in the Palmer House, with the thunderstorm raging outside, he saw when they were finished how fragile this wild, crude, superstitious woman was.

And it was her appealing fragility that bound him to her. Passionate women Burke had known before, but none who were so devastatingly vulnerable.

In a way she had civilized him. After her, there could be no other woman. She was more than enough. And while he had once been one of the most ruthless of the legal powerbrokers – 'the smartest crooked lawyer in town,'

Dick Daley, no admirer of Burke, had once said – he gradually pulled back from the game. He loved it with every fibre of his being, but he loved Brigid more. He could not take the risk of going to jail and leaving her unprotected.

What a shame they did not have children of their own. Her half-made sons had too much of Clancy in them ever to amount to anything. The only one in the family up to her was Noele . . . and she was not really . . .

Burke did not want to think about that ingenious, winning, delightfully impertinent, and possibly very dangerous child.

He felt no guilt about anything he had done. Indeed, for the past six years he had been a model of probity. As for the things before that . . . well, they were over and done with.

The only problem was the dreams.

And he knew that he would have them tonight.

He kissed his love, now sleeping quietly, and prepared to face the terrors of the night.

If anyone threatened Brigid again, he would stop at nothing to protect her. God – if there was one – should expect nothing else from him.

James III

They were parked in Flame, in front of the Farrell house on Jefferson Avenue. Noele nestled close to Jaimie Burns. The same fingers that had stolen the pigskin from the frustrated Hurricanes now stroked the tense muscles in the back of her neck with infinite delicacy. Noele was deeply worried. As she often was.

'What's up, MN?' he asked.

'Don't stop,' she pleaded.

'I wasn't planning to.'

When Jaimie was a little boy, his father had been away

in Vietnam – before he ran for Congress – and Jaimie had
been very close to his mother. He had learned to be sensitive to women and gentle with them. Most useful skills in
dealing with the dazzling, unpredictable, and utterly
delightful Mary Noele Farrell. At one moment she was, if
not the bossy bitch she frequently called herself, at least
very much in charge of everything and everybody. And
the next moment she was a terrified affection sponge
whom you could not love too much or too tenderly. Jaimie
was pleased that he was one of the very few people who
had been permitted to be close to the sponge, and indeed
to provide vast amounts of affection for her. It beat inter-
cepting passes.

'Do you think Danny Farrell might be still alive?' she
asked suddenly.

She could still surprise Jaimie. His fingers stopped dead
in their tracks.

'Don't stop,' she said, repeating her order.

'He's been dead for eighteen years, Noele. All the prisoners were released when Nixon visited China.'

She cuddled closer to him.

'There's something terribly wrong, Jaimie. I just know it.
I feel it. They're all lying to me. They tell me different
things about Grandpa Clancy's death – he was drunk, he
wasn't drunk, he was a little drunk. And different things
about Danny, too. He was a genius, he was a bum, he was
Peter Pan, he was a great man. They're afraid of him even
though they all say he's dead.'

'The world says he's dead too.'

She pounded on his chest. 'I know, but why do they get
so shifty-eyed and dishonest whenever I talk about him?'

Jaimie Burns had as much lust for the bodies of pretty
young women as any man his age, maybe a little bit more.
And he had been well aware that when Noele was in one
of her 'collapse' moods – as she was tonight – she was
intensely sensual and might possibly be lured off to bed. It
was a very attractive possibility, made unattractive by the
certainty that the guilt and the anguish of the next day
would probably shatter their friendship.

As he said to his father when the congressman worried

about the relationship, Noele was a speculation in a future commodity.

'Delayed gratification,' he'd told the congressman, who was impressed with the words his son was learning in college.

'A long delay,' said James II.

'A gratification worth waiting for,' replied James III.

'I think you may love her,' his mother laughed, encouraging him, as her laughter always did, because it contained so much respect and affection.

'Tell me about it,' her son said.

DANCE
THREE

Galliard

'A gay, rollicking sixteenth-century dance of Italian origin . . . frequently coupled with a pavane.'

Irene

There was laughter coming from Tommy Taylor's room. At last someone was making the little boy laugh. Her curiosity and her sorrow that she had never borne a boy child drove Irene to peek in the door of the hospital room.

Her brother-in-law, Monsignor John Farrell, was shadow-boxing with the leukemia victim, and pretending to lose.

'Tommy never beat up a monsignor before,' John explained, winking at her.

Irene's two volunteer afternoons at the hospital, visiting old people and children, were the high point of her week. With the sick she was, somehow, both gracious and graceful. But Tommy had always been immune to her laughter and her stories.

And John had cracked him in five minutes.

He was good with kids, except for teenagers, who were turned over completely to the resilient Father McNamara. Almost every afternoon he could be seen in the school-yard, talking and joking with the students as they poured out of the school – in far more disorderly ranks than would have been tolerated in her day at St Praxides.

Tommy hugged John when it was time to leave and then hugged Irene for good measure.

'I'll be back in a minute, Tommy,' she promised.

The little boy grinned happily. 'I'll wait for you.'

'What are his chances?' she asked John as they walked down the freshly scrubbed corridor to the elevator. The hospital smelled of disinfectant, as did all Catholic hospitals – the price of having floors so clean that one can eat off them.

John threw up his hands in uncertainty. 'They think a remission is beginning. With some luck he could live until they find better cures than they have now. The parents are the problem.'

'They don't come very often. . . .'

He reached into the inside pocket of his carefully fitted jacket and pulled out a stack of the postcards Little Company of Mary Hospital sent to parishes about sick parishioners.

'Crises like a sick kid can tear a marriage apart. Ace – Father McNamara – says that as soon as the diagnosis is made both parents should go into therapy.' He shrugged. 'I suppose he's right. . . .'

'Could I buy you a cup of coffee?' Irene said, feeling that for once she was on her ground and not Farrell ground.

'I was thinking of making the same offer, but I've got five more patients to visit, two wakes this afternoon, two more this evening, a couple of marriage instructions, and a meeting of the parish school board.'

'With a schedule like that, how do you find time for the TV programme?'

He laughed, the winning John Farrell laugh that the women of the parish of every age adored. 'I wing it, Irene. What else?'

He was, God knows, a hardworking priest, taking up the slack for the two curates the parish used to have – one lost to the priest shortage and the other represented by the usually invisible Father Miller. About his love of his parish and people, there could be no doubt.

'You'll wear yourself out. How long has it been since you've had a vacation?'

'A couple of years now, but I'm going to try to get away for a week after Christmas.' He laughed winningly again, but it was wasted on her. 'By the way, has Roger said anything more about running for governor? Can't you talk him out of it?'

'Last night we were riding down the Ryan, coming

home from the concert, and he talked about the Taylor homes. We built some of those high-rise public housing slums. Roger feels the need to do something about such problems.'

There was no real love between Roger and Irene and not a large amount of affection, either. But sex and a common household made them at least companions, and she was an occasional sounding board for his efforts to recapture the political dedication that had animated him during the 1960s.

'I thought he gave up on politics after 1968,' John said. 'Kennedy's death, the convention, McCarthy's making a fool of himself. . . . Weren't those too much for my brother's precious idealism?'

How little they understood each other.

'I certainly can't stop him,' Irene said, 'and Brigid won't. I think she wants a son as governor, even if she won't admit it.'

An elevator door opened, but the car was filled with white- and blue-gowned doctors and nurses. John let the door close.

'Governors don't get re-elected. . . .' He bit his lip thoughtfully. 'Is Noele against the race?'

'She hasn't said. Still has Danny Farrell on her mind, I think.'

'That's all we need, isn't it?' He jabbed the elevator button. 'She's so young, so naive. . . . Were we ever that young, Irene?'

'I don't think you or Roger were. I might have been for a couple of weeks.'

'And Danny?'

'Danny never did grow up,' Irene said, instantly regretting her words.

The elevator door opened. John gripped her shoulder and brushed his lips against her cheek, reasonably close to her mouth but not too close – Monsignor John Farrell was with a woman parishioner who was also an in-law.

He was wearing a very pleasant male cologne.

'See you in church, Irene.'

And he disappeared behind the quickly closing elevator door.

His rough-hewn masculinity, emphasized by the cologne, stirred an extra heartbeat or two. Sweet-smelling bastard, Irene thought. And then reproved herself. He meant well, and he worked so damned hard.

We were all born middle-aged.

Except Danny.

She hurried back to Tommy's room, hoping that the nun in charge of the floor would not see her tears.

Tommy saw them. 'Don't cry, Mrs Farrell,' he said as she hugged him again. 'We'll be all right.'

She cried a few moments more, nevertheless, for Tommy's hope and for her own despair.

Noele

She felt her jaw tighten. Ever since he'd been hired, the parish's Director of Music, a thin, waspish, bald man with a slight stutter, had been trying to muscle in on the 9:15 teenage folk Mass, with some help from Father Miller, who vanished whenever Noele was around. Guitar music, the DOM had assured Uncle Monsignor, was no longer sanctioned in the best church-music circles. That meant he had come into a head-on conflict with Noele in her role as vice president of the High Club and principal guitarist of the folk group.

Noele forced her jaw to relax. Jaimie said that she was even more scary than usual when her jaw turned hard. Noele did not want to be a domineering woman – well, not most of the time. And she had to be particularly charming today at lunch with Jaimie's parents, because she had a very big favour to ask Congressman Burns.

Nonetheless, this morning's Mass had to be salvaged. Like her grandmother Brigid, Noele firmly believed that things that were worth doing ought to be done properly, even if it meant that she had to take charge and see that they were done properly. (Keeping one's room neat didn't count, because neatness in the room wasn't important.)

You don't have a proper teenage folk Mass when the DOM and two other retards sing a Mozart trio during Communion. Noele had nothing personal against Mozart, poor man; however, a Mozart trio during Communion wiped out the congregation's enthusiasm for singing, which the folk group had diligently stirred up earlier in the Mass. It was hard enough to get Catholics to sing in church as it was without pouring water on a weak fire with old Wolfgang Amadeus.

Moreover, the final hymn was 'Lord of the Dance,' Noele's favourite. She couldn't bear to have it sung listlessly.

Father Ace, who said the 9:15 Mass every Sunday, gave the final blessing. As he was urging the congregation to go forth in the peace of Christ, Noele in a vanilla wraparound dress with a green belt that the kids said made her look totally like Jamie Lee Curtis in *Halloween*, slipped up to the microphone on the left-hand side of the sanctuary, beating the slow-moving Director of Music by three feet.

'Our final hymn is "Lord of the Dance."' Michele Carmody and the other kids began to hum the familiar melody, which was the same as that of 'Simple Gifts.' Noele plunged on, like a dolphin that has surfaced and then dives back into the water. 'Our lives are a dance, and our friends and families are our dancing partners, and God is the head of the dance. He calls the tunes, and directs the music, and invites us all to dance. Sometimes He even interrupts our normal dances so that He can dance just with us. Let's all sing it like we were dancing so that God will know that we are ready to dance with Him whenever He wants.'

Congressman and Mrs Burns and all the little Burns kids in the second row of the church looked startled. Jaimie rolled his Robert Redford eyes. Father Ace laughed, and behind her the Director of Music coughed as if he were ready to die. Noele didn't budge an inch. Standing at the microphone, strumming vigorously on her guitar, she led the thousand assembled Christians in a rendition of 'Lord of the Dance' that made the walls of the long, cool, modern church shake with excitement.

I danced in the morning
When the world was begun,
I danced in the moon
And the stars and the sun.
I came down from heaven
And I danced on the earth,
At Bethlehem
I had My birth.
Dance, then,
Wherever you may be,
I am the Lord
Of the Dance, said He.
I'll lead you all
Wherever you may be,
I'll lead you all
In the Dance, said He.

I danced for the scribes
And the Pharisees,
But they would not dance,
They wouldn't follow Me.
I danced for the fisherman,
For James and John,
They came with Me
And the dance went on.

I danced on a Friday
When the sky turned black,
It's hard to dance
With the devil on your back.
They buried My body
And they thought I'd gone,
But I am the dance
And I still go on.

They cut Me down
And I leap up high,
I am the life
That'll never, never die.

I live in you
If you live in Me,
I am the Lord
Of the Dance, said He.

Dance, then,
Wherever you may be,
I am the Lord
Of the Dance, said He.
I'll lead you all
Wherever you may be,
I'll lead you all
In the Dance, said He.

As soon as the song was over Noele slipped away from the
folk group, dodging the Director of Music, with whom she
did not want to argue, and Father Ace, with whom she did
not want to banter. There were more important things to
be accomplished this Sunday morning.

Out of the corner of her eye, however, as she made for
the Burnses' Lincoln, she saw her uncle surrounded by
parishioners who paused to shake his hand before they
raced for their cars, newspapers, Sunday breakfast, and
the Chicago Bears on TV. They were telling him how much
they liked 'Lord of the Dance.' That would show the nerdy
Director of Music.

'Way out, Noele,' said Mrs Burns, who was sooo cool,
even though Noele had beaten her in a golf match at
Grand Beach last summer.

'You made the church come alive,' boomed the congressman. 'That was a profound experience.'

Always running for office.

Jaimie hugged her and announced, 'That's my Noele.'
Which really jazzed her.

Jaimie Burns was Noele's first serious boyfriend. He did
indeed have Redford eyes and wavy blond hair, and Noele
became really fenced when someone suggested that his
face was too thin and his body too skinny.

Nor did she like it when they said that she was the boss
and he a dreamer who did what she told him. Like, it was

Jaimie, not she, who thought of looking up the *New York Times* and *Time* magazine indexes for information about Danny Farrell. He really was totally practical, even if sometimes he acted a little like a space cadet.

What's more, he respected her, which made him really sweet.

At first he had accused her of being a Nancy Drew because of her detective work about the disappearance of Danny Farrell, but nevertheless, he had patiently combed through the *Time* magazine and *New York Times* volumes in the Notre Dame Library seeking information for her. There was very little to be found: A Chinese picture of the plane that might be a U-2, a denial by the American State Department that there were intelligence flights over western China, a denial from the CIA that anyone named Daniel Farrell worked for the agency, a brief editorial in *The New York Times* questioning the advisability of such flights, especially when Chinese assistance might be useful in mitigating the conflict in Vietnam, an article in *Time* about an American missionary who was released from a prison camp in China after Henry Kissinger's first visit with a passing reference to an 'American U-2 pilot' whom the missionary had seen briefly in prison. A rundown in the *Times* of Americans who had been held prisoner by the Chinese, concluding that all those who were still alive had been released. Daniel X. Farrell, a Chicagoan who was probably an agent of the CIA, the *Times* said, was presumed to be dead.

Presumed. Noele had snorted when she read the material that Jaimie had delivered. 'The last anyone heard of him was through the missionary, and he saw him alive. Who does the presuming?'

'Call the missionary,' said Jaimie, his dreamy blue eyes kind of absorbing her.

'Of course I'll call the missionary,' Noele had replied crisply, though she would never have thought of it herself.

But the Presbyterian missionary society told her that the Reverend Doctor Cameron had died two years before. Noele wondered why her family had never sought him out. In her bones Noele knew that the two family tragedies, Clancy's death and Danny's disappearance, were connected.

Otherwise why would all the members of her family give different descriptions of Danny Farrell and different accounts of Clancy Farrell's death?

'Aren't you playing with fire, opening Pandora's box, rushing in where angels fear to tread?' asked Jaimie Burns, a long question for him.

Normally Jaimie was content to sit quietly and watch Noele's act with wide-eyed fascination and utter such profundities as 'You astonish me,' or, when he was really astonished, 'You overwhelm me.'

He was not much given to pawing, or even to kissing. In fact, Noele usually had to kiss him good night first, though, when he did begin to kiss, Jaimie Burns's lips came alive with breathtaking intensity.

The night she'd wept in his arms after he had decked the two zods in South Bend, Noele realized that she could easily become 'way gone' on him . . . and that she might not mind spending the rest of her life in his arms.

But she was not going to make the mistake her mother and grandmother had and get married as a teenager. Not that Jaimie Burns seemed to have either marriage or getting her in bed with him that much on his mind.

'I have to find out, Jaimie,' she said.

'Why?'

'What if he's still alive?'

Jaimie answered with another question. 'What if he's still alive and comes home and it turns out he killed your grandfather?'

A question that had lurked in the back of her own mind, like a menace in the night, unacknowledged and frightening.

'I don't believe he did that,' she said hotly, defending a man she had never met and who was probably dead anyway.

Why do I care?

'But he might have.' Jaimie could be very stubborn and tough when he wanted to. The nerd.

'What if he did?' She shifted her tactics, still not knowing why she simply had to defend Danny Farrell. 'Wouldn't eighteen years in China be enough punishment?'

Jaimie nodded thoughtfully. 'My father might be able to help,' he said. 'He's on the intelligence subcommittee –'

'Really?' Why hadn't she known that?

'I'll talk to him.'

'No, it's my responsibility.'

'You overwhelm me,' said Jaimie Burns.

He was rewarded with a brief kiss and responded with a much longer one of his own, which Noele would later remark to Eileen Kelly was 'really excellent!'

It was a pleasant memory as they drove to the club for breakfast and she prepared her tactics of enlisting Congressman Burns in her campaign to free Danny Farrell.

Ace

Dick McNamara hung up his alb with the careful precision he had learned as a chaplain at the San Diego boot camp.

'Yes sir, Captain, sir.' He laughed to himself.

The folk Mass had been a show and a half. The best homily likely to be heard in St Praxides for many a year. And from a kid who was all tied up in emotional knots by a strange, almost spooky, search for her own identity.

If she thinks there's something strange with her identity, there probably is.

'A young woman of some determination,' Ace said with a wide grin, greeting the pastor as he strode fretfully into the sacristy.

'I hope she'll grow out of it,' John said, and sighed. 'Right now, though, she's used to having her own way. Most of the parishioners seem amused, but there will be a lot of raised eyebrows at the breakfast tables all around the Neighbourhood. They'll say that if she wasn't my niece, she wouldn't dare be so bold.'

You are transparent, Ace thought. I like you, and you're a good priest. But you are so afraid of what people might say, especially parishioners and your fellow priests. Still trying to please Brigid, I suppose.

'I hope she doesn't grow out of it. Most of the Irish women-leader types peak out at sixteen. The world resents so much insight and vitality in someone so young. Like Irene.'

Memories of the time when McNamara was the young priest in the neighbourhood and John and Irene were kids flickered briefly in Ace's brain. She had done a lot of stupid things to escape her genius. A silly summer fling with a confused and bitter seminarian was one of the silliest.

And for ten years she had avoided him, as though she had let him down. Poor, foolish kid.

What a curious crowd to have produced Noele: Brigid, with her guilt and her superstition; John, with his transparent but harmless vanity; Roger, with his faintly bent idealism: Danny, a doomed genius; Irene, drifting ever more deeply into a dreamworld where she mourned for something she had lost.

So much promise and so much possibility when they were young. And all the opportunities wasted. Happiness offered and rejected. And the damn Neighbourhood, with its magic hold on anyone who had experienced it. Yourself included, Richard McNamara.

'I wasn't aware that you had such a high opinion of my sister-in-law,' John said stiffly. 'And don't think the world will pressure Noele into anything she doesn't want to do.'

'It will try,' Ace said, but mentally phrased it in the appropriate marine language.

'By the way' – the pastor seemed to be caressing the collection basket, with its mountain of bills and envelopes –'has she been asking you about our family past?'

'Half the kids in the neighbourhood are doing the family history term paper. And I happened to be around here when the parents were teenagers.'

'What has she told you about us?' John snapped nervously.

Ace hid behind laughter, his favourite mask. 'What are you hiding, Monsignor, sir?'

'Sorry, Ace.' The pastor quickly recovered himself. 'There's been a lot of tragedy in the family. . . .'

'All on the record, as far as I know.'

'Sure.' John picked up the collection basket to take it to the rectory.

'The kid thinks she runs the parish.'

'Maybe,' said Ace McNamara mysteriously, 'she *is* the parish.'

Noele

Noele loved brunch at the Club with the Burns clan – three sons and four daughters – with the hunger of an only child who missed brothers and sisters. But there was too much commotion during the orange juice, bacon and eggs, french toast, pancakes, and strawberries and cream to talk about Daniel Farrell. Constituents had to shake hands with the congressman, and Notre Dame fans had to congratulate Jaimie on his touchdown interception against Michigan. Mrs Burns, a pretty woman in her early forties, had to talk to Noele about going away to college, which she would soon be doing. And the congressman was more interested in the Director of Music than in finding out the 'something important' that Noele wanted to ask him.

'He seems somewhat, uh, unsympathetic to young people,' said Congressman Burns, as massive and as animated a man as his son was slim and mystical.

'Tell me about it,' said Noele.

'I'm sure he complained about you to the pastor before the eleven o'clock Mass. He's the kind of fellow, I suspect, who would use your relationship to the monsignor against you. But you have the votes, young woman. Half the adults who come to the nine fifteen Mass do so because they want to see you directing the folk group. If Monsignor gets rid of you, he's going to lose a lot of his constituency.'

'Male half, anyway,' said Jaimie.

It was only after brunch that Noele was finally able to corner the congressman as they walked through the lobby to the club. Both paused spontaneously to look out over the eighteenth green, bathed in the golden light of the prolonged Indian summer and framed by red, yellow, and purple leaves.

It reminded Noele of the inside of a cathedral late in the afternoon, even though she'd never been in a cathedral late in the afternoon.

'All right, young woman, what's on your mind?' asked the congressman, as if he were dealing with an interesting but faintly troublesome constituent.

'Since you're on the intelligence committee' – Noele took a deep breath – 'I want you to find out from the CIA whether Danny Farrell is still alive.'

The congressman could not have appeared more astonished if his young constituent had asked for the United States embassy in Katmandu.

'Danny was killed eighteen years ago!'

'Was he?' Noele poured out the story she had pieced together from the Xeroxes his son had provided. 'So you see, there was a big change from the time the Presbyterian missionary said he was still alive to the time *The New York Times* said he must be presumed dead. I want to know what happened and why he must be presumed dead.'

The congressman's hands were jammed into the pockets of his light brown tailor-made suit and his high forehead wrinkled in scepticism. 'You shouldn't play Nancy Drew, young lady.'

'The next thing you're going to tell me is that I shouldn't open Pandora's box or rush in where angels fear to tread.'

The congressman cocked an appreciative eyebrow. 'You're a very interesting girl, Noele.'

'Jaimie says I'm overwhelming. But we're not talking about me . . . and there are a lot of other strange things too. His mother's death –'

'Does your family know you're doing this?' the congressman asked suspiciously.

''Course they do. I've interviewed all of them. A lot of the kids, like, have to do this term paper. I'm really cranking along on mine.'

'You think he's still alive.' The congressman was jingling coins in both his pockets.

Noele was enthusiastic. 'I think it would be, like, terrible if he were alive and everyone forgot about him. You know?'

'I don't know. . . .' The congressman hesitated.

'It wouldn't do any harm just to kind of nose around, would it, Congressman?' She tried her most appealing smile.

'It might, Noele; it might do a lot of harm to you and to others. But I will kind of nose around about kind of nosing around and see what I can do.'

Noele sailed out of the Country Club as if she were Hercule Poirot, Roderick Alleyn, and Lew Archer all rolled into one.

And none of them ever got hurt.

Or if they did, they recovered quickly.

John

John was still preoccupied with memories of Irene and Danny when they were young when he taped his programme later in the week. The guest was a militantly feminist nun who had written a book called *Chauvinism and Peace*. He wondered how it was possible to make something beautiful and attractive like peace seem angry, hateful, and vicious. Yet Celeste had done that easily.

John was certainly sympathetic to the women's movement, and could hold his charming own with virtually every feminist guest he interviewed. Sister Celeste, however, had rolled over him as if she'd been a steam engine.

'I would hardly expect a priest to understand either women or peace. The church will appeal to modern women only if it rids itself of oppressors like you.'

John knew he had done badly, though he supposed that

his regular viewers would be sympathetic and give him points for patience. That was the danger of involvement in what he called the 'television apostolate.' You began to worry more about your image and about the audience's reaction to you than you did about the religious purpose that had brought you to television in the first place.

And he did care about what they thought of him. He did care about his image. At first he used no makeup. Now he was fastidious about what kind and how much: 'Protect me from the glare,' he would lamely rationalize.

Vanity of vanities, he told himself; all his vanity.

He sighed as he parked his Buick Skylark in the rectory garage and pulled down the garage door. A picture of Irene flashed momentarily in his brain, a sharp, vivid, enormously attractive picture. He was *objectifying* her, as Sister Celeste would have said, thinking of her as an attractive object instead of as a person.

It was too late, anyway – too late for all of them. They were all caught living out the results of decisions they and others had made long ago, and he was not sure they'd had the freedom to choose anyway.

His associate pastor, Father Jerry Miller, was sitting at a lunch table in the rectory dining room when John Farrell entered. Jerry was a late 1960s radical, born and ordained out of due season, feminine in his manner, semiliterate in his vocabulary and grammar, and utterly ineffective in the ministry.

The people of St Praxides, however, were remarkably patient and tolerant of him, arguing that he worked hard (which was not true) and was good at arranging flowers on the altar (which was). The parishioners were charitable, John reasoned. He ought to be charitable too.

'Like, I mean, did you read, you know, Dads Fogarty's article in *Upturn*? Like, I mean, it was really, you know, funny.'

In the old days if the pastor didn't like the grammar and vocabulary of a curate, he could simply tell him to shut up.

'I haven't got to the mail yet,' John said heavily.

'Like, I mean, you know, it's the most; it's a make-believe interview between Monsignor Harold and an "actress for Jesus" on TV. Dads has you down perfectly. Like, the phone's been ringing all morning, you know, priests calling up to tell you about it.'

John felt slightly sick to his stomach. Dads Fogarty had been a few years ahead of him in the seminary, a pastor who was reported to make the lives of his associates miserable and run his parish with an iron hand. Nonetheless, he had a reputation, undeserved it seemed to John, for being a humourist without equal in the clergy. When he or Terry Quirk, a younger and more vicious, if more gifted, satirist – also with nothing better to do – clobbered you in the newsletter of the Association of Chicago Priests you became the laughingstock of the diocese. Unable to fight their psychopathic leader, the clergy of Chicago stayed alive by eating their own.

'I imagine I will get to read it sometime this afternoon,' John said with forced nonchalance.

'You'd better read it soon; I mean, the phone calls are going to start right after lunch.'

Indeed, John Farrell did read the article as soon as he went to his study. He was only halfway through it when one of his classmates called. Dads Fogarty's victims never received any sympathy. They were momentarily outside the law, and you could with perfect taste and charity gloat over their predicament.

Which was just what his classmate did. 'Boy, does Dads have your mannerisms down perfectly. You'll never dare say "in the deepest sense of the term" again, will you, John?'

'They tell me three quarters of a million people watch the programme,' John replied icily. 'I don't imagine many of them read *Upturn*.'

His classmate ignored the response. 'I'd go easy on the androgyny of God, too, if I were you.'

John Farrell sighed. As one of his hilarities, Dads Fogarty had spelled androgyny as though it were andro-*genie*.

'If it's an important theological concept, and I think it is, I'll certainly continue to use it. Now, if you don't mind, I have an appointment . . .'

Screw the bastards, Danny would have said, just as he had when John told him during his seminary days that he was being ridiculed by some of his classmates because of the family's wealth.

He reread the Fogarty article. It was not funny. . . . It did not even begin to measure up as satire. It was simply nasty, vicious, heavy-handed ridicule. Balloonhead Mortimer had been right. The 'guys' were closing in. Again John Farrell felt sick to his stomach. He opened the small icebox next to the television set, put three ice cubes in a tumbler, and poured himself one very tall glass of Scotch.

Which was the greater sin, vanity or envy?

He would either cave in to the pressures of the clerical culture – far more of a threat than the cardinal's psychopathic rage – or become a permanent outcast among the men who were the most important people in his life outside of his own family. There wasn't much in the way of an intermediate option.

Damn you, Dan Farrell, why aren't you here when I need you? Why did you have to die on me?

The people of the parish seemed to like his programme. In fact, they even seemed a little proud that their pastor was on television.

But from the parishioners, John knew, there would be, and there could be, no consolation and no defence against the animus of his fellow priests.

He opened the rest of the mail but paid little attention to its contents.

He also had to do something about Noele and the folk Mass.

Then he had an idea. His hands began to sweat. Instead of talking to Noele, he would talk to her mother first – not on the telephone, but at home.

Roger

'This place kind of reminds me of the coffee shop at the Tel Aviv Hilton,' said Mick Gerety, looking somewhat disdainfully at the oak-panelled, pennant-decorated wall of the Faculty Club.

'It sure isn't the old Morrison Hotel,' added Angie Spina. 'They all look smart. But I bet not one of them could deliver a precinct if his life depended on it.'

'And to make matters worse, a lot of them wouldn't even think delivering a precinct is important.'

'You like it here, Rodge?' Spina asked, glancing around the dining room, in which there were two Nobel Prize winners, one former cabinet member, and some of the world's most distinguished scholars. 'Doesn't it get kind of dull?'

Roger winced at the name Rodge, which always annoyed him. He would have to get used to it if he were going into the rough and tumble of elective politics. 'It's like everything else, Angelo. Some good days, some bad days.'

'Yeah, well, I think you'll like Springfield better. And between you and me, Rodge, Springfield is only the start. Mick here and I think all you need to run for the roses is a few breaks.'

Roger laughed easily. 'Let's worry about that bridge when we come to it.' It was a bridge that Roger would not have been averse to crossing, however, should they ever come to it.

Gerety and Spina were not organization politicians, although Spina had good connections with the organization, and Gerety good connections with the liberal Independents. Since the death of the Mayor (the only *real* mayor) the organization no longer even appeared to speak with one voice.

In the lacuna after the demise of strong central leadership, powerbrokers like Angie Spina and Mick Gerety dealt with the organization and the other political, social, and civic groups to put together temporary and ad hoc coalitions, either to elect a candidate or accomplish a goal, like planning a World's Fair or scheduling an auto race in Grant Park. Mick was a successful lawyer, Angie the successful president of Atlantic Import Company, and both were involved in politics not for money, and not even for power, but for the sheer love of the game – a fact that made them far more attractive to Roger Farrell than to other politicians, either Regulars or Reformers. The former were interested only in money and power, and the latter were interested only in ideology. Roger had far more respect for gamesmen.

'The point is, Dr Farrell' – Gerety winked at the formal title – 'that there's no end to the possibilities for somebody with your special gifts and background at a time like this. With a few breaks we can win Springfield. And with a few breaks after that . . . well, who knows?'

They were both tall, handsome men, their black hair turning attractively silver, one with dark skin, the other with fair skin. Slick, expensively tailored products of the new Catholic affluent class. They could as easily be, Roger thought to himself, two monsignors on a mission from the Vatican.

'I find the idea of Springfield challenging and the idea of Washington terrifying,' Roger said modestly.

'That's all we need, Rodge.' Spina waved his hand expressively, flashing some very expensive rings – both the hand and the rings reminders of Taylor Street in a man who had otherwise pretty much left the old neighbourhood behind. 'We're just exploring possibilities, that's all. Just exploring possibilities.'

'People are going to ask' – Gerety's wink was that of the classical Irish pol – 'why you're giving up tenure at this place for a job where you'll be lucky if you're re-elected once.' He shrugged ever so slightly. 'What should we tell them?'

Roger hesitated, ordering his thoughts as he did before a classroom lecture for which he had not prepared.

'I'll give as honest an answer as I can, and you'll have to figure out what to do with it. I was deeply involved in the Young Christian Students when I was at St Ignatius High

School. In those days, back in the late 1950s, we believed that the Catholic layman's mission was to represent the Church in the, uh, temporal order, as we called it then. And we were told we would be most effective in that mission if we were professionally competent. I went into political science at Notre Dame thinking it was the route into politics. I discovered it was the route into graduate school; in those days if you had good marks and could write a decent English sentence —'

'You should have been a lawyer.' Gerety laughed.

'I know that's the traditional way in,' Roger said, and laughed somewhat uneasily with him. 'But if I'd gone to law school, my mother would have wanted me to come into the company and . . . well, I guess I didn't find that very appealing. Too idealistic, I suppose.'

Their faces were expressionless.

'If you're running for governor,' Spina said tonelessly, 'it's just as well that you weren't too closely linked with Burke Kennedy at that time.'

'Or the firm, for that matter,' Gerety added.

'Not that it's a problem now,' Gerety murmured, filling up the awkward pause.

'So I've always had this sense that politics was a form of vocation, a commitment,' Roger continued, ignoring their delicate allusion to his stepfather, as he was supposed to ignore it, 'that I wanted to make and someday would make.'

God, does that sound hypocritical. Yet I meant it . . . or at least I did once. I don't know what I mean anymore.

'That's great public service motive,' Angelo said enthusiastically, 'but from a professor and not a businessman, so the words are a little different.'

They both seemed pleased, neither sceptical about nor impressed by his idealism. They probably did not care whether he was sincere or not.

'Will your wife go along with the campaign, Roger?' Gerety asked cautiously. 'I mean, there are demands that will be made of her. She'll lose a lot of her privacy . . . that sort of thing.'

'Irene will accept my decision,' he said primly. He had never bothered to consider the question of Irene's reaction.

'Will she campaign?' Spina leaned forward. 'She's a stunning woman, Rodge; she could be a great asset to the team.'

Roger hesitated. 'I'm afraid she's not much of a public speaker. She'll be quite visible, of course. I assume that'll be enough?'

'Sure, sure,' Spina said easily. 'And the kid. What's her name? Noele? No drug problems there or anything like that?'

Roger grinned. 'Nothing like that at all. Indeed, Angie, if you even suggested that in her presence, you might be in very serious trouble. You wouldn't want her to campaign, would you? She's been known to give impromptu homilies in church on Sunday.'

Gerety laughed uneasily. 'Precocious kids can be a problem to a candidate.'

'Not Noele.'

Not unless someone makes her mad. I'll have to say a word to her.

'There's one thing we've got to be up front about, Roger.' Mick Gerety bent over his chocolate ice cream as his waiter – a divinity-school doctoral candidate – filled the coffee cups. 'We've got to explore the possibility that you might not be clean. There isn't any nice way to say it, so I'll just say it bluntly.'

'Clean?' Roger was amused.

'Yeah, there's no point in the three of us or anybody else getting involved in a campaign when we might find out three, six months, down the turnpike that you have some great big scandal in your past.'

'That's certainly up front, Mick. What kind of scandal?'

'Well.' Gerety shifted in his chair. 'It varies. Adlai Stevenson had some trouble back in 1952 because he was divorced. That wouldn't make any difference today. Neither would women, so long as you weren't into kinky things or people with mob connections, like Jack Kennedy. But we could have trouble with fraud, murder, rape, drugs, even psychiatric treatment, like that poor guy Eagleton.'

'I see.'

'We hate to bring this sort of crap up,' Spina said fret-fully. 'But with the papers being the way they are these days, if you know what I mean . . .'

'Bill Wells and his political people over at the *Star Herald* are almost in our camp,' Gerety added, again with the slight, nervous shrug. 'But they have to sell newspapers, even if it means doing in someone that Bill personally likes. You know these Chicago circulation wars.'

'I understand completely,' Roger said suavely. 'I'm sure Steve Bilko will have enough fun with my being a profes-sor in politics as it is. Of course, there was my mother and Burke Kennedy. For a long time they were what my broth-er the priest used to call public and notorious sinners. I don't suppose that matters, since if it did we wouldn't be sitting here.'

'Family's all right,' Gerety said quickly, 'as long as there's nothing really bad. You know what I mean.'

'I can't guarantee all my father's and grandfather's busi-ness practices,' Roger said.

'Statute of limitations.' Mick Gerety waved an imperious legal hand. 'Unless you're talking about murder.'

Roger laughed, hoping that he did not sound nervous. 'I've probably bored a lot of people to death, comes with being a professor. In fact, though, I have led a pretty dull and blameless life. It's hard to do much else when you're a university faculty member. But it wouldn't hurt to do a little checking on family history.'

'We'd appreciate that,' Gerety said. 'Before we step into public, where the media people will go after us like those man-eating fish in South America.'

'The piranha,' Roger said, then kicked himself for acting like a know-it-all.

'Yeah, well, Governor, give us a ring in a day or two and let us know for sure.'

Both the operators grinned. They were confident that they had a candidate, and that he was a winner.

Governor Farrell. It had a pleasant ring.

And what if the next time they met he told them that there probably had been a murder? It was made to look like an accident. The man who most likely ordered the crime is dead. I had nothing to do with it, though I have suspected the crime for a long time. No proof, but a reporter might dig up some pretty strong suspicions.

'And,' he would add hesitantly, 'the firm might have been involved.'

There would be no wink in Gerety's ice-blue eyes. 'It would raise the character issue, like Chappaquiddick: If you knew about it and did not do anything . . .'

No one would call him Governor Farrell again.

In a few days there would be a call saying they were getting a lot of pressure from some of their friends to go with someone else.

I won't tell them now. I'll think about it. Reread the papers. No reason to make a decision this moment.

Already he was cheating.

Roger Farrell smiled pleasantly as he walked down the broad staircase of the Faculty Club with his two guests. The danger of the horror story – so long as it was an appropriate and modest danger – would make the race for governor even more enjoyable.

Like the enjoyment of being caught with Martha Clay.

Congressman Burns

'Clancy Farrell was one of the weakest human beings from whom I ever had to take campaign contributions, a jellyfish, oily and greasy and sometimes dangerous,' exploded James McDowell Burns, former congressman of the Third District of the Great State of Illinois. 'Burke Kennedy may be kinky. But Brigid really improved her situation when she dumped Clancy. Can't blame her in the least. Can't blame Burke, either. Gorgeous woman. Still is, as a matter of fact.'

There were three James M. Burnses. The first was the former representative who was always called James, a stalwart seventy-year-old with a big head, on which there had not been much in the way of hair for forty of his seventy years, and a mellow voice, which had marked him, according to those who knew, as the greatest Irish political orator in Illinois in the twentieth century.

When he had stepped down at the age of sixty, after twelve terms in the United States House of Representatives, he was promptly succeeded by his son, James M. Burns, Jr. (called Jimmy by everyone but his wife, who called him Jim, save on those rare occasions when she was angry at him, and then he was Junior), the incumbent congressman, who had no oratory skills at all, but could read a budget with a colder eye and question a bureaucrat with more devastating precision than almost any member of the House.

James M. Burns III was Jaimie, even when his mother was angry at him, which was practically never, since in her view he was practically perfect. Jaimie was an apparently lacklustre young man who displayed no energy whatsoever, save in the presence of either a pigskin or Noele Farrell.

'The daughter-in-law and granddaughter aren't bad either,' said Jimmy Burns. 'Irene in a spring dress is still one of the greatest distractions to religious devotion in the recent history of St Praxides. And that young redhead has our Jaimie quite bewitched.'

The present and former congressmen were having lunch at the Chicago Athletic Club, on the fifth floor, overlooking a brown but sundrenched patch of Grant Park and the sparkling blue lake beyond. The House of Representatives had awarded itself a long weekend, and the present congressman was mending fences in his district.

The club was old and conservative and solid, which is to say that it was having a hard time, since the younger generation was flocking to such dubious places as the East Bank Club, where they mixed sex, swimming, and other modernities.

The ex-congressman complained vocally about the mess that 'damn fool' had made of the Art Institute. 'Same damn fool who built that monstrosity in Colorado Springs.'

The incumbent chewed on a celery stalk and remained silent. He rather liked the addition to the Institute. And the architect's wife was a sometime political ally. But his constituents did not like it, those who bothered to notice it.

So, as wise politicians do when their friends are on both sides, he said nothing at all.

The heavy maroon curtains that framed the park and the lake ought to have been replaced two years ago. Nonetheless, even though it was in decline, the dining room was a good place to mend fences with a certain generation of South Side Irish business and professional men – a vanishing breed, thought the congressman with a sigh.

He continued on the subject of Noele Farrell.

'That girl is a doll. She reminds me in a way of poor Danny Farrell. The other day she informed us that the solution to all the Jimmys in our family will be for there to be a *Seamus* in the next generation and then announced the name was Norman Irish, a hibernization of *Jacques*.' He sighed again. 'I don't know what's getting into kids these days. I agree with you about the others, though. I suppose I'd support Roger if he goes for governor, since he's in my district. But I don't like him, and I don't think I trust him. A bit too much of the poseur, if you ask me.'

His father's vocal range was in two tones, loud and louder, and it was the latter he used to comment on Roger Farrell as governor. 'Goddamned intellectual snob. And not that much to be snobbish about, either. They started in the sewers and never really have been clean since. It was a miracle that old Bill Farrell didn't end up in jail, where he belonged. And Clancy had been a vacillating prick most of the time. He never would have taken over the firm if Martin, who was a decent man, had not been killed in the war. When his mother started whispering in Clancy's ear or he had too much to drink, he thought he was the Lord God Himself and could do anything he pleased. No one was sorry when he died, especially not Brigid, or her boyfriend Burke Kennedy.'

'Would Martin have inherited the firm if he had lived?'

'A lot of talk about it in those days. Bill died before Martin, so nothing came of the talk, especially after Martin's wife, Florence, died.'

The congressman, having finished his lean hamburger

without a bun, relaxed in his chair, fighting off a temptation to order dessert. 'They certainly weren't much interested in finding out what happened to Marty's son when he
disappeared, were they?'

'Danny?' His father eyed him shrewdly. 'What do you
mean?'

'Did they push you to find out what happened to him?
They were heavy contributors to your campaigns.'

James Burns chewed reflectively on his steak. 'They
went through the motions, nothing more. And heaven
knows, that Brigid has never been shy about asking for
favours or using her clout. I kind of suspected that they
thought he might have defected. Maybe someone from the
CIA planted that notion in their heads.'

'Why would he defect? The U-2 was not much of a secret
even to the Chinese by that time.'

'Who knows? He was a crazy kid. Not a sewer type, like
the others, but still a little daft. And they tossed him out of
the Navy because he intervened to protect a black seaman
who was being railroaded into the brig by some redneck
CO. That was back in the days when you could push
black sailors around and have the Navy on your side. Or
he might have been a CIA double agent, spying on the
Chinese for us and then getting himself shot when the
Chinese found out.'

'Convenient for the Farrells to have him out of the way,
though, wasn't it? No one to challenge our pastor's and
our next governor's inheritance?'

'You remember Danny, don't you? Not that kind of person. Why the interest in him, anyway?'

'Noele is writing a term paper.'

'And you're worried about a teenage term paper?' the
retired congressman exploded.

'What do you think it would do to the Democratic party
if Roger runs for governor and the papers find out there
was something fishy about Danny's disappearance? What
if he was a traitor? And what if his family, for reasons we
don't know, was glad to be rid of him? As you said, they
come from the sewer.'

The ex-congressman scowled. 'That all happened a long

time ago. How would anybody find out what really went on?'

'All too easily, Dad; a sixteen-year-old girl dug up enough information to make me suspicious, and one question to you here at lunch makes me even more suspicious.'

'You don't think Dan is still alive?'

'Of course not. The issue is not whether he is still alive; the issue is whether his family was glad to have him dead. Or whether maybe he was a defector or a double or triple agent. Can you imagine what that would do to the whole Democratic ticket?'

'We don't need that.' The former congressman shook his head grimly. 'And especially you don't need it.'

'Tell me about it,' said Jimmy Burns.

Brigid

Brigid almost never went out to lunch. Instead she would eat a small salad and drink a cup of tea in her cluttered office at Farrell & Sons' headquarters in Blue Island, a suburb south of Chicago. A light lunch and a brisk walk around the perimeters of the firm's vast 'yard' were Brigid's only concessions to maintaining her physical health. 'I was lucky with my genes,' she would explain, 'and I'm not going to risk my luck with dangerous things like exercise and diets.'

Sometimes she shared her salad with a staff member with whom she had business. Her companion today was a fellow immigrant from the west of Ireland named Hugh McCauley, a wrinkled little red-faced leprechaun of dubious vintage who was technically an assistant general manager and actually Brigid's political contact and payoff man.

'Business is not good, Biddy.' Hugh sighed a west-of-Ireland sigh, a sound like the advent of a serious asthma attack. 'Not good at all.'

'We've survived bad times before, Hughie,' she said, taking a cigarette out of her purse and searching for a match.

Hugh had learned long ago that she could never find a match. He flicked his Bic for her, knowing she would grind her cigarette into the ashtray after one or two puffs.

'Ah, we have. But in those days there were ways of dividing up the business and keeping the cut-rate boys out. Now, with the kikes and even the niggers undercutting us and the government watching every move we make, we can't maintain the old standards.'

The old standards were a set of arrangements by which the traditional, politically connected construction companies divided the business among themselves by none too gently rigging bids, with, of course, the connivance of the politicians. Everyone had done it and no one minded until the People of the United States, represented by a United States Attorney for the Northern District of Illinois looking for publicity and a career as an elected official, had indicted a score or so of upstanding and civic-minded contractors, all of them Irish, all of them Catholic, and all of them pillars of their party and their parish.

Brigid had evaded indictment and a possible term in jail only because of some devious dealings by Burke. Politicians were still bribed, Democrats and Republicans alike, but the techniques of bribery were much more complex and the competition in the construction marketplace substantially more intense.

'What does the man in DuPage County want?' Brigid came bluntly to the point, not sharing Hughie's Irish love for the indirect and allusive approach.

She ground out her cigarette.

'Your man in DuPage County claims he has a lot of very heavy expenses, campaigns, education for his children, charities . . .'

'How much?' Brigid insisted.

Hughie shrugged. 'Half a million dollars in cash, up front, to be deposited in a numbered account in a Swiss bank.'

'The holy saints preserve us,' Brigid exclaimed prayerfully, 'a politician in DuPage County with a numbered account in a Swiss bank. What's the world coming to? No, Hughie, not one penny.'

'We need the work, Biddy; with this Reagan budget . . .'

'Damn Reagan and damn his budget and damn DuPage County.' Brigid slammed the desk with the palm of her hand. 'We'll survive, Hughie. I'm not going to run the risk of a grand jury looking at us and finding something while my boy is running for governor.'

'Ah, 'tis true, Biddy.' Hugh flipped his head mournfully. 'As soon as he announces, I suppose they'll be all over us.'

'Well, they can't lay a finger on us, can they?' Brigid said decisively. 'And I intend to keep it that way.'

After Hugh had left and her young black secretary had taken away the remains of lunch, Brigid returned to her computer output with this month's payroll for the firm. They needed the business even more than Hughie realized. They'd survive, of course, but these were the worst times she had ever seen.

At last, woman, you've been forced to be virtuous, if only to get your son elected governor.

Your sons are not quite what you wanted, but they'll do. Besides, they're yours.

Thanks be to God for the statute of limitations. If they investigated some of the things we did in the 1950s in this office, it would be the end of all of us.

And there's a lot of other things they might look at, too, but reporters are too dumb to think of them. I wish it were as easy to fool God. And again Brigid saw the vast black pit which was certainly waiting for her.

My damn body got me into it. I didn't know what fucking was like until Burke came along. Then I couldn't give it up. Poor Clancy. He was no good at screwing at all. Could hardly get it up unless he beat me.

She remembered the night at the lake, a heavy silent summer night save for the noise of the crickets, when Danny had found her on the floor with her torn nightgown soaked in blood. He had held her in his arms and sworn vengeance against Clancy.

She shook her head in dismay. And, you old whore, you liked being in his arms, just as you liked being in his father's arms the month before he married Flossie. And you're still sorry you didn't let him screw you that night, and yourself knowing all the time how much he loved Floss.

She went back to the payroll, her pencil moving hesitantly down a column of numbers.

Hell is too good for the likes of you.

Roger

Joseph Kramer was sitting in Roger's outer office in the new concrete block building in which the University housed its government department. He was taking copious notes on Roger Farrell's doctoral dissertation, comparing the political theories of Niccolò Machiavelli, Vilfredo Pareto, and Benedetto Croce.

'You may be the first person who's read that dissertation since my doctoral committee,' Roger said, laughing lightly. 'And I'm not sure of *them*.'

'I think it's important to understand how a man's ethical thinking has developed.' Kramer had the big smile of an intellectually handicapped archangel.

'You certainly are a thorough researcher, especially for a three-thousand-word article.'

'A responsible journalist tries to be precise,' Kramer said piously.

'I'm sure Mrs Marshfield will be of every assistance to you in seeing how my manuscripts turn into articles and books.' Roger nodded toward his secretary, who was staring vacantly out the window. At the salaries the University paid secretaries, you were lucky if they could speak English, let alone read and write.

'Won't you, Henrietta?'

Henrietta's nod of agreement was something less than enthusiastic.

'Well, then, if you'll excuse me, Mr Kramer. . . .' Roger opened the lock on his personal file cabinet and withdrew from the second drawer a small metal file box, which was also locked with a padlock and a combination. He closed the drawer of the larger cabinet, locked it, and went into his inner office.

On the whole he felt that his confidential papers were safer at the office with Henrietta than at the house with Irene. While Irene wasn't very intelligent, she might understand some of the contents of the neatly ordered manila folder under *F* inside the safe. There was not the slightest possibility that Henrietta could understand them, even if she were able to read them, which was doubtful.

On his desk were two notes that 'Miss Clee' had called. Henrietta was not much at spelling either.

He tore the notes up. I'm a middle-aged professor infatuated with a thirty-two-year-old woman. I must restrain myself for a while. What kind of love . . . To hell with analysis. Enjoy it while you can.

He paused before opening the folder. He had never quite been able to add notes about his father's death to the file. If he were honest with himself and with future generations – Noele's children, perhaps – he ought to complete the story that had begun in 1944 and had its denouement in the autumn of 1963.

He pressed his fingers against his temples and shuddered. His father had begun with an attack on the Kennedys and then turned to the Conlons, making poor Irene weep. Danny had lost his temper, a rare enough event. Then Clancy began to talk about the past. John scoffed in disbelief. Danny listened in stunned silence. And Roger was terrified at the possibility that his father's drunken ravings might be the truth.

A few hours later Roger and John stared at Clancy's dead body, listening to his mother's account of what had happened and Burke's grim plan for coping with it.

What else was there to do?

Then Danny came back into the house, his lips pressed

tightly together, his face parchment white. The body was being carried down the steps into the autumn darkness. Captain Nolan and Doctor Keefe had been bribed. The matter was concluded.

Danny said not a single word. Perhaps he thought he was justified in what he had done. And perhaps he was.

He left Chicago the afternoon of the funeral Mass. Roger could not find the courage to talk to him about what had happened. Brigid warned him to stay away from 'the poor man.'

Roger shook his head, trying to clear the images away.

Keefe and Nolan were the weak links. Yet they would not risk losing their comfortable incomes from Farrell construction – as well as admit to obstruction of justice.

It was not the death of 1963 that might be the problem, but the death of 1944.

He opened the file: the clippings and correspondence he had found among his father's papers, his own notes, further clippings, and the single memo from Burke: 'For God's sake, Clancy, forget it!'

His father's picture and Uncle Martin's, identical twins, and yet even as young men the rough black Irish good looks that were part of the family heritage made Martin look strong and Clancy somehow feeble and artificial.

Yet he was not a bad man. It was not his fault that he was ineffectual. He was generous to such liberal politicians as Adlai Stevenson and Paul Douglas, told wonderful stories to his sons, took them to ball games a dozen times every summer, talked sports with them at the supper table every night, did his best to be a friend and companion to them.

He was ineffectual as a father, too, but out of the natural sympathy that children have for the feeble, they pretended that he was a buddy.

No, not a bad man. Yet the conclusion from the file must be that under certain circumstances Clancy could be a monster, especially when his demented mother, Blanche, goaded him into action with the charge that he was not manly. As though she herself were not responsible . . .

Roger shuddered. There was no point living through the horror of such recollections again.

Yet he could not stay away from the folder. Often he would awake in the middle of the night and resolve to finish it. Perhaps there was expiation to be found in truth.

What would the press say if they knew that the father of a reform candidate for governor had been so deeply involved with a cheap crook who had once been the outfit's most feared enforcer?

He thumbed through the clippings and the notes. Marsallo ('The Marshal') had come a long way. From petty torturer to protégé of the Mob's most respected senior leader. Crazy now, they said.

Yet it was all long ago; the connections were thin, and even his own conclusions were speculative. Clancy's outbursts the night of his death was the only proof, and even John did not believe it was any more than drunken braggadocio, similar to Clancy's claim to be a war hero who had secretly worked for the OSS.

He closed the folder. . . . No, there was nothing there that was any serious threat. If a reporter were able to put all the pieces together, he might have some kind of story, but a quick and relaxed denial would dispose of it. And no reporter had been in the corner at the Club that dreadful night. . . .

Florence's picture slipped out.

He could hardly bear to look at her. She would be over sixty now, not as well preserved as Brigid, but still probably an attractive woman. The fire that had appealed to Martin and that Dan had kept alive for nineteen years more would still be burning.

She was wearing a formal gown, for a prom or debutante ball, perhaps. So young and so lovely to die.

And such a senseless death. She had only asked a question, not made any threats. . . .

He opened the file again and glanced at the conclusion of his memo to 'future Farrells.'

'Let me take this opportunity to plead with you, if not for forgiveness, at least for understanding. You will think that my father was a monster. And so it will seem from this story and from other stories I could also tell you. Yet in fact, in everyday life he did not seem evil to his sons. He

was generous to us and to the church and to a wide variety
of charities. He drank more than was necessary and more
than was proper, but I do not think he could have been
considered at the time of his death an alcoholic. He was an
enthusiastic sports fan and loved to play softball with the
two of us, though, in truth, he was not very good in
sports. He was weak and ineffectual in most of the things
he attempted but well-meaning, save when he felt personally threatened; then he fought like a cornered animal,
ruthlessly and viciously, though with neither wisdom nor
strength.

'I don't believe that my brother John and I ever loved
him. Nonetheless, it is not an exaggeration to say that we
genuinely liked him most of the time, save when he was
drunk or swept up in the emotions of one of his rare temper tantrums. One could not, finally, love or respect
Clancy Farrell as a father, but one could enjoy his company
as a child like oneself.

'All of this is by way of trying to persuade you, Farrell
descendants of the future, that you must not think my
father was thoroughly evil. If, as I believe likely, he was
the agent of great harm to others, he was an agent acting
with greatly diminished moral responsibility, somewhat
more to blame for what happened than would have been a
bolt of lightning or a collapsed wall, but substantially less
to blame than would have been a free and mature adult.'

Roger Farrell hunched over his desk, face in his hands,
and sobbed bitterly, as he often did when he thought of
the enormous human suffering that had plagued his
family. The sordid sins of the past were being expiated by
the misery and destruction of the last forty years. Would it
ever stop? Was there more suffering ahead of them?
Would Noele be harmed? He pounded his desk. God
damn it, nothing would touch her – nothing.

Gradually he regained his self-control, placed the folder
inside his grey, portable safe, and closed the door, noting
absently the words Confidential. For the Eyes of Roger Farrell
Only, which he had printed in large red letters on the folder.

It's the only scandal that could embarrass us. It will

never become public. Yes, I have made up my mind; I am going to have a go at the governorship. That means I will have to lie to Mick and Angie and tell them there is nothing to threaten us from my past. A Young Christian Student from two decades ago, filled with idealism and even a sense of vocation. And you begin your pursuit of political power with a lie.

It probably won't be the last.

His office phone rang. 'Mr Farrell.'

'Roger, Martha. I think I've finally reworked the conclusion so it makes sense. I want to put it in the mail tonight. Could you stop over late this afternoon for a drink and reassure me?'

Roger Farrell smiled to himself. It was three thirty. Why waste any time? He had established his virtue by keeping her at bay for two days. 'I'll come right over,' he said briskly, thinking of himself as an alcoholic who was exulting over the fact that he had stayed out of a tavern for two days.

Today he would be an extraterrestrial who kidnapped a housewife from a supermarket. Just what he needed after coming up out of the family cesspool.

'I don't want to cut short your working day,' she protested.

'Who works in this department after three o'clock in the afternoon?'

Two and one-half, perhaps three, hours of amusements with the frightened and then enchanted prisoner, and then push her off his flying saucer, after some brief, justifying remarks on her concluding chapter.

On the way out of his office, already imagining the delightful pleas he would soon compel his earthling captive to breathe, Roger deposited the portable safe, the Florence Farrell folder with its 'confidential' label on top, in his personal filing cabinet and closed the door.

Enough of the Farrells for one day.

But not quite enough. Alongside the happily groaning Martha Clay, who was more than content with her brief imprisonment in his space vehicle, he was haunted by the expression on Danny Farrell's face on the cold and rainy day when they returned Clancy's body to the earth from which it had come.

John

Just as John was parking his Buick Skylark in front of his brother's house, Irene drove up behind him in her Datsun sports car, a vehicle that made him nervous. Somehow it did not seem proper for the pastor's sister-in-law to drive a high-performance car. She was burdened with several bags of groceries that John courteously offered to help carry into the house. In a beige autumn dress – Irene preferred dresses to suits – she appeared to John as she always did, a naked woman with a few garments that had been hastily thrown on and that might at any moment drop away.

'You look a little under-the-weather, John,' she said. 'Let me mix you a drink, and then we can talk about this folk Mass crisis.'

His martini was very dry, and very generous, as presumably was her own. Irene's drinking made him nervous. She was, he thought, pre-alcoholic; at least she was a quiet drunk, even quieter than when she was sober.

She sat next to him on the couch in her elaborately antique parlour. 'The folk Mass isn't that serious, is it?'

'Oh, no, it's not the folk Mass at all.' The hint of sympathy in her liquid brown eyes overwhelmed him. He poured out the whole story: the TV programme, the envy of his fellow priests, and the priest association newsletter. In response he expected her to say what any sensible person would say under the circumstances: that it was ridiculous to worry about such things.

But Irene did not dismiss his troubles as foolish. 'May I see the newsletter?' she asked quietly.

So eagerly that his hands trembled, he took the paper

out of his inside jacket pocket and gave it to her. Irene looked in her purse for reading glasses, and with a martini in one hand she read the newsletter very carefully.

'What an awful man,' she said finally. 'It isn't funny at all. How can priests think it's funny? It's cruel and sick. I'm so sorry for you. It's not fair. You work very hard on that programme. These terrible people should support you and not make fun of you.'

'I suppose criticism and envy go with the territory,' he said, dissolving in the delightful warmth of her compassion.

'Not in the church, it shouldn't. And you mean to tell me that this nickname, "Slick," is sticking to you? You're Slick Farrell?'

'I'm afraid so.' He folded the newsletter and put it back into his pocket.

'Another drink?' Not waiting for an answer, Irene took their glasses to the bar, filled them, and returned to the coffee table.

'Are you going to give up the programme, John?'

'What do you think?' He was astounded that he would care what his sister-in-law thought.

She pondered his question carefully, holding her drink at her chin as if she wanted to solve the problem before sipping any more vodka.

'I think you ought to tell the whole lot of them to go to hell,' she said fiercely. 'The people of the archdiocese must like your programme or it wouldn't have high ratings. And as long as we like it, why should you care what a bunch of envious priests think?'

An Irene who was thoughtful, intelligent, and spoiling for a fight was not exactly what John had expected. Had she been that way in the summer of 1963? Not that he could recall. Maybe he had been too horny to notice.

'Well, perhaps you're right. Maybe I – at least – ought to finish out the present contract. Now, about the teenage Mass?' he said, changing the subject before he could consider the implications of his change of mind.

Irene drank deeply from her martini glass. 'Since I'm being so bold this afternoon –' He glimpsed a breathtaking

gleam of white teeth and a spectacular movement of graceful breasts as she spoke '– let me be blunt about that subject, too. Mr Creepy Crumb – I know that's not his real
name, but it's the only one I hear around this house – is
trying to manipulate you. He's telling you and others that
if Noele weren't your niece, you'd cancel the folk music
group. He's playing on your sense of fairness, John; he
knows darn well that if she weren't your niece you would
tell him to leave that group alone without a moment's hesi-
tation. Teenagers who otherwise might not bother going to
church love that Mass, and so do a lot of adults. If you cancel them because he's trying to blackmail you, you may
please him, but you are going to offend a lot of other
people – and, of course, they'll be like the priests who
admire what you do on television, and you'll never hear
from them.'

What had happened to Irene this afternoon? 'You're saying that I ought not to discriminate against Noele because
she's my niece?'

Irene laughed, another rare event. 'Yes, and I'm also
saying, Monsignor John Farrell, that if you want to have a
real fight on your hands, try to cancel the folk Mass. Mr
Creepy Crumb is a pushover compared to your niece. And
you would be much wiser to fight this awful Dads Fogarty
person' – she gestured contemptuously at the newsletter –
'than to fight my Christmas child.'

John felt that chains had been torn off his legs. 'You're
right, Irene, absolutely right. I ought to sign you up as my
spiritual director.'

Irene coloured faintly. 'I don't think I'd make much of a
spiritual director, John. I'd offer you another drink,
but . . .'

'Can't have a pastor driving back to the rectory drunk,'
John said, and rose somewhat shakily to his feet. 'I'd better
finish off some work before supper.'

As he stood up to leave, another worry popped into his
worry-crammed mind.

'Is Noele finished with her term paper yet?'

'I think so.' Irene hesitated. 'She hasn't asked me any
more questions lately. They bring up painful memories

. . . and I wonder if we ought to have told her –'

'About California?' She had never once mentioned that subject to him. Feeling enormous compassion for her, he stilled the words that almost came to his lips. His hand squeezing her shoulder lightly, he said, 'Don't torment yourself, Renie.'

'Thanks, John.' She kissed him lightly on the cheek as he was leaving, a routine sign of affection that had occurred many, many times before. As he tottered toward his car in the rapidly falling darkness of an autumn afternoon, John thought that the kiss had meant a little more this time than it ever had before.

Be careful, he told himself. You could fall in love with the woman again.

Noele

Noele Farrell parked her car, Flame, on Ninety-fifth Street in front of the small, white, brick cottage in which Dr Michael Keefe had dispensed the wisdom of medical sciences for forty-five years. She had assigned a willing Jaimie to interview his grandfather about Martin and Clancy Farrell when they were young. She would tackle Doctor Keefe about the night of Clancy's death.

It was not fair. James Burns was a cute old man, who told wonderful stories about the past. Doctor Keefe was your all-time classic nerd.

She checked her notes on the legal-size yellow pad. Grams had said that she and her husband had been tired after the fight and had come home from the club immediately after dinner, and that he had gone right up to bed, still complaining about Danny.

That could have been no later than ten thirty.

Yet the time of death on the certificate Jaimie had obtained from the County Recorder's office said one thirty.

Doctor Keefe had signed the certificate three hours after Clancy fell down the stairs. All right, suppose that Grams was wrong. Suppose that they came home from the club later. There was no way they wouldn't have been home by eleven thirty. A half hour to call Burke at the most, another half hour to find the doctor, who, after all, lived in the parish. . . . Why the extra hour?

And where were John and Roger all that time? If they had known about their father's death, wouldn't they have called another doctor? Come to think of it, why didn't Burke call another doctor? Why have the dead body lying on the floor?

So either he had died much later than seemed possible if Grams was telling the truth, or there had been a long delay. . . . And why would there be such a delay?

To cover up for Danny?

She pounded the steering wheel of Flame in dissatisfaction. I'm obsessive about Danny Farrell, she realized.

Well, after this conversation is over, I'm going to stop.

The terrible feeling of loneliness had returned only once since the Notre Dame-Miami game. Maybe it would never come back.

She slammed the door of Flame in disgust at herself.

She was still disgusted when she entered the cramped waiting room of Dr Keefe's office. There were two pregnant women, a seventh-grade boy who looked like he had a bad stomachache, and one very old man waiting in the office, leaving a single empty chair for herself. It was that way every time you came to Dr Keefe's. She was an hour late for her appointment, knowing that the doctor was never punctual and she would still have to wait for another hour. She removed her boring trigonometry homework from her book sack and began to puzzle over sines, cosines, and tangents.

Dr Keefe was reputed by those over forty in the neighbourhood to be a 'wonder' and to 'have forgotten what those bright young kids out of medical school will never learn.' Noele suspected that he had forgotten practically everything about medicine. And she agreed with her mother that Doctor Keefe was a dirty old man.

But it wasn't a matter of health that brought Noele to his office.

Finally, just fifteen minutes before she ought to have been home for supper, she was admitted to the doctor's disorderly office, which smelled of stale disinfectant. He was a wiry little old man with a lean, pale face and several strands of yellow-white hair hanging over his forehead. Noele shuddered.

'Well, young woman,' he wheezed, 'what brings you to my office on this lovely fall day?'

'I'm not pregnant or anything like that.' Noele thought his leer was disgusting. 'I'm writing a family history term paper and I am particularly interested in Grandfather Clancy Farrell. I want to do a page or two about his death, and I wonder if you could tell me some of the details.'

It was an enormous fib.

The leer disappeared immediately from the old doctor's face and was replaced by an expression of demented cunning.

'Not much to tell. I'm sure your grandma told you about it. Poor man came home from dinner at the club on Sunday evening, climbed up to the top of the steps, tripped, fell down the steps, and landed on his head.'

'They left the club early in the evening, Grams said.' Noele fiddled with her legal-size pad. 'And poor Clancy fell down the stairs about ten thirty?'

The doctor's filmy eyes flickered in surprise. 'Closer to eleven, as I remember it.'

Noele sprang her trap. 'Then why does the death certificate say that the time of death was one thirty?'

'Let me see that thing.' He grabbed it from her and twisted it in his hands. 'Well, that's the time I signed it. . . .' He hesitated. 'I was at the hospital delivering a baby. Took them a long time to get to me. . . .'

He was making it up. Grams had not told her the truth about the time of death. It was probably closer to twelve. An hour to get Burke and her sons, a forty-five minute ride for Uncle John from his parish, and the doctor and the police. . . . Why would Grams lie to me?

'Two hours. . . .'

The watery-eyed old goat considered her suspiciously. 'What's the point in asking all these questions, young woman? You sound like you're trying to conduct a murder investigation.'

Noele laughed disarmingly. 'A fine detective I'd make, Dr Keefe. I don't suspect anything. I'm just trying to figure out how people behave in time of crisis.'

'It's easy to see that you are young and inexperienced,' the doctor snapped. 'Someday a tragedy will occur in your life, and you will realize that people don't always act logically at such times. Your poor grandmother was beside herself with grief. There was her husband at the bottom of the stairs, his eyes wide open, blood pouring out of his head – he'd banged up against the railing at the foot of the steps. She couldn't reach Father John at his rectory, she couldn't get through to your dad at the club because the line was busy, and Danny – that worthless scoundrel – was driving around drunk in somebody's car. She didn't know what to do when I wasn't home, my wife – God have mercy on her' – he crossed himself devoutly – 'was away on vacation. I was delivering a baby in Little Company Hospital. It was only when your father finally arrived that Brigid was able to pull herself together. They called me at the hospital, and then Captain Nolan at the Gresham Station, so nobody would be asking the kind of funny questions you're asking, young woman!'

He was a quick and clever liar. But three hours, even two hours, were too much. Were there not neighbours who could have gone over to the club to tell Roger? Were there not other doctors? The neighbourhood was filled with doctors, one out of every ten men, according to Uncle Monsignor.

There was either a deliberate delay in calling a doctor or the death had occurred much later. And in that case Grams had lied. Why lie, unless something terrible happened between ten thirty and midnight?

'And it was only when Uncle Monsignor came that they thought about a priest?'

'He got there only half an hour or so before I did. Why

should they think about calling a priest from St Praxides when they have a priest in the family?'

Because if you call another priest, you might give away your cover.

Grams had lied, and Doctor Keefe was trying to protect her lie, even though Noele had surprised him.

What had happened between ten thirty and midnight?

'And his death was an accident?'

'Of course it was an accident,' he said impatiently. 'Doesn't the death certificate say that?'

But then why would Grams lie to me?

'Okay, Doc.' She gave him her very best smile. 'I guess that's all I need to know. I'm going home now and finish the term paper tonight after supper.'

'I don't know what's happening in Catholic schools these days,' the doctor grumbled, and stood halfway up in his chair. Then he added, 'I think we'd all be much better off if we left the dead alone.'

'So do I,' said Noele at the door. 'Oh, by the way, was Dan Farrell there when you arrived?'

Again the old doctor hesitated. 'He came in just as I was finishing. Looking pale and kind of guilty. He had a big fight with your grandfather earlier in the evening.'

'Not drunk anymore?'

'Death sobered him up.'

He either thinks that Danny killed Clarence, or he wants me to think that he thinks Danny killed him.

Back in the front seat of Flame she pondered her notes. Clancy Farrell had died sometime between ten o'clock and one o'clock on Sunday night – well, make that sometime between ten thirty and twelve thirty. Dr Keefe had been summoned from Little Company Hospital between one and one thirty and came to the house almost immediately. Uncle Monsignor had arrived a little bit before that. A forty-five-minute drive from his parish on the North West Side. He must have arrived back at the rectory at a quarter to twelve and picked up the phone then.

Something had happened between a quarter to eleven and a quarter to twelve.

Maybe she should forget the whole thing. The family

history term paper had started out as a lark. Then it had become a fascinating mystery, the kind Miss Marple solved in her cute little village of St Mary Mead. Now it was turning ugly.

There was one very simple explanation. Danny had dropped Moms off, come to the house, and then killed Clancy. Everyone else, including Doctor Keefe, was conspiring to cover up for Danny by pretending that the death had been earlier, when Danny was still with Moms.

Ask Moms about the time she went home? But would she tell me the truth? She loved him, I think, and would still want to protect his reputation. Her parents, who might know what time she really came home, are dead. She could claim that she was with Danny till he showed up after one o'clock. . . .

Something strange had happened that Sunday evening in the late autumn of 1963. Gramps, everyone said, was a nice man until he lost his temper. Maybe he had lost his temper that night and done something that made someone want to kill him – his wife, or his son, or his nephew Danny.

Or Burke. Maybe Burkie was tired of sharing Grams with him. She hesitated. Or maybe even Moms. But Moms couldn't hurt a fly. Brigid could hurt a fly, and so could Roger and so even could Monsignor John, if he were pushed hard enough. Probably Cousin Danny could too.

Maybe they were all protecting him. They all loved him. Then he disappeared, and there was no need to protect him anymore. Couldn't blame them for being relieved.

What had he and Clancy fought about earlier? Just the Kennedy family and the federal investigation of the firm? You don't kill people for that sort of an argument.

Even if he'd done it – she was still defending him – he must have had a good reason.

A good reason for murder?

Maybe it was self-defence.

A young pilot defending himself against a weak, middle-aged man?

Or revenge.

Revenge for what?

It had been a long time ago. Dr Keefe was probably right. The dead should be left alone.

Noele stuffed her yellow pad into her book sack, turned over the ignition to the car, and flipped on the lights. She felt heavy and discouraged. There was a trace of the loneliness teasing at the back of her head. She ought to leave the whole mess alone. She was being a giddy teenager, pretending that real life was like an Agatha Christie mystery story.

If you want me to do it, she informed the One in Charge, you're going to have to send me a sign.

So there.

What kind of sign?

Oh, I don't know, any kind of sign. A rose or something yukky like that.

The light changed to red. Noele was hemmed in by a van.

Geek, she said half aloud.

The light changed and the van moved ahead, its back door flapping in the wind.

They should lock it, she said righteously. Nerds.

A car cut in front of the van, and it slammed to a hasty stop.

Noele screamed as she lunged for her brakes.

Flame rose to the occasion and halted a few inches behind the van. The swinging door hesitated above Flame's hood. *Mount Greenwood Florists.*

What you'd expect from yukky Mounties.

The van lurched forward, the door swung drunkenly, and a bundle fell on Flame's waiting hood.

Flakes!

She pulled into a gasoline station and climbed out of the car. It was only when her fingers were about to touch the package that she knew what would be in it.

Totally excessive, she said hotly. I asked only for one, not a bouquet!

Well, I don't have to do it, anyway. She slipped Flame into the flow of the Ninety-fifth Street traffic. She would forget about the whole thing.

After she got a full report from Jaimie.

And talked to Captain Nolan.

DANCE
FOUR

Saraband

DCI

'Mr Radford is here, sir,' said the lean young man who was the administrative assistant to the Director of the Central Intelligence Agency.

'Ask him to come in, please,' said the DCI heavily.

A tall, muscular, bearded young man, one of the more recent models of the Harvard graduates who flocked, generation after generation, from Cambridge to Langley, Radford was the DCI's 'man.' He was the instrument by which the Director could turn over every stone in the Company's past or present to discover what kind of worms were crawling around under it. Radford's blood was reported to measure only slightly above freezing, and his blue eyes suggested a temperature much below freezing. No one argued with Radford; no one tried to hide anything from him. No one spoke to him when it could possibly be avoided.

In other words, Radford was an absolutely first-rate hatchet man. But the Director, a Wall Street lawyer inexperienced in recent intelligence operations, was as ill at ease with him as anyone else.

'Sit down, Radford,' he said. It was possible that Radford had a first name, but the DCI had never been tempted to learn it. 'I have a problem out of the past for you to look at.'

'Oh?' Radford's voice never betrayed emotion.

The Director knew that he was the most popular and respected man to preside over the Agency in a decade because, as the insiders conceded, he was tougher than any of them. He felt that the reputation was deserved. Wall Street was tougher than the shadow world any day. But if Radford was frightened of him, he did not show it.

'We had operations out of Japan over China until the middle sixties, didn't we?'

'I believe so,' Radford agreed cautiously.

He knew damn well there were such operations, that several pilots had been lost in China and that one of them had come back alive. And contemplated running for congress. Wouldn't that be nice. A former employee of the Company sitting on a congressional committee?

'You may remember an incident in 1965, when the Chinese reported shooting down a U-2 over Sinkiang,' the Director continued. 'We, of course, denied the plane was ours and claimed that we knew nothing about the pilot. Does it ring any bells?'

'Faintly,' said Radford.

'So everybody agreed he was dead. The Chinese said he was dead, and I guess we had no reason to think otherwise. Then in 1971, when the Chinese were releasing everybody, a Presbyterian missionary who came home reported seeing the fellow.' The Director unnecessarily glanced at the sheet of paper in front of him. 'Daniel Farrell . . . in a prison camp in western China. It made one or two of the newspapers, and then apparently was forgotten. If the Company did anything about the missionary's report, it didn't make the papers. The missionary is dead now, of course. He was an old man then.'

'Wouldn't the Chinese have released Farrell when they released everyone else?' Radford's eyes remained icy.

'Sure; why not? Only I want to know some more of the details. What we did about the missionary's report. Whether we ever asked the Chinese about this man, Farrell. And if we didn't, why we didn't.'

Radford was silent, waiting for an explanation, if one were to be offered.

'You know Congressman Burns, don't you, Radford?'

An ever-so-slight lift of a blond eyebrow. 'One of our

more intelligent friends on the Hill. Sympathetic, but not a naïf.'

'Chicago Irish politicians are never naive, Radford.' The Director was proud of himself for scoring one of his occasional points against his young assistant. 'Anyway, Jim Burns wants to know if we are sure that Farrell is dead. He also wants to know whether we are certain that there are no worms under that particular rock that might be turned up if somebody took a hard look at it. It seems that Farrell's cousin is probably going to run for governor in Illinois. The congressman is uneasy, by his own admission, that something might turn up on the Farrell affair during the election campaign.'

'A reporter could remember the U-2 incident, dig up some facts about the Presbyterian missionary, and maybe smoke out something else even more embarrassing,' Radford said tonelessly.

'Precisely. If a reporter shows up here asking about Daniel Farrell, I want to know all there is to know, what I have to tell him, and what I have to try to hide, if anything.'

Radford considered silently.

'I don't like it any more than you do,' the Director continued. 'Something doesn't smell right. Burns thinks the Farrell family was less than diligent in pushing us to find out what happened to this pilot.'

For the first time since the DCI had known him, Radford blinked. 'There's probably nothing at all under that rock, chief,' he said.

It was also the first time the Director had heard him use the word *probably*.

'I tend to agree with you. But we would look awfully silly, Radford, if someone else turns up the rock first and finds there is something under it. Get on it.'

'Yes, chief,' he said as he slipped out the door.

Despite his height and weight, Radford moved with the speed and grace of a predatory cat. The Director wondered why he thought of a black panther every time his strapping Harvard-trained assistant departed from his office.

Irene

Irene could not sleep. She lay next to her husband in bed, craving affectionate contact and wishing that she might at least touch his hand. Roger Farrell did not like physical contact unless they were making love. But Irene's need to touch and be touched was so powerful that she would have been delighted to be held in a man's arms while she was asleep every night, even if there had been no sex between them.

Roger was a skilful enough lover. He knew how to arouse her, to bring her to climax, and to settle and reassure her after lovemaking. But Irene often felt that Roger made love as though he were performing before a group of judges who would hold up cards and numbers on them after he was finished, like the judges at Olympic diving and gymnastic events. And when the applause died down, Irene was left alone, pleasured indeed, but feeling that the depths of her passions had not even been approached.

'It takes me a long time,' she had said once to her lover.

'And you're worth waiting for,' he'd said tenderly.

But that was long ago, before she had made an irreparable mess of her life.

Roger was less patient. After they made love, physical contact was brought to a decisive end, and she dared not touch him in bed until the next time. While she could not calculate Roger's schedule, she knew that their lovemaking was scheduled according to a formula, as was everything else in his life. And she was reasonably confident that the schedule for her was not correlated – the word he would use – with the schedule for his mistress.

Was that woman unsatisfied too?

Feeling mean, Irene hoped that she was.

There had been a scene at the supper table that evening. Roger had curtly informed his wife and daughter that he intended to run for governor and, in his most professorial tone, had tried to lay down rules for the campaign – how they should dress, what they should say to the papers, how Noele should keep a low profile and Irene a high profile. He was so taken up with his own importance that he did not notice the gathering storm on the Christmas child's face.

'You never asked me whether I wanted you to run for governor, Roger,' Irene said mildly.

'You never objected,' he replied with some asperity.

'I'm not sure I could get used to being the first lady of Illinois,' she replied knowing she would do whatever he wanted.

'Your friends Angie and Mick sound like total retards to me,' Noele shouted. 'They're not going to tell me how to be a teenager.'

And she soared out of the room, like a comet blazing across the winter sky.

'Have I been pompous?' Roger asked hesitantly.

'Even for you.'

'I'd better apologize.' He wiped his lips, folded his napkin carefully, and followed Noele out of the room.

He didn't apologize to *me*, Irene thought, but I suppose he'll make love to me tonight. That'll be the only apology I get.

The exchange with John that afternoon had troubled her deeply. He had always seemed a bit of a pompous ass, even as a seminarian with whom she temporarily thought she was in love, mostly because he was a kind of forbidden fruit. Now, as the pastor of St Praxides, he was someone to whom she was polite and respectful because he was a priest and a brother-in-law, but hardly a man to be considered as a troubled, vulnerable, and attractive male.

Yet that afternoon he had not been nearly as egotistical in his male insecurity as most men. In fact, he'd been rather charming, graceful, and astonishingly honest in his vulnerability. His need for sympathy had won instant response from her. And her response, spontaneous and unconsidered, had triggered an even more disarming self-revelation.

Irene was used to the imaginary undressing men routinely performed on women like her. Sometimes it was flattering, sometimes infuriating, mostly only 'boring,' as Noele would have said. But the look in John's eyes when she climbed out of the car was quite flattering. Pleased with his admiration, she had been a little more gracious to him than she ordinarily might have been. And thus encouraged, he had spilled his story of unhappiness. Poor man.

I could like him, she thought, shifting uneasily on her side of the bed. I could like him a lot.

I can't let that happen. I've had enough trouble with male members of the Farrell family as it is. I don't need a romance with a Farrell priest.

But if he were in love with me, he would never let me out of his arms. He would apologize if he hurt my feelings.

Like Danny, had he lived.

Roger

Roger was complacent as he drifted into a pleasant sleep. Normally he would not have made love to his wife the same day he had committed adultery. It was aesthetically unsatisfactory. But sex had been a way to soothe Irene's hurt feelings. He had been a damn fool to behave so insensitively – precisely the sort of behaviour he found so offensive in other academics.

He knew, however, that Noele was not so easily appeased. You had to reason with her. And reasoning with a stubborn, wilful young woman was not easy. Still, he would have to contain her, no matter how much effort was required.

Curiously, Martha had mentioned Noele that afternoon. She'd been clinging to him after they'd made love, using some new techniques and fantasies he had not tried before, including the idea of Martha as a young man as well as a young woman, a brain-crackling fantasy that increased greatly his affection for her.

'I would like to have a child of yours,' she had said, pressing against him as if the oxygen she breathed had to pass through his body first. 'Your daughter is so beautiful.'

It was the first hint of domesticity in their relationship, and it shocked Roger into momentary speechlessness.

'I thought your principles were against motherhood,' he stammered.

'Oh, they are.' She kissed his chest. 'But because I've chosen not to bring children into this unhappy world doesn't mean that I'm so inhuman as not to have regrets. I wish there was enough justice for women in the world so that it would be possible for me to have a daughter like Nicole.'

'Noele,' he said mechanically. Would she actually run the risk of pregnancy? Not that there was much chance . . .

'You're not angry with me?' she asked meekly.

'Of course not. In another set of circumstances, I would be happy to father a child of yours.'

In a lonely corner of his soul he had to admit that he spoke the truth. Martha was an obsession, a fantasy, an object, and a love – indeed so much of each that he could not pause to figure out what she meant in the other three roles.

And Irene was merely a wife.

At the last moment of wakefulness he perceived a troubling thought lingering at the outer reaches of his consciousness. He struggled to identify it. Something he had overlooked. Something terribly important. . . .

Brigid

'You wear me out, woman,' Burke murmured contentedly.

'Good enough for you,' Brigid said, cuddling even closer

to her husband. The forgetfulness, the oblivion of pleasure, passed quickly. 'I wish we were young and could fuck twelve times in a night. I heard one of the young women at work claiming that she and her boyfriend had done it twelve times in one night. Do you think that's possible, Burke?'

He laughed. 'Possible but remarkable.'

Brigid sighed her familiar west-of-Ireland sigh. 'The world comes back too quickly.'

Burke was always patient with her fears. 'Terrible things have happened, Bridie, but I don't think we did anything we didn't have to do. Even loving each other. . . .'

'A fine argument that will be when you plead our case before Himself,' Brigid said, and sniffed.

Burke was not altogether sure there was a Himself before whom he would have to plead. Yet with the passage of time even he was beginning to have doubts about his doubts. 'I think I can make a damn persuasive case for both of us. Maybe not enough to prevent a guilty verdict, but with mitigating circumstances and time off for good behaviour.'

'Ah, I hope so. But I doubt it. I think Himself will throw us out of court, and there's no appeal.' There was silence for a time, and then Brigid began again. 'I'm afraid of what might come out during Roger's election campaign.'

Burke was not quite asleep. 'Everything's covered, Bridie. The only one who can hurt us is Tim Nolan, and I don't think he's going to risk interfering with his pensions, especially since we've given him a raise. And besides, no one can touch the killer now.'

'Tim was in from the beginning, wasn't he?'

'That's why the greedy SOB receives two pensions from us, one for each cover-up.' He tightened his arms around her protectively. 'We're perfectly safe, Bridie, in this world, and if there is a next one, I think I can make a case there too.'

Poor Burke thought he understood everything, but she hadn't trusted him with the full story. He would never have revealed it, yet it was safer if only two people knew what actually happened.

'I don't like those questions Noele asked Doctor Keefe. She must suspect that Clancy died later than I told her.'

'It doesn't matter, does it? There's no one left to protect.'

Ah, but there was.

The picture was seared in her brain, never to be erased. She was huddled against the wall in the upstairs hallway. Her dress torn away. Clancy's cane flailing at her. The worst beating ever. He was furious because of the romance between Danny and Irene. *He's going to kill me this time,* she had thought. *It would be a welcome relief.* Then the cane was snatched from Clancy's hands and was slashing him across the face.

She saw him stumble back against the railing, lose his footing, and then career head over heels down the steps, his head bouncing off the post at the foot of the staircase with a sickening thud, blood pouring out on the new carpet.

Then more lies. They never seemed to stop. Lies, lies, lies.

She huddled even closer to Burke, who was now sound asleep.

Roger

Roger ran his finger along the slim curve of Martha's back, his chest moving rapidly up and down in self-satisfied breathlessness. A smooth back, a slim little ass, trim legs. From the rear she could indeed be boy or girl, and she was enjoyable as both. She luxuriated in any sexual innovation he proposed, justifying it by the ideology of sexual freedom and loving it as a passionately aroused woman. She did not have the proportions of a *Playboy* centrefold, but a *Playboy* fantasy she had become. Yet the more he used her as a fantasy object, the more tender and protective he felt toward her during the sweetness of their afterglow affection.

A little bisexuality never hurt anyone, he told himself, knowing full well that he would be assaulted by enormous guilt on the way back to the neighbourhood. Martha was a source of greater pleasure than any of the others. And hence a source of greater guilt. And oddly, greater love.

So it must necessarily be in a universe ruled, if not by justice, at least by a rough proportionality.

His campaign for the governorship was beginning to move. He had decided to announce in early December, just before the meeting of the State Democratic Slate-Making Committee; he had been assured privately that all the powerbrokers would support him and that there would be only token opposition in the March Democratic primary.

Even the mayor had sent an ambiguous message of noninterference. The mayor was not to be trusted and might easily turn against him if she thought there was a possibility he could align himself with her political enemy in the next mayoral campaign. But Mick Gerety had assured her in Roger's name that he would take a hands-off position in Chicago politics. Still, as Mick said, 'Assurances are not enough for herself. You would have to deposit a gallon of your blood, your right arm, and possibly certain more intimate organs too. But I think she'll stay out of this one. Hell, a primary battle against one of her people would be good for you.'

Roger was about to leave on a whirlwind tour of speaking engagements, many of them in sleepy little Downstate towns or in dull industrial cities whose existence he would have preferred not to consider, and he would have to endure a few days without the delights of Martha.

The talks in Chicago had been successful so far. His audiences were warm and responsive. They laughed at his jokes and cheered enthusiastically for his programmes – on the whole, a much better reaction than he could have expected from graduate students at the University.

His faculty colleagues had been remarkably tolerant of his descent into the mess of elective politics. It was an amusing quirk in his behaviour, they thought, much like his Roman Catholicism. He was, of course, expected to take a leave of absence from the department. And some of his colleagues were doubtless already murmuring behind his back that this 'episode' was proof that he was not, after all, a serious scholar. What else can you expect of a Roman Catholic? some of them would say.

But they would not make such comments too loudly, because by voting him a full professor in the political science department, they had by definition decided that he was a serious scholar.

There were some murmurings of protest from other departments, most notably the Committee on Social Theory, that his political speeches had already lowered the standards of the University – a mortal sin in that community. However, others somewhat more pragmatically argued that the University could well use a friend in Springfield.

He was still meeting with his classes, of course; the classroom was never a time-consuming activity for a full professor. One was expected to discuss one's own work and tell anecdotes in lecture courses and, in seminars, to listen without appearing to be bored to student presentations of research they had done for your monographs. His students, in any event, were delighted to learn something about practical politics in a political science course.

During the month of November, he was waging, along with his own campaign, a vigorous battle for the promotion of Martha Clay, a campaign he had raised to a matter of high principle in public discussion of her. Perhaps she was a marginal case for tenure, but so, by the standards of the present, were half the tenured faculty of his department and most of her male peers who were likely to be promoted.

He had been able to swing three votes at the final meeting of the tenured faculty, two abstentions and one positive vote, so that the vote in her favour was seven to four. The opposition came from a peculiar alliance of Marxists and behaviourists, the former because they thought her perspective was 'incorrect' and the latter because they thought, quite properly, that her use of empirical data was abominable.

The letter of transmission to the dean was moderately strong. Thus the dean, one of the great memo-initialing clerks of the century, was not being given a clear signal that the department wanted to be overruled. His dilemma, therefore, would be quite difficult, especially since the 'standards'-bearing crusaders of the Committee on Social Theory were already mobilizing their considerable resources against Martha, as they did against anyone reputed to be a threat to 'standards.' Still, now she at least had a chance, which is more than Roger would have given her a couple of months ago. And that chance exorcised much of his continuing guilt over their affair, an affair which, he had begun to realize, was getting out of hand because of the enormous sweetness of his bisexual fantasies.

He would not, he could not, follow the path of other academics who allowed themselves to be captured by their transient mistresses. Noele, the governorship, Irene – all would be lost. Yet he was, he had to admit, utterly and completely besotted with Martha. She was the first woman since the daydreams of his adolescence to preoccupy him during all his waking hours and invade his dreams at night.

She rolled over on her back and looked up at him with soft eyes and a satisfied smile. 'Will you always love me, Roger?'

It was a cheerleader/senior prom question. 'I can't imagine ever not loving you,' he equivocated. Domesticity rears its ugly head again.

'I'm not talking about marriage,' she said. 'I dread the thought of ever losing you.'

'We both believe in total freedom, don't we?' Roger replied, falling back into his usual line of defence.

He would not, he supposed, tire of her for a long time. On the contrary, the curve of satisfaction was going up rather than down. It might, arguably, be very difficult to give her up. Yet a gubernatorial candidate could hardly afford a scandal; and even though he had paid little attention to Irene recently, she was still his wife.

'Certainly.' She propped her head up on her elbow. 'I'm not making any claim. We're both totally and absolutely free.'

Only they were not, Roger realized. The body makes demands of its own, regardless of ideologies. That's why I feel so tender toward her at this moment that I would give up almost anything to make her happy. Fortunately for me – and for her, too – this moment will pass. Separation will be an agonizing problem for me somewhere down the road.

And the thought of walking down the road tickled a spot in the back of his mind, which reminded him intermittently that he had forgotten something terribly important, something potentially very dangerous. What was it?

Noele

It was a really excellent pep rally, Noele told Jaimie Burns, using the favourite superlative of her generation.

Jaimie shrugged indifferently. He was totally unjazzed about football before and after the game. Pep rallies and victory dances were bummers. Only the crunching tackle of a halfback, a ball snatched out of the hands of an unwary wide receiver at the last moment, or best of all, a lazy, spiralling punt arriving in his arm at about the same time tacklers headed for his legs could stir him.

Jaimie had earned a new nickname, which Noele thought was horrid and of which he was inordinately proud, even though Noele insisted that the reporter had mixed his metaphors.

With the unpredictable grace and dazzling speed of a fire racing across the bogs of Ireland, the Fighting Irish's Freshman Free Safety, Jim Burns, raced across the turf here at the Meadowlands this afternoon, said the newspaper story, *sinking the Navy's chances of obtaining a rare victory against their traditional foes from South Bend. Wherever the Middies threw the football, there was Jim Burns, blocking, tackling, and picking off passes, four of them to be exact, not only matching the Notre Dame record, but depriving the Navy of two almost certain TD's. Asked by someone after final obsequies for the Navy whether his interceptions were 'Hail Mary' catches, Burns, the son of a congressman from Chicago, replied with a typically laconic comment, 'As my girl friend would say, The Mother of Jesus is on the side of those who practise the longest.'*

'I never said it,' Noele protested.

'You would have if you'd been there.'

'What does *laconic* mean?'

'Totally cas.'

So Jaimie was a hero and was now Bogfire Burns and had to stand on the platform during the pep rally.

Noele did not have the heart to tell him that Brigid said bog fires travelled very slowly, 'Like molasses in January, child.'

After the pep rally they went for a long walk along the shore of the tiny moonlit lake in the centre of the Notre Dame campus. She was spending the night before tomorrow's season finale against the Trojans of Southern Cal with friends in one of the women's dorms.

Jaimie recounted, with precise detail, his conversation with his grandfather.

'Why would William Farrell leave his company and all his money to Clancy when he knew that he was such a terrible space cadet?' she asked after Jaimie had described the reputation of the Farrell twins and the rumours of dishonesty and incompetence in the firm's construction of defence plants. 'Wouldn't Martin be the one to take over the company when he came back from the war?'

'Granddad said that Martin wasn't especially interested in business. And besides, he was William's favourite son and Clancy was Blanche's, and Blanche always had her way. There were rumours that Bill Farrell was so angry about the government investigation back in 1943 that he was going to change the will, but apparently he never did.'

'Hmm. . . . Well, I guess it didn't matter. Martin died, and Clancy would have inherited anyway.'

Jaimie thought for a moment. 'Not necessarily. Martin was killed in action after his father's death. If the will had been changed . . . let me see . . . yeah, Martin's son would have inherited everything.'

'A little boy?'

'That doesn't matter.'

'Like, wow! Now we have two motives, one for which he might have killed and another for which he might have been killed.'

'No, you don't,' he argued. 'You have one gratuitous speculation about a will no one says ever existed.'

'What's *gratuitous* mean? Oh, never mind. Has your father said anything about the CIA?'

'It means "way out," and Dad hasn't said a thing.'

'What if he's alive?' Noele said soberly.

'What if he is? And what if he comes back and kills someone else?'

'He'd never do that!' Noele said, flaring instantly. 'Anyway, if he's still alive, I'll get him out of China. I suppose you don't think I can do that?'

'I think you can do anything you want to,' Jaimie said fervently. 'That's why you totally overwhelm me.'

So Noele kissed him, which under the circumstances was the only thing to do. Noele noted to herself once again that, like her mother, she was a very sensuous person. More sensuous maybe than Jaimie, who was nonetheless a very good kisser.

Then something melted inside of Noele. She felt herself dissolving into a unity with Jaimie. They were now one person – Noele/Jaimie – and that person was caught in an incandescent electrical current.

She was losing herself to him. And she wanted to.

'Hold me tight, Jaimie . . .' she pleaded.

He did. As if she were a Trojan tight end he was trying to tackle.

'. . . forever.'

Jaimie laughed, but he hung on.

'I'm afraid, so afraid.' The words tumbled out before she knew what they were.

She was fighting to keep away the loneliness that was

suddenly all around her, blotting out the lake and the moonlight and the campus and even Jaimie.

'I'll take care of you, Noele, no matter what.'

If he wants me this minute, he can have me. . . .

Jaimie ended the embrace, as he usually did. 'So you're going to try to interview Captain Nolan?' he asked.

'You know me too well,' Noele protested.

He patted her rump with about the same degree of affection he had patted the strong side safety when that young man had blitzed an opposing quarterback. 'For sure.'

John

The parish council was debating whether the lunches and dinners served to members of the parish staff who happened to be in the rectory at mealtime ought to be considered part of their salary and subject to withholding tax. The discussion had deteriorated into an alley fight between Geraldine Leopold, a member of the parish council who worked for the IRS, and Martina O'Rourke, a former nun who was director of the religious education programme for students attending non-Catholic schools.

It was the kind of personality fight masquerading as an intellectual argument that made John wonder whether democracy in the church was a good thing. Eddie O'Reilly, a razor-sharp young lawyer, had already provided a solution to the problem. Such meals were professional meetings of the parish staff and could not properly be considered part of their recompense. He was sure if the matter arose – and that was most unlikely – that the IRS would agree. Nonetheless the two angry and frustrated middle-aged women had to be permitted to fight it out to the end, one complaining about 'clerical discounts' and the other protesting the 'oppression of our capitalist economy.' In due course someone would demand the question, and there would be a vote overwhelmingly in favour of O'Reilly's solution. But no one was yet ready to brave the wrath of women by demanding the question.

John had little patience for the debate. He had been denounced in the TV section of the Chicago *Star Herald* that morning, and the phone had been ringing all day with calls from clergymen who, under the pretence of seeking information from him but with every intention of gloating over his plight, asked: 'Did you see what the *Star Herald* had to say about you?'

Larry Rieves, the TV columnist, wrote all his columns from a perspective of high moral outrage, a perspective that enabled him to say that a programme was popular though its ratings were low, and unpopular though its ratings were high, and then a few weeks later come back and celebrate the accuracy of his self-fulfilling prophecy.

In his latest attack, that morning, Rieves had congratulated himself on the waning popularity of *The Monsignor Farrell Show*. Viewers, he said, were growing tired, just as he had predicted, of Farrell's shallow posturing. Moreover, they were sceptical about whether a priest whose brother was running for governor ought to continue to have access to prime-time television. Finally, many of the Catholics of Chicago, influenced by the insightful criticism of their clergy, were being turned off by Monsignor Farrell, and hence were turning him off.

Much of the remaining two thirds of the column was devoted to comments from an anonymous but 'influential' Chicago priest. John Farrell was 'on an ego trip'; he was 'hungry for publicity.' Everyone knew that he was 'just interested in promoting himself and making money' and that he was 'neglecting his parish in order to devote his attention to the programme.'

Monsignor Mortimer, of course.

It was also asserted that John Farrell didn't really care anymore about the people of his parish. He was, in fact, thinking of leaving the priesthood, and had been offered a position as a host of a major New York talk show.

(Inconsistent with declining popularity, it would seem, but Rieves was never bothered by consistency.)

Finally, Rieves reported that a committee of St Praxides parishioners were planning to submit a formal request that Monsignor Farrell choose between the parish and his television programme. 'We have a good parish here,' Rieves wrote, quoting an anonymous member of the community. 'Racial integration is working fine. We don't need to have it spoiled by a controversial pastor.'

John was numb after he read the column, and then frightened. In the midst of the gloating calls from other priests, there were a few phone calls from anxious parishioners wondering what was going on. And to make matters worse, virtually every member of the parish council, as they came into the rectory for the meeting, asked whether he 'saw the job that Rieves did on you this morning.'

He did not want to be 'controversial.' Once that word was applied to a priest, he was finished with his fellow priests and his parishioners. John had been able to survive the trauma of the day only because Irene was the first one on the phone. She told him briskly that his only answer ought to be that his ratings had gone up, not down, and that everything else in the Rieves column was just as untrue as what he had said about the ratings.

It turned out to be a very effective answer, but John realized for the first time in his life that the press could lie about him with impunity. And his clerical adversaries had probably put Rieves up to it. Your enemies might persuade the media to attack your reputation and you would not be able to defend yourself. The media could stamp you with an image totally at odds with what you really were, and you would be stuck with that image for the rest of your life.

He desperately wanted to talk to Irene again, confident that his adolescent lustful fantasies had been wiped out by genuine respect and friendship. A conversation with her over a drink – no, not a drink, she was drinking too much these days – over a cup of coffee after the parish council meeting would relax him and help him to sleep.

He signalled Eddie O'Reilly somewhat impatiently with his eyes, and the young man caught his instruction and moved the question.

John ignored the wrathful looks of Geraldine Leopold and Martina O'Rourke.

Would that they were the only ones he had to fear.

DCI.

Radford was in his office early on the Monday morning after the Thanksgiving weekend, something less than his usual confident self.

'It's bad, chief,' he said, using an adjective the Director had never heard before on his lips.

'You'd better tell me the whole thing.'

Radford considered the brown Virginia fields outside the windows of the Director's spacious office and then turned and sat in the chair in front of his vast desk. 'It was a termination, the sort of thing we used to call termination with extreme prejudice.'

'We executed Daniel Farrell?'

'The mechanics, the medics, and the technicians all knew that he was a condemned man, every bit as much as the prison staff does when someone is being electrocuted. His fuel supply was half of what it should have been, the ejection mechanism was fixed so it wouldn't work, all the top-secret material had been taken off the plane, the explosive that would destroy the aircraft was rigged to respond to the ejection trigger. If Farrell tried to eject, the aircraft should have exploded.'

'Only it didn't.' The Director felt a disturbing sensation in the pit of his stomach.

'Apparently not, if the photographs we have of the wreckage are authentic. Our people tell me they certainly appear to be.'

'Why was he terminated? Who ordered it? My predecessor of happy memory?'

'No one ordered it,' Radford snapped. 'No one here had anything against Farrell. He was a superb pilot, apparently quite trustworthy. The mission security chief claimed to have instructions from us. Indeed, he showed the mission director all the required documentation. It was murder, chief, pure and simple. Cleverly faked orders for termination on the grounds that Farrell was selling secrets to the Soviet Resident in Tokyo.'

'And then?'

'Nothing for a year and a half. Then the mission security chief retired early and moved to Mexico with a very large sum of money. One of the technicians on the team – which was disbanded shortly after the crash – smelled a rat and went to the inspector general. There was an investigation.'

'And the highest authorities in the Company decided to do nothing about it,' said the Director, knowing all too well what was likely to have happened in his office in the late sixties and early seventies.

'That's right. And the last thing we wanted here was some poor old missionary suggesting that Farrell was still alive.'

'What a mess. We would be in deep trouble if this story were ever leaked.'

Radford spread his massive hands in a gesture of frustration and impotence. 'There's worse, chief. Farrell was still alive when the Chinese were releasing all of our prisoners ten years ago. They asked us if we wanted him back, and we told them no.'

'In God's name, why?' the Director exploded.

'The members of the team that made the decision are gone now, chief, but I imagine you can guess why. Farrell must have known his plane had been sabotaged. The Company didn't want a U-2 pilot returning after an attempt to terminate him. Much less did we want anyone to open a can of worms about a mission security chief who might be guilty of attempted murder.'

'And the mission chief is dead now?' the Director asked, drumming his fingers nervously on his massive oak desk.

'How did you know that?' Radford grinned crookedly. 'Natural causes, as far as I know; and incidentally, there is considerable evidence of suspicious links in his past. In fact, he seems to have been one of the unofficial channels of communication the Company used to maintain those links.'

'One of those Mafia types that Donovan brought in during the war with the assistance of his friends Cardinal Spellman and Frankie Costello?'

Radford nodded.

'Will we ever get that monkey off our back?' the DCI snapped irritably.

Radford did not comment. Much of his job consisted in taming monkeys out of the past who would not get off the Company's back.

The Director considered the problem carefully. 'So the Central Intelligence Agency, acting through its duly appointed and approved mission security chief, carried out a hit contract – for reasons, I suppose, we don't know and can no longer learn?'

'Precisely,' Radford agreed sombrely.

'And like a lot of our dirty tricks in those years, we buried it along with Farrell?'

'Exactly.'

'Are you sure it's completely buried?'

Radford shrugged imperceptibly. 'It would be awfully hard for anyone here to dig it up without your authority. I suppose the syndicate go-betweens know, and whoever ordered the hit, but they're not likely to talk about it.'

'Is Farrell still alive?'

'Probably not.'

'Probably won't do.'

Radford nodded.

Of course it wouldn't do. If Daniel Xavier Farrell were still alive, he might appear at any time, released in some unfathomable Chinese gesture. You could never be quite sure what the Chinese would do. And the longer he was in prison before he was released, the greater the media outrage when he finally did surface.

Radford stirred in his chair. 'There's a cocktail party later on this week where I'll bump into the Chinese Resident. We'll exchange information politely and indirectly. Do you want me to ask about Farrell?'

'Is the Resident likely to understand at this point we're only looking for information?'

'Those people' – Radford shrugged – 'make the Japanese look transparent. It's anybody's guess, chief.'

'You think we ought to leave well enough alone?'

Radford was his old familiar cold-eyed self. 'The Company has left well enough alone on the Farrell case for the last sixteen years and got away with it.'

'I know,' sighed the Director.

Radford waited silently for his chief's decision. The DCI searched for a few words from the ethics class he had attended in a small liberal arts college many years before.

'Talk to the Resident,' he said.

Irene

Noele and her mother had a furious fight. Irene became edgy every December. The greyness of winter depressed her. Dresses were replaced by thick skirts or slacks and sweaters, which made men stare at her even more intently. The responsibilities of Christmas shopping, Christmas card lists, and the annual Christmas party that Roger insisted they give for their friends weighed heavily upon her. She told herself that a woman with no job and help in her home every day of the week should be able to cope with the holiday season.

However, her ability to cope diminished with each passing day. She had read an article in the life-style section of the paper the previous year about people who become depressed at Christmastime. It had seemed like a perfect description of herself.

Roger was busy in the campaign, so busy that he hardly

seemed aware of her existence, even in bed at night. And Noele was going through a particularly difficult adolescent phase. She snapped Irene's head off every time her mother asked where she was going, where she had been, or why she had been out so late.

'I'm sure that I'm old enough to take care of myself,' Noele had ranted after having been mildly castigated for coming home late on a Sunday evening after the last football weekend with Jaimie at Notre Dame. 'And I'm sure nobody was asking those kinds of questions when you were my age.'

'I'm sure' was a new teenage expression indicating ironic anger. It was also an absolutely certain sign Noele was in one of her bitchy moods. Irene had no idea what was bugging the child. And she did not know how to begin to try to find out.

The battle on this cold Saturday morning in early December as snow flurries pirouetted on Jefferson Avenue was about the condition of Noele's room, a subject about which they engaged in listless combat at least once a week.

Irene had threatened that there would be no Christmas dances or Christmas dates for Noele if she didn't put her room in order. 'I simply won't let people come into this house for Daddy's Christmas party and run the risk of their seeing that we have a pigsty on the second floor.'

'I'm sure they'll go up there just to look for my pigsty,' Noele fired back.

'Whether they look for it or not, young woman, you're going to clean up your room, and you're going to do it now. I'm really very angry at you.'

'Don't say you're angry,' Noele snapped back. 'Say you're disappointed in me.'

'I am *not* disappointed. I'm angry,' Irene shouted. 'What's more, you better shape up and act like a presentable young woman. Your father is going to be running for governor, and he can't have a dork for a daughter.' I try to reprimand her, Irene thought, and I use her own ridiculous slang.

'He has a dork for a wife. Why not a dork daughter, too?'

She wanted to hit the little brat.

'You will not go to the Christmas dance, and that's final!'

'I want Roger to be governor.' Noele seemed inclined to negotiate, as she often was after an outburst. 'But I'm sure a neat room won't elect him.'

'I'll be the judge of that,' Irene said, furious at her own impotence.

'And I'm sure you're tough enough to prevent me from going to the Christmas dance, even if I don't clean it up,' Noele responded.

'You just try me and find out,' Irene shouted furiously.

She knew that if she did work up enough nerve to ban Christmas activities for Noele, Roger would overrule her.

'You're a terrible disciplinarian, Moms,' Noele said contemptuously. 'You can't make anything stick. I'm sure Roger will let me go to the Christmas dance, particularly the Notre Dame Club of Chicago dance, no matter what you say.'

The child was perfectly right. 'Noele Marie Brigid Farrell,' Irene ordered, the full name a sign of her anger. 'You go to your room this instant. If you act like a nine-year-old, I will treat you like a nine-year-old. This *instant!*'

Surprisingly enough, Noele obeyed, slamming up the stairs like an outraged company of infantry. Irene soon heard the noise of furious movement from her daughter's room. Using all three of her names still worked, Irene mused. I don't quite know why. Maybe it's a signal that I'm still bigger than she is and the time for her to fight back has been temporarily terminated.

Maybe I would have been better off if I'd fought back that way when I was her age.

The door bell rang. John Farrell with new troubles. Irene straightened her dress, fluffed up her hair, inspected her face carefully in the large mirror in the hallway, and opened the door. She kissed John lightly as she admitted him to the house. Externally it was the same sisterly kiss that they had exchanged many times before, but both of them knew it was an expression of affection that was taking on deeper and more dangerous meaning. Irene was thrilled and stimulated by the danger.

'Too early for a drink?' she asked as she ushered John into the parlour.

He hesitated, and then said, 'I guess I could do with one, even if it's only eleven thirty.'

John was pale and thin. She wondered how much weight he had lost since the persecution had begun. 'Confusion to our enemies,' she said, toasting him with what she hoped was something of a crooked grin. Then she sat on the chair next to the couch where he was sitting. Noele was in the house, and they ought not to be too close.

'Their numbers grow,' John said. 'I suppose this is significant.' He gave her a four-colour advertising brochure announcing an archdiocesan workshop on communication – two days of seminars, lectures, and discussion of the role of the mass media in the ministry of the church.

Irene glanced over the programme and its list of participants – the director of Vatican Radio and the head of the Papal Office of Social Communication; an anchorman from Washington; a film director from Hollywood, of whom she had never heard, with a long string of film credits; Monsignor Mortimer, director of the Catholic Television Channel; and a number of 'Archdiocesan media specialists.'

'Someone's missing,' she said ruefully.

'I ought not to be surprised.' John's eyes were sad, and his face was lined and gaunt, looking the way Irene imagined an ex-convict's would. 'I was invited to some of the preparatory meetings last spring, and then didn't hear a word about the project. I figured it had been dropped.'

'Is it important to you, John?' She tried to sound warm and sympathetic.

'I suppose it ought not to be.' He spread his hands out in a motion of dejection. 'The church and the archdiocese have been my life since I first went to the seminary almost thirty years ago. Everything I've done has been directed to the service of the archdiocese. I didn't want to take the damn TV office. The cardinal had to insist. Every priest I know pleaded with me to take the talk show. And now they all think I'm on an ego trip and have begun to pretend

I don't exist. . . . I simply don't understand it.'

'Envy,' Irene said bluntly.

My poor dear, she thought. Your vanity is injured. But vanity is a vice that hurts no one. Envy hurts everyone.

John looked up from his folded hands. 'Is that it, Irene? Is it really envy? Or am I really on an ego trip? Sometimes I'm not sure myself. God knows, I don't want to be controversial.'

'Don't be ridiculous. Of course you're not on an ego trip. And how can you accomplish anything worthwhile without being controversial?'

Maybe someday I'll tell him the whole truth about himself, but he's not ready for that yet.

'And it keeps up. Read this column by Parson Rails.'

Irene had never paid much attention to the *Star Herald*'s religion column, which appeared every Saturday. She could not remember having heard of Parson Rails.

TV PRIESTS WOULD NOT HAVE BEEN ACCEPTED IN THE OLD DAYS DOWNSTATE, the headline read.

Irene glanced through the article. 'This is silly, John. Who cares whether the parish priest in the town where he grew up was popular with everyone, even this columnist's Protestant mother, because he fried the chicken himself at the annual chicken roast on Labour Day weekends?'

'Parson Rails is good at nostalgia . . . old-time religion.'

'But this is the age of television, and we don't live in small towns downstate. Parson Rails is as bad as that little toad who does book reviews for the *Star Herald*. What's his name?'

John seemed surprised that she read book reviews. 'Manny Sizer? Some people think he's the most mean-spirited, petty, envious critic in America.'

'And when he tries to destroy a book, it is a sure sign that it will be an enormous success in Chicago. Why take such vile creatures seriously?'

'I know it's just one more sign of the pressure building up against me. And it's finally got to the parish. You know the Arthur Kellys? They have a different priest at their house once a week for dinner. Well, they've apparently formed a committee of parishioners to request that I either give up the programme or resign as pastor.' His hands were trembling as he put the brochure for the television workshop and the newspaper clipping back into his coat pocket.

Do you want the cheers of your audience or the support of your people? How unfair it is, poor, simple, innocent man, that you can't have both. Why don't you have an ego implanted in a concrete silo like your brother?

Or like your goddamned cousin Danny?

'You shouldn't pay any attention to them, John. I'm sure they couldn't gather twenty votes against you in the parish.'

'I think they could probably get a lot more. Every parish has malcontents, and once they begin to organize, they can make a lot of noise – just as Rieves has been saying in his column.'

'John, there will be one hundred parishioners in support of you for every one against you. They can organize too, you know. Eddie O'Reilly would love a good fight.'

'I wonder. . . .'

Noele bounced down the stairs dressed in brown corduroy knickers and brown stockings and light brown shirt with fluffy ruffles. Over an arm was draped the matching corduroy jacket.

'Hi, Uncle Monsignor. Larry Rieves is a creep. And if anybody tries to organize a committee against you, I'll have the High Club picket their homes.'

Irene and John laughed spontaneously, both wondering how she knew what they were talking about.

Noele grinned. 'It will be really excellent. I'm sure we'll show those yuk-heads who run this parish.'

'Mary Noele Brigid Farrell, of course,' John said.

'I have an appointment with Father/Captain/Doctor Ace, Mother. I'll finish my room when I come back.' Noele hesitated, as if asking for permission.

'Father McNamara merits dress-up clothes and your uncle doesn't?'

'Really, Mo-ther, Uncle Monsignor is a relative, and Father/Captain/Doctor Ace isn't.'

'Well, you look very pretty, Noele.' Her mother gave in. 'But I still want that room cleaned.'

'As soon as I get back. This is a really important problem I have to solve.'

'Thank you for cleaning it,' she said.

Noele stopped in midflight and turned to consider her mother carefully. The little computer under her red hair was whirling.

'Anytime, Moms.' She threw up her hands in a gesture of mock majesty, like a precinct captain who had done someone a great favour.

From an obnoxious little bitch to my sweet Christmas child in a few moments, Irene thought. How I wish I were like her.

Noele ran out of the house and into the street, having apparently decided that snow flurries or not, she would walk to the rectory. Of course, she had to show off her new brown corduroy suit.

'Come over to the window, John, and watch her,' Irene said.

As Noele moved down the street, trenchcoat open so as to display her new clothes, hands jauntily stuffed into the pockets, an entourage of dogs assembled to follow her. First a languid Irish setter, then a disheartened bloodhound, a happy-go-lucky black Labrador, and finally a yapping schnauzer.

'In order of their appearance, John, the dogs are Melissa, Poindexter, Sebastian, and Heather. She'll probably collect five or six more before she gets to the rectory. Every time the child walks down the street, she's followed by all the dogs and the little children in the neighbourhood. See, there's the McCarthy girl, and Josie Holloway's little boy will be right behind her. My Christmas child attracts, among other things, dogs and little children.'

'Has she finished the term paper?' John turned away from the street and looked at Irene.

'I think so. She doesn't talk about it anymore. But you never know with that child.'

They returned to their pre-luncheon martinis, but this time Irene sat closer to John on the coach, just far enough away so that their knees were not touching.

'Will we ever be able to tell her the truth?' Irene asked sadly.

'I don't see how we can, Irene. Not ever.' The lines on

John's face seemed to deepen, and his eyes turn hard and distant. 'I'm sure it would tear her apart.'

'Yet sometimes I wonder if she doesn't already know, deep down inside. Maybe she's already listened in to our thoughts about that terrible day when we . . . when we found her.'

'I hope to God she hasn't,' John prayed fervently.

They were both silent for a moment, as if on a private visit to the Blessed Sacrament in an empty church.

'You're going to challenge the Kellys head on, aren't you?' she asked, breaking the silence between them. 'And do you really want Noele to throw a picket line around their house?'

'No, I won't do that,' John said briskly. 'But I'm going to ask Eddie O'Reilly to propose a resolution at a special meeting of the parish council, a resolution supporting me and recommending a parishwide petition. That will silence the Kellys in a hurry.'

'That's a real Farrell!' Irene hugged him impetuously. He embraced her in return. And then, as if he were terribly weary, he rested his head momentarily on her shoulder.

A delightfully powerless languor crept into Irene's body. She had never committed adultery before. Only two men had ever possessed her. This man could be the third. He needed her. He probably had to have her. And she wanted him.

John Farrell lifted his head as if to pull away from her, but she put her hand on the back of his neck and held his face against her breasts a few moments longer. 'Don't worry, John. It's all right. Nothing bad is going to happen.'

He sighed softly, as if he would be content to remain in her embrace for the rest of his life.

It all depends, Irene thought to herself, what I mean by *bad*.

Noele

'Like the Murphys' Hobie Cat the summer before last?'

Noele's face felt very warm. 'I was a tomboy then,' she

said, trying to defend herself.

She and Eileen Kelly had got themselves into a real lot of trouble by kind of borrowing the Murphys' brand-new beach boat and drifting several miles down the shore.

'You're not a tomboy anymore?' Father Ace's eyes were dancing now.

'Only privately,' Noele answered, and sniffed.

Father Ace laughed the way he always did, joyously enough to make the rectory windowpanes shake. 'Come on, MN.,' he said, 'what makes you so certain that your grandfather was killed?'

'I know he was. I just absolutely know he was.'

'And Danny Farrell killed him?'

'Stop sounding like a district attorney. You're supposed to be the sympathetic counsellor.' Noele sighed in distress. 'No, Father, I don't think so. But he might have . . . Anyway, what did he and Gramps fight about all the time?'

Father McNamara pushed his hands into his Marine Corps fatigue trousers, his standard uniform for when he was talking to teenagers.

'I can't remember that they fought, to tell you the truth. Of course, a lot of things go on in the Neighbourhood that we don't hear about in the rectory. And Danny was a comedian, not a fighter. . . .'

'Was it about the firm?'

'Stop peeking in my head.' Father Ace was accustomed to Noele's apparent ability to read other people's thoughts. 'There *was* a nasty rumour in the parish, among the old-timers, that Clancy had cheated his brother out of the control of the firm. It doesn't make much sense, though. Martin was killed in the war. Danny might have thought the firm was his by right.'

'Wouldn't Brigid have given him the money if he'd asked?'

Father Ace dismissed the dim recollections of the past. 'I'm sorry I ever brought it up, Noele. Of course she would have. He would have had not motive at all.'

'Except maybe to get even.'

'Get even for what?'

'Oh, I don't know, Father. I just know I have to find out.'

'Still the Jane Marple of Beverly?'

'Cordelia Gray,' Noele said indignantly.

'And you're not going to leave the family skeletons alone until you rattle them all? Even if they fall on you?'

'I guess not,' she said slowly. 'I have to. I don't know why I have to. . . . It's, like, I'm nobody until I find out.'

She could not quite tell him about the horrible feeling of loneliness. He would have wanted to send her to a shrink.

'What happened when you tried to turn the Murphys' boat around?'

'We discovered we couldn't drift back in the direction we came.'

'Yeah,' said Father Ace.

DCI

'You saw the Chinese Resident last night?'

'He was very charming. They're quite charming these days, you know.'

'So I gathered,' said the Director drily. 'He knew about the Farrell case?'

'If he didn't, he pretended to.' A faint frown blemished Radford's handsome face. 'Bobbed his head up and down like a marionette and repeated six or seven times, "Understand, understand," and didn't lose his painted-on smile.'

'A language barrier?' asked the chief.

'He was three years ahead of me at Harvard. He speaks English perfectly.'

'So he understands that we're simply making discreet inquiries about the facts of the Farrell situation?'

'I didn't say that, chief.' Radford rubbed the arm of his leather chair. 'I have no idea whether he's ever heard of

Farrell. But I don't think they're going to do anything hasty to embarrass us.'

'And how did you leave it at the end of the conversation?'

'He said they would take care of everything.'

'That sounds ominous, doesn't it?'

'Not necessarily. At any rate, the Resident said we have nothing to worry about.'

The Director had other problems that morning. There were some very strange troop movements going on in southern Africa. Daniel Farrell was only a minor responsibility.

'So we have nothing to worry about? I wonder if Farrell ought to be worrying if he is still alive.'

Roger

On the way home from O'Hare he was finally able to place the gnawing sensation of having overlooked something important.

Maybe he had not locked either his portable safe or his personal file cabinet.

That would have been childishly irresponsible.

He had been in so great a hurry to blot out the memories of the past with the delights of the present. Martha would make him forget Florence Carey.

He smiled at himself, a self-mocking, contemptuous smile. A Freudian would have said that he had done it deliberately to run the risk of exposing the family past so he would not have to run for governor.

He told the cab driver to head for the University instead of the neighbourhood.

Certainly he had locked both the safe and the file.

He had a lecture to the Knights of Columbus Council in the western suburbs that night. Roger hesitated. It could wait till tomorrow.

Nonetheless, it was time to eliminate that nagging peripheral worry definitively.

At the University he told the cabby to wait, and ran across the street to the government department building, leaning into the chilly December west wind.

Mrs Marshfield was on the telephone when he walked into the outer office. She was always on the telephone. She did not bother to look up or even to acknowledge his presence. One thing he had to say about Mrs Marshfield: She didn't do any less work in his absence than she did in his presence.

Casually he looked for the key to his personal filing cabinet, opened it, and removed the portable safe.

He had not spun the combination lock.

With trembling fingers, he flipped the top of the lid and thumbed through the files.

The *Farrell, Florence Carey* file was missing. There had to be some mistake. He went through the files again. He found it at the bottom of the filing cabinet drawer, underneath his old tax returns. But he had not put it there. It had been taken out of the safe and then returned to the cabinet drawer.

With quivering fingers he opened the folder. The materials were out of order. His memo was at the end of the clippings, not at the beginning. Someone had been reading them.

'Mrs Marshfield,' he said, his voice quivering. 'Has anybody been in this file cabinet?'

'I am on the telephone,' she replied haughtily.

Roger leaped across the room, grabbed the telephone out of her hands, and slammed down the receiver. 'I don't give a goddamn what you're doing. Answer my question. Has anyone been in my personal filing cabinet?'

'Of course they have,' she said, now a wounded martyr. 'That boy from the magazine. You told me to cooperate with him. I made copies for him.'

'He was to see my manuscripts; I didn't tell you to permit him in my confidential papers!'

'You didn't tell me to keep him out, did you?'

DANCE
FIVE

Allemande

'It is a more heavie daunce than the galliard, fitlie representing the nature of the people whose name it carieth so that no extraordinary motions are used in the dancing of it.'

'A Plaine and Easie Introduction
to Practicall Musicke'
T. Morley

Irene

She should not have come to the rectory for the meeting of the Spring Luncheon Committee of the Women's Altar Guild. John Farrell was certain to be there, and he was becoming a delightful obsession. But how could she avoid the meeting, she asked herself piously. She was the chairman of the committee because in a weak moment she had acceded to the request of Mrs Riordan, the perennial president of the WAG, to chair this year's 'event.'

Spring luncheons were always the same, a search by newly middle-class Irish housewives for upper-middle-class respectability, a clumsy imitation of the spring luncheons of Protestant church groups. Even though the Irish in the Neighbourhood had long since caught up economically, the older women, like Mrs Riordan, were unaware of that fact. They were also unaware that the Protestants were abandoning spring luncheons, replacing them with matinee concerts at Orchestra Hall. Mrs Riordan didn't know that there was an Orchestra Hall, or indeed what an orchestra hall was.

So there would be a badly prepared meal and a dull fashion show at some expensive downtown hotel, the Drake or the Ritz-Carlton (the latter if the more progressive group within the guild won the annual debate about a site for the 'event'), and the women of the parish – such as bothered to come –would drink too much, flirt with the clergy, and weave their tipsy way home in the early stages of the rush hour. It was astonishing that none of them had piled up the family Cadillac after a spring luncheon.

Guardian angels working overtime.

'How do you stand it, John?' Irene asked.

She and John were in the knotty-pine meeting room in the rectory basement, finalizing the plans for the major event of the WAG year. It was customary for the pastor and the chairman to make the final decisions after the women of the committee had consumed most of the pastor's afternoon with foolish and occasionally angry suggestions.

'The argument used to be that these things brought in four or five thousand dollars that we wouldn't get any other way.' John leaned back in his chair, strong and handsome – a Roger with broader shoulders and more masculinity. 'Now we do it because we've always done it and because old dears like Mrs Riordan would probably lose their faith if we stopped doing it.'

'A High Club for matrons?'

'Something like that.' John pushed himself out of his chair. 'Goes with the territory. Every Catholic parish has to have one. Come upstairs and have a drink with me. We can't let the afternoon be a complete waste.'

Irene knew she should hesitate and then decline. 'Wonderful idea!' she said.

All she wanted from John, she had told herself repeatedly, was affection and friendship. The reaction of her body to his presence, the sad eyes, the unruly lock of hair falling over his pale face, the intense line of his mouth, was not to be taken seriously. He was her brother-in-law and a priest, a pompous and stuffy man who had never treated her as anything more than a beautiful object.

Yet, standing now in the pastor's suite in St Praxides rectory – the holy priest's house of her childhood – she wanted to be naked for him in front of all those popes and cardinals on the wall. Ridiculous horny bitch.

'Any more harassment from the clergy?' she asked as John was preparing the drinks.

'An anonymous letter this time,' he called from the other room. 'Mailed to every priest in the diocese.'

Irene walked into the wet bar, where John was putting the final touches on a large pitcher of martinis. The thrill of their physical closeness triggered with astonishing speed powerful reactions in her body. She bit her lip, trying to assert control of mind over flesh.

'What did it say?'

'I tore it up. I could have sued him if it had been signed. He charged that I was using parish money to pay the expenses of the programme and then taking a salary from the programme. Also said I was "carrying on" with the associate producer.'

'My God,' exclaimed Irene. 'What do you do with the money, John?'

'I contribute it to the parish. I don't have to, of course, but the Farrells have more than enough money. Damn fool clergy don't realize how a television station works.'

He poured a quarter of the contents of the martini pitcher over the ice in a tumbler marked with the initials JWF.

'Are you going to reply?'

'Damned if I do and damned if I don't. If I reply, my priestly brothers will say that because I'm taking the charge seriously, there must be a little bit of fire with all that smoke. And if I don't reply, they'll say the charges have to be true; otherwise I would have replied.'

He filled a second glass and, giving her the first one, toasted her silently.

'What are you going to do?'

'I'm going to reply. But I'm not going to tell them either what my salary is on the programme – it's only two hundred a week for twenty-six weeks – nor am I going to tell them that I give it to the parish. Jesus did say that the left hand should not know what the right hand is doing.'

'Oh, John,' she murmured softly.

She knew as she said it that the tone of sympathy in her voice was provocative for both of them. And she didn't care. He was her brother-in-law, a priest, a man she had often despised, and they were in the pastor's suite in a rectory, but none of that mattered.

They walked back to his parlour in silence and sat next to each other on one of his absurd leather couches. Ecclesiastical pomposity!

She should be on the other side of the room, as far away

from him as possible. In a desperate attempt to break the dangerous emotions that had oozed into the room, she changed the subject. 'You know about Noele's visit to Doctor Keefe?'

John's face, which had been momentarily soft and childlike as it basked in the warmth of her sympathy, quickly hardened. 'Yes indeed. Brigid called me as soon as she heard from the doctor. My God, Irene, can't you contain the child?'

'You and your brother and your mother have spoiled her rotten all her life, and you expect me to contain her?' she replied hotly.

John smiled sheepishly. 'I'm sorry, Irene.'

'You should be sorry. I order her to stop, but she won't obey me because she has always been able to appeal to her father when I give her a command. Roger reasons with her in his ponderous professorial way. She nods solemnly, collects Jaimie Burns, and does what she damn well pleases.'

'We have to stop her.' John spread his hands as though in a plea. 'Everyone would be hurt.'

'That's all I've heard for weeks,' Irene said impatiently. 'But no one will tell me why. Or are you trying to hide some family secret that I don't know?'

'You know one secret, isn't that enough?' John's voice was cruel momentarily, and then it turned gentle again. 'Take my word for it, Irene; you're better off not knowing. The Farrells could all be in danger.'

'Most of all my poor Christmas child.'

'All the more reason to stop her.'

Irene nodded sadly. At least she had dissipated the sexual tension between the two of them.

'She thinks Danny is still alive.'

'What?'

Instead of the anger she would have expected, John seemed sad, as though he too wished that Danny were still alive. After all these years all of us still love him.

'How do you know she does? Has she told you?'

'No, but I can tell. I *am* her mother, you know.'

'Indeed, I do,' he said with some irony.

'She has his old Annapolis graduation picture in a brand-new silver frame hanging above her bed, almost as if he were the Sacred Heart. . . .'

'That's spooky, Irene.'

'I know it's spooky. Do you think . . . he might be alive?' she asked hesitantly, for the first time admitting to herself that the question might be asked.

'Of course not.' He waved his hand brusquely.

'But . . . ?'

'But if he were,' John said solemnly, 'we'd all be in very deep trouble, wouldn't we?'

No one more than I, Irene thought sadly.

Roger

The office of the president of the Catholic college at which Joe Kramer was a student seemed ill-suited to his enormous physical energy, an energy that in Roger's cynical opinion he had increasingly substituted in the last few years for doing his homework. The high ceilings, blue walls, cluttered desk, cramped space, and photographs of the president with ecclesiastical and political dignitaries all suggested a more leisurely era when he had not been an international celebrity, characterized by some of his enemies as the Vicar of Bray because of his ability to make friends with every chief executive of the republic for the last two decades.

'We do not tolerate that sort of thing here,' said the president decisively.

'I'm glad to hear it,' Roger said. 'However, Father, I must point out the young man was working on an assignment for your magazine with an expense account provided by the magazine. Thus I would assume the school is legally responsible for what has occurred.'

'What really has occurred Roger? It seems to me that he had permission to go through your files?'

'He asked to see the drafts of my books and articles, to learn how I worked. I did not give him permission to look at, much less make copies of, my personal and confidential notes,' Roger said wearily, wondering how often it would be necessary to repeat this fact. 'Admittedly, my secretary gave him the key to my personal files. Quite apart from that, however, he surely had no authorization from me or from anyone to remove copies of my personal papers from my office.'

'I understand,' said the president. 'The issue, then, is not so much entering your file as copying the documents and, of course, taking them with him.'

'Taking them across state lines, making it a possible federal offence.'

'Naturally,' the president said smoothly. 'Our goal is not to prosecute the young man. Our goal, rather, is to seek the return of the documents and to preserve the good name of the school.'

'I have no desire to bring charges,' Roger said, sighing. 'The documents could be embarrassing for my campaign for governor.'

The president held up his hand. 'I'm not interested in what is in the documents, Roger; your distinguished academic career speaks for itself. I only seek a happy solution to our problem.'

A carefully rehearsed speech, a little too bland, a little too pat.

'Then you'll speak to the young man and have him return the documents?'

'I can make no promises.' The president shifted some papers on the blotter in front of him. 'I'll tell him that we don't do those sorts of things here and that if he wishes to continue to be a member of the college community, he must return the copies of your papers. But I'll have to be very judicious. I don't want to back the young man into a corner where he may do something desperate.'

Roger felt as if he were a criminal pleading to a gentle and sympathetic but faintly supercilious judge.

'I'll leave the tactics to you, Father. Neither the school

nor my political career will benefit from the continuation of this situation.'

'Yes, of course,' said the president, extending his hand cordially. 'But the college has survived many terrible crises, as I'm sure you know, Roger.'

Noele

Mrs Timothy Nolan was a tiny woman with snow-white hair, a baby face, and the loud voice of the deaf. She was also a complainer and a fussbudget, though Noele suspected old age had not caused either condition.

On impulse and without telling anyone, not even Jaimie, Noele had ridden her bike up Jefferson Avenue to the Nolan house in the woods, despite the icy north wind that was cutting through the bare trees of the Forest Preserve. A teenager on a bicycle in a *totally* cool white-down jacket, she calculated, would be less of a threat than a teenager in an automobile.

Mrs Nolan had permitted her into the house with obvious reservations. She offered Noele no pot of tea, seemingly forgetting that the reason for the visit was Noele's wish to talk to her husband 'about a term paper I'm writing,' and launched immediately into an attack on crazy teenage drivers. Then she switched to the subject of her husband's health – 'six heart attacks and two strokes, my dear' – and what a terrible trial 'the poor man's health' had been to her.

Almost, Noele thought, as if she'd be happy when he's dead.

Finally Noele was admitted to Captain Nolan's 'library.' A dark, dingy room smelling of cigar smoke and lined with shelves of books that looked as if they hadn't been moved since they had been placed in their proper positions thirty years before. The captain, a little old man as fragile as a porcelain doll, was sitting in a corner in a deep chair, hiding behind a cloud of cigar smoke and watching a soap opera on a large colour-television screen with the sound turned off.

'What do you want, young woman?' he bellowed, doubtless assuming that she was as deaf as his wife. His head reminded Noele of an Easter egg on which the dyes had not worked very well. But his voice was loud and clear, even though it indeed seemed that, as his wife had put it, Timothy Nolan had 'one foot in the grave.'

'I'm Noele Farrell,' she began, determined to be her most charming and innocent teenage self.

'I know who you are,' the captain said, considering her carefully, his lecherous old eyes snatching at her sweater and jeans.

'And I'm writing a family-history term paper,' she continued, repelled by the way the old gelhead was looking at her.

'No good will come of that,' the captain said, smiling affably.

Noele took a very deep breath. 'And I wanted to know more about how Clancy Farrell died.'

She expected the captain to become very angry. Instead, he continued to puff on his cigar and watch the television screen with intense concentration.

'Don't know what you're talking about,' he said finally. 'It was an accidental death, full investigation.'

No, there wasn't a full investigation. You're lying. Aloud she said, 'How could there have been a full investigation if Doctor Keefe signed the death certificate that night?'

The old man's tiny eyes flickered dangerously. 'I did the investigating myself afterward. Informal like, so there would be no police record to embarrass anyone.'

'You're afraid of me, aren't you, Captain Nolan?' she said implacably.

'Get out of here, young woman,' the old man bellowed. 'Margie! God damn the woman; where is she? Get this brat out of here.'

Noele stood up. 'Really, Captain Nolan, don't be gross.

I'm leaving I don't like to associate with crooked cops any more than I have to, even when they are senile old men.'

'Senile, am I?' the captain screamed. 'Crooked, am I? The Nolans were always a lot more honest than the Farrells. It's your family that's crooked, kid. Now get out of here.'

'At least we didn't violate our oath of office,' said Noele haughtily, standing at her chair but not leaving. There had to be more information to pry out of this wicked, angry, frightened old man.

'Oath of office, huh? You'd better be real careful, kid. Another Farrell woman asked too many questions and got herself very dead. Marge! Get this brat out of here!'

Noele's world stood still for a moment. She felt light-headed and dizzy, as if she had been dieting for days. The smell of Tim Nolan's room made her sick to her stomach.

Captain Nolan was coughing, small wonder with all that cigar smoke. His wife, who had heard none of his shouting, dashed into the room at the first hint of a cough.

'Go away. You Farrells are nothing but trouble, always trouble. Can't you see that the poor man is having another attack!'

'I'm sure I don't want to stay here any longer, Mrs Nolan,' Noele said, rushing out of the room through the parlour into the cold, clear, December sunlight.

Riding home on her bike, Noele wished the family-history term paper had never been assigned.

Someone killed Danny's mother.

My God!

It was half exclamation, half prayer.

She called Jaimie's number at Notre Dame as soon as she had rushed upstairs to her room.

'I need more newspaper clippings, Jaimie. Would you be a dear and check up on the death of Florence Carey Farrell in an auto accident in 1944? And anything else you can find out about who was involved in the accident?'

Jaimie was silent for a moment.

'If you want me to, MN,' he said finally.

'I do. I think I have a motive for a revenge killing.'

Did she want to convict Danny Farrell of avenging his mother's death?

No, of course not.

Then the loneliness came back, as though Florence Farrell's ghost had come into Noele's room.

Was it the loneliness of a restless ghost she felt?

Burke

The phone was clammy from the chill sweat on Burke's hand when he hung up.

She's only a child, he told himself. I can't let anything happen to her. Yet in the jungle in which Burke lived, one chose one's woman over a child if one had to.

He walked to his window and watched the crowds hurrying across the Daley Civic Centre plaza. That first word was rarely used in City Hall now. Herself did not like to hear the word *Daley*. She had even moved the official Christmas tree up to the river so there would be no chance that people would associate Daley and Christmas.

Would nothing stop the child?

First there had been Doctor Keefe, who always guessed more than he knew and who knew too much to begin with. Then, dear God, Tim Nolan, of all the dangerous old men in the world. Who else might she have called?

The Marshal? Please, God, not that madman.

The outfit would have to be careful. Her boyfriend's father was a powerful man on the Hill.

Then Burke felt a cold stab of fear. Chairman of the House Intelligence Subcommittee. Had Noele talked to him?

He rushed back to his desk, flipped frantically through his book of confidential phone numbers, and dialed a 202 number.

'Jim? . . . Burke Kennedy here. . . . Yeah, I know. . . . Hope you get home by Christmas. . . . See you at the party for Noele, I suppose. . . . Oh, yeah, great kid . . .

kind of hard on her being an only child. . . . Say, did you find out anything from the Company about Dan Farrell? . . . We had to admire her spunk for asking and kind of wondered . . .'

There was dead silence at the other end of the line while the shrewd mind of Jim Burns pondered that bolt from the blue.

And then came the only answer that Burke could have expected, a carefully vague response that told him nothing.

'Yeah, I know how the Company is about such things. . . . Sure, he's dead, Jim. . . . You know Bridie . . . Irish mothers never stop hoping. . . .'

Again the fleeting wish that she had borne him a son.

'Well, thanks, Jim. Give my best to Jane. Merry Christmas. . . .'

After he had hung up, Burke Kennedy slumped over his desk, head in hands.

There will never be peace. Never.

Roger

'I realize you're doing your best, Father,' Roger said wearily into the telephone. 'But you must understand that I'm under enormous pressure. And the young man's ethical dilemma is very difficult for me to understand.'

And now Noele had bearded Tim Nolan in his den. The child has an unerring instinct for stirring up the pot, the cop who . . .

'He claims that the materials are his property,' the president said, 'now that he has them. He also states that there was no theft because he removed only copies, not the originals.'

'How in God's name can he claim that? Not a court in the country would agree that I lose rights to my documents because they have been copied. Don't you teach the Ten Commandments there anymore?'

'I'm only repeating his position.' There was reproach in the president's voice. 'He feels you relinquished possession of the property when you permitted him to come into your office. He also feels that because you are a major public figure and a success, you are a legitimate target for investigative reporting.'

'Which means because I have a few dollars it is moral to steal from me.'

Nolan looks like an innocent old man, but he's pure poison. She could get herself killed. And I have to worry about this stupid little prick.

'I'm only trying to explain, Roger. He feels he has a solemn obligation to make these matters public and that if he did not do so he would be violating his professional ethics.'

He and Irene had had a flaming row about the Nolan visit. Uncharacteristically she had fought back, telling him that it was his responsibility, not hers.

'Forgive me for being ill-tempered, but as I said, this strain is devastating. I appreciate your efforts very much.'

Roger realized that he was a fine one to talk about the Ten Commandments. Another hour – he glanced at his watch – well, another forty-five minutes, he'd violate the sixth commandment, commit adultery once again with Martha Clay.

And in the pleasure of bizarre fantasies he would forget the family past.

But not entirely. When he made love to Martha, he often thought of Dan Farrell, doubtless because Dan used to poke fun at him for his obsession with women, as if he knew that Roger was trying to prove his masculinity.

'If it has skirts on, you'll chase it,' Danny would say in his phony Irish brogue. 'Though, sure, you don't seem to like women with proper size tits at all, at all.'

'I'll leave them all for you,' Roger would reply crisply.

He felt guilty about these fantasies, but told himself that as an adulterer, he wasn't adding much to his guilt by permitting himself gay images in the course of lovemaking. In any case, as a trained social scientist he knew that human sexuality was enormously complicated. We're all, he told himself, polymorphously perverse. I might as well enjoy it while I can.

The quarter was over and tomorrow Martha would return to Boston for Christmas with her parents. She would also see her former husband. 'You see your wife every day, Roger, and I don't object to that,' she had argued persuasively. 'Do we have a double standard?'

Martha's promotion was in trouble. The dean had taken him aside at the Faculty Club the day before yesterday to say that he had sent the appointment on to the provost with 'the strongest recommendation I could in all conscience give.' The dean's 'in all conscience' meant a lukewarm recommendation. 'Do you think that Mrs Clay would consider a compromise solution?'

Roger's ears perked up. The University was talking compromise. Then all was not lost.

'You mean a term appointment as associate professor with a review in several years?' In other words, promotion but not tenure.

'Well, obviously I can't speak for the provost,' the dean said, 'or for the president, but perhaps something along those lines could be worked out if we can find the funds to support such an appointment.'

The University could find funds for anything it really wanted to do, despite its annual poor-mouthing.

'That's a very interesting possibility, Winston. Let me make some discreet inquiries among members of my department.'

But first he would have to consult with Martha, as the dean well knew. She might be offended by the compromise and consider it a degrading, chauvinist insult and reject it out of hand. More likely, she would swallow her principles and accept five more years of employment. She might very well lose in an all-out confrontation, and you don't get paid $28,000 a year for moral victories.

Now unbearably eager to have her again, Roger left his office hastily. How many other faculty members were also departing early to take their pleasure with their current female slaves before the Christmas season would impose a moratorium on such amusements?

He would have to terminate the liaison eventually. If Martha left at the end of the academic year with perhaps a lawsuit against the University, the relationship would end in an easy and natural fashion.

As he walked over to her apartment Roger reflected that it was odd that he would no longer be in trouble with the voters if he was guilty of flagrant adultery. The electorate more or less accepted such aberrations from its political leaders. But he could lose the governorship because a young man had violated all the canons of responsible journalistic ethics and found materials relating to a crime committed in the distant past.

Was there no room left for morality and truth in the world? The full truth could destroy him and his family. It could even threaten his daughter's life.

But who was he to complain?

John

December's second Sunday dinner at Brigid's seemed like a century in purgatory. Irene, as she always did at Brigid's, slipped back into her role of passive and insipid housewife. Roger and Brigid patronized her as usual, and John found himself tempted to fit into that routine.

How many times had he insulted her in the last fifteen years? What a pompous, arrogant fool he must have seemed. How could such a lively, sensuous woman have put up with it?

He longed for the warm solid feel of her in his arms. The desire he always felt for her now contained respect and admiration and sympathy, which made her more attractive and even more dangerous. They had come very close in the rectory the other day, too close. He must not permit himself to be alone with her again.

The glum atmosphere around the dinner table was

aggravated by the family's unease about Noele. She and Jaimie were at a Christmas dance, and Brigid took the opportunity to interrogate Roger.

'Are you sure we'll have no more of this term paper nonsense from the child?' she demanded sharply.

'Of course. I had a long talk with her.'

'A pity the child's mother can't keep her under control.'

The child's mother, treated like a piece of the furniture, acted as if she were just that, speaking not a word in her own defence, hardly seeming to hear the insult.

'Can I have a word with you outside as we leave?' Roger whispered as they adjourned from the supper table.

'Sure,' John agreed, expecting to hear more about Noele's escapades.

'We have another problem. A young college reporter has taken some papers from my office that could create a lot of trouble.'

'What kind of papers?' John demanded, incensed by his brother's dry academic pose.

'Basically some material I found in Dad's files after the funeral. Documents dealing with the death of Florence Farrell. And some other materials of my own in which I pursued the subject.'

John tried to comprehend. 'Do you mean Dad was telling the truth that night?'

'Danny believed it, didn't he?' Roger said lightly.

'I don't think I ever did, though, did you? I thought it was more BS, like the stories about the OSS during the war.'

'I take it as almost certain that our beloved father was afraid that Florence might challenge the will. Probably at the urging of our equally beloved grandmother, he made arrangements to have her removed. I wrote this conclusion down in a memo that was part of the material the young man removed from my office.'

'My God.' John was so horrified that his voice choked.

Roger smiled lightly, as though he were mildly amused by the species Homo Farrellensis.

'Tim Nolan was involved then too. Not only did he protect Danny from the consequences of his action, he also protected Clancy from the consequences of his earlier action. I fear that Noele has guessed some of this. Why else would she go to Nolan?'

John Farrell would not have known how to answer the question of whether he loved his brother, Roger. He was offended by Roger's intellectual posing, and now by his treatment of Irene. Nevertheless, he respected his brother's brilliant intelligence and quick wit.

Love, he would have said to a questioner, didn't matter. You were loyal to your family, especially when they were in trouble, maybe only when they were in trouble, and Roger was in trouble.

'Why the hell did you write that memo?' John asked, masking loyalty, as the Irish often do, with impatience. 'That was a damn fool thing to do. Besides, are you sure it was Dad? Arranging a murder . . . ? That's the sort of thing Burke would do.'

'What motive?' Roger gestured hopelessly.

'Protecting Mother. What other motive is there in Burke's life?'

'Impossible,' said Roger.

You want to believe it was Dad, John thought, but why?

It was cold in front of the old house; the thermometer was well below freezing and heading toward zero. John had not worn a topcoat, preferring the image of the busy parish priest dashing about without a coat.

Now he was shaking, only partly because of the cold winter night.

'I felt that we had to leave some sort of message to those who would come after us,' Roger continued. 'What if one day someone stumbled on the whole story? A child of Noele's, for example, doing a term paper twenty years in the future.'

'The whole world is likely to stumble on it now,' John said gruffly.

'I suppose. And to make matters worse, there is an involvement with the Mob. That could be very dangerous.'

'What are you doing about it? Can't you find somebody to steal the papers back? Couldn't Burke have some of his friends pay a little visit in this case?'

'Don't think I haven't thought of it. However,' he said, laughing, 'I am a candidate for governor, you know, and I have to watch myself. Anyway, the president of the college is going to work it out. I just thought I'd alert you.'

'Let me know if there is anything I can do to help.' John was sympathetic if also helpless.

'If you hear the slightest hint that Noele is still mucking around, let me know. You can imagine how dangerous that would be, especially now.'

John nodded his agreement. 'I wonder if Dick McNamara might not be a bad influence on her. You know what a romantic he is about youthful enthusiasm.'

'Don't we both,' said Roger drily. 'Are you going to try to get rid of him?'

'I might . . . though he didn't have much influence on Dan, and Dan didn't want to grow up either.'

'When Noele looks at me with those terrible green eyes and asks me what the family acts so guilty about, I'm not so sure who's grown-up and who isn't.'

Before John could reply to that ominous statement, his mother and Irene appeared in the doorway.

'Monsignor John, get in your car and go home to the rectory,' Brigid ordered him as if he were a five-year-old. 'You stay out on a night like this without a coat on, and you're likely to get pneumonia.'

'Some things don't change.' Roger laughed.

'Some of us, I guess, are immune to pneumonia.'

'Good night, John,' Irene said softly as she joined her husband.

Did Roger realize how fortunate he was? Probably not. None of us ever does until it's too late.

St Praxides rectory was empty and lonely when he returned to it.

James III

Noele's piquant, usually mobile face was frozen in an expression of horror, as if she had just seen a child die in an accident. Jaimie touched her chin. Her eyes turned toward him as if he were a stranger. Recognition returned, slowly at first, then with a rush.

'Oh, Jaimie,' she said weakly.

The fire was burning in the old-fashioned fireplace of the congressman's study, and the smell of the family Christmas tree drifted in from the next room. The stereo was playing carols, and they were surrounded by the sights, the sounds, the smells, the warmth of Christmas. Noele, in blue sweater and slacks, looked like someone's special Christmas present.

Except for the sadness on her face and the single tear that flowed from each eye.

Jaimie caressed her face with the tips of the fingers of one hand and gathered up the clippings on Rocco 'The Marshal' Marsallo from his father's worn brown leather couch with the other.

'He enjoys beating people to death with a basketball bat,' she said, still not quite believing what she had read.

'There are people like that,' Jaimie said lamely.

'And burning women with cigarette butts – forty burns on that one poor girl.'

'He's evil,' Jaimie agreed.

He had not wanted to show her his new stack of Xeroxes; a few small clips on the accidental death of Florence Carey, the arrest of the driver of the truck, Rocco Marsallo, and his conviction on a charge of involuntary manslaughter. Nor had he wanted to show her the big collection of articles on the rise of Marsallo in the Mob after his six-month jail term in 1946: enforcer, hit man, torturer, ruler of a prostitution and pornography empire, senior leader in the Mob, and now retired Mob crazy.

There was yet another collection on the dubious police career of Timothy Nolan – charges of Mob links, investigations, threats of indictments, promotions, rumours of bribes. A very bent cop.

But Noele had bugged him for the clippings. And he had finally given in.

'Danny's mother was killed by that man,' she said, pulling her face back from his fingertips.

'It might have been an accident. . . .'

'Sure, and Tim Nolan might have accidentally been the cop who arrested him, accidentally said that a Farrell woman had asked two many questions and was killed. Only he didn't say that she was accidentally killed. She asked questions about her son's inheritance and was killed.'

'Maybe.'

'What else could explain it?' she asked, searching desperately for another explanation.

Jaimie began to stroke her long, soft hair, and she smiled gratefully.

'Suppose the questions about the will would have led to a government investigation and sent Brigid to jail. Wouldn't Burke have a motive for protecting her even then?'

Noele nodded thoughtfully. 'They have been sleeping together for a long, long time, and he would do anything to protect her.'

'And you don't know that Danny ever found out that his mother was killed by a Mob punk.'

'Well, then who pushed Clancy down the stairs?' Now she was touching his face, with the respect and reverence due to a sacred vessel.

Jaimie tried to keep his thinking clear and his voice steady. 'Maybe he fell, like everyone told you, or . . .'

'Or what?'

'Maybe your grandmother pushed him.'

Instantly her hand abandoned his face.

'What a terrible thing to say,' she complained. 'Why would Grams do that?'

'I didn't want to tell you this, but . . . well, my grandfather said that there were rumours in the old days that Clancy beat her.'

'Why?' The deep freeze returned to her face.

'Maybe because he was angry about Burke and . . . well' – he squirmed – 'some men only enjoy sex if they . . .'

'SM,' said Noele promptly.

'Something like that,' said Jaimie, embarrassed, as he often was by Noele's sexual knowledge.

'So you think Burke and Brigid were responsible?'

'Not necessarily. I'm only pointing out that you can't prove for certain that there were murders or, if there were, who were the killers. You can make cases against almost anyone. And it has been such a long time, you can't prove anything. Besides, who else is there to talk to?'

Noele put her arms around him and laid her head on his chest.

'So you want me to forget about it all.'

'At least till after Christmas.' He held her close, but gently, as though she were a china doll. The most he could expect was an agreement to leave it alone for a time.

'And the CIA hasn't reported to your father?'

'He says they probably won't. And that means they found nothing. That's the way they work.'

She kissed him, and he responded. In a moment their lips were working automatically and fervently.

If this keeps up, thought Jaimie, I'm going to want to take off her sweater and kiss her everywhere.

Reluctantly he disentangled himself and pulled her off of the couch.

'Back to decorating the tree,' he said.

'Right,' she said, none too enthusiastically.

'And no more Farrell family skeletons till after Christmas.'

'Right.'

Jaimie patted her rump affectionately. 'That's my girl.'

'Right.' She giggled as she jumped to escape a second swat.

And as soon as she got out of this house, Jaimie knew, she'd be right back on the case.

Irene

The hum of the blow dryer down the hallway meant that Irene's privacy was over. Noele was home from school early this afternoon. The gymnastics meet had been cancelled, and Noele's fury would be the sole conversational topic at supper, supplanting even Roger's pontifications about his campaign.

God, he was insufferable.

She sighed, sounding to herself a bit like Brigid. The new story she was working on was coming slowly. She was trying to revise the character of Father Tom, the priest who had appeared intermittently in some of her earlier stories – most notably 'The Buying of the Baby.' He had been a supercilious and insensitive man in the other stories. Now it was necessary to picture him as vulnerable, sensitive, and loving, while maintaining some kind of consistency, a difficult challenge technically, as well as a difficult burden to her personally.

The new story was about a married woman who was strongly attracted to Father Tom. She was trying to capture on paper her conflicting emotions while recalling how their eyes locked and unlocked across the dining table at Brigid's last Sunday night.

Dressed only in her underwear, she was stretched out on the chaise longue in her bedroom, enjoying the warmth from a furnace that refused to attend to its thermostat. The house was as warm as she liked it, and Roger could not complain about the temperature being over sixty-eight.

Had Father Tom changed? Or had her heroine and alter ego, Lorraine, changed?

What was he like in 'The Buying of the Baby'?

She took 'The Buying of the Baby' out of its folder and reread the ending.

> Father Tom extended the envelope to the tense young man.
>
> He took it quickly, began to look inside as if about to

count the bills, and then, shamefaced, stuffed it into the pocket of his old tweed jacket.

'Everything will work out for the best,' Father Tom said blandly, for the tenth time that day.

Lorraine wondered how any man could be so unfeeling. Cash was being exchanged for a beautiful red-haired, green-eyed child. The mother would weep all night, blaming the father for his failure, and he, suffering more acutely, would not be able to weep and would have to blame himself.

And Lorraine would hold the crying child in her arms and ask herself once again if they had done the right thing.

John, Irene now understood, was not the Father Tom of the story. He was hurting that day as much as the rest of us. He has hurt all his life, but he hides his pain under a mask of clerical urbanity. Sometimes so well that he forgets he hurts.

Unfortunately, masks become the person if they are worn often and long enough.

'Hi, Moms.' Noele charged into Irene's room clad in a huge, quilted white robe, her long hair still wet and limp. 'Wow,' she said, and whistled in approval. 'You say *my* underwear is what whores wear.'

'If you come into my room once more without knocking, young woman,' Irene said, acutely embarrassed, 'I'll ground you for two months. How many times do I have to tell you –'

'Okay, okay.' Noele would humour her mother this afternoon. 'Still I think you look really *excellent*. What are you doing? Writing another story? Can I see it?' She reached for the manuscript.

Irene quickly closed the folder in her lap.

'Can't blame me for trying.' Noele grinned. 'Someday you're going to break down and let me find out what a really excellent writer you are, right?'

The Christmas child was gone as suddenly as she had appeared, leaving her mother embarrassed, humiliated, and frightened.

She is so innocent and fresh, Irene thought. And how quickly her innocence would be destroyed if she read this story. Everyone seems to be worried that she might be hurt if she continues to ask questions about the past. Who could hurt Noele?

No one -- except me.

Rising from the chaise longue, Irene donned a robe and carried the folder with both the stories down the hallway to her office. She would put it in the leather binder with her other stories in the secret compartment of her desk.

She had the usual trouble with the old-fashioned lock of the secret drawer. The key jammed just as the phone rang. Hastily she stuffed the folder into the centre drawer of her desk.

It was Mrs Riordan with a long and complicated question about the spring luncheon.

Roger

At the end of the exam period the University had the vitality of a cemetery, especially if, like Roger Farrell, you were waiting anxiously for a telephone call from a college president and wondering whether your suddenly docile daughter had in fact pulled back from the brushfire she had lit.

Roger had been moved by the intensity of his brother's reaction on the previous Sunday evening. John wanted to help. In fact, he wanted desperately, almost pathetically, to help, even if he could express that desire only in hostility over Roger's stupidity at having collected the dangerous documents and written the telltale memo.

We Irish are a strange people, so good at hiding strong affection for one another. Well, there was nothing much John could do.

And what would he think if Roger were to tell him that

his predicament might be a punishment for his own sinfulness?

Bless me, brother, for I have sinned. I have committed adultery repeatedly with some special perversity added. Do you want to hear the details of my perversity, brother? I think you would find them rather amusing. I have tried to obtain a tenure appointment for my mistress at the University, one for which she is only marginally qualified. That is why, dear brother, God has sent Joseph Kramer to plague me. I am a man of outstanding public ethical principles and shabby private principles. What is happening to me is something I richly deserve.

The phone rang. A long-distance call, but by the time the operator at the other end got back to her party, the connection was broken.

What would his mother and Burke say if he had to tell them about the memo? They would both be furious, of course. Why did he have to put something that foolish in writing? Damned academic posturing, they would say.

And what if John were right? What if Burke had put out the contract on Florence? It was certainly possible. There was a lot of bullshit in poor Dad. He might have made up the cruel story he shouted at Danny that night because he was so angry at him for consorting with 'the little Conlon bitch.'

But somehow the thought that Burke had disposed of Florence with Brigid's consent was even more intolerable to Roger than the suspicion that his father had done it. Yet if Brigid were threatened with jail – even remotely threatened – Burke would strike with deadly swiftness.

The phone rang again.

'I think I can promise you a happy Christmas, Roger,' said the president of the college. 'Mr Kramer returned the papers to me this afternoon, and I put them in an envelope and sent them to you at your office at the University, special delivery. Our crisis is over.'

'Any copies?' Roger asked nervously.

'He assures me that there are no copies,' the president said calmly. 'We'll all have much to give thanks for at the Midnight Mass on Christmas Eve.'

Roger felt as if a mountain range had been lifted from him.

'I'm enormously grateful to you, Father. You may be sure I will not forget you or the college.'

Well, it was over, thank God. Heaven's punishment for the sins of Roger Farrell had been surprisingly mild.

Even though it was forty-five minutes before quitting time, Mrs Marshfield had long since left, thoughtfully locking the correspondence that he dictated in her desk so he would not know what, if anything, she had finished.

The phone rang just as he was leaving the office.

'Hello, Roger. This is Lawrence.'

The provost at the University referred to himself either as 'the provost' or as 'Lawrence,' the latter a certain signal that you had become part of the University community. Such a favour did not come with tenure, or even with the full professorate. It appeared to Roger that it was bestowed only on those who ate lunch at one of the round tables in the Faculty Club.

'Good afternoon, Lawrence. I hope you're enjoying the weather on St Maarten.'

'It does wonders for Penny's health,' the provost replied uneasily. Like other University administrators he justified the flight from Chicago cold at the end of the quarter on the grounds of his wife's health. 'Actually I'm calling you about the Martha Clay case – in a very informal and confidential manner. I trust you understand.'

The provost spoke with a dry little rasp, much as if he expected to die of TB before the conversation was over.

Roger understood. The provost will make a compromise offer, and I'll say it won't work. They will turn Martha down, and by spring it will all be over.

All for the best, I guess.

'Of course, Lawrence,' he purred in reassurance. He knew there would follow a long and rambling reflection, as though the provost were talking to himself.

'The Mrs Clay case is a complex one, if I may speak in all candor. This University will not accept the imposition of quotas by outside authority. Neither, however, can we afford to overreact and reject a promising younger scholar merely because we wish to swim against the tide of quotas. Moreover, Mrs Clay comes to us with a moderately strong endorsement from her own department. On the other hand, some of the most distinguished members of the department are not enthusiastic about the prospects of her future scholarship. And Winston's letter of transmittal was hardly reassuring. You understand my problem, Roger?'

Roger mumbled reassuringly.

'These are difficult times for the University.' The times were always difficult. 'And the president and I are convinced we do not need another public controversy, especially when the evidence is not clearly weighted against a lifetime appointment. . . .' There was another pause, during which Roger was supposed to admire the provost's wisdom under pressure. 'Therefore, I'm inclined now in a tentative sort of way to forward this matter to the president, appending my own cautiously positive recommendation, along with that of the dean. I fear I cannot offer you this as my definitive conclusion on the Mrs Clay case because, of course, I will have to read the whole dossier.' The provost, whose publication record in thirty years of academic service was one thin book and two articles, didn't read anything, not even the *Chicago Tribune*.

'Her case is obviously a marginal one,' the provost rambled on. 'But sometimes the University administration has to go with its instincts and, of course, with the instinct of faculty members whose judgement it trusts.'

'I certainly appreciate your trust in my judgement, Lawrence.' Roger put his hand over the telephone and muttered 'Stupid cowardly bastard. You're afraid to take on somebody who might be governor.'

'I hardly need to add,' the provost plodded on, 'that this is all very preliminary, tentative, and confidential. I'm sure that our conversation will be between ourselves and you won't share it with any of our mutual colleagues, even the dean – and especially with Mrs Clay.'

Don't tell the dean, because he'll have a fit.

'I believe Mrs Clay has gone to her parents' home in Massachusetts for Christmas,' Roger said, implying that of course he would not have her phone number, and even if he had, he would not dream of disturbing her Christmas relaxation – quite likely with her former husband, who was some kind of engineer at MIT.

'Quite, quite,' said the provost, with just a faint whiff of his self-image as someone rather like a master in a prestigious college at Cambridge University, a CP Snow character who combined both cultures.

I should feel joyous, I've won, Roger told himself, and yet somehow I don't.

The Lord gives and the Lord takes away. In this case it would have been better if he had taken Martha away.

Nonetheless, he permitted himself a vision of the fantasy he would have with her when she returned and he told her the good news.

Brigid

Brigid loved gimmicks, whether they were microwave ovens or personal computers. She argued that they made life more convenient. In fact, she loved to play with them, probably because she had had so few toys as a little girl.

Her newest toy was a giant-screen television that enabled her to watch her son interview a bearded peace-activist priest in something larger than life-size. She was dismayed by John's diffidence in dealing with the poor fool, who spoke with much feeling but no intelligence.

'You do look a little vain on the large screen, John,' she told her absent son. 'And if you were here you probably would be telling me the large screen is a needless luxury, and yourself not knowing what it's like to have to use an outdoor loo for the first fourteen years of your life.'

Burke came in to the TV room, a brandy snifter in either hand, both of them filled almost to the brim. He pushed the button on the television cabinet, instantly extinguishing Monsignor John Farrell. 'I know I'm the one who said we have nothing to worry about, Bridie. But I think we've got troubles.'

She had known there would be troubles eventually. Once more it would be necessary to crush her emotions and respond to the trouble with ruthless cunning. No, it would never stop. 'What kind of troubles?'

'Noele.' Burke sank wearily into the chair next to her and extended the brandy snifter. 'You know that I'm fond of her, Bridie, but right now I have to say she's a nosy little bitch who ought to be spanked.'

'Oh, my God, what now?'

'I found out more of the details of her conversation with Tim Nolan. He had a bit too much to drink and called me today to say he thinks Noele smells something about Flossie's death. Tim says he just about had another heart attack.'

'I wouldn't mind the son of a bitch having a heart attack,' Brigid said fervently.

'Nor I.' Burke swallowed a huge gulp of brandy and made a pained face. He thought it was barbaric to drink brandy the way she did, as if it were Pepsi-Cola. 'But it's not Nolan I'm worried about. I'm almost certain he called the Marshal. And God knows what that lunatic might do.'

'The holy saints preserve us!' Brigid felt dizzy. She put the brandy snifter on the arm of her chair and clamped her hands over her eyes.

'We've got to put a stop to it, Bridie,' Burke insisted. 'Even if Roger wasn't in a political campaign right now, none of us can afford to have this box of dynamite opened again. You know that.'

I know it even better than you do, darling, Brigid thought to herself. 'What do you think we ought to do?'

'Someone ought to have a good firm talk with Noele and lay down the law.'

'We've tried that.' Brigid shook her head. 'It works for a while. But Roger isn't tough enough and the woman is worthless. The child is stubborn, more stubborn than anyone in the family, myself included.'

Burke swallowed his brandy angrily. 'Then what would you suggest?'

'I think we should have a summit meeting between now and Christmas and work out a strategy with everyone.'

'What kind of strategy?' Burke squinted suspiciously.

'Make sure that all of us – you and me, John and Roger – agree what our story is and then have someone sit down with her and tell Noele a good deal of the truth.'

'The truth?' Burke interrupted in dismay. 'How can we tell the truth?'

He looks so old tonight, Brigid thought sadly.

'Admit that Danny Farrell was drunk and that he had a fight with Clancy and pushed him down the stairs. We felt we had to cover it up because it wasn't really murder, only involuntary manslaughter, and the family already had too many scandals.'

'That's close enough to the truth,' Burke said thoughtfully. 'If she'll believe it. The kid is scary. There's something not quite right about her.'

'Nonsense,' Brigid said briskly. 'She's just very smart and very tough.' Smarter and tougher than she knows, smarter and tougher than she ought to be for her own good.

'It might work,' he admitted grudgingly. 'And we keep quiet about the earlier matter?'

'Indeed we do.'

She drank the rest of her brandy with a single swallow and coughed as the brandy robbed her of her breath.

'You never were temperate, were you, woman?' Burke permitted himself a grin, which turned into a flattering leer. 'And who's going to talk to her?'

'Well,' Brigid said after an expressive west-of-Ireland sigh, 'certainly not the woman. She's as soft as shit. And to tell you the truth, my son the television interviewer isn't much better. Either me or Roger. Noele respects us both. And I think when she understands what Danny did, she'll lose interest in him – an adolescent love affair, and a sick one at that, if you ask me.'

Burke drained his brandy glass and looked at it wistfully. 'It's either another glass of brandy tonight or you, my dear.'

'Then don't touch the brandy,' she said decisively.

Burke put his hand on her shoulder. It was strong, demanding. She felt herself melt.

'Hellish ironies,' he said softly.

'And the fires are just getting warm,' Brigid agreed.

Irene

The first December cold snap had come – a nasty, snow-coated Canadian thug with a bitter snarl. A strong wind that rattled the windows and crept through every tiny crack in the house. Irene huddled under a thick robe, preferring warm clothes to a hot room during the wintertime. But she hardly noticed the howling wind, because she was so furious about John's pathetic performance. He caved in to every self-righteous, Catholic ideologue who managed to muscle his way onto the programme. His ratings would go down after tonight's show. The peace activist was an angry, hate-filled man who would admit no ambiguity, no nuance, no possibility that anyone who disagreed with his call for immediate, total, and unilateral American disarmament could possibly be in good faith.

'Damn it, John,' she said angrily to the television screen, 'you know better than that!'

Working on her new short story had exorcised most of the tantalizing heat from Irene's bloodstream. It had been replaced by a numbing chill, much worse than the cold outside her 'office' window. The murky half-light in which she had lived so long and in which she had fallen in love with her brother-in-law had been replaced by a cruel, implacable glare, like the harsh lights of a television studio.

At last she saw herself, her husband, and her brother-in-law with brutal clarity. John was a confused, troubled man needing acceptance by his clerical cronies more than he did a woman. If Dads Fogarty wrote something nice about him, he would quickly be cured of his infatuation with her.

Roger was a man of unusual emotional needs married to a woman who did not ignite those emotions. So he found satisfaction with a string of young mistresses. She would probably be a much better sexual match with John than with Roger. But there was no future in such a love affair. Although the experience of sexually initiating a vulnerable and handsome forty-two-year-old male virgin would set Lorraine afire, that character lived in a make-believe world where there were no risks of pain on the morrow.

Irene saw herself with pitiless clarity. She was a stupid fool who had lived her whole life mourning for a dead man. And she had tried to escape and to console herself for her failures by writing stories no one else would read.

Tomorrow she would burn them all.

The interview was coming to an end. John, curly locks slightly askew, leaned towards his guest, his soft blue eyes glittering. Could they be glittering dangerously?

'I'm very grateful to you for appearing with us today, Brother,' he began lightly. 'And for sharing with us your interesting, challenging, and disturbing point of view. I want to say one thing, however, to you and to the viewers. A great many of us have been concerned about the nuclear arms race for a long time. In fact, I even wrote an article in the *Homiletic and Pastoral Review* seventeen years ago on the subject. In my opinion you have a very naive view of an intricate problem for which there are no clear and easy answers. We have thought about it much longer than you have, prayed over it more than you have, and agonized over it much more intensely than you have.

'Candidly, Brother, I don't need to be told by you that the nuclear arms race is dangerous. Nor do you have any right to assume that your solution is the only one that any decent Christian could possibly advocate. You must forgive me for it, Brother, but I think you an arrogant, self-righteous prig who substitutes enthusiastic dogma for intelligence and understanding.'

Irene was as startled as was the speechless peace

activist. She flicked off the TV and punched John's personal rectory number on her phone, hoping to talk to him before anyone else was able to reach him.

'You're one tough son of a bitch, John,' she said when he answered. 'That was awesome.'

'You'd better not use that language around your daughter.' John laughed, patently delighted by her enthusiasm.

'I know what you should do, John,' she said in a rush of confident words: 'Challenge Larry Rieves and Parson Rails and Dads Fogarty to come on your programme and interview you with all their snide objections. You'd annihilate them.'

'Rieves would never do it. He's a stumblebum. He knows he'd lose all his credibility if he went on television, so he resolutely refuses to appear on anyone's programme.'

'Challenge Rieves first. And, when he won't do it, ask the *Tribune* to send a reporter over who will really give you hell. And then fight back.'

There was silence for a moment at the other end of the line. 'I really appreciate your confidence in me, Irene,' John said, sounding very much like a love-struck teenager, much more infatuated even than poor Jaimie Burns.

'Confidence be damned,' Irene replied sharply. 'It has nothing to do with confidence. You're good at it, John. Better than you realize, better than the rest of us comprehend. Let yourself get angry. Fight back on your programme, and win!'

She leaned forward on the edge of her chair as if she were poised for combat.

'Funny thing, Irene. You're beginning to sound like Danny. Do I get time to think about it?'

She was glad he could not see the heat that flooded into her face. 'And even time to ask Father Ace.'

I think you cared for Danny in your way as much as I did in mine. Oh, God, how I let him down!

After she had hung up, Roger came into the room with elaborate casualness. They chatted for a while. And then he began to paw her, his hands creeping beneath her robe.

Yes, of course; his mistress was probably away for Christmas break. Well, that's what wives are for, to provide sexual release when the mistress is unavailable.

In their bedroom Irene pretended at first to enjoy the interlude of love. Then Roger's persistent persuasion and her own traitorously sensual body made her response more than pretence. Roger had perhaps learned a few new tricks from his new mistress. But as crushing sweetness leaped up her spine to her brain and then cascaded throughout her body, Irene fantasized that the lover of the night was not her husband, but his brother.

A brother who resembled in mysterious ways his cousin Danny.

Brigid

The first big winter storm had swept through Chicago, dropping a foot of wet snow on an unwary city and then, like a drunken Christmas reveller, caroused across the lake to add two more feet on the Michigan shore.

They would shovel out more quickly on the other side, Brigid knew, even if they didn't have mayors to reelect.

There was no hope for their neighbourhood. The Nineteenth Ward was on the wrong political side again. Nonetheless, even if it meant that her two sons had to slog through the snow on foot, the meeting would not be postponed.

The martinis and the old fashioneds were mixed and distributed, and her family sat around the comfortable, old-fashioned parlour, the same parlour in which her first husband had died violently. Lord have mercy on him, she thought, mentally crossing herself.

Burke was tired and grim, John preoccupied, and Roger nervous and jittery. A fine crowd to deal with a family crisis.

'We have a serious problem, gentlemen,' Brigid began, trying to light a cigarette as she talked and receiving assistance from her husband. 'Unless we can resolve it and resolve it soon, we may be in very deep trouble. The name of the problem is Noele. Roger, this family history project of hers has gotten completely out of hand. You must put a stop to it.'

'She's not an easy young woman to stop, Mother,' Roger said mildly.

'I'm not unaware of that,' Brigid snapped. 'Nonetheless, she must be stopped for her own good. She's been asking about Florence's death. And there are no statutes of limitation on murder.'

'Then it was murder?' John's face turned pale.

'We suspect so,' Burke said gravely. 'We've always suspected so, though we have no proof other than your father's terror at the possibility that the will would be challenged.'

'And his claim to Danny that night,' Roger added softly.

'It will never end. We keep getting in deeper and deeper,' John said bluntly, echoing Brigid's own thoughts.

'Rather late in the day for you to think of that, isn't it, old boy?' Roger asked sardonically.

'It'll be the fault of your damn permissive theories of child rearing,' John replied sharply. 'Sit down and talk it out. You've never been able to give Noele an order and tan her hide when she disobeys.'

'You're in no position to tell a married man how to rear his children,' Roger flared back, now thoroughly angry.

'His children, indeed,' John responded viciously.

'Both of you shut your stupid mouths,' Brigid ordered imperiously. 'We have to protect the child.'

John sighed. 'Yes, of course. You must have something in mind, Mother. If you don't, it'll be the first time in your life that you haven't.'

Brigid was surprised by the bit of nastiness from her clerical son. The boy would have been much better off if he had been nasty as a child.

'Of course I have something in mind. Someone has to do the thinking in this family. I know there is a difference of opinion among us' – Brigid heard the brogue creeping into her voice, as it did when she was especially tense – 'as to whether Noele is fey or just smart. I incline to the latter view. In either case, she will not be easy to fool. Therefore I propose that she be told the truth. Not all the truth, heaven knows.'

'We Farrells never tell all the truth,' Roger said with a smirk on his lips.

'Roger, do stop sounding like an academic jackass for a few moments, would you please?' Burke said. 'This is scarcely a matter for university irony.'

'I wasn't aware of being ironic,' Roger responded stiffly.

'Will you both be quiet!' Brigid commanded. 'And listen to me. Roger, you have to sit down with your daughter in the very near future and tell her that she must stop asking questions about our family history because there are events in our past that could do us enormous harm if they came into the open. Tell her bluntly, since she's already guessed it, that Danny killed Clancy. But tell her that it was a drunken fight, an accident, and that Danny really wasn't responsible.' She stubbed out another cigarette, permitting herself only one puff. 'So we covered up for him because there were already enough black marks on his record after he was thrown out of the Navy. We all thought that he should have another chance. Dr Keefe and Captain Nolan cooperated with us because they agreed that Danny wasn't really responsible and that a charge of reckless homicide or involuntary manslaughter would have made too much trouble for everybody – especially Danny. Then God, or the Chinese, or someone intervened, and Danny never got a second chance. Once he was dead, there was no point in reopening the investigation of Clarence's death, and the matter, however tragic for everyone, was over, finished, done.'

'That's fundamentally the truth,' Burke pointed out.

'Fundamentally.' Roger sipped his Scotch and water. 'A few points missing that our fey and/or smart little redhead may have already figured out.'

'More lies, more lies, more lies.' John groaned.

'Neither of you is being very constructive.' Brigid was

peremptory with them. 'We're not exactly lying, John. We're only telling part of the truth.'

'And what am I to tell her about Florence?'

'Nothing, unless she asks. If she gives up on Dan, we don't have to worry about what went before.'

'And if she does ask?'

'Tell her that we are convinced it was an accident. And that we did not prosecute Rocco Marsallo on a manslaughter charge because we could not afford in those days to offend the Mob.'

'Or now, either.' Roger smiled thinly.

Brigid ignored him, though she felt a powerful impulse to slap his face, as she had often done when he'd been bold and impudent as a little boy. 'Once you tell her what Danny did, that should end her crush on him, and we'll be out of the woods.'

'Not nearly enough truth, not nearly enough truth,' John said, sighing.

'I do not need, Monsignor,' Brigid said ruthlessly, 'a sermon from you on religious obligation. I take it we all agree that our responsibility is to protect Noele from her own foolishness. Has anyone a better suggestion?'

'Not I,' said Burke, staring moodily at his brandy.

'Under the circumstances, no.' Roger shrugged indifferently. 'I'll make it a point to talk to her, though she did tell me that she had received an *A* on the family-history term paper, and that, as far as she was concerned, the project was closed.'

'John?' Brigid watched her priest-son carefully.

'I rather think,' he spoke softly and very slowly, 'that perhaps we ought to tell Noele everything, the entire truth.'

'Do you really mean that?' Brigid's eyes locked with his.

'No.' John sighed. 'You're right, Mother, as always. Telling the whole truth now would do more harm than good –'

'– to everyone.' Brigid finished the sentence for him.

'Yes,' John agreed. 'To everyone.'

John

John sank to his knees on the prie-dieu next to his bed as soon as he returned from the Confirmation service in Evergreen Park. The wood seemed to cut into his knees. He had discarded long ago, in a burst of penitential spirit, the plush purple cushion.

It had been unwise to go to the Confirmation at Holy Saviour in Greenwood Park. Indeed, the pastor of the parish seemed quite astonished when John blithely walked into the dining room in the rectory basement. The cardinal shook hands with him in a characteristic show of phony sincerity. 'Hello there, John. Good to see you again. Great work you're doing on that television programme. We really enjoyed it the other night. You gave that peace fanatic what he deserved. Keep up the good work.'

After fifteen years of psychopathic administration in the archdiocese of Chicago, the hypocrisy of the cardinal's compliments was so patent no one bothered to be shocked or upset by it. Nor did John believe for a moment the cardinal had in fact watched the programme. Someone else had told him about it, probably Jim Mortimer, whose balloonhead could be seen floating about the other side of the dining room in an aura of self-importance.

Mortimer may also have told the cardinal that the studio had been inundated with phone calls praising Monsignor Farrell's tough honesty. So the cardinal would back off for a bit, only to return later for the kill with the dogged persistence of a grizzly bear stalking its prey.

The brave, honest, and outspoken John Farrell, object of his sister-in-law's confidence and admiration.

Many of the other clergy present at the dinner were less hypocritical than the cardinal. After a sufficient amount of liquor had flowed, they either joshed him, with cruel heavy-handedness, about his 'feud' with Larry Rieves, or asked him archly about his slipping ratings (which in fact were fluctuating up and down, but were still considerably ahead of the other three channels at that hour). A few extolled the success of the mass communications workshop and wondered, innocently, if John were to believe them, why he had not been there. As always when the sanctions of clerical culture were being applied, their attitude was a mixture of veiled self-righteousness and partronizing wit. They were like mourners at the wake of a family member who had been killed robbing a bank.

John decided to escape quickly after the dinner and not even lend the dignity of his purple robes to the procession into the church at the beginning of Confirmation. The clergy would not, of course, remain for the ceremony, but would proceed out of the church and back to the rectory for more drinks and bridge or poker and a long night of loud and vulgar masculine conviviality. John wanted no part of it. He packed his cassock into its suitcase, left the rectory, and strode towards his black Buick as if he were running from a house of ill repute.

Henry McKeon, a lean, balding pastor perhaps fifteen years older than John, headed him off in the parking lot. 'I think what you're doing on television is fantastic, John,' the older man said vigorously. 'Don't let the bastards get you down. *Invidia Clericalis* is the devil's own work. Remember there's a lot of us out there in the diocese who are cheering for you, even if most of us are afraid to open our mouths.'

With a lump in his throat John thanked McKeon for his kind word. But on his way back to the Neighbourhood, while flakes from a light snow flurry assaulted his Buick, he asked himself what good one supporter did when there were so many opponents. Doubtless McKeon was right. There were a lot of other silent allies, men who would come out of the woodwork when he gave up his programme and write him letters saying how sorry they were that he had been forced to quit. Not a word of encouragement from any of them, however, when it counted.

Kneeling now at his bedside, John realized that Hank McKeon's reassurance became one more heavy weight in the burden he felt he was carrying. Irene still continued to haunt him. He had been careful not to be alone with her since those deliciously awkward moments in the rectory. Yet her presence at Brigid's at the monthly family dinner had been a torment. She was both inaccessibly distant and immediately available – a haunting, mystical, mysterious presence and a demanding physical challenge.

He tried to persuade himself that the maddening mixture of lust and love he felt for her was diminishing. But then the warmth of her voice on the telephone, the curve of her throat at the dinner table, or merely the imagined click of her heels on the steps to the second floor of the rectory would send a stab of desire racing through his body that paralyzed both his heart and his brain.

His fears for Noele made his need for her mother even more imperious. Someone must protect the two of them. They were both in danger and did not know it. Two innocent, vulnerable women, victims of the Farrell family's lust and greed and of his own cowardly irresponsibility, now possible targets for a man who liked to torture beautiful women.

'Dear God,' he begged the figure on the crucifix above, 'forgive us, forgive us, forgive us.'

Roger

The first statewide survey was far more encouraging than Roger had dared hope. The incumbent governor had become unpopular, as all incumbent governors must, because the machinery of state government doesn't work. The pollster, doubly cautious because a professional in political science was to read his rather simpleminded report, said it was altogether possible that Roger could win the election with very little campaigning, so long as he stayed out of trouble and avoided 'dangerous' comments to the press.

'Stay out of trouble, ha,' Roger said sardonically, tossing the five-page report aside.

He had given his pre-Christmas address to a group of

downtown businessmen who met once a month for an early dinner and even earlier cocktails. Most of them were a little tuned out but were responsive to his vague promise of a 'new, creative, and responsible approach to the relationships between federal and state government.' They interpreted that to mean less federal and more state regulation of business, not yet comprehending that the state bureaucracy could be and doubtless would be more rigid and mindless in their regulatory requirements than the federal government.

Although he was dead tired when he and Irene finally got home from the Country Club Christmas Dance, long after midnight, he resolved to wait up until Noele returned. It would be reckless in the extreme not to carry out his mother's plan as quickly as possible. He also intended to make love to Irene, after discreetly hinting to her that the dress she had worn at the dance was a bit too revealing. He did not particularly relish watching middle-aged drunks ogle his wife.

Glancing out the window of his study, he saw the lights of an auto reflected on driveway snow and heard a car door slam. He glanced at his watch. One forty-five. Noele was, thank God, not a night owl.

A moment later the lights shifted on the driveway as the car left. Not much prolonged farewell affection between Noele and her lanky, inscrutable boyfriend.

She would come to his study, as she always did at the end of an evening when the lights were still on. But tonight he heard her footsteps in the parlour and then on the staircase. Well, there comes a time, I suppose, when daughters don't kiss their fathers good night. 'Did you forget something?' he asked genially.

Halfway up the stairs she glanced over the railing. 'Oh, Roger, I didn't know you were still awake.'

She backed down the stairs, leaned over the railing, and pecked at his forehead.

She was wearing a dark red dress with a broad white sash, the dress precariously kept in place with thin straps. Everything about her glowed – dress, flaming hair, deep green eyes, fair complexion, neat young shoulders and chest. Her trim, lithe womanliness, fleetingly revealed in the quick movement when she leaped toward him, appealed to Roger far more than his wife's overstated charms.

Despite the vigour of her youthful glow, Noele seemed worried – a mask settled on her face when she wasn't talking.

'Something wrong, Snowflake? Have a fight with Jaimie?'

Noele was astonished. 'REALLY, *ROGER*, who could fight with Jaimie Burns?'

He hesitated. The child was not in the mood to talk. A rare enough circumstance. Yet he had to talk to her.

Now.

He did not want to face Brigid's wrath.

'Still working on the family history thing?'

'It's all done. Sister Kung Fu gave me an *A*,' she said impatiently, as if he were a very annoying little boy. 'I told you that.'

'I'm sorry, Snowflake. I forgot. I guess I'm tired too, and I've been doing a lot of speaking. You're going to have to be more patient with me while I work out this governor thing.'

She smiled affectionately. 'Governor Roger. I think that's totally cool. For sure. Don't worry about me, Governor Roger. I'll be in your camp all the way.' She leaned over the railing to kiss him again; then she ran quickly up the stairs, neatly deflecting Roger's scheme to tell her the truth about Danny Farrell.

Irene

It was already nine thirty, and Irene was still lingering over her breakfast, drinking a third cup of coffee, eating an extra bite of toast, reading the *Star Herald*, and dreading the ten thirty meeting of the hospital volunteers' governing board. She loved visiting the sick, particularly the elderly sick, who had no one else to visit them. Somehow they found her radiant and smiled whenever she came into their rooms. But the governing board, one of the bitchiest groups of women she had ever met, was another matter. In a few moments she would have to go upstairs, put on her dress, and drive over to the hospital to explain to the governing board that no, she didn't want to run for president of the organization, without telling them that the real reason was that she could not stand having to meet with them every month.

She had dreamed of Danny again. The dreams came almost every night now. Before Noele's family-history project, she had never remembered the dreams in the morning. She dreamed of him the way he looked in the old Grand Beach photographs and then later in his ensign's whites. He was such a strange young man, a crazy mixture of deadly serious genius and mad comic. No wonder my parents didn't like him. I would be suspicious of a boy like that who was dating Noele.

If he had lived, he would have blown his life too, just as she had.

Once she'd asked him why he avoided Father McNamara. 'You're two of a kind,' she argued.

'Aye,' he said, escaping into his wonderful fake brogue. 'That's why I stay away from the man. He'd read me too well.'

'Maybe he could help with your writing. He's been a big help to me.'

'Ah, no, I don't want to face him till I have something worthwhile to show him.'

'And when will that be?'

He kissed her soundly. 'Sooner than you think, and later than you expect.'

That's the way he was. . . .

Irene had stayed in bed later than usual that morning. Although she had not touched a drop of liquor at the dance the night before, she still had a headache. She was sick almost every morning lately. For a few days she teased herself with the thought that she might be pregnant.

But that was almost impossible.

Or was it? Maybe Roger's recent randiness was not merely a sign that his mistress was away for the interim at the University. Maybe he had the faint hope that Noele's long demanded little brother would be a campaign bonus.

Bastard.

She was fed up with his endless nagging: she wore the wrong clothes, she drank too much, she said stupid things, nothing she did was right. Everyone else thought she was beautiful at the dance. Some one of these days there would be an explosion.

No, there wouldn't. She had threatened such explosions to herself since the first months of their marriage, and they never occurred.

She turned a page of the newspaper and came to Larry Rieves's column. Oh, no. He's gone after John again.

PRIEST INTERVIEWER IN MORE TROUBLE, the headline read. Rieves had interviewed John's last guest. Brother Shawn Plotke accused Monsignor Farrell of unfairness, insensitivity, lack of moral courage, and indifference to the problems of nuclear destruction. 'What else can you expect from a monsignor born with a silver spoon in his mouth?' asked Plotke.

Brother Shawn, however, was the only one of John's critics who did not hide under anonymity. Rieves quoted several more bitter denunciations from participants in the archdiocese's mass communications workshop.

One 'highly placed church official' even suggested that if 'Monsignor Farrell continues to disgrace the church with his television performance, it may be necessary to take ecclesiastial action against him.'

On another page Parson Rails returned again to his Downstate origins to spin a parable about a preacher who became so popular as a guest speaker that he no longer prepared sermons for his own congregation. His contract was finally renewed when he agreed to 'stay home and preach to his own people.'

'Smug hypocrite,' Irene snapped, dropping the paper on her breakfast table with shaking fingers, scarcely noticing that she had smeared the sports page with butter.

John had to fight back. Only if he challenged Rieves to come on the programme and interview him could he maintain his self-respect and dignity.

Reluctantly Irene shoved the chair away from the breakfast table and glanced at her watch. She usually cleared the table before the cleaning woman came in the morning – she felt guilty if she didn't. Well, today she would live with her guilt. In her bedroom, as she absently unfastened the belt of her robe and let the garment drop to the floor, she looked out the window and shivered at the sight of the sun-sparkled, snow-lined driveway. Bitter cold outside again. Then she saw the squat, black shape of John's Skylark.

Irene removed the skirt of her dress from its coat hanger. Time stood still. Then the despair she had discovered as she wrote her last short story exploded inside her. Her life was an utter waste. The man she loved was dead. She did not and could not love her husband, any more than he could love her. The only good thing she had ever done had turned out to have a bitter taste, through her own fault. No one would miss her when she was gone, and she would leave nothing of importance behind.

She was as damned as Brigid.

She dropped the skirt on her bed and put her robe back on, knotting the belt loosely. She had nothing more to lose. There was an attractive male virgin awaiting the wonders of initiation.

She ran down the stairs to greet him. John's eyes jumped with surprise when she opened the door. He stepped inside and they swayed in each other's arms, body pressing against body in a frantic attempt to become one. Their kisses ignited like tiny fires on a dry prairie, fires that merged and spread as if driven by a high wind. Then they were on the couch, John's face torn with an agony of desire. Irene moaning in anticipation of pleasure. His fingers were underneath her robe, bringing light and peace to her eager body. Despite his intense need, he was gentle and considerate, a naturally skilled lover.

She had not expected that, she told herself, as if observing their desperate embrace from a great distance. I thought you would be a brute, ravishing a woman for the pleasure of triumph. But you are sweet and tender.

Her robe slipped away. Oh, yes, strip me. Take all of me. I want to be yours. Make me come alive with longing and love. You know what I want and need. Just like Danny.

Danny, always Danny.

Reluctantly she pulled away. 'We shouldn't, John,' she pleaded hoping that he would not hear.

But he heard.

Only a priest, she thought as they drew apart, would have the self-discipline and the generosity to stop.

I am a tease. And you are a good priest, pompous and vain, but still a good priest. I'm so sorry I have done this to you.

God damn you, Danny Farrell. Won't you ever leave me alone?

Brigid

Burke and Brigid were watching *The Monsignor Farrell Show* on the Saturday before Christmas.

'Some of you may know,' John said as he wrapped up the show, 'that there's been a bit of criticism of this programme by some of my clerical colleagues and by a prominent Chicago TV critic. It seems to me only fair to give them an opportunity to make this criticism on the air. So I'm going to invite Monsignor James Mortimer, the Director of the Chicago Catholic Television Channel, as a representative of the archdiocese, and Mr Lawrence Rieves, *Star Herald* columnist, to co-host this programme next week, as a kind of Christmas present for the viewing audience.'

John was smiling cheerfully. 'And the guest to be interviewed will be Monsignor John Farrell. Mr Rieves and

Monsignor Mortimer can ask me any question they wish, no hold barred. This may sound like a kind of modern equivalent of the old Irish offer to step out into the alley and settle matters. And, in fact,' he said, grinning, 'it is just that. But I can assure the viewers that there will be no physical violence next week, in keeping with the Christmas spirit. There may, however, be lots of good conversation, which is what we try to offer you every Saturday evening.

'I assume that both Monsignor Mortimer and Mr Rieves will accept my invitation. If they don't, I won't disappoint the viewers who are spoiling for a good old-fashioned alley brawl. I'll find another priest and another journalist who, I guarantee, will give me a harder time than I've ever given any guest on this show. And so, peace on earth, Merry Christmas to all, and to all a good night. I'm John Farrell.'

'My God in heaven!' exploded Burke.

'What the hell has happened to the boy?' Brigid asked in total amazement. 'He hasn't done anything like that since the days Danny egged him on to devilment.'

'If I didn't know him better, I'd think he was getting a good fucking from someone – like the kind you'll be getting in a few minutes if you ask politely enough.'

Brigid chuckled. 'No fear of that, Burke, no fear of that at all.'

Roger

The Chicago Press Club is shrouded in subterranean darkness. It is made to seem all the more mysterious because its walls are covered with mirrors. One can never really be sure whether one is seeing one's own likeness in the mirror or real people on the other side of the room. The effect created is one of a secret meeting place of a band of Renaissance plotters – poisoners, thieves, and murderers.

In other words the membership of the Chicago Press Club.

Here men decide on the news before it happens, malign the reputations of public personages to curry favour with the arbiters of journalistic taste, assign book reviews to known enemies, cook up schemes of entrapment, abase themselves to visiting firemen from New York, plan sexual seductions of one kind or another, congratulate one another on their knowledge, sophistication, and cynicism, and drown their sorrows in expensive booze.

Anything to escape the cruel fate of going into the winter cold to cover a story.

Roger was lunching there on the day before Christmas Eve with Bill Wells, the editor of the *Star Herald*. The invitation came from Wells, a handsome man whose good looks and liberal ideology made many Chicagoans think of him as a dashing and able young journalist.

It was also alleged that he would like to be a United States Senator, even though an endorsement from his paper had been the kiss of death for many a candidate.

'Those people over at the *Star Herald* are important,' Mick Gerety had said. 'We need their endorsement.'

'How many precincts can Wells deliver?' Roger replied with a wink.

Mick winked back. 'You're learning, Governor. Real quick. Almost too quick.'

The book on Wells was that it took him a long time to get to the subject. He would mumble inaudibly over several drinks before he worked up enough courage to say what was really on his mind.

'Your brother certainly chopped off Larry Rieves's balls the other night, Governor,' he said with a faint, carefully practised smile.

'I didn't even see it. But from the way my wife described it, it hardly sounded like the John Farrell I've known for the last four decades.'

Not the total truth. John on occasion displayed considerable fire, although never before such disciplined fire.

'The men and women in the city room have put up

posters advertising the Rieves-Farrell fight.' Wells stirred his martini thoughtfully.

'Will Rieves really go on?'

Wells laughed. 'No more than Jim Mortimer. Your brother would eat them alive, with Parson Rails thrown in for dessert. But I hear he's invited Neal Marlowe of the *Tribune*, one of the most hard-nosed city hall reporters in town, and young Mick Murphy, the president of the Priest Association. Both of them can be counted on to give him a very hard time. It should be the best entertainment of the Christmas season.

'It's a gutsy move,' Wells continued. 'If he loses, they'll cancel his contract in the next two or three weeks. But if he wins, no one will dare touch him for years. And I'm sure he's smart enough to tell both Marlowe and Murphy to do everything they can to get him fired.'

There was an awkward pause. Roger was becoming uneasy. Wells had not invited him to lunch to talk about his brother.

'How's the campaign going, Roger?' He spoke so softly, his eyes on the empty martini glass, that Roger barely heard the words.

'Not all that bad; it's too early to tell, but I think we have a good chance.'

Wells did not look up from his martini. 'A kid from one of the Catholic colleges came up to see me last week looking for a job. He claimed to have some interesting information about your family that he would give us if we hired him as a full-time reporter. He said that the president of the college would fire him if he knew that we'd got our hands on the papers.'

Roger felt the blood draining from his face and his stomach muscles tighten. Was that the way women feel when they are about to be raped for the second time? 'Did you look at what he had?'

Wells raised an eyebrow. 'Of course, why not?'

'He had no permission to copy that material from my files.'

'I didn't know that.'

'How in the hell do you think he obtained those papers?' Roger demanded hotly.

'The public has a right to know, Roger,' Wells responded soothingly.

'Does your paper routinely review personal documents that are copied from citizens' files?'

'As editor of the paper that will almost certainly endorse you in March and in November, I felt that I would be acting in your name.'

'So?'

'So, of course, we didn't see a story in it. Neither did the opposition. On the basis of evidence that seems to us rather thin, you wrote a memo suggesting that your father may have ordered the execution of your aunt almost forty years ago, and that perhaps your mother and stepfather knew of it. That isn't really much of a story, even by contemporary standards.'

'And if you had better evidence?'

'That might be another matter, Roger,' Wells said lightly, 'but I don't see where the evidence could come from. It would be a one-day sensation, though it would sell newspapers that day. . . . Even if we brought in the name of Rocco Marsallo, "The Marshal," that would only make it a two-day sensation.'

If it was all so minor, why had Wells bothered to invite him to lunch? He felt that he had no choice but to be utterly candid. 'Do you think I ought to withdraw from the race, Bill?'

Wells munched thoughtfully on a celery strip.

'If that stuff is floating around out there, somebody will get hold of it. The governor is bound to find out about it, and his people will start snooping. Then all the papers and all the television channels in the state will take a good hard look at your family. Frankly, Roger, there's probably nothing in that file that would generate an indictment if your father was still alive. But with that as a beginning, we would have no choice but to make the Farrell family look like Chicago's Borgias. To tell you the truth, Roger, there have been a lot of rumours about your family for years. Your mother and Burke Kennedy are no worse than a lot of other folks in the construction business, but they have been notably more colourful than the rest of them. Better copy, if you know what I mean.'

'None of this, of course, has anything to do either with my own personal life or with my qualifications to be governor?'

'Hell, no!' Wells was now neatly dissecting a carrot stalk.

'You're as clean as a whistle, but once the family scandal avalanche begins to boom, you're going to get swept away too.'

For some reason Roger thought of Danny. He'd think of some way to get me out of this scrape, just as he always had when we were kids. He'd know how to protect the women from Rocco Marsallo, too. Damn, why did he have to die on us?

'Can anybody survive this sort of thing?' Roger asked. 'Can anyone run for public office if they are subjected to such scrutiny?'

Wells shrugged negligently. 'It sells newspapers and improves TV ratings.'

A point that Roger told himself that Niccolò Machiavelli would have appreciated. But from a self-professed liberal who demanded the highest standard of ethics from public servants?

'I guess I'll have to think about it very seriously, Bill. I'll let you know.'

'Mind you, Roger. You'd make a better governor than anyone who's likely to run. It would be a shame if we had to do you in.'

'But you sell newspapers.'

'And the public has a right to know,' Wells said delicately, breaking a piece of Ry-Krisp in half.

Well, Roger decided, it had been a pleasant campaign while it lasted.

DCI

The Director was stuffing documents into his briefcase, determined to leave at three PM. No matter what peculiar Russian sounds the snoops had picked up, the world would have to survive without him while his family escaped to the Virgin Islands for the Christmas holidays.

Radford was standing in the doorway. What did he do at Christmas? Did Radford believe in Christmas? Did Radford have a family? The Director trusted that he would be dispensed from wanting to know the answers to those questions.

'If it's anything serious, Radford, I don't want to hear it.'

'I don't think it's serious, sir. I saw our Chinese friend again last night.'

'Oh?'

'He told me that the Farrell matter had arranged itself.'

'Arranged itself? Does he think we're French?'

'One never knows with those folks.'

'All right, Radford, I'm in a hurry. Tell me what you think it means.'

'My guess is they misunderstood our message and anticipated our wishes. Farrell, in other words, *was* still alive. And he isn't alive anymore.'

'I thought they had given up quick executions.'

'Not when one of their loyal allies seems to be requesting such an execution.'

'That isn't what we requested.'

'No sir, it was not. But it's what they thought we wanted. It's probably what they would have wanted in our circumstances.'

'And you think it's all for the best?'

Radford was his usual icy self. 'One could imagine worse outcomes, sir, from the point of view of the Company, of course. Perhaps even from Farrell's point of view. But then we'll never know that, will we, sir?'

Might Radford have requested the Chinese to eliminate the Farrell problem? Not likely. He never exceeded instructions. Not as far as the Director knew, anyway.

'Well, that's that, I suppose,' he said sombrely. Daniel Farrell's ghost would haunt him through the Christmas vacation. 'I'll speak to Jim Burns when Congress comes back next month. Merry Christmas, Radford.'

'Merry Christmas, sir.'

DANCE
SIX

Gigue

Then on the cross hanged I was
Where a spear to my heart did glance
There issued forth water and blood
To call my true love to the dance.

'My Dancing Day'
A Medieval Good Friday Carol

John

'You have a remarkable appetite this morning,' Ace McNamara said, looking up from his copy of *The New York Times*. He had moved into St Praxides rectory for the Christmas rush. 'You have the Christmas spirit a day early? Or is it just the fun of telling off your critics on the programme?'

John laughed heartily. 'A clear conscience, a happy parish, and a week off after the first of the year. What more does a pastor need at Christmastime?'

He was in love, that's why he felt so good. And even if the love had not been consummated yet, it surely would be soon. Irene loved him as much as he loved her. Only the memory of Danny Farrell stood between them. And if he were kind enough, and considerate enough, and understanding enough, that memory would fade.

Perhaps someday he would confide in the Ace. But right now he felt no guilt, no regret, no sense of sin. Only exuberance. The pastor of St Praxides would soon have a mistress. So what? He was neither the first nor the last priest in the history of the Catholic Church to stray from the most narrow path of virtue. And in the sweetness of his love for Irene, stolen documents, ancient crimes, lingering guilt, meant nothing.

'So you're going south after the first of the year and leaving the parish in charge of the old Navy chaplain? Dangerous business,' said the Ace. 'By the time you return, Jerry and I will have moved the rectory across the street.'

'I doubt that. You'll be lucky if you see him.'

'At least he doesn't work any more when you're around than he does when you're not here.'

'Incidentally,' John asked, changing a distasteful subject, 'are you coming to Noele's birthday party the day after Christmas?'

'Does anyone in this community have a choice? Turning down an invitation to MN's St Stephen's Day reception is lese majesty, at a minimum.'

'I wish you wouldn't encourage her into thinking she's something special,' John said with sudden irritability. 'She's not special, you know; she's no different from any other dizzy teenage female. And she causes us a considerable amount of trouble. That term paper –'

'A call for you, Father,' the housekeeper interrupted him. 'Your sister-in-law, I believe.'

'I'll take it upstairs, Maeve.'

He stood up abruptly from the table. 'See you later on in the day.'

'Sure,' said the Ace. 'Say hello to Irene for me. And tell her she's not special either.'

As he dashed up the stairs, John wondered if McNamara was baffled by the apparent transformation in him. They had known each other a long time. And the Ace was a very shrewd customer.

Irene

Irene hung up the phone. Why had she called him? Some stupidity about Noele's party. No, that wasn't the reason at all. She was as much in love as he was.

There had been an article a few months ago in *McCall's* about 'romantic love,' infatuation, amorous obsession. She had thrown it aside in disgust. That sort of thing happened only to teenagers like Noele and Jaimie. But now it had happened to her. She was more in love with John than Noele was in love with Jaimie.

The article said that the longer the tension of unfulfilled romantic love lasted, the worse the pangs became. And then when the lovers finally possess each other, they quickly fall out of romantic love and either part or settle down to the ordinariness of everyday life.

In her head she knew that she and John did not love each other in any mature and responsible way. They were two lonely, troubled people, conscious of their own mortality, trying to cling to each other for a few moments of warmth on their way to eternal cold. She knew, too, that it was a replay of their adolescent love affair, all the more powerful and demanding because they were older. Nonetheless, after a few romps in bed they would both be cured.

Why not romp in bed then?

Why not find an excuse to go away at Christmas and spend a week in bed together? Get it out of their systems. That's what John wanted. But priest that he was, he was afraid to pressure her.

The damn fool. Why not insist?

He had a reason for not insisting, Irene knew. He had been trained to think about others, even if he often didn't know what that meant.

And why won't I agree to sneak away with him for a week of sex and sun?

Because I'm haunted, that's why. I'm haunted by a dead man.

Noele

The day before Christmas Eve was gross. In the morning there was to be a gymnastics meet at Sacred Heart in Lisle.

Then Noele would have to race back for folk music practise in the church at twelve o'clock, then home to wrap her Christmas presents, fix up her bedroom '– spotlessly clean, see, Mo-*ther* –' and finish the decorations for her birthday party the day after Christmas.

And in the middle of all that find time to wash her hair, which was a *mess*.

After all that, she would have to take Jaimie Burns's present (an Aran Isle sweater, specially made in his size) to his house, and then dash over to Grams's for Christmas Eve supper, then back for another practise with the choir, and finally a breakfast after Midnight Mass at the Burnses'. TOO much. And now Flame was on another one of his strikes.

Noele dashed into the house. Roger had gone downtown on the Rock Island for a meeting, so both the Seville and the Datsun were in the garage (and the yukky old Mercedes, which no way would Noele touch). But Moms, typically, was not around when she was needed, and the maid had no idea where she'd gone.

That WOMAN! Noele protested.

Well, she kept the spare set of keys for the Seville in the little antique desk in her office. She'd never really told Noele not to take those keys. So, Noele argued to herself, it would be all right to take them. She *had* to drive to the match at Lisle if she was going to be back in time for choir practise.

She bounded up the stairs and down the hallway to Moms's little office, with its cute antique furniture. She opened the desk drawer and snatched up the keys. 'If you're angry, Moms, I'll apologize.'

There was a small stack of neatly typed pages under the keys. Noele glanced at them. The title in capital letters on the first page read 'The Buying of the Baby.'

She hesitated. Moms had never shown her one of the stories. They were always locked up carefully. But here was a story that wasn't locked up. Moms had casually left it in a drawer where JUST ANYONE could see it. Then probably she wouldn't mind if someone else read it. AFTER ALL, what kind of a mother wouldn't share at least one of her short stories with her own daughter?

Feeling quite sneaky despite her rationalization, Noele

sat on the edge of the little antique desk and began to read the story.

Moms wrote very well. The story of a woman and a priest, Lorraine and Father Tom, going to the town of La Puente outside of Los Angeles to buy a baby, was crisp and sardonic. Father Tom was the brother of Lorraine's husband, Alfred, who refused to participate in the actual purchase of the baby, although he had approved of it.

Alfred! Noele felt the blood draining away from her face and her head. Her fingers trembled as she turned the pages. The room became warm, like a sauna someone had turned on without warning.

The description was vivid – the tiny house in which the young couple lived from whom the baby was to be purchased, poor people hemmed in with mortgages and desperately needing the money – scraggly lawn, unpainted walls, cracked window, a car on concrete blocks in the driveway. The woman's name was Marsha and there was anguish in her voice as she said, 'If the war gets worse in Vietnam, then there will be more jobs in aerospace, and they'll be hiring engineers at Lockheed again. Then Herbert will have a job, and we can get back on our feet.'

Father Tom, a model of ecclesiastical discretion, gave Herbert the crisp, white envelope bulging with hundred-dollar bills 'as though they were representatives of the American and Russian government meeting at a bridge between East and West Berlin to exchange prisoners of war.'

Nice image, Noele thought mechanically as she turned another page.

The baby was traded for the envelope. Herbert glanced inside, not counting the bills, but estimating them, and Marsha laid the baby gently in Lorraine's arms. She drew the blanket away from the baby's head to make sure that her head was red. Everyone but Father Tom was crying.

'It will all work out for the best,' he said unctuously.

Noele sat numbly at the desk, absently rearranging the pages of the story into a neat stack, aligning the edges by tapping the pile on the desk and then sliding it back into the drawer from which she had taken it.

She closed the desk drawer and, keys in hand, ran down the stairs and out into the cheerfully sunny winter day. She drove to Sacred Heart and led her team to victory with her best performance ever on the parallel bars, directed the folk group practise with determined vigour, wrapped all her presents neatly, cleaned up her room, dashed over to the Burnses', kissed Jaimie Burns vigorously when she gave him his sweater, ate supper silently at Grams's house, sang loudly at Midnight Mass, sipped half a glass of champagne at the Burnses' breakfast, and then came back to her own home and in the quiet of her totally neat room sobbed herself hysterically to sleep.

Roger

His arms locked around his wife, his breath coming in deep and heavy sighs, Roger groped for understanding, feeling that he was an explorer lost in a mysterious jungle.

'Did I hurt you?' he asked tentatively.

'Of course not,' she murmured, her fingers sinking more deeply into his buttocks.

It had begun as routine 'after Midnight Mass' love. Then they had both become two different persons. His passive, submissive, compliant wife turned into a fiery aggressor who had pushed him to the outer limits of tolerable pleasure. In response, for the first time in their marriage, he gave himself completely and without restraint to her. The paralyzing sweetness of sex with Martha seemed trivial in comparison.

'What happened to us?' he managed to say.

'Politics makes you hungry,' she replied.

Perhaps she was right. The heady excitement of the campaign trail might be making him a different person.

He took one of her hands in his own and held it tightly. 'I love you, Irene,' he said.

How many times had he spoken these words before, not really meaning them. Perhaps he didn't mean them now, either. One wild fling in bed did not transform a lifetime.

But it might be a turning point.

Her other hand began to tease him into arousal. He felt himself respond very quickly.

'More?' he breathed in astonishment, unable to understand either her caresses or his response.

'A lot more,' she said fervently.

I will not let them hurt her, he found himself thinking as he pressed her against the mattress, throwing all his physical strength into his new attack.

Loving tenderness seemed to burst his rib cage apart.

Their screams of pleasure exploded at the same time.

'Sleepy?' he asked a few minutes later.

'Uh-huh.'

'Can I tell you a story?'

'Of course.' This time she sought his hand and held it tightly.

'I may have to give up the campaign.'

Irene was instantly awake. 'Why?'

'The newspapers have some personal papers of mine, copied without permission in my office. I'm afraid my father hired a young hoodlum to kill Florence and Danny because he was afraid that my grandfather's will would be contested. Mother and Burke may have been involved too.'

He had no idea how his wife would respond.

She turned on the light and peered intently at him. She touched his face lightly.

'Dear God,' she breathed. 'Is that why everyone was so terrified when Noele started asking questions about the past?'

He nodded sadly. 'There may be some danger for all of us. The killer is a Mob enforcer.'

'Do you want to be governor, Roger?' she asked, tracing the outlines of his face as if to make sure they were real.

'I guess so,' he said, chuckling ironically. 'As much as I've ever wanted anything, and as you well know, I don't normally want anything very much.'

'Then don't quit.' She kissed him with slow, loving affection.

At that moment his wife's beautiful breasts, pressed against his chest, did not seem at all excessive.

'What's happening to our family?' Roger asked. 'John turns into a fighter, you turn into a wanton – and that's a compliment – and I'm half tempted to turn into a crusader.'

'Maybe it's the ghost of Danny Farrell. Maybe Noele has called him back from another world with her term paper.'

'You'll stand by me, no matter what happens?' Roger could hardly believe that he had said anything that romantic.

She pulled the sweat-drenched sheet away from him. 'Only if you come into the bathroom and take a warm, sudsy shower with me – a long, leisurely one, too.'

'At this hour on Christmas morning?' he protested. She had never suggested anything remotely like it before.

'What better time?'

'Sounds,' Roger said, astonishing himself again, 'like a wonderful idea.'

Irene

There was something wrong with Noele. Irene had been so preoccupied with the split of her personality into despair and sensuality that she had hardly noticed her red and green Christmas child.

Irene thought that perhaps she was as guilty of adultery as Roger. One man aroused her, another man made love to her, and a third man's ghost lived in the other two.

But guilt did not seem to stick. She was pleasantly exhausted by her nonstop orgy with Roger. And if he wasn't the only lover in her bed, he was still present. If they continued to enjoy each other as they had the last two nights, the barriers might collapse and they might even become friends.

But Irene was not sure that she wanted such a change.

As she pondered the new mysteries in her life she became vaguely and then sharply aware that the Christmas child was not happy on Christmas day nor St Stephen's day, her 'official' birthday party day. She seemed to be living on a planet in a different galaxy, perhaps in a different universe. All the motions were there, the winning smiles, the courtesy, the friendliness – she remained very much the reigning monarch of St Praxides. Yet something was missing. One did not hear 'Mo-*ther*' or 'Tell me about it,' or 'Really!' or 'I'm sure.' The contentious and forceful part of the Christmas child's personality seemed to have dried up, like a Christmas tree deprived of water.

A fight with Jaimie Burns? That did not seem likely. In a room full of guests, he stood at a discreet distance from her, like a modern Lancelot ready to crack the skull of anyone who dared disturb her peace and contentment. Conflict with her friends? Eileen was buzzing around like a vice-regent in the presence of a queen bee. Trouble in school? Noele never had trouble in school.

If there was something truly bothering the new seventeen-year-old, would she confide in her mother? Irene knew with a wrenching pain in her heart that, whatever the pretences that Noele might attempt, there was no trust between the two of them. Impulsively she sought out the one man in the room who she could be certain would not fall in love with her.

'Hello, Father McNamara,' she said to the Ace, who was pontificating to a crowd of Jaimie's friends about boot camp – her first words to him in fifteen years.

The blue eyes had seen terrible pain in Vietnam, but they still danced, and his laugh was as quick as ever.

'Haven't seen you lately, Renie,' he said, and grinned. 'How was that first semester at St Mary's?'

'Really yukky.'

The boys dissolved into laughter, and then, sensing that they were not needed, disappeared.

'I'm sorry,' Irene went on. 'I . . . I guess I just blew it.'

'What?' He feigned genuine surprise.

'My life.'

'Broken old woman.' He took a strong drink from his glass of Jameson's.

There was an awkward pause as they both hunted for bland words.

'You look tired,' he said tentatively. 'Are you going to have some time off after Christmas?'

'The Rafertys have offered us their house in Tucson the week after next. I don't know whether the Governor' – the word came out without any irony – 'can get away. But I may go.'

'The whole clan will be out of town. The pastor to Puerto Rico, Brigid and Burke to their usual retreat in Acapulco.'

'It might improve the parish to be rid of us for a while. Are you going away?'

'I've had enough tropics for one lifetime.'

'Can I come see you?' Irene blurted out the frightening words.

'Anytime, Renie.'

He didn't even ask why. But perhaps he already knew. He inclined his glass of Jameson's toward the birthday queen. 'Something bothering her today, do you think?'

'Do you think so?'

'Watch. Hey, MN,' he bellowed in his deliberate South Side shanty Irish voice. 'When do we get something to eat?'

Noele turned away momentarily from former congress-man Burns and smiled sweetly. 'In a few minutes, Father McNamara.'

'That's not her,' Ace said. 'No way, José.'

'I suppose it's a phase she's going through. They always seem to be in phases.'

'Yeah,' Ace agreed. 'Probably just a phase. But it worries me. Something's wrong.'

Brigid

No matter how many parties she attended in the Neighbourhood, Brigid could never quite get over the feeling that she was an outsider, even at her grand-daughter's birthday party: Muggins permitted to peer at the window of the great house and amuse those who really belonged. So she was always irritable at a Neighbourhood party, even though she did her best to be charming and fooled everyone but Burke. They should have moved out of the Neighbourhood long ago. They had enough money to live in Lake Forest. When the boys left, John to his first assignment on the North Side, Roger to graduate school, Danny – Danny to China – she should have listened to Burke and moved away. But she argued that it was close to the firm. In fact, she wanted to prove to her neighbours that she was something more than an illiterate immigrant girl.

And now most of those she wanted to convince were dead.

As soon she would be.

Noele's young friends, so presentable and grown-up in their good clothes, made her even more uncomfortable. Not so long ago they were infants. And Noele herself, so quiet and subdued – not like her usual self at all. I never could understand what goes on in that pretty redhead's mind, she thought; what does she see with those scary green eyes. She's all that's left now. Everything we've done was done for her. Yet she doesn't seem to care.

Why must she poke around in the past? Doesn't she realize how easily a young woman can die. Like Florence.

What would be left then for any of us?

Brigid realized that she had been drinking too much. She felt dizzy and slightly sick. The noise of the party made her head ache. Infernal kids. I'll lie down upstairs for a moment, she thought. And then Burke can take me home.

She met the woman in the upstairs hallway, pretty in a pale green dress and still soft as shit.

'Did Roger talk to the child yet?' she said, forgetting in her irritability that Irene did not know about the family meeting.

'I have no idea what you're talking about,' Irene replied sharply, trying to walk by Brigid.

'Why aren't you able to control the child? What kind of a mother are you?'

'A mother who can't stop her in-laws from spoiling her daughter,' Irene responded tartly.

Ah, a little more fight than normal.

'And a wife who is incapable of giving her husband a good fuck.' Brigid wished she could have chopped off her tongue. Why had she said anything that stupid?

'A husband whose mother so dominates his life that he wouldn't know a good fuck if he saw it. And I know what you're trying to hide,' Irene shouted. 'You and your husband and your lover killed Florence Carey.'

'That's a lie.' Brigid was insane with rage. 'The only killer in our family was Danny. Your previous lover killed my husband.'

Irene stared at her in shattered disbelief. 'He did not, you evil old bitch.'

Then she crumpled like a piece of tissue paper drifting toward the floor. Sobbing, she turned away and rushed down the hallway to her bedroom. She slammed the door shut.

Brigid felt something slam in her heart.

And that, Maeve, she told herself, using her real name, is one of the worst things you've ever done, you goddamned fool.

Ace

The tears poured down her fresh young cheeks, and though she was not yet hysterical she was closer to hysteria than Ace had ever expected.

'I know I'm a terrible person for reading the story,' Noele said, sobbing.

He chose his words very carefully. He must follow his instincts, as he had in Vietnam – where when someone shouted 'Duck!' he ducked without asking why, and was still alive as a result. 'The story,' he responded, 'is not necessarily true, MN.'

'I wanted to find out who I am, and you and Jaimie and everyone else said I should stay away from it. Now I've found out, and I wish I hadn't.'

That explained Noele's odd behaviour at her birthday party, which had so concerned both Irene and him. Did Renie know she had read the story? Perhaps that's why she had asked to see him.

'Stories are stories, Noele. They may be made up out of real experiences, but they're not necessarily true.'

She dried her eyes with a twisted piece of tissue. 'You haven't read it.'

'Your face is so much like your mother's,' he said slowly. 'Same bones, same shape, same gorgeous beauty.'

She smiled through her tears. 'Nerd!'

'I'm serious. You do look your mother's daughter. And I've never seen a father/daughter relationship closer than the one between you and Roger. Anyway, there's nothing wrong with being adopted. You're still you.'

'Whoever that is,' she said wryly. 'Oh, I know, Father Ace, that's what I tell other kids who are totally into a snit because they're adopted. Still . . .'

'Then what are you going to do about it. Ask your parents?'

She shook her head. 'I don't know what to do.'

He hesitated again. His loyalties were under cross pressures. What the hell!

'Why don't you talk to your uncle. . . .'

'Monsignor John?'

'Why not?'

Noele dabbed her eyes with the tissue and smiled. 'Why didn't I think about that?'

'What about Danny Farrell?' he asked, wondering if that issue was still alive.

Noele waved the question aside. 'Oh, I'm finished with all that, Father Ace. It doesn't, seem, like, important anymore.'

'Not convinced he's still alive?'

She considered thoughtfully, her tear-stained face wrinkled in a deep frown. 'Not anymore,' she said hesitantly. 'I did once, kind of. But now . . . Do you think Uncle Monsignor will tell me the truth?'

'Of course.'

'Well, I guess I'll have to wait until he comes home from Puerto Rico. Right?'

'Right.'

Poor John, thought the Ace. Happy New Year, Monsignor.

Burke

The Farrells sat around the large-screen television in Brigid's parlour watching with astonishment as John took on two of the toughest interviewers who had ever appeared on Chicago television. Neal Marlowe, a veteran political correspondent, and 'Father Micky' Murphy, a tough, red-haired Irish gamecock from Cannaryville, Back of the Yards. They had been told to give Monsignor Farrell a hard time and were enjoying every minute of the combat.

So too, surprisingly, was John.

'Doesn't it all come down, John,' said the frowning little red-haired priest, 'to a question of whether being a television personality is compatible with being a priest? Don't you think your brother priests are right to be offended at your prostitution of the Roman collar for commercial purposes? Didn't Father Fogarty really speak the truth when he suggested in our newsletter that you're a slick, smooth copout who's using the priesthood as a vehicle for a monumental ego trip?'

'How could anybody be slick and still fight with you, Micky?' John asked with a cheerful laugh. 'Actually, I asked Dads Fogarty if he wanted to come on instead of you or along with you. But apparently he only takes on targets who can't fight back. I was raised in an era of the church, Micky, when seminarians were told that priests should strive to be the best in everything they do because Jesus, whom we represent, deserves the best. I feel I represent the catholicity of the church and the priesthood on this programme by the questions I ask. My presence here is witness to the church's concern about the mass media and their influence on modern culture. If I didn't think that as a priest I brought a special and unique contribution to the role of talk show host, I'd get off the air tomorrow. I'm disappointed that some of my fellow priests disagree with me, of course. But I still intend to do my best and to follow my own conscience, the way any good priest should.'

All very impressive, thought Burke heavily, but trivial compared to what we're facing. Both of her sons are weaklings, unable to protect her, not even able to comprehend the danger she's in. The kid has more sense than you.

'Yeah, but Father – I mean Monsignor.' Marlowe grinned crookedly. Through the whole programme he had deliberately confused *Father* and *Monsignor* to see if he could throw John off balance. 'Geez, what's a priest doing on television?'

'Hey, Neal,' John said, 'why don't you call me John and forget about the formal title?' Laughter from the studio audience.

'Okay, Monsignor, I mean, John,' Neal Marlowe said ruefully.

Very funny, Burke mumbled to himself – clever, handsome TV priest. Your father was clever and handsome too, but he didn't have any balls either.

'I'm trying to do on television just exactly what Jesus tried to do when he preached in the temple, and what Saint Paul tried to do when he walked up to the statue of the unknown God in the Acropolis and claimed to represent him. I'm nowhere as good at it as Jesus or Saint

Paul, but I try. And if Larry Rieves doesn't like it, he's always welcome any week of the year to come on this programme and take my place!'

Danny Farrell at least had balls, Burke thought. He was ready to fight for what he believed, poor dumb bastard. Not as slick as you or Roger, but a fighter. I almost wish he were back. We need fighters now. And I'm the only one left.

And I'm old and tired. Too tired maybe.

'I cannot believe my eyes and ears,' Brigid said when the programme was over. 'Something has happened to that boy.'

'I tell you, Bridie,' Burke said, repeating his crude joke, 'he's screwing somebody.'

Noele, who had been moody and withdrawn all through the programme, exploded. 'Burkie, that's the most gross thing I've ever heard you say. I'm sure humans don't have to have sex to be passionate.'

'I'm sorry,' Burke apologized quickly. 'And if I ever needed proof that virginity and fire are not incompatible, you just gave it to me, Noele.'

She was not to be appeased. 'I don't want any of your cheap compliments. I demand that you apologize.'

Burke surrendered easily. 'All right, Noele, I apologize.'

Noele, quite uncharacteristically, was not gracious in victory. 'That's better,' she snapped, and then retreated again to her strange, faraway mood.

One fighter I forgot about, Burke thought ruefully.

'What's eating the child?' he asked Brigid as the others were collecting their coats. 'Has Roger talked to her? Did he tell her about Flossie?'

'He says he's talked to her, but I'm not sure. I don't think the damn fool is telling the truth.'

They stood at the front door watching as Roger caught up with his wife at the door, took her hand, and walked toward the car after their daughter, who had stormed out of the house without saying goodbye either to Brigid or to Burke.

It's all coming apart, Burke thought helplessly. The curtain is rising on the final act.

Noele

The phone rang. Noele ignored it and continued to type a book report on the new TRS-80 model III that the family had given her for a Christmas present. The phone kept ringing.

'Oh, damn it!' she exploded. 'Can't anybody else in the house answer the phone?'

She picked it up and in her most acidly charming voice said, 'Farrell residence, Mary Noele speaking.' There was a heavy breathing sound on the line.

'Come on, who is it?' Noele demanded impatiently.

The heavy breathing continued. Noele slammed the receiver down.

The phone rang again. She picked it up. 'What the hell do you want?'

'You mind your own business, or you'll get your tits cut off,' said a muzzled voice. The line clicked.

A gross, obscene phone call. Other girls in the Neighbourhood got them too. Scary, but not serious.

Except it was ugly instead of sexy.

Maybe it was a wrong number.

Her hands felt very cold.

Roger

He leaned against the door of Martha Clay's office, a very tiny concrete cubbyhole on the fifth floor of Green Hall. Assistant professors, especially when they were women, were assigned the sort of office space that in the good old days of the late 1960s had been given to junior research assistants. Ah, for the years of the government gravy train.

'Welcome back, Professor Clay. I hope you had a nice vacation.'

Martha looked up from the journal she was reading. 'A wonderful vacation!' she exclaimed. Then, as though realizing his feelings might be hurt, she quickly added, 'But, of course, it's nice to be back.'

'And it's nice to have you back.' So, another reconciliation with the husband? Well, she would get over that quickly enough. 'I'm not supposed to tell you this' – Roger looked discreetly either way down the dimly lit corridor – 'but the provost hinted to me – and the phone call was from Saint Maarten, so it must have been important – that they will renew your appointment. Nothing official, of course, but the provost reads the auguries pretty well.'

'A five-year term appointment?' she asked expectantly.

So she would have settled for the compromise? 'No. They were ready to give in without a fight. The whole works. As they put it, a lifetime appointment in the University.'

Martha smiled complacently. 'Well, it's certainly nice to win. I suppose we should postpone the formal celebration until the news is official. You never can know with those chauvinists in administration. Somebody might remind them I'm a woman.'

'Oh, I think they know that. The provost kept calling you Mrs Clay. Anyway, I thought we might celebrate informally later on this afternoon, despite the snowstorm.'

He let his suggestion of a tryst hang momentarily in the air while Martha glanced out of the window at the mantle of new-fallen snow.

Did he want to reassure himself that he could still be dominant in a sexual relationship? Perhaps.

'I'd love to, Roger, but I have a meeting of the faculty women's committee and then a graduate student party – the beginning of a semester, you know. I don't suppose you'll be able to attend.'

'No, I guess not. I'm technically on leave of absence already.' His wife had been out of town for a week, and Roger was lonely, despite daily phone conversations with her.

'Let's try something tomorrow night or the next night,' she said brightly. 'Whenever you're free.'

'I have a speech in Rock Island tomorrow evening. I could be free late afternoon the next day.'

Sex with her would not compare to the ecstasy with Irene at Christmastime, but it was safe. Odd that a wife would be terrifying in bed and a mistress reassuring. He was deeply in love with two women. The thought of losing either hurt like an exposed dental nerve. Yet if he was not very cautious now, he might lose both.

'My apartment about three thirty, then?' She smiled invitingly.

'Woman, you have yourself a deal.' Yet as he walked back to his office Roger was worried. There was a false note somewhere in the conversation. Martha was not as enthusiastic as she had been before Christmas. Women's committee meetings would not have been an excuse then. Whether he lost her might not depend completely on his actions. And that somehow did not seem fair.

Back in his office he rolled typing paper into his IBM typewriter. His basic political speech needed some modification. A little more substance, Mick Gerety had said.

If it had not been for Mick's insistence that he couldn't cancel speeches now, even though he was unopposed in the primary, Roger would have escaped to Tucson with Irene. His usually predictable wife had now become wildly unpredictable. Sometimes she was devastatingly affectionate and other times distant, prickly, contentious.

Last night she had been cheerful and seemed genuinely happy to hear from him. The night before she had had no time to talk. He did not need a turbulent relationship with Irene during a campaign that still had eleven months to run.

And he still had not talked to Noele. Brigid saw through his repeated lies and was furious with him.

Roger typed out a paragraph of frightening facts about the deterioration of the Illinois economy vis à vis the Sun Belt states. Irene was in the Sun Belt. What had happened between them? An interlude, a passing phenomenon. It could not survive. She was the devouring mother goddess for a few nights, that was all.

But, dear God in heaven, what magic nights they'd been!

He typed a few more sentences. The Irene who came back would be the old Irene, unappealing and unthreatening.

And the Noele problem was not as serious as Brigid made it out to be. The term paper was over. She had received her *A* in social studies and was now worrying about the PSAT. On the fringes of his consciousness Roger heard a warning that from Noele silence did not mean that a quest was over. Before he could attend to the warning voice, his phone rang.

'A man on the phone says he wants to talk to you,' the ineffable Mrs Marshfield announced, as though she could not believe that the man actually wanted to talk to him.

'Mr Farrell,' he said politely.

'Bill Wells here, Roger. I hadn't heard from you, so I assumed you were going ahead with the race.'

'That's right, Bill,' Roger said, trying to sound smooth and confident. 'I'll have to take my chances on what comes out. If the people don't want me as their governor, the place to indicate that decision is in the ballot booth, not in the editorial columns of newspapers.'

Wells was silent for a moment. 'That's a pretty hard-nosed stand, Roger.'

'I don't think I have much choice, Bill.'

'I suppose not. . . . Well, I hear your friend from the magazine was over at the opposition again, looking for a job. They offered him a two-hundred-and-fifty-dollar kill fee for his article, but the kid didn't take it. He still thinks he's a combination Woodward and Bernstein of the 1980s.'

'My decision is final, Bill. I'm in this race to the bitter end. Thanks for keeping me informed.'

Roger felt ill. It was a dirty, messy world. Maybe he should have been the priest instead of John.

What was he thinking about when the phone rang?

Oh, yes, Noele. And her moods. *Boring* was her latest word. School, the High Club, the folk Mass, ballet lessons, gymnastics – everything was boring. Would she find his story about Danny boring too? No telling how she would react.

He tried to corner her as soon as he came home, but she had to baby-sit at the Foleys'.

Finally, at 11:30, she walked into his study, sat back wearily in the easy chair, and composed herself, as though she were a novice about to hear a sermon from the archbishop.

'All right, what is it you want to talk about?'

Roger wet his lips with his tongue. 'It's sort of about that family history term paper you were doing.'

'Oh, that! Roger, I finished that at the beginning of December.' She was braiding her long hair, a sure sign that she was *really bored*.

'We've talked about it in the family, Snowflake, and we feel you have a right to know what really happened the night your grandfather died, both because you are a part of the family and because we want you to understand why it's something that we are careful about.'

Noele said nothing.

'The truth is . . .' He sighed, again feeling the pain and horror of that terrible night. 'Damn it, Noele, this isn't easy to talk about; my father had his faults, heaven knows, and he wasn't very good to your grandmother. But he was my father.'

His genuine anguish merited him no sympathy. 'I know he wasn't very nice to Grams,' Noele said coldly.

'I'll come to the point then; Danny killed my father. That's the simple and honest truth, Noele.'

'I know that,' she said impatiently.

'Do you want to know why he did it?'

'If you want to tell me. I don't *have* to know.'

'It was a foolish fight. Both of them had too much to drink that night. And when my father was very drunk he became quite . . . well, let's say outspoken. And Danny had a hot temper too. They had had an argument earlier in the evening, and it started up again when they came home, upstairs in the room that's Burke's study now. My father hit Danny with a cane. Danny grabbed the cane away from him and swung it back. My father ran out of the room, tripped at the edge of the stairs, and tumbled down the staircase.'

'How horrible,' said Noele tonelessly. She wasn't giving much away.

'When the police came, it looked like an accident, and Mom and Father John and I, well . . . we felt sorry for Danny, we knew he was going off on a very dangerous job, and that he would do much more for the country working for the CIA than sitting in the jail down in Joliet. You see, Noele, it wasn't murder, not in the legal sense. They would have called it involuntary manslaughter or something like that, and he would have had a year or two in jail. Danny knew we were protecting him, but he wasn't even able to say thank you. Not even to me, and I was his closest friend.'

Roger's voice trembled at the memory of how much Danny's ultimate ingratitude hurt.

'Then he went to the training camp for the CIA out west. And was dead a few months later.'

'*If* he's dead,' Noele said sullenly.

'Noele,' Roger almost screamed, 'he *is* dead.'

'If you say so, Roger.'

There's something else on her mind. What is it? It doesn't matter. I've got to finish this thing. Roger rushed on with the story.

'It would not have brought Dad back to life, but it would have destroyed Dan completely. We thought that, well, maybe if he left the country and worked for the CIA for a couple of years and came back, maybe he would be grown-up and maybe . . . I don't know what, Noele, but do you understand?'

She nodded. 'Yes, Roger, I understand.'

'So you see why we would rather leave the whole thing just the way it was,' he concluded in frustrated desperation. 'And why we don't want to pursue that term paper any further.'

'I told you, Roger,' she said quietly. 'I'm finished with the term paper. It's boring.'

Irene

Irene hung up the phone and rolled over and faced the comforting warmth of the sunlight and her carefully oiled flesh. The Rafertys had been good enough to lend her their house in Tucson, which they hardly ever used anyway. For much of the week she had basked at the poolside in the foothills of the Santa Catalina mountains, revelling in the warmth and the peace. Only Roger knew where she was. He called her every day to pour out his dreams of what he would do as governor, idealistic fantasies of the sort that had attracted her when she'd met him at Berkeley, after she had run away from home.

The dreams had been wiped out in the tragedies of 1968 – the King and Kennedy murders, the Democratic convention riots, the election of Nixon. He had taken refuge behind the pose of the detached, faintly amused academic.

And now the dreams were back again, and so was something purporting to be love. It would not last; it was merely an episode, albeit a spectacularly passionate one.

Her one extra drink on Christmas Eve had triggered·it. She was a sensual mother again, a confidante who could nurse his wounds, a substitute for Brigid, but a passing one.

The same role she played for his brother the priest.

Both furiously passionate men when they were aroused, but lacking the sensitivity that Danny . . .

Always thinking of Danny.

When we began together, Danny knew little more about women's needs than they do now. But he set out to learn and learned very quickly indeed. I was a seminar for him on how to be tender and sweet to a woman, when to be fiercely passionate, and when to be delicately gentle. It was embarrassing – and terribly erotic – the way he watched me and studied me. All the better to hide his real self, of course.

She should not think of Danny. She was here for the

peace and the warmth, a naked body on an inflated mattress with a pool into which she could occasionally jump and a full pitcher of martinis.

She did not leave the house except for two trips to a shopping mall for food. No sight-seeing, no shopping, no contact with anyone.

All of her problems would be waiting for her when she returned. But for a few glorious days she could forget about them.

A surprise? Well, not exactly. An interlude rather.

'There are still surprises in life, Renie,' Father McNamara had said. 'That's what Christmas means.'

'Noele was a surprise,' she said to him, laughing. 'There haven't been any good ones since then.'

'None that you've noticed,' he said, grinning.

It had been a strange conversation. She had not mentioned Brigid's accusation about Danny or her dangerous romance with John or even her hidden stories. Rather, she had begun by apologizing for having let Father McNamara down by her failure to amount to anything.

'And I was so disappointed that I joined the foreign legion.'

'Silly, I didn't mean that. But you were counting on us, weren't you?'

'Only to be happy.' He laughed again. He laughed all the time, just as he did in the old days. 'It was your idea to be a writer, but you had to make it my idea, which turned it into an obligation you had to obey. And then I became your father, and you ran away from me.'

'Didn't you want me to write?'

'I didn't even know you could write until you showed me your stories. You were good at it. Probably still are. And writing would make you happy. But that's not the only way. God, unlike the South Side Irish, is a pluralist.'

'I suppose.'

'You don't want to give up your obligation to please me, do you? Okay, I'll cooperate. I'm a broken man, destroyed because Renie Conlon . . .'

She was laughing as loudly as he. Then she tried to change the subject. 'Does Noele feel an obligation to please you?'

'The other way around. And you're trying to change the subject.'

She could speak about none of the worries that plagued her, and he did not force her to. A typically Irish plea for help without help being mentioned or any plea made.

But he heard her and told her by his laughter that he was there when she needed him.

Like all the Farrells, she was recklessly running head on for disaster. She would need him all right. And soon.

'You're beautiful.'

'John. . . .' He was dimly visible through her sun-shades. She should dash for something to cover herself, but lethargy and heat robbed her of her energy. 'What are you doing here?'

'I found out where you were. I'm going back to Chicago from the Caribbean via Arizona.'

He stood over her, dressed in light blue slacks and a sport jacket, arms folded somberly, like a conquering warrior.

'I want you, Irene.'

'I want you, too.'

He sat next to her at the poolside and began to kiss and caress her. His lips explored her breasts, a child suckling its mother. She drew him close and hugged him with gentle passion.

Yes, yes, yes. Why not? It didn't matter. Nothing mattered anymore.

'Oh, Danny . . .' she murmured.

He drew away from her.

Oh, my God . . .

And he laughed. 'You're not ready yet, Irene?'

'I need more time.' I must need more time, otherwise why would I make such a terrible mistake. And he's not angry with me. He's patient with me, as he was with poor Tommy Taylor.

'And we both need cooling off.'

He rolled her into the pool and dived in after her, clothes and all – and was in those moments even more like Danny.

Later, huddled in a towel and sipping a martini, she

told him the truth about himself. 'You pretend to be a liberal in the parish, John, but you're really an authoritarian. And you're desperately dependent on the approval of other priests and the people of your parish, so much so that at times you don't have any character at all.'

'No clothes left on me,' he said lightly, though he was badly hurt.

'Let me finish. And everyone knows those things, and they still love you, because you are kind and good and generous.'

'You love me?'

'Of course I do.'

He gripped her hand fiercely. 'The way everyone else does?'

'No, the way a woman loves a man.'

He relaxed his grip. 'I can wait, Irene.'

'I didn't mean that.' What did she mean? Her head was whirling – too much vodka, too much sexual arousal. 'Anyone can make love to me. Not anyone can be a priest.'

'What's a priest?' he demanded.

'Someone who can love you without having to screw you.'

He turned away from her, his eyes scanning the distant mountains bathed in the purple hues of twilight.

Now, why did I say that, Irene thought. I'm drunk. But that doesn't mean I'm wrong. I've only made matters worse. I should have let him make love to me. Then he would get over me quickly. Now . . .

And why did I think he was Danny?

Noele

Jaimie Burns spent the first two weeks in January skiing at Steamboat Springs with his roommate, DeWitt Carlisle, and returned with a gorgeous tan.

'Just look at you,' Noele complained at Red's hamburger stand after Friday night High Club. 'And I look as pale as a ghost.'

'A very beautiful ghost,' Jaimie assured her.

'You must have done all kinds of bad things in Steamboat Springs to start paying me compliments.'

'I didn't do anything bad,' Jaimie said cheerfully.

'I'll have a Tab and french fries,' she told Red, who always insisted on serving her personally.

'The usual,' Red said.

'Tell me about it,' Noele smiled at him.

'I'm accused of playing around with coeds in the mountains, and you're flirting with Red.'

'Don't be gross. Do you want to hear the end of the Danny Farrell story?'

Jaimie was instantly serious. 'You bet I do.'

So Noele told him about her conversation with Roger.

'You sound like you don't believe it.' Jaimie had been watching her intently.

'I sort of believe it, Jaimie. I mean, I don't think Roger's *totally* lying to me. But there are a lot of things I don't understand.' She wasn't going to tell Jaimie yet about the short story 'Buying the Baby,' not yet, maybe not ever.

She had, however, figured out what she would do. As soon as Uncle John came back from Puerto Rico or wherever he was she was going to confront him and demand the whole truth. *Then* she would talk to Father Ace and *maybe* tell Jaimie the whole thing. After that she would have to make lots of decisions.

'Did you ask your father about Florence Farrell's death?'

Noele sighed. 'No. He would say it was an accident. And if I pushed him, he'd probably tell me that Clancy arranged it, even if that wasn't true. Clancy is dead and Burkie is alive.'

'You think it might have been Burke?'

'Like you said, Burke would do anything to protect Grams . . . anything.'

'So, what now?' Jaimie's hand closed on hers.

Gosh, there was a lot of strength in those hands. No wonder he could intercept passes like he was black. She thought she might tell him about the weird phone calls but decided there was no reason to worry him. She could cope by herself.

She was going to have to learn to cope by herself.

'I'm going to think about it a little bit more, then talk to Father Ace, and talk to you again, and then it's all over. . . . Oh, thanks, Red, but that's too many french fries.'

Jaimie tilted her chin up so he could look her directly in the eyes.

'There's something I guess I better tell you. Dad called me in Steamboat. The CIA talked to him. Danny is dead. He was a prisoner for a long time, but now he's dead.'

'Yes, he's dead,' she said slowly. 'I guess I've known that for some time now. Maybe I should forget about him.'

She felt the same way she had when she'd been a tomboy and was into fence-climbing. She wanted to be free of Danny; she wanted to believe that he was dead so she could forget about him and worry about herself. But she couldn't quite climb to the top of the Danny Farrell fence. She might say she knew he was dead. But she did not fully believe her own words, not quite, not yet.

'Make me a promise?' Jaimie said, his hand even tighter on hers.

'Sure.'

'Don't do anything big without talking to me about it first.'

'Really!' Noele exclaimed, meaning there was no way she could do anything serious without talking to Jaimie.

Yet she knew that she didn't completely trust anyone anymore, not even Jaimie.

And she was still numb, as numb as she had been on Christmas Eve when she'd read the story.

Nosy little bitch. It serves you right.

She was the only one in the house when Jaimie dropped her off that night. Roger was giving a talk someplace and Moms was still in Arizona. She had pulled the blankets up to her chin when the phone rang. Even before she answered it she knew who it was.

Again the heavy breathing and then the threat. 'We'll cut off your tits and then shove them up your cunt.'

John

Ace and John were sitting at the rectory lunch table after the 12:15 PM Mass, Ace devouring the 'Week in Review' section of the Sunday *New York Times*, John reading the entertainment section of the *Chicago Tribune*.

'Your suntan is a reproach to me for my sinfulness,' the Ace said as he peeled an orange – part of a gift package John had brought back from his trip.

'Puerto Rico is a wonderful place; I can recommend it thoroughly.'

John decided not to fly from Arizona to Florida and then back to Chicago. Only a few people knew that he was supposed to be in Puerto Rico, and they were not likely to be on the plane from Tucson.

On the crowded DC-10 returning to Chicago, he did not feel the slightest guilt. He was in love. His lover was hesitant. He would be sensitive to her hesitancy as long as was necessary. Then he would have her.

Afterward?

He would worry about that bridge when he came to it. No, he was worrying about it now. Guilt was catching up. He had to talk to someone.

'Dick, would you mind coming upstairs?' he blurted impulsively. 'I'd like to talk to you for a few minutes.'

'Sure.' Ace folded his *New York Times* neatly – the Navy had taught him to do all things neatly – and followed him up the stairs.

John carefully closed the door to his suite and, without asking, mixed two drinks. A vodka martini for himself – one of the many tastes he shared with Irene – and Jameson's neat for Father McNamara.

He put the three bottles on the coffee table.

The two men sat opposite each other on imposing leather armchairs that, John had thought, created the right ambience for a pastor of St Praxides.

Now the chairs and the couches seemed dull and pompous.

'The guys getting to you?' Ace said sympathetically.

'God, yes,' John replied, happy to have a chance to talk about that problem, though it was not what was encroaching upon his sanity.

'You'd better make up your mind, John,' the Ace said slowly. 'You're at a turning point now. If you go on with your programme, particularly if it is syndicated around the country, you'll be a pariah in the priesthood for the rest of your life.'

'You too?' John said in surprise.

'I'm not telling you to quit; I'm merely saying what will happen. You'll become the victim of collective envy neurosis. Your motives will be questioned. Your personality and character will be distorted so that you will not recognize yourself. Your friends and your family will be called upon to defend you by almost every priest and nun they encounter. Any attempts you make to reply will be twisted to fit the neurosis. You will become a myth that many of your fellow priests will love to hate. And even those who are free of the neurosis will tell you that you shouldn't expect anything else.'

'You'll turn me into a paranoid,' John said sombrely.

'No, I'm just warning you that a lot of paranoids will be chasing you.' McNamara grinned, though not very enthusiastically, at his own joke. 'Envy is maybe the third most powerful human motive, after hunger and sex. We have no monopoly on it in the priesthood. Hell, you never hear a word about it in psychology classes because their profession is riddled by it too. It's the fault that even the analysts won't discuss.'

'Are we worse?' John asked, seeing with terrible clarity that McNamara was saying nothing but the simple truth.

'Probably. Our reward structure is pretty thin; and we're socialized into it in the seminary because it's a very useful means of imposing control. Ruins talent, of course, but our leaders don't want talent anyway.'

'So if I go ahead I better be sure that my friends and family are enough to support me?'

'Don't even count on your friends.' The Ace emptied his glass of Jameson's and filled it again. 'The negative myth will stick to you for the rest of your life. Some of your friends will secretly envy you and others will succumb to pressure to go along with the myth.'

'You too?' John said softly.

The Ace grinned. 'Naw, I'm the kind that stays bought. A bottle of Jameson's every weekend and Captain McNamara will go ashore with the first wave of marines.'

'I suppose the programme's connected with the other thing I want to talk about,' John said, trying to muster the courage he needed to talk about Irene. 'I'm in love, Dick.'

'Huh?' McNamara was obviously utterly surprised.

'I wasn't in the Caribbean all the time. I was somewhere else with a woman. I didn't go to bed with her, not yet. . . .' John saw how petty, almost comic, it all was. How many times must a priest trained in psychology have heard the same words?

'Do you plan to leave the priesthood?' The Ace's eyes were hooded, and his voice neutral.

'I don't know. I . . . I don't think we could ever be married. When I tell you who, you'll understand.'

'There's no need for me to know that.'

'Yes, there is.'

'Oh?'

'Irene.'

A flicker in the former chaplain's eyes showed that he was surprised. Or perhaps impressed.

'Maybe you'd better tell me all about it,' said Father McNamara.

So John told him everything, all the way back to his grandfather's death and the first battle of the Philippine Sea.

'The priesthood was an escape for me. I felt that by being a good priest I was making up for the bad things that have happened. Even before Irene the priesthood was slipping through my fingers. If I'd stayed off that damn television programme I'd still be an accepted and admired member of the prebyterate. I wouldn't have had to turn to Irene.'

'Too simple, John,' Ace protested, his usually mobile face grim and sombre. 'You're at an age when almost anything could push you into a love affair. Don't blame the TV programme. And don't blame the family for your vocation. You didn't become a priest to expiate.'

'They've made a lot of sacrifices for me. I owe them something.' Before Ace could ask what that meant, John's personal phone rang. Reluctantly he answered it.

'Noele.' He tried to be bright and cheerful. 'Good to talk to you again. Sure, tomorrow night at eight o'clock? Far be it from me to interfere with the gymnastics meet. Everything okay?'

I'm so preoccupied with myself, he thought guiltily as he hung up the phone, that I forget the danger she could be in if those papers are ever published.

'Something's bugging her too,' he said to Dick McNamara.

'I wouldn't worry all that much about Noele.' McNamara smiled for the first time in their conversation. 'She may have some hard times ahead, but she can take care of herself.'

'And I can't?'

The Ace buried his head in his hands for a moment, searching for a response. 'What happens, John, is that either a man leaves the priesthood or he works the woman out of his system.'

'What will happen to me?'

'You'll survive; I worry about Irene, a beautiful and gifted woman who probably doesn't love her husband, and almost certainly feels she has wasted her life. Now she's in love with a man who is a surrogate for her dead lover.'

'I'm a surrogate for Danny?'

Ace turned in surprise from the bar, where he was pouring himself his third Irish whiskey. 'Certainly, John. You mean you haven't figured that out yet?'

Ace

He looked out the window of the tiny guest room in the rectory. The snow was beginning to melt under a quiet winter sun, one of the phoney thaws that would tease Chicago for the next two months. The asphalt on the Courts was still covered. No teenagers there today.

Poor John. At a crossroads in the priesthood. Faced by massive rejection from his colleagues and in love at the same time. Randy and romantic, obsessed with a foolish love and unaware that Noele was going to hit him with a massive two-by-four.

John was a survivor. Transparent, vain, generous, pompous, kind – and a survivor.

Again Ace wondered how such a family of self-preoccupied cowards could have produced a Noele.

Genetic mistake? Perhaps not. Danny was a Farrell too. He was not a coward. And not a survivor either. Despite the warmth of his room Ace shivered.

Why did all the Farrells have to turn away stubbornly from the possibilities life offered them and settle on such dull terms of respectability and social approval?

Roger would make the gubernatorial race look like an academic bore, John would turn an important career in mass communications into a fearsome battle with clerical culture, Irene would continue to bury her talent.

And Danny had died young because of some foolish notions of chivalry.

But they had not yet got to Noele.

Not yet, but she was weakening.

What a fool Irene had been to leave the story where Noele could read it. Almost as if she wanted to be caught.

Brigid

It took several days for the warmth of the Mexican sun to melt away her weariness. 'We're going to Acapulco,' Burke had said to her at supper on January second. It was not an idea for discussion or a suggestion. It was an order. She'd been too tired to argue.

Brigid had never learned to swim, and her fair skin blistered with the first ray of sun. But she loved to look at the sea, lying with Burke in the shade of their patio in a house in the hills overlooking the beach, holding hands like young lovers.

'The woman is not as young as she used to be,' she said, and sighed. 'It'll take at least another week before I'm ready to go home. I could lie here in the warmth forever.'

'Maybe we ought to, Bridie.' Burke sat up and leaned against the post supporting the canopy over their heads. 'Maybe it's time for you to relax and realize that the world won't rush in and destroy you if you stop working.'

'Give up the firm?'

'Retire, relax and enjoy. For most of your life you've been running – from a cruel father, and a cruel husband, and a cruel foster son who threatened to kill you. Farrell and Sons has never protected you from the demons, has it?'

'No, you're the only protection I have, Burke,' she said quickly.

'It's time to stop running, Bridie.'

'Is it, now?' she said hotly, her voice tinged with brogue. 'Should we stop running and let the truth catch up with us? I don't know about you, but I'm too old to go to jail. How can we relax with all the evil things we've done still on our consciences? I work to forget about them.'

'We could try to forget,' he said lamely. 'Travel . . . get away from Chicago.'

'Run out on the firm during a recession? And what about Noele? She's mine, the only grandchild I'll ever have. If the truth catches up – and, God help us, it might – who will protect her if I'm not there?'

'Stop thinking about that,' he said impatiently. 'The whole matter is closed.'

'Maybe it is and maybe it isn't,' she said furiously. 'All of us are bent on our own destruction. We're going to save the Almighty the task of punishing us by doing it ourselves!'

And then, sorry about her anger, she tried to compromise. 'Anyway, will you think this conversation a success if I promise you that I'll think very seriously about it?'

'An enormous success. One that I rarely expect in an initial conversation with you.'

She swung at him fiercely. 'You're a terrible man, Burke Kennedy.'

He grabbed her hand and held it. 'And you are a very soft and vulnerable woman, Bridie.'

'I know that look in your eye,' she said, pretending to escape. 'I know what you have on your mind.'

He slid the straps of her bathing suit off both her shoulders. 'Do you, now?'

The holiday had turned Burke into a young buck. He tugged savagely at her swimsuit.

Brigid was frightened by his hunger – and delighted. It was like the room in the Palmer House once again. A terrible, terrible man, no respect for a decent woman at all, she thought, sighing in abject resignation.

Thank God he still wants me. Dear God, don't take him away from me. Please don't. Not yet.

Not ever.

Despite the banter and the laughter and the pleasure under the cloudless sky, Brigid was as frightened as she had been on the cold winter morning when her father woke her up to send her away from her home forever.

Roger

The fire in his study fireplace had died down to embers. There was a black-and-white French Foreign Legion movie on television, to which he was paying no attention, but he was too physically exhausted to turn the set off. A gubernatorial candidate should have a remote control for his TV, he told himself.

Chicago was reeling under ten inches of snow. O'Hare was closed, and Irene's plane had been diverted to Minneapolis and then to Milwaukee. She had phoned from Milwaukee saying that she was boarding a bus that would bring her into the Chicago loop. There were only snow flurries north of the Wisconsin line. 'Don't wait up for me,' she'd said. 'I may not be home until noon tomorrow.'

'I'll wait,' he said briefly. He was both afraid of her return and eager for it.

'Suit yourself,' she had said, every bit as briefly.

It had been a terrible day. The 'Farrell for Governor' campaign headquarters had opened for its first full day of work. Channel 6's TV cameras discovered chaos, as its assignment editor knew it would. The telephones were out of order, the duplicating machine broke down, the door to the men's room was jammed shut, several boxes of mailing lists were mysteriously lost, the computerized research system was not functioning, the candidate himself was in everyone's way.

'Not a very good beginning, is it Dr Farrell?' asked a tall young blonde with a microphone in her hand.

'Republicans have the smooth beginnings, Ms Hennessey,' he had countered, chuckling, 'and Democrats have the strong endings.'

'Then you're predicting that you will be the next governor of the state of Illinois?' she demanded, doing her best to sound like a hardnosed news veteran.

She was a lovely young thing, fair Irish. Politics had its own slave markets. . . .

'Of course.' He chuckled again. Have to watch that. Not the same chuckle too many times. 'That's why I'm running. Now, if you'll excuse me, Maryjane, I must find out why no one thought of assigning an office to me.'

He smiled cheerfully, and he hoped handsomely, at the red light above the lens of the video camera, and waited till the red light flicked off. Then he winked at Maryjane Hennessey and said, 'I'm not sure anyone here knows what state this is.'

Five minutes later Mick and Angie came into his office, their faces as long as the Mississippi River.

They've found out about Joe Kramer.

'We've been hearing things on the street, Governor,' Mick said sombrely.

'Why the hell did you let those papers out of your office?' asked Angie.

Roger heard almost none of their arguments. His mind was elsewhere – worrying about Noele and Brigid and Irene. His wife wanted him to stay in the race. She did not know enough about the Marshal to be frightened of him. Perhaps he should withdraw.

Quit.

He hesitated. Prudence dictated that he withdraw. To stay in the race would be like trying to broad-jump the Grand Canyon.

'What is done is done, gentlemen,' he said crisply. 'I'm in this race to stay, whatever happens to those stolen papers. If someone wants to run as a write-in candidate in the primary, that's up to them. I'll stay in the race. If the governor uses those papers against me in the fall election, I'll stay in the race then, too. Is that clear?'

'It ain't going to help us,' said Mick grudgingly.

'I hardly thought it would.'

'You're staying in for keeps, no matter what the press says?' Angie asked.

'To the bitter, bitter end, Angelo.' It was a decision that he himself was making at that very moment. Damn Irene.

'Got to admire your guts, Governor,' Mick said. 'Maybe we can keep it out of the paper, and maybe with a few breaks you can turn it around even if it gets in the papers.'

Roger smiled benignly. 'Michael, it's your job to create the breaks!'

That afternoon he stopped in his office at the University before dropping in at cocktail hour to visit Martha Clay. There was a note on his desk saying that the provost had called. Roger returned the call promptly.

'I'm afraid we've run into a little snag in the case of Mrs Clay, Roger.'

'This has been a day for snags,' Roger said easily. 'You should have been down at my campaign office, Lawrence.'

He heard a dry little rasping laugh. The provost was not ready yet to officially acknowledge that a member of his faculty was actually running for governor.

'Three members of the Committee on Social Theory,' he began with the solemnity of one reading a papal encyclical, 'have submitted a memo to the dean with copies to me and to the president invoking the Shils report against Mrs Clay. I won't detain you, Roger, with the contents of the memo, but I'll be happy to send it to you in faculty exchange.'

Invoking the Shils report was like quoting scripture before an auto-da-fé.

'Don't bother, Lawrence. I'm sure I know what's in it without reading it. No discussion of Mrs Clay's work, high praise for the standards set for the University in the past, for the wisdom of the Shils report, and a warning about the too easy gift of lifelong appointments.'

Once Roger had asked at the round table whether Shils himself would have measured up to the standards of his sacred writ. There had been no laughter, no smiles, no reaction of any sort.

Blasphemy.

'As you know,' Lawrence continued sonorously, 'there is a tradition in this University of treating memos from the Committee on Social Theory with great respect.'

Respect? More like reverence. The members of the committee rarely published anything. And they rarely met classes. Rather, they existed in a lofty heaven of intellectual abstraction, and accepted as a matter of right the commonly held conviction that their physical presence alone brought the Univeristy so much distinction that it was only slightly inferior to Harvard. Their principal activity was meddling in the appointments of other departments in the name of maintaining the same lofty standards of academic productivity and teaching excellence that they maintained themselves.

'How important is this snag going to be?'

The provost hesitated. 'The president is quite disturbed by it, as you may imagine. Candidly, Roger, I'm not certain.'

Roger decided to play his high card. 'Lawrence, I find this outrageous. The government department at this University is distinguished and indeed internationally respected. The majority of the tenured faculty after mature deliberation has made a recommendation. The dean has approved this recommendation. I had an informal communication with you in which you told me you were disposed to transmit our recommendations favourably to the president. Now I'm told another unit of the University, unqualified in any way of which I'm aware to make judgements in the field of political science, has chosen to attempt to override our recommendation. I cannot be responsible, Lawrence, for the consequences of this situation.'

A brave idealist as a gubernatorial candidate and a shrewd manipulator working, with dubious motives, for the promotion of his lover. Maybe I would be for her, he told himself, even if I was not obsessed with her. It's a marginal case. There are no strong, positive reasons for expecting that she will be a distinguished or productive member of the University faculty. Yet with a little effort she could easily be as productive as several members of the committee.

'I understand your dismay,' said the provost, who had called to see whether Roger proposed to make trouble and learned that he did indeed propose to make trouble. 'I assume that you have reason to believe you are not speaking only for yourself?'

Roger laughed bleakly. 'You've been at this University for a long time, Lawrence. How the hell do you think government is going to react? Even those of us who had doubts about Mrs Clay will be furious.'

They would be furious only if Roger goaded them to fury, which he was perfectly prepared to do for the love of his mistress.

I am losing control, he told himself. I don't know what I'm doing anymore. I'm like a railroad engine that has jumped the tracks.

'I see,' said the provost.

When they met later in the afternoon, the mistress in question seemed both undismayed and unimpressed by Roger's account of the conversation. 'More hazing,' she said, relaxing comfortably in his embrace.

They had renewed their love affair; yet it was not quite the relationship it used to be. Was it that Martha's abandonment was a little less total? Or was he comparing her unfavourably to his wife?

Afterwards they were sipping white wine in her bedroom, partially dressed.

'Have you ever considered the possibility, Roger,' she said in her best academic tone, 'that you might have bisexual propensities?'

With considerable effort he managed not to choke on the white wine. 'I suppose that all of us are bisexual in part,' he said. 'You'd know more about that because you're more of a Freudian than I am.'

It was one thing for him to revel in kinky fantasies, and quite another for the young woman to catch him at it. What the hell kind of game was she playing now?

'Sometimes when you're making love to me' – she was as matter of fact and dispassionate as if they were discussing similarities in Machiavellian and Marxist theory – 'I sense you are thinking of me rather more as an attractive boy than as a woman. I'm liberated enough not to mind that; actually, I find it rather stimulating. But it is altogether possible, you know, that it would be healthy for you to seek some sexual release with members of your own sex.'

The rules of intellectualism demanded that he keep the discussion on the same abstract level on which she had placed it. 'It's a possibility, of course, and I'll certainly have to take your insight seriously. But I do indeed find you attractive as a woman, Martha. You can take that as a given.'

'Now you're being defensive, Roger. I'm not saying you're gay.' She permitted herself a tiny academic smile, rather like the provost's. 'I've had more than enough experience to know that you're not – even though, surely, there would be nothing objectionable if you were. I'm merely suggesting that you ought to explore the possibility that some sexual release with men might be morally beneficial for you. I know I'm not gay in any permanent sense of the word. Nonetheless my own lesbian interludes have been very constructive for me.'

Lesbian interludes, he thought derisively. You and someone in your consciousness-raising group played with each other's tits so you both could talk knowingly about 'gay sex.'

'I appreciate your candor on the subject, Martha. Let me give it some thought.'

'No need to report back to me.' Again the tiny, provostlike smile. 'More wine?'

The implication was that the homosexual tendency in his personality was so powerful that his mistress could not help but notice it. And if he had yet to experience sexual satisfaction with men, the reason was that he was more repressed and less liberated than she. An infuriating but also frightening suggestion. What if she were right?

And both the fact that she had challenged him and the possibility that the challenge might be valid undercut some of his love for her, as waves undercut a pine-covered bluff. Maybe that was what she intended to happen.

How much time had she spent over Christmas with her ex-husband? Or was he an ex? Was the divorce final?

As he waited for his wife by the light of the dying fire in his study, Roger considered the question of his hetero-sexuality – objectively, as a good full professor must. He enjoyed the all-male company of the round table of the Faculty Club. And the camaraderie of his golf partners at the Country Club. The only 'crush' he could remember in his life was Danny Farrell, and that relationship, while close and intense, had never been overtly physical.

Save in one incident.

And the crush had never ended. Even though Danny was dead.

He had to admit that he did find the physical appearance of handsome young men attractive although not, on the whole, nearly as attractive as the physical appearance of handsome young women. But maybe he was repressing?

No one could deny that in the Christmas week he had been quite heterosexual with his wife.

But he was ambivalent about continuing such activities.

He groaned aloud. Damn the woman. She'll be able to tell all her feminist bitch friends that I have an interest in young men, which, while not morally objectionable to her, made it very difficult for her to relate to me.

Was she looking for a way out?

And after I went out on a limb with the provost for her.

What a hell of a thing to think. The runaway engine is charging down the embankment.

'Good morning, Governor.' He was startled. He had fallen asleep. Irene was leaning provocatively in the doorway of his study in a beige suit that accentuated her glorious suntan.

She peeled off her jacket and flipped it playfully at him. 'You look like you want what your mother would delicately call a good fuck.'

He was overjoyed at the instant and spontaneous reaction of his body to her suggestion.

John

'Sorry to keep you waiting, Noele,' he apologized. 'It's been a busy night in the rectory.'

'No rush, Uncle Monsignor,' Noele said listlessly.

'When I was a young priest, we had orders to close down all rectory offices by ten-thirty and be in our rooms by eleven. Nobody would dare to begin a conversation at eleven fifteen.'

'Really?' she said, displaying almost no interest.

'And there was a diocesan rule that we were supposed to be in the rectory every night by eleven o'clock. A lot of people didn't keep it, but my first pastor insisted.'

Noele was momentarily disconcerted. 'Eleven o'clock? You mean you had to be in the rectory every night by eleven o'clock? Were you?'

'I didn't miss a single night in the first four years I was a priest. It had its advantages. I always had an excuse to get out of a boring meeting or party.'

Noele seemed very thoughtful.

'I'm sure you didn't come here to talk about old-fashioned clerical rules,' he said.

'I want to know who I am,' Noele said, her voice a sorrowful whisper.

'I don't understand. You're Noele Marie Farrell, daughter of Roger and Irene Farrell.'

'No, I'm not. You and Moms bought me from an out-of-work aerospace engineer in California when I was a baby.'

'Did your mother tell you that?' The words burst from John's lips.

'Of course not,' his niece replied haughtily. 'I *know*, Uncle Monsignor. And don't try to lie to me anymore. I *know*.'

'It's not as bad as it seems, Noele.' He groped for words of explanation about the past. 'And don't judge any of us too harshly.'

'Who is my mother? Who is my father?' she demanded.

'Curiously enough, Noele, your mother and father are your mother and father. We did buy you, but we bought you back from a couple who had adopted you. Please give me a chance to explain.'

Her swamp-fire eyes were pitiless. 'Explain.'

'As you probably guessed, your mother was in love with Danny Farrell. Your father was too. Not the same way, of course, but he worshipped the ground that Dan Farrell walked on. And when Danny died, well, your mother and father were drawn to each other. Then Roger went back to graduate school in Berkeley. And Irene simply disappeared. People in the neighbourhood thought that she'd had her fill of being ridiculed by her parents and by her brothers and sisters. She was carrying you then, Noele. Roger's child. But she felt that there wasn't any love between her and Roger. She also was afraid of the antagonism between her family and ours. So you were born in California, Noele, the daughter of a mother who could have easily ended your life with an abortion. She was afraid to tell anyone and was convinced that she would fail you as a parent. So you were adopted by a young aerospace engineer and his wife, who'd been told, erroneously, as it turned out, that they would not have any children. Do you understand?'

Noele was as grave as the bishop's master of ceremonies at a solemn pontifical Mass. 'So far.'

The words were coming quickly and smoothly now. 'Your mother and father met again in California. They bumped into each other at a peace rally at Berkeley and discovered that they did indeed love each other after all. It was a quick decision, I went to California to marry them. And then your mother told us about you.'

John rubbed his hand across his forehead. 'God in heaven, Noele, the three of us sat there at a cheap little Mexican restaurant in Berkeley and cried about you. We agreed that we had to find some way to get you back.

'I made some inquiries, found out who the family was, and discovered they were under tremendous financial pressure. It was a tough decision for everyone, Noele. What we did may seem terribly cruel to the couple who adopted you. We felt we had to do it.'

The green eyes were now awash with tears, the swamp fire extinguished.

'I didn't mean to make you cry,' John said wearily. 'But didn't it work out for the best? You were reunited with your mother and father who, it turned out, could not have any more children. The people who took care of you for the first ten months of your life later had four children of their own. He is now the president of his own electronics firm. He started the firm with the money –'

'With the money you gave him to buy me?' Tears were streaming down her face, but she was smiling.

'You are the one who must judge us, Noele. Forgive us if you can.'

'There's nothing for me to forgive.' She grinned at him, the bumptious director of the folk group again.

Lord, how resilient they are.

'And you're not angry?'

'How could I possibly stay angry at you, Uncle Monsignor?' She hugged him briskly. And then, almost as an afterthought, she added, 'One question though: Do you think Mother married Roger mostly so she could buy me back?'

A bolt of lightning across the night sky after the storm had cleared.

'She married your father, Noele, because she discovered that she loved him all along. And he discovered the same thing.'

Noele nodded solemnly. 'I suppose so.'

A few moments later, on his prie-dieu, the image of the happy youngster bounding down the steps and across the snow-covered street to her red car fresh in his brain, he prayed, 'Forgive me. She was sad, and I made her happy, just like we made Brigid happy with the same story. Isn't the truth often what we want it to be?'

Irene

She sat at her desk in a heavy robe staring hypnotically at the chilly winter landscape outside her window. It was fifteen below zero, a bitter cold mid-January day, even though the sky was clear and the sun deceptively bright.

She was still working on her story about the married woman who had an affair with her brother-in-law, who was a priest, a story that subtly explored the possibility that the two lovers re-enforced each other, the heroine's passion for the brother igniting a passion her heroine had never felt for her husband.

She opened her secret file and placed the typed pages neatly on her desk. Then she removed an old Cross pen from an austere holder in front of her. She read the first sentence of the manuscript and tried to replace a comma with a semicolon.

The pen was out of ink. She sighed, resenting as she always did the need to replace the cartridge. She opened the drawer in the centre of her desk and then sat up abruptly. Her short story 'The Buying of the Baby,' was in the drawer, underneath the spare keys to the Seville. It must have been there for weeks.

What a stupid and unthinking thing to do. Suppose Roger had read it. Or Noele. . . . She examined the pages very carefully. They seemed in order and, as well as she could remember them, in the same position in which she had left them in the drawer. But her memory for such things was poor. Anybody might have read the story.

Shivering, she slipped the manuscript into the leather case, restored it to the secret compartment of her desk, and returned uneasily to her story.

She was trying to write an intensely erotic tale without explicit description, all the more powerful in its sexuality, she hoped, precisely because there were no clinical details.

She reread the story with a critical eye, occasionally altering a word or inserting a sentence, until she reached the last page.

So she knelt in front of him and teased him lovingly. Numbed by physical exhaustion, guilt, and the worry of flying through a snowstorm, Lorraine was free of all restraint. 'I've never loved you as much as I love you tonight.' The words tumbled out of her mouth as if spoken by a stranger. Yet at that moment they were the total truth of her life.

In her small precise hand she wrote a new and final paragraph; she would retype the page later.

When they are young, men use love about which they know very little, to obtain sex, about which they know much. Women use sex, about which they know little, to obtain love, about which they know much. And as they mature, if they mature, most men and women are able to share in the perspective of the other. Neither Lorraine nor the two men whose needs she had used to anneal her pain would ever be anything but adolescents.

In fleeing from despair to sensuality, Lorraine had become a whore.

She reread the two paragraphs, pen in hand, and considered adding two final sentences, which were screaming inside her skull.

'Sensuality would depart soon. There would remain only despair.'

She scrawled wild circles across the page. A dishonest story. There was no mention of the fourth person in the parallelogram, the man Lorraine loved, the corpse who had her sealed up in his own unmarked tomb.

DCI

A bottle of beer reassuring his hand, the Director relaxed in front of his television to watch Notre Dame play George-town. Beer and basketball – hardly the image he had created for himself at the Company. But he'd played basketball in college and enjoyed the rich, New York accent of Al McGuire as he conducted a coaching seminar illustrating the mistakes of Digger Phelps and John Thompsen.

The red phone next to his chair rang. He sighed and picked it up. What were the Russians doing now?

'Radford, chief. Sorry to interrupt the game.'

How did Radford know he was watching the game? 'Yes,' the Director said crossly.

'I have some rather surprising information for you.'

Brigid

The family was arranged around the dinner table, with the exception of Noele, who had been excused to watch the end of the Notre Dame–Georgetown game and Jaimie's six-foot-eleven-inch black roommate, DeWitt Carlisle. (According to Noele they had stopped counting his I.Q. at 175, and he was totally cute.)

Brigid glanced around the table. The family was off-key again tonight. Irene solemn, John restless and hyperactive, Roger as moody as she had ever seen him, even Burke glum and unreadable.

Perhaps they all realized that they were skating toward the edge of the pit.

After John had led the grace, Brigid, mostly to placate Burke, made the suggestion that she retire from the firm and embark on a 'career change,' which meant, 'if I'm to believe my husband, that I'll make a career of doing practically nothing, but enjoying it all.'

'Now that's not fair, Bridie,' Burke said stiffly.

'I know it's not fair. But I'll confess to everyone that the prospect of spending another month or two in Mexico is extremely attractive.'

'Then what would you do?' John asked. 'You're a young woman, Mother, why retire from life?'

'The intention isn't that she retire from life, but merely from the firm. The firm isn't life,' Burke insisted.

'A rather shocking view to hear from you, Burke,' Roger said. 'Do you think Mother is ready to be a grand dame, wandering around on some world tour?'

'I think Burke feels that I'll stay a younger woman longer if I escape some of the madness of the firm.' Brigid knew that her sons would resist her retirement. 'And you, my dear?' She nodded at Irene, not altogether sure why, except that the woman had shown some spunk lately.

'Oh, I didn't know that I was supposed to vote. I think you should do exactly what you want to do, Brigid.'

'And what do you think that is?' she persisted.

'I think you want to do both.' Irene smiled faintly and then relapsed into the faraway world in which she spent so much of her time.

'A very perceptive answer.' Brigid looked around the room and prepared to tell her family exactly how she proposed to do both.

Noele entered the dining room. Ah, the child is beautiful, Brigid thought. And the peat shines in her eyes.

But there was something about the glow on her face and the brilliance of the fire in her eyes that stirred fear in the deep substratum of superstition that existed, rock hard, at the core of Brigid's personality.

'The game over?' Roger asked cheerfully.

'There was a news brief on television after the game ended,' Noele said, and Brigid heard the sound of fairy dance music in her voice. 'It will probably interest all of you. The American Embassy in Beijing has reported that the last American held prisoner in China has been released. He was an alleged employee of the Central Intelligence Agency, shot down on a U-2 flight in 1964. His name is Daniel Farrell, and his last known address was Chicago, Illinois.'

DANCE
SEVEN

Bolero

'Danced by one dancer or a couple, it includes many brilliant and intricate steps, quick movements, and a sudden stop in a characteristic position with one arm held arched over the head.'

Roger

The following week, after the Super Bowl game, there was a brief glimpse of Danny Farrell on the NBC Sunday Night News. Dressed in a grey suit, he stood in front of the American Embassy in Beijing, silver-haired, slender, smiling.

'He looks totally like Paul Newman. Look at those awesome eyes!' Noele exclaimed.

'Are you an employee of the Central Intelligence Agency, Mr Farrell?' asked the journalist who was interviewing him.

The lean, handsome face came alive; the blue eyes glowed. 'Of what?'

'The CIA,' the reporter insisted.

A wide leprechaunish grin lit Danny's face. 'Never heard of the organization. What does it do?'

'I mean, *really*, he has Paul Newman's eyes,' Noele insisted. 'Don't you think so, Grams?'

'Hush, child,' said the weeping Brigid.

'Is it true that you were flying a U-2 over China when you were shot down eighteen years ago?'

'That's what the local authorities say.'

'What were you doing in that plane, sir?'

'Taking pictures.'

'For whom?'

'For an American news magazine that I hear is dead now.'

'Do you feel, sir, like someone who's come back from the dead?'

'Nope, I feel like the rest of the world has come back from the dead. Me, I've been alive all along.'

'What have you been doing the past week, Mr Farrell?'

'Reading back issues of *Time* magazine.'

'Are there any changes in American society that disappoint you?'

'Sure are. The miniskirt is gone!'

'What kept you going through the years in Chinese prison?'

The leprechaun grin brightened. 'Religious faith.'

Jane Pauley was back on the screen. 'Farrell will return to the United States in the middle of the week for, as he puts it, conferences with the executives of the news magazine that went out of business a long time ago. Most Washington reporters believe that the conference will occur at the headquarters of the Central Intelligence Agency in Langley, Virginia.'

'Same old Danny,' John said, as though he could not believe what he had seen and heard.

'Is he?' said Roger thoughtfully. 'I wonder.'

Brigid was in tears. 'Would you look at the colour of his hair. Ah, the poor, poor boyo.'

'No, not a boy,' Burke said solemnly. 'Not anymore.'

Irene, looking like a widow at a wake, said nothing.

'I still think he looks like Paul Newman,' Noele said in a tone that refused to admit the possibility of disagreement. 'Really.'

DCI

Radford leaned back in his chair, loosened his tie, took out his handkerchief, and wiped his forehead. 'Chief, I know damn well you have a bottle of bourbon in that hidden cabinet in your desk,' he said. 'Pour me a double one. Neat, straight up, and quick.'

It was the first time that the Director had seen Radford even slightly rattled.

'Wonderland,' Radford said, gulping down half of the tumbler of the Old Fitz the Director had poured for him.

'Certifiably mad?'

Radford leaned forward. 'Let me put it this way, chief. If Dan Farrell had come back from that mission and if he'd stayed with the Company, he might have your job now, and all the rest of us might be locked up in an asylum.'

'Indeed,' said the DCI.

'I told him, of course, that we would consider that he has been on the payroll for the last eighteen years with a pay scale commensurate with the usual promotions plus the interest that would have accrued from investments over that period of time.'

'That's a big chunk of money,' the Director said nervously. 'What did he say to that?'

'He said, "Tom" – he either called me Tom or General all through our conversations – "Tom, that's not nearly enough to keep me quiet if I want to tell the whole story, and entirely too much if I don't."'

'Is he going to embarrass us?'

'He claims he won't. He asked who ordered his termination – he'd figured that out – and suggested that if the man was still around he ought to be fired because he'd made a mess of it.'

The DCI frowned. 'And this novel he's writing? Is it about us?'

'It's about an Irish Catholic family in Chicago. Not his own family, either, or so he says. He claims that he has every word of the novel in his head. That all he has to do is get to a typewriter to put it down. He also says that the Company won't be mentioned once. Then he added, with that funny laugh of his, "not in this novel, anyway, General."'

'What do our shrinks say? Was he brainwashed?'

'He didn't object to our using some hypnotism to probe into his unconscious. Apparently he was subject to no more pressures than anyone else in China during the Great Proletarian Cultural Revolution. The Chinese released him from prison seven years ago and sent him to a commune in Hunan province, where he was an agricultural worker and also a member of the local defence militia. It would seem that he was pretty well integrated into the society. He speaks Chinese fluently and is providing us with some interesting information about how the country works. The shrinks say he was able to make a reasonably satisfactory adjustment to a totally different culture and come out of it suddenly without any immediate or obvious trauma. They tell me that at one level he's a shrewd, flexible guy and that the comedy act is one of the masks he hides behind to survive, a life-long defence mechanism that happened to be very useful for the last eighteen years.'

The Director lifted the bourbon bottle from his desk and filled Radford's glass again. He also filled his own.

'What are the other levels?'

'The first one is the comedian, the stage mick and the phony brogue and the quick wink of the eye. Then there's talent approaching genius, a first-rate flyer, naval officer, and practically anything else he wants to be. But there's anger and fear at the core. It's the personality he went to China with and the one he came out with, and everything is intensified because of the China experience.'

'Anger at whom?'

'Currently at these two people.' Radford shuffled through a stack of colour photos of the Farrell family. The Director was once again amazed at how the Company could find pictures of people at a minute's notice. 'This is Burke Kennedy, his stepfather. Or, rather, his foster step-father. Married the aunt who raised him. Was her lover for years. A powerful and corrupt political lawyer. One of our shrinks says there's a rivalry there for the foster mother's love. Oedipal thing.'

There was a moment of silence as both of them pondered a possibility they did not want to articulate.

'And the other one?'

'This woman. Irene Conlon Farrell. He apparently loved her very much. She married his foster brother – cousin actually – after Farrell was shot down. The same shrink thinks he resents her betrayal.'

'An incredibly lovely woman. . . . Might he kill her?'

Radford nodded grimly. 'Might and then again might not. One of our men says that he is obsessed with vengeance, and the other says Farrell is the kind of person who copes with anger by diffusing it. Typical psychiatric report. They have it both ways. But the hypnotism indicates powerful anger at both of them.'

'We have a potential time bomb on our hands, then?'

'Probably a crisis down the road in a few months.'

'That's all we need.' The Director thoughtfully considered his glass of bourbon. 'What if he explodes on us in six months or a year?'

'And tries to bring us down in the explosion just like we tried to bring him down?'

'Precisely.'

'Maybe whoever tried to kill him before will solve our problem for us.'

Irene

Chris Wallace was interviewing Dan Farrell on the Washington segment of the *Today Show*. Irene watched, her heart beating rapidly, her mind trying unsuccessfully, as it had for the last two weeks, to make sense out of Danny's return and to decide how she should respond to him.

'Now, Mr Farrell,' said the boyishly handsome Wallace, 'you were flying a U-2 over Sinkiang when the aircraft malfunctioned. Aren't those aircraft normally operated by the Air Force or Central Intelligence Agency?'

'So they tell me,' Danny said brightly.

'And you're sticking to your story that you obtained one of those aircraft to take pictures?'

'That's what the planes are for, Chris.'

Oh, God, how many times she'd seen that impish smile. Especially when she tried to break through the protective layers of his personality. Their relationship had been the opposite of the ones she now had with his foster brothers. She listened to them talk about their problems. Danny listened to her, always the sensitive, sympathetic, tender friend. And when she tried to be a friend to him, he would flee, sometimes psychologically, with a wink and a grin, and sometimes physically, by disappearing for days or not writing from the Carrier for weeks. A woman could be his mistress, even his lover, but Danny took flight when she wanted to be his friend.

'And how did you obtain it?'

Danny winked. 'That'd be telling.'

'So you continue to deny that you were an employee of either the Central Intelligence Agency or the United States Air Force?'

'If I were a CIA employee, do you think I would admit it to you?' Danny asked genially.

When he smiled he looked healthy and happy. When his face was in repose, however, he seemed drawn, weary, distracted.

'Why do Irishmen always answer a question by asking another one?' Wallace asked.

'Do we really?' Danny responded.

'And you say that the novel that you composed in your head in China has nothing to do either with the Chinese prison camp or with the Central Intelligence Agency?'

'Not this novel, anyway.'

'Do you have a publisher yet?'

'Not yet. Know any good ones?'

'You've been home from China now for two weeks, more or less out of sight. Where have you been?'

'I was recuperating in a rest home in Virginia.'

'Near Langley?'

Danny smiled again. 'I think that's what they said the name of the town was.'

'And now your plans are to go home to Chicago and finish the novel. Will it be good to go home?'

'It sure will.'

'Did you ever come to enjoy it in China, Mr Farrell?'

There was a long pause. Danny's face filled the whole screen, blank and expressionless.

'Not for one single moment, Chris Wallace.'

'I wish you had stayed in China,' Irene screamed at the TV screen, and began to sob hysterically.

Brigid

'We've got to give him a chance, Burke. You saw him on television. He doesn't seem angry at all. And you heard him on the telephone today. It's the same old Danny.'

'That's exactly what I'm worried about, Bridie,' Burke said nervously. 'But I'm willing to wait and see. Emotions were running high that night, and it was a long time ago. Nevertheless, I'm going to keep a close eye on him. And I'm not going to let him or anyone else hurt you.'

'Promise you won't do anything without discussing it with me first.'

Burke hesitated.

'God damn it, Burke, promise me!'

He shrugged in resignation. 'All right, Bridie, I promise.'

'And' – she held her breath – 'promise me you won't even mention Clancy's death to him.'

'Why that promise?' He regarded her quizzically. 'Oh, all right. In a way, the boy did us a favour. And there never was any point in arguing with you.'

She sighed to herself. Now I must make Roger promise the same thing.

I'm so happy he's back that I could die from joy. And so worried that I could die from fear.

John

The Farrell brothers stood silently in the pastor's suite watching a snow plough clear the Courts, both of them wondering whether Danny would return to the scene of his former athletic triumphs.

'Will he still play basketball?' Roger asked absently.

'I suppose,' John murmured.

His relationship with Irene was certainly finished. Danny would replace him again, damn him.

'I hope he doesn't plan to move back into the neighbourhood,' Roger said, turning away from the window.

'Don't count on it,' John replied gloomily. 'You'll talk to him about whether we should meet him at the airport?'

Roger nodded. 'I'm getting a lot of free campaign publicity out of it. Angelo Spina says that money couldn't buy it.'

John laughed hollowly. 'I suppose that you've wished many times, just as I have, that he was still alive.'

'And now, just like you, I'm not so sure that it's a good thing.'

'Happy to have him back, of course.' John sank into one of his horrible, tasteless leather chairs. 'Make you a drink?'

'Not now, thanks. Oh, sure, happy to have him back. God knows it will be great to see him.' Roger beamed enthusiastically, and then quickly became sombre again. 'And afraid of the disruption.'

'Primal chaos,' John agreed. 'And we don't know what the new creation will be. If any.'

You have a wife to lose. And maybe I . . .

'Irene is taking it well,' Roger said thoughtfully.

'Oh?'

'She seems quite self-contained. Doesn't mention him. Noele does all the talking.'

'That young woman will bear watching,' John warned.

'You're telling me.'

Noele

Noele was totally edged.

I mean, I didn't think he'd be *short*. Sure he looks like Paul Newman – blue eyes, curly silver hair, cute baby face. But I never expected he'd be like, *short*.

Really!

Not as short as she was – 'almost' five four – but maybe only an inch taller than Moms, who was five eight. She sighed. And he kind of scrunches down in that grubby old jacket so he looks even shorter. I'll have to do something about his posture.

Noele decided she would call him Daniel save on those occasions when it was time for him to 'act right.' Then he would be called Daniel Xavier.

Danny had asked by telephone that his family wait for him at their home rather than meet him at O'Hare. By the time the taxi pulled up in front of the old house, he had shed the mass media.

But Noele watched the reunion with an eye that was as penetrating as the lens of a TV camera.

First Brigid, both of them crying, both of them cooing words of endearment in an Irish brogue. Daniel Xavier was a bit of a fraud, but he knew how to cope with Grams – lay it on thick, real thick.

Sometimes his eyes were not Paul Newman's. Nor Robert Redford's, either. Kind of like someone old, the man who was Lawrence of Arabia on the late-night movie.

Then a warm handshake for Burke. 'Congratulations to you, Burke. Sorry I couldn't be here for the ceremony, but I had some business out of town.'

They didn't like each other very much, Noele decided. And maybe they still don't.

Then an embrace, from a quarterback playing his last game, for Monsignor John. 'And, Brigid, now you have a son that's a monsignor and himself a television personality and the pastor of our parish, too. Jackie, it's good to see you again. I hope you'll give me a few weeks before you draft me into service as head usher.'

And, of course, you'd be his *head* usher.

'Things have changed in the church, Danny.' Uncle Monsignor was not his usual suave self. He stumbled over the words. 'You could be head lector at Mass. Or a leader of song, like Noele.'

'Not much money in that, is there?'

It was an act, Noele decided, carefully planned, well executed, and not meaning a thing. Underneath all the congeniality and charm there was another Daniel Farrell who had to be watched. He gave himself away when his eyes glowed intermittently, like the brights being clicked on and off by a driver on a country road at night.

He was nervous and frightened and lonely.

And angry too.

He kissed Moms's hand, and she blushed deep red, something she almost never did. 'Irene, you're more beautiful than ever. I'll have to confess that coming down in the cab I hoped and prayed that you and herself here would not have grown too old. Now I see that the two of you have both improved with time, like the best of French burgundies.'

Oh, *barf*!

'If you think that about me,' Moms said, still blushing, half pleased, half angry, 'it must be because you haven't seen an American woman in a long, long time.'

Daniel laughed enthusiastically. 'I sure haven't, but even the ones I have seen don't compare to you, Irene. And Roger' – an embrace for him almost as enthusiastic as for Grams – 'the next governor of the state of Illinois. I always knew you'd come to no good – a politician with a Ph.D. I hope you find your old cousin a cushy job where he doesn't have to do an honest day's work for the rest of his life. Hey, I'm not even registered in the state anymore. Can a man come back from the dead and vote in a primary election?'

'I'm sure we can get the board of election commissioners to work something out for you,' Roger said. He was the only one in the room who was genuinely happy. He must really have liked Danny when they were kids together.

And now it's my turn. Be cool, Noele, she quoted DeWitt Carlisle's favourite instruction to her.

'I can't really believe that this beautiful queen out of an ancient Irish legend is my niece,' Danny began.

'Cousin,' Noele corrected him.

He tilted her chin back and brushed his lips against hers. Noele felt very weak in the knees.

'I'm told I owe you a very great debt of gratitude, flame-haired Irish goddess.'

For one of the few occasions in her life Noele was speechless.

'How so?' Roger asked him.

'If that Company for which I didn't work is telling the truth, Noele talked to her boyfriend, who talked to his father, who's a congressman, who talked to the president of the Company, who had one of his aides talk to the Chinese. I think I already resent the boyfriend, by the way.'

'I talked to the congressman myself,' Noele flared, feeling her face grow very warm.

'You didn't tell us that, honey,' Brigid protested.

They were not altogether pleased with her.

'I didn't think it was A.G.B.D.,' Noele replied, trying to regain her balance and finding it very difficult as long as he kept his stubborn forefinger gently on her chin and stared admiringly into her eyes.

'A.G.B.D.?' Danny asked, his fingers caressing her chin. 'Isn't that the Jesuit motto?'

'No, that's A.M.D.G. A.G.B.D. means "any great big deal."' I am, like, totally jazzed, she told herself. Really phased out.

'Of course not. No great big deal. Just get the battered old cousin out of China, a small good deed before supper-time.' He winked at her wickedly.

'Really,' she stammered.

Noele recovered some of her cool by the time her family gathered around the dinner table and turned the TV camera in her head back on.

Roger was indeed the only one who was completely pleased at Daniel's return. Burke was wary and suspicious. Brigid was uncharacteristically anxious. John's eyes were darting nervously, and Moms was still blushing. You're a strange man, Daniel Xavier Farrell. You've come home and disturbed all of these people's lives. I'm not sure they think I did them a favour at all by talking to Congressman Burns.

'What are you planning to do now that you're back, Danny?' Burke asked.

'Try to stay out of trouble, counsellor,' Daniel said, and wolfed down the mashed potatoes as if he were trying to make up for the eighteen years of not eating them.

'Don't talk when you have food in your mouth,' Noele told him.

He winked mischievously at her, but finished the potatoes.

'Are you going to live in the Neighbourhood?' John asked pointedly.

'I've got a room down at the Drake, though I'm told the Mayfair Regent or the Ritz-Carlton are the places to stay. I thought I might rent one of those old houses over on Mandrake Parkway or Dalton Road while I'm working on my novel.'

'Whitehall,' Noele said.

'Huh?' Danny's fork was poised over a second helping of potatoes.

'Really cool people stay at the Whitehall.'

'See how much I'm learning!' He plunged into the potatoes.

'Do you have a publisher?' Moms asked eagerly.

'Sure.' His eyes zoomed quickly around the table as if to drink in her face. 'That was the reason for doing the *Today Show*. There was a publisher on the phone by noon; I showed him the first thirty pages that I'd written out, and he gave me a contract and an advance on the spot. I'll finish the book here in the neighbourhood and then decide what to make of the rest of my life.'

'Then you probably will move elsewhere?' Uncle Monsignor seemed eager to get rid of Danny.

'You'll have a lot of catching up to do,' Grams said.

Daniel put his potato fork down.

'Look, I'm not thinking of trying to catch up, and I'm not thinking of beginning again where I left off eighteen years ago.' He was anxiously rubbing his fingers against one another, struggling to keep his tension under control. 'It will take time for me to get used to being alive again. All of you go on living your own lives and don't worry about me.' He grinned boyishly. 'Of course, you can cook me supper occasionally with lots of roast beef and potatoes, Bridie, Irene, and you, too, Noele. You know how to cook?'

'I'm sure, Daniel Xavier.'

'*I'm sure*,' said Moms, laughing nervously, 'is a warning sign. Proceed further at your own risk.'

'Mo-*ther*,' Noele howled.

'And when you call me Daniel Xavier, does that mean I'm about to get in real trouble?'

'It means,' she snapped, 'that you'd better start acting right.'

Everyone laughed except Noele, who didn't see what was so funny.

'I really mean what I said,' Danny went on, waving his hands expansively, like the Pope giving a blessing. Or maybe absolution. 'For me it's a completely new life. For you, it's life as usual. And neither should interfere with the other.'

Everyone around the table murmured agreement and approval and relief. Everyone, that is, but Noele.

Fat chance, she thought.

He left for his room at the Drake before anyone else was ready to depart. 'I have a lot of sleep to catch up on,' he explained.

He touched Noele's long red hair at the doorway. 'Never in my wildest dreams in China did I expect to come home to find such a gorgeous young woman in the family.'

'Really,' Noele huffed, but her knees were wobbly again.

And you don't erase the past that easily, Daniel Xavier. No way, José. We're going to see a lot of you.

And there's going to be a lot of trouble.

Ace

He leaned on his broom. 'Well, MN, have you found your identity now that your cousin is home?'

'Geek,' she responded. 'And stop loafing. I'm not going to do *all* the cleaning up after your teenagers.'

As veep of the High Club, Noele was responsible for the clean-up crew that collected the broken Coke bottles and swept up the mess at the end of the evening after the five hundred adolescents deserted the parish hall for Red's and other hot-dog stands around the neighbourhood.

In the old days the priest didn't have to work. That was before the Vatican Council and Noele Farrell.

'What's he like?'

'You KNOW.'

'Yeah, but I want to hear your opinion. . . . All right, all right, I'm pushing the broom.'

'WELL, he's SHORT!'

'You're not exactly a Valkyrie, MN.'

'Be SERIOUS. . . . Anyway, he's also sweet and cute and funny and nice and about as mature as Micky Kelly.'

'Eileen's little brother?'

'No, he's even less mature.'

'Uh-huh. And how did the rest of the family react?'

'Totally weird. Burkie and Grams are afraid, Moms is embarrassed, John twitches a lot, and Roger acts kind of goofy. I think they all wanted him to be alive and now, like, wish that he had never come back.'

'A lot of mystery still?'

'Don't stop sweeping. . . .' They were pushing their two brooms together. 'He doesn't know who he is, so how is his coming back to help me find out who I am?'

'You mean that if you solve the mystery, Danny will grow up and you will know who you are too.'

'I mean' – she pounded the broom against the wall –'we'll know why all the Farrells are so geeky.'

I'm not sure, Dick McNamara thought, I want to know why.

Brigid

Danny was on his second helping of watercress soup at the L'Escargot restaurant in the Allerton Hotel. 'I can't get over how classy this city has become,' he said between gulps of the soup. 'I'll have to take your word for it, Burke, that this was an elite French restaurant when it was over on Halsted. My generation didn't go to elite French restaurants on Halsted or anywhere else. We didn't know much about good wine either.'

He put down the soup spoon long enough to sip the Chenin Blanc Burke had ordered. 'Watercress soup and Chenin Blanc and the Allerton, which used to have a cafeteria in the basement for high school kids. I tell you the city's getting elegant. New buildings, new hotels, new people. . . . It's great to be back!'

L'Escargot was Brigid's choice, even though Danny had requested home-cooked meat and potatoes. She had learned to cultivate a taste for French food, and L'Escargot was her favourite bistro, as she called it. The restaurant's blond wood, the easy friendliness of its staff, and the medium buzz of conversation protected her from the feeling of being intimidated, as she was in other French restaurants.

'Some of them other places,' she insisted, 'are like high-class funeral homes. You're afraid to talk because you might say something vulgar.'

She and Burke were beginning to relax under the glow of Danny's persistent charm. The crisis had not passed yet, but Brigid was hopeful now that it would be manageable.

'And I can't get over the way you look, Bridie. You must have one hell of a sex life; that's the only way I can explain how you're more gorgeous than you were eighteen years ago.'

That cracked Burke up. 'Ah,' he said, faking an Irish brogue, 'sure, the woman's a good lay.'

Brigid felt her face grow hot. 'Shush, now. Both of you. That's locker-room talk and not to be heard in the presence of a decent woman in a public place.'

'Go on with you,' Danny said. 'Decent woman or not, you're pleased as punch to hear two men talking about you that way.'

'You shouldn't be so explicit. 'Tis a shocking bad use of language,' she persisted.

'It's worked out so far,' said Burke. 'Of course, you can't tell what the woman will be like a month from now. She works too hard. Maybe you'll join me in trying to persuade her to resign from the firm and live like a person of leisure.'

'Ah, I can see her in the Doge's palace or the Uffizi or the Louvre. Of course, you'll have a hard time, Burke, keeping her from eating popcorn.'

'Both of you shut your flannel mouths,' Brigid ordered, by no means displeased with the flattery.

Burke explained briefly the condition of the firm and the reasons he was urging Brigid to retire and the possible arrangements of administering the firm after her retirement.

'It'll all be yours, Danny, someday. We've taken good care of it,' she said, suddenly feeling sad for all the suffering of the years.

He did not respond to what she had said. 'Ah, no . . . no more wine. I promised that if I got out of China I'd only drink wine and not much of that.'

'And who did you promise?' Brigid asked.

'God, who else?'

Danny walked to Holy Name Cathedral every morning, even in the sub-zero January cold, to go to Mass, behaviour she would not have expected from him, not even after eighteen years in China.

'Would you ever be interested in becoming president of the firm?' Burke asked tentatively. 'The woman, of course, would have to approve, but it does make sense. It isn't a full-time job, at least not necessarily. You could write your book and still have a bit of an active business life, too.'

Danny did not look at either of them directly. 'Can I take a rain check for a few months?'

'There's no rush,' said Burke soothingly. 'Think about it.'

'I will, though I have to think about dessert first.'

'At least you didn't say no,' Brigid observed, watching him closely.

Danny grinned up at her mischievously. 'That I didn't, woman; that I didn't.'

'Do you trust him now?' she asked Burke anxiously as they drove home in their Mercedes through the quiet and bitterly cold streets of Chicago.

'He was really your favourite, wasn't he?' Burke said. They were silent for a moment; then he continued. 'What's done is done, Bridie; we weren't responsible, and there would have been no good of us doing anything after it happened.'

'Then why don't you trust him?'

'I'll tell you why. When I was in Sicily before the war, I drove to the foot of Mount Etna. There was a little whiff of smoke curling up from its cone. Peaceful, even charming smoke. How could anything that mild be a threat? Then you realized that at any time, without a bit of warning, that goddamned mountain was going to blow its stack.'

Burke

Burke searched in the dark for his sleeping wife's breast, found it, and touched it lightly. She sighed contentedly.

After a certain age, on some nights, even the small pleasures of a woman were almost unbearably sweet.

Slipping under the thin cover of lace, he moved his fingers softly against her flesh, brushing against a nipple, but very gently so as not to wake her. She was so tired.

And for a minute or two there was only peace.

Not enough peace to permit sleep, however. He had forgotten how likable Danny was. There had always been a rivalry between the two of them, lover and favourite son. Yet it had been hard to resent Danny, even in the old days.

And now he was a brave man returned from a living hell and still able to laugh.

Yet behind that laugh, underneath Danny's smooth urbanity, Burke was convinced that there was terrible anger, a pent-up rage repressed for almost two decades and about to explode like a boiler whose safety valve was clogged.

Much of that anger, Burke assumed, was directed at him. It could be seen lurking behind those twinkling silver-blue eyes. Yet there were times when he looked away from Brigid, as though he could not stand the sight of her. She trusted him completely and was utterly defenceless against him.

Her nipple was now hard at his fingertip. A little more pressure, and she would awaken, aroused and ready for him. He moved his finger away. Her sleep was more important than his lust.

Love and lust, how they intertwined. Long ago he gave up trying to separate them in his reaction to her.

But he did love her and would destroy anyone who was a threat to her.

I don't trust him. I never will.

He eased her nightgown back into place and turned over to face away from her, his imagination filled with a grim vision: two wild beasts pawing in a forest clearing, waiting for the other to attack.

Noele

Flame did not like cold weather any more than Noele. So he slid and squished in protest down Jefferson Avenue as she tried to combine automobile safety, a subject on which she was obsessive, with the need not to be late for school. Then at Ninety-third Street she saw Danny, in an old Windbreaker and summer jeans, labouring against the wind as he ploughed through the partially shovelled side-walks.

'Daniel Xavier Farrell, what are you doing out there in a morning like this without a hat or a proper coat on?'

'Can I have a rid, Mother?' He grinned wickedly at her.

'You get in Flame this minute,' she told him. When he was in the car she demanded, 'Don't you have enough money to buy a car or a proper coat?'

'To tell you the truth, pretty cousin, I never want to see a quilted coat again. And as for a car, what do you think I ought to buy?'

'I tell Moms,' she said promptly, 'that she's silly to be driving a Datsun when she can afford a Porsche. Moms really loves sports cars. Kind of weird. Doesn't fit her personality. Anyway, why don't you buy a Porsche and take her riding with you?'

Out of the corner of her eye she could see that she'd embarrassed Danny. So maybe he was still in love with Moms after all these years. That was yucky.

'I've been so busy pounding away on my book that I haven't had time for the really important things, like buying a car. Will you come with me and help me buy a Porsche?'

'Really!'

'Fine.' Danny leaned back in his seat and relaxed. 'Driving a Porsche will be almost as much fun as driving a U-2.'

'I hope you don't crack the car up too,' Noele said, and sniffed like a mother whose son had destroyed a bicycle.

'I didn't really crack it up,' he said easily, as though he were totally unfazed by Noele's hunt for information. 'The plane flamed out, which means the jet engine stopped working. Then I tried to eject. The ejection mechanism didn't work either. That was the bad news. The good news was that the destruct mechanism, which was supposed to go off sixty seconds after I ejected, also didn't work; and the MIGs that came up after me couldn't shoot straight, so I glided the thing down on land in one of their deserts. It doesn't have wheels you know, it lands on slides.'

'Sure, you dropped the wheels after you'd taken off.' Noele knew all that there was to know about the U-2. 'But it wasn't an accident, then?'

'That's right. The people at the Honourable Company claim that a termination order had been given on me. That means that the mission security chief in Japan, acting on Washington's orders, or so he said, told the technicians that I was no longer a useful employee of the Company. So they sabotaged the plane, and I was supposed to be killed. I think maybe one or two of the technicians had their doubts and gave me a fighting chance.'

Noele was outraged. 'How dare they give such an order?'

'Oh, they might have done it if they thought I was selling information to somebody who was our enemy then. But the men who run the Company now say there were never any instructions from Washington to terminate. The mission security chief made up the order on his own. They say he retired a few months later and moved to Mexico, where he lived far beyond any income that the Company knew he had. I kind of think this crowd is telling the truth, though you never can tell about the Honourable Company.'

'You mean that somebody paid him to get rid of you?' Noele could scarcely believe her ears.

'It kind of sounds that way.' Danny shrugged philosophically, like a man whose horse had quit halfway through the race. You win some and you lose some.

She turned off Glenwood Drive and up Mandrake Parkway, carefully negotiating the slippery street to the top of the hill. She stopped Flame in front of the old stucco house Danny had rented.

'Don't you realize that whoever tried to kill you once might try again?'

'You're reading too many mystery stories, Noele.'

'It was not a fictional killer who paid off the mission security chief.'

'I suppose not,' Danny Farrell agreed indifferently.

'Daniel Xavier,' she said, thumping Flame's steering wheel, 'you simply have to grow up. You should buy neat clothes and live a regular life and stand up straight and not feel sorry for yourself and care about whether someone tries to kill you and –'

'Do you order Jaimie Burns around that way?'

'Airhead.' She hit his arm, hard. 'And anyway, Jaimie doesn't need to be told to act like a grown-up.'

'Why do you care about me?' he asked softly, almost as if there were tears in his voice.

'Because you're my cousin, and we thought you were dead but you're not.' She was unaccountably running out of breath. 'And I want to keep you alive, that's why.'

'Angry at me?'

She thumped the steering wheel again. 'Tell me about it. You're impossible.'

'Your family could have told you that long ago.'

He kissed her lightly, slipped out of the car, and shuffled through the snow to his house, head down, shoulders bent.

She was going to be late for school. That didn't matter. The poor dear man needs me.

It was several minutes before her face stopped burning and she was able to turn over the ignition key and stir a reluctant Flame back into action.

Roger

'If you would dress up in something besides a Windbreaker and a sweater,' Roger said, 'I could take you to lunch in one of our more elegant clubs, or a swinging place like the East Bank.'

Danny, who as a young man could not walk into a room without attracting attention, had drifted around the Farrell for Governor headquarters without anyone noticing him. The years in China had taught him the art of being invisible. 'Let's go somewhere and grab a hamburger,' he said. 'I'm not up to fancy eating clubs yet.'

It was a mid-February false spring day. Temperatures had soared to the fifties. The ice and snow were melting.

Secretaries were eating their lunches on the benches in the Dearborn Street plazas. A few musical groups had turned up to provide lunch-hour entertainment and prove that summer could not be all that far away. For once Danny's disreputable Windbreaker suited the weather.

He strolled with Roger along Dearborn, commenting about the transformation of the street since he had seen it last. He chuckled at the Miro and laughed outright at the Picasso across the street in the Daley Civic Centre, which in the Byrne administration, Roger explained, was usually called the Chicago Civic Centre.

'Himself was taken in on that one,' Danny observed. 'He fell for Picasso's joke. But then I suppose if you have to fall for somebody's joke, it might as well be Picasso's.'

It had been a tense morning at campaign headquarters. Mick Gerety, his face as long as the Tri State Expressway, was waiting for Roger in his office. The 'Kramer Papers' had fallen into the hands of one Rodney Weaver, the editor of a small weekly magazine called the *Chicago Informer*. Weaver, a 1960s liberal, was agonizing about whether or not to publish the papers.

'That means he'll wait until after the primary,' Mick said gloomily. 'And then the rest of the Chicago media, which haven't touched the story so far, will have to report the *Informer* story.'

In Roger's opinion the story was going to come out eventually anyway, and it was probably just as well to get it out in the open immediately after the primary instead of right before the November election. By summer the issue would be not his family history but the governor's incompetencies.

Gerety was still grumpy. 'There may be some question of the soundness of your judgment in putting that stuff in writing in the first place.'

Somewhere deep inside Roger's brain a demon was advising him to get out of the race now and return to the gentle indolence of the round table at the Faculty Club. How in the hell had he gotten mixed up in such a roughhouse?

'We'll just have to fight it out. That's all, Mick. And by

the way, how did you like me with Radigan again last night?'

'You were tough, Governor,' Gerety admitted grudgingly. 'And you're going to have to be tough.'

Tim Radigan was a gravel-voiced news commentator on one of the radio stations, a choleric and obtuse shanty Irishman whose sense of fairness had disappeared with the 1933 Century of Progress World's Fair.

How long can I continue to be tough? Roger wondered.

He had thought about confiding in Danny, but that would have meant discussing Danny's mother's death and his own father's death. Roger wanted to touch neither subject.

They walked farther down Dearborn Street. Danny howled with joy at the sight of the great red Caldar mobile in the Federal Building Plaza. He left Roger behind and ran over to embrace one of its great scarlet arms.

'She's one of the most beautiful of her species I've ever seen!' he exclaimed, his voice faking religious awe.

'And what species is that?'

Danny turned to him in feigned astonishment. 'Why, of course, she's a rare, benign, red tarantula, isn't she?'

'Most Chicagoans think she's a flamingo.'

They bought a hamburger at a small shop across from the Dirksen building and then found a bench in the plaza. 'What the hell's eating you, Danny?' Roger asked bluntly.

'Fear,' Dan mumbled through a mouth filled with hamburger and bun. 'I'm scared silly, Roger; haven't you figured that out yet? There hasn't been a night since I left China that I haven't wished that I'd wake up the next day and find myself back in that commune. It wasn't a nice place, but you didn't have to make any decisions. And you didn't have to take care of yourself.'

'You give a great imitation of not being afraid,' Roger said, squeezing the last bit of catsup out of its little plastic bag and over the remaining half of his hamburger.

'Hey, remember me? Danny Farrell, the inseparable buddy of your youth? Of course I put on a good act. Even eighteen years in China couldn't change that. Just the same, I'm scared shitless. Maybe I shouldn't have come back to the Neighbourhood and reopened all the old wounds. I don't know.'

He finished his hamburger and wiped his fingers on a paper napkin, which he jammed with the rest of the debris into the pocket of his Windbreaker.

Roger hunted for words and couldn't find them.

'You have nothing to worry about, Roger.' Danny hunched over and stared at the plaza concrete. 'Brigid and Burke asked me about taking over the firm. But there's not a chance of that. I'd go to pieces the first time I had a tough decision to make. And what you and Renie and Noele have going is too perfect for me to spoil. I'll never mess with that. Or anything else. Maybe I ought to get out of here. My publisher says he can find me an apartment in the Big Apple, as it's called these days.'

'An apartment with a built-in woman?' It was the sort of crack Roger would have made twenty years ago.

Danny's laugh this time had a touch of bitterness in it. 'I wouldn't know what to do with one, Roger. I got out of the habit. Anyway, remember what I said: I'll never interfere with anything in the family. That's all over and done with.'

'As Harry Truman said, Danny, never say never, because never is a long time.'

'I guess.' He frowned and then dismissed the length of time that never might be with an obvious change of subject. 'Hey, what were the 1960s like, I mean, after I left? I keep reading about them, but I can't get a fix. You were an idealist then, and you are one now. You haven't changed.'

'I was out of it for a long time, Dan. The disillusionment after 1968 was terrible. We thought then that politics mattered. But when everyone was killed and the war went on anyway, all of us, the radicals and the liberals and even the Catholic moderates like myself bugged out. And now some of us are coming back in, but we're still walking on eggshells.'

'Don't bug out this time, Roger. You'll never have peace with yourself if you do.'

'And you're the one who uses fear as an excuse,' he shot back.

Danny cocked a quizzical eyebrow. 'A point for your side, Roger. But don't do as I do; do as I say.'

And Roger heard the sound of an escape hatch clanging shut.

He left Danny to return to his office at the University to pick up his mail. There was a note from Lawrence promising a decision in the Mrs Clay matter any day. Martha Clay was at a woman's social science meeting in Davenport, which seemed to Roger a strange place for radical feminist scholars to assemble. He missed her, even though he was now longing for the end of their relationship. The sting of pressure was too great to give up, yet he longed to be free of it.

Since Danny's return, his relationship with Irene had returned to its old familiar pattern of occasional and restrained passion.

Conversation at the dinner table that night was dominated, as usual, by Noele. And her subject, as usual in recent weeks, was Danny. She approved 'totally' of his new Porsche. But his clothes and his posture and his attitude toward life were still 'geeky.' Roger glanced at Irene occasionally to see how she was reacting to their daughter's fascination with Danny. But Irene did not seem even to notice it.

After dinner Roger worked on a campaign speech for a while and then resolved that this was the time to say things to Irene that he knew he had to say, no matter how difficult it might be. She was lying in bed reading the latest Book-of-the-Month Club novel when he entered their bedroom. A patronizing comment about her literary taste died on his lips, as patronizing comments had been dying for some time now. And her Bonwit's eroticism had become unbearably appealing.

He sat on the edge of the bed. 'Mind a few minutes of serious talk?' he asked tentatively.

She folded the dust jacket into the book, put it aside, and removed her reading glasses. 'The BOMC judges left their taste outside the door when they chose this one.'

'There's no good way to begin this, Irene. So I'll begin it the only way I know how. Do you want me to move out?'

'Of the house?' She was astonished.

'No, I mean out of our bedroom.'

'Oh.'

'We should have talked about this before, you know.'

'I know, Roger,' she sighed. 'I admire your courage in bringing it up. But nothing has changed, has it? Danny is confused and frightened and uncertain, and I think not a bit interested in me.'

'I suppose not. But I want you to know, Irene, that you are perfectly free to do whatever you want to do.'

Irene lay back on the pillows watching him intently. 'Do you love Danny so much that you're willing to give up your wife to him?'

Roger winced, as if someone had plunged a knife into his chest. 'I suppose I deserve that, Irene, but it's not altogether fair. I love you so much that I value your freedom more than my own happiness.'

She sat up and took his hand. 'Forgive me, darling, for being a bitch. I knew that's what you meant.'

'I do love you, Irene,' he said passionately, the fervour of Christmas Eve returning. 'And I'll always regret it took me so many years to find out how much you deserve to be loved.'

'That's very beautiful, Roger,' she said, tears forming in her eyes. 'It took me a long time to discover you, too.'

She pressed his hand against her breast and he caressed it gently. For a few seconds the sweetness of their contact was almost unbearable. Then she released his hand, and he withdrew it from her smooth skin.

So quickly did the fires die out.

Could he really give her up?

Would it be up to him to choose?

Irene

She encountered Danny for the first time without other members of the family in the supermarket on Ninety-fifth

Street. He wore an obviously new blue and gold Notre Dame Windbreaker.

'I see that Noele at least persuaded you to wear a proper jacket,' she said to him as he was trying to make a decision between brands of frozen orange juice. 'Don't buy either of those, Danny. It's much better in the bottle.'

He smiled shyly. 'Maybe I could hire you as a shopping adviser.'

'I'm surprised you even have time to shop. You're so involved with your novel that we don't see much more of you than we did when you were in China.'

'You can see plenty of me this Saturday night. I let John talk me into appearing on his TV programme. What's happened to my two foster brothers, or cousins, or whatever I should call them? Roger's running for public office and turns out to be a feisty candidate. John's thumbing his nose at church authorities and apparently enjoying it.'

'And to make the turn-about complete, you've become a recluse.'

Danny terrified her. His eyes dominated her whenever they were together, sometimes undressing and stroking her, other times ripping her to pieces in cold, vengeful fury.

God knows he had reason to hate her.

But worse than the hatred was the mixture of anger and affection. He cannot make up his mind about me, Irene thought. But no matter which he decides, I'm defenceless.

And she liked the terror of her defencelessness. At least she still mattered to him.

He put his hands in the pockets of his Windbreaker and bowed his head. 'What's over is over, Irene,' he said softly.

'I understand.'

But you don't really mean it, do you, Danny? You may kill me. You may make love to me. You may do both, but it's not over.

'Sometimes I think it would have been better if I'd stayed in China.'

'Never!' The word exploded from her lips.

He grinned sheepishly. 'You sound like Noele.'

'Someday, Danny, you're going to have to write a novel about what it's like to come back from the dead.'

'Maybe. Do you still write, Irene?'

'A little bit.'

'Can I see it?'

'If I can see your novel.'

'I'll think about that. You're not in it, Irene.' And there was murderous rage in his eyes.

'I'm disappointed,' she said, fighting to keep an answering burst of anger under control.

'Am I in your stories?'

Her anger melted. Make up your mind about me, please, Danny.

'Of course you are.'

Roger

'Do you want to lay down the rules, Maryjane?' Roger ushered Danny and the reporter into a booth in the River-view Room of the East Bank Club. The frozen North Branch of the Chicago River shone in sub-zero winter sunlight, a rough sheet of uncut crystal.

'Sure, Governor.' She ticked off her regulations on her fingers. 'Number one, I pay the bill, two, everything is off the record, and three, no passes.'

They were her guests for lunch, and after showing them around the club, Maryjane had changed from her East Bank uniform of leotards (white), tights (red), and running trunks (blue) to a loosely fitting heather-green sweater dress with a matching scarf. How to look sexy and at the same time coolly professional on the coldest day of the year.

Folklore reported that women were more likely to stroll around in the buff in their locker room at East Bank than anywhere else in the city. Roger permitted himself to

imagine Maryjane that way, a pleasant mixture of boyish-
ness and girlishness, tall, slender, and athletic, a different
kind of bisexual fantasy object from Martha, a new interest
and challenge.

'Ms Hennessey doesn't believe in sexual freedom,' he
explained to Danny.

'Sexual exploitation, both ways,' she said brusquely.

'I'm happy to hear that,' Danny said genially. 'Is that
opinion shared by all the lovely women running around
this place in varying states of, uh, dishabille?'

'God, you *are* a writer; and no, it isn't. You like the East
Bank?'

'A temple of three dramatic changes since I went on my
little trip – physical fitness, feminism, and sexual open-
ness, whatever that is.'

'That's good. Do you mind if I take notes, just for my
own memory?' She pulled out a large spiral ring binder.
'Do you approve of those changes? And what did you do
for sex in China?'

Roger had forgotten the electricity that so quickly leaped
between Danny and a woman. A hint of a smile, a flash of
an eye, a courteous attentiveness, and women began to
glow.

His magic worked with Maryjane in thirty seconds.

Damn him.

'I don't disapprove,' Danny said disarmingly. 'And the
Chinese control population the way the Irish did in the last
century. They abolished sex. After a while you hardly
notice. There are more temptations in this Taj Mahal of
physical culture in a single day than in a whole year in a
Chinese commune.'

'Do you plan to marry? What do you think of American
women?' Maryjane could hardly contain her questions –
and felt no need to link them in any logical order.

Dan laughed. 'I have no plans to marry. I think
American women are gorgeous, even more so now that
they are independent and aggressive. And I'm fascinated
by this place: rooms for serious weight lifting, beautiful
women in tight clothes, other rooms for medieval torture
machines, others where young men and women jump

about and sing, tennis courts, beautiful women in loose clothes, handball courts, squash courts, beautiful women in almost no clothes at all, people running around a track with earphones on their heads.'

Maryjane grinned sheepishly. She had had a Walkman in her hand as she'd rushed by them on the track.

'You mean exercise classes and exercise machines . . .'

'A swimming pool with the most charmingly indiscreet costumes, a singles bar in the middle of a three-storey atrium, marvellous food, politicians and journalists at almost every table. Where else but Chicago could you have so many different purposes served under one roof?'

'You're being satirical. . . .' Her ball-point pen hesitated, and she cocked an eyebrow in doubt.

'I'm celebrating a monumental plush-carpeted marble mausoleum of cultural diversity,' Danny replied. 'Why shouldn't one set of walls contain the most advanced methods of both losing weight and putting it on? All the highest virtues and all the most pleasant vices? Seriously, Maryjane, I love it, even if I'm too old and decrepit to fit in.'

'You'd fit in fine,' she protested hotly.

Oh, God, Danny, you ought to be ashamed of yourself.

'I'm afraid I couldn't compete with all the swingers – that is the word, isn't it? – in their fancy, faded, fanny-hugging jeans.'

'Alliteration,' Maryjane said. 'Let me get that down.' She scribbled frantically.

And so it went. Despite her youthful bounce and vitality, Maryjane Hennessey was clear-eyed and clear-headed about the celebrities of the city. Yet Danny dazzled her completely. When she shook hands with him at the end of the lunch, during which Roger said practically nothing, there was hopeless adoration in her lively brown eyes.

She would be much better in bed, Roger decided, than Martha Clay – and was, in all probability, quite unattainable.

'Bastard,' he muttered to Danny as they left the humming buzz of forced camaraderie on the main floor of the club and descended to the silent caverns of the parking garage.

'Envious?' Danny asked innocently. 'You're not interested in her, are you?'

'Of course not.'

'Well, neither am I.' Danny was grim. 'Or in anyone else, for that matter. It's kind of nice, though, to know I'm not totally a retard, as my lovely cousin says I am.'

'Did you mean that about not marrying?' Roger opened the door of the Mercedes.

How could he say to Danny that friendship between men was much more important and much more stable than the endless sexual games men played with women? How hint that he would rather eat lunch with him than with the lovely blonde Maryjane?

He could not say it. He would never risk a replay of his humiliation in the movie theatre thirty year ago.

'I'd be a bad risk.'

The gate opened, and Roger drove up the ramp. Demented cold assaulted the Mercedes and made them both shiver. Roger turned on the heater.

'Don't worry, Roger. You have her. I don't.'

'Maryjane?' he said, surprised by the sudden twist of the conversation.

'Of course not.'

'We thought you were dead, Dan. Otherwise . . .' His voice trailed off into silence.

'No problem,' Danny said, looking away from him and out the window of the car, as if he were studying intently the freezing pedestrians. 'No problem at all.'

Yes it is, Danny. Yes it is. And it's going to get worse.

*

Noele

'This is a rather special experience for me tonight,' the monsignor said. 'My guest is my cousin, Daniel Farrell, who was held prisoner in China for eighteen years due to circumstances that we won't be able to discuss tonight. But everyone in our family, and I suspect a lot of people in your families too, saw him on television last month after the Notre Dame–Georgetown game. And many of us were fascinated to hear Danny say that it was religious faith that kept him going through the seeming hopelessness of the long years as a prisoner. Could you tell us more about that, Danny?'

'I'm sure you, of all people, remember, Monsignor,' he replied in mock seriousness, 'that I was not exactly a pious youth. There was the time, if you remember, when . . .'

'He isn't going to,' Noele said indignantly. Her eyes were glued to the TV screen, absorbing every detail of Danny's appearance.

'Hush,' her mother said.

He looked respectable enough. His suit was pressed, and he was sitting up fairly straight. But he wasn't going to tell that *gross* story about putting warm-up jackets on the statues of St Praxides on Holy Thursday. But that's exactly what he did.

'I think they may want to revoke my ordination after hearing that story,' John responded with a chuckle. 'But let's get back to your religious faith and China.'

Danny spoke slowly, as though choosing his words carefully – even though he had gone over the whole thing with Noele the night before.

'The point of the story was that I wasn't in fact the holiest kid in the neighbourhood by a long shot. In fact, I sometimes thought God had dealt me a pretty rotten hand. My father was killed in the Second World War, as you know. And my mother was killed by a runaway truck. But I was raised a Catholic and thought that, on the whole, being a Catholic was a pretty good thing. Then I found out that my Chinese friends weren't going to kill me, and that I might spend a long, long time as a prisoner in a land I didn't know and didn't particularly like. I decided I'd start praying to Whom It May Concern, if to no one else. I sort of got into the habit. A lot of times I thought it was a mistake. Because if I didn't believe in Him – my niece would insist I throw in "or Her" – I would have certainly killed myself. Sometimes I was very angry He – sorry, Noele, *She* – wouldn't let me die and wouldn't let me give up

—306—

hope, even when I wanted to. . . .'

'The NERVE of him!' Noele exploded, secretly jazzed to hear her name mentioned on television and eagerly anticipating Jaimie's reaction.

The conversation continued with both of the Farrells saying exactly the right things and making all kinds of points for God and religion and faith and charity. Noele was unimpressed. The two of them talked about God, and they certainly believed in God. But something was missing. They had faith all right, but not enough faith to straighten out the Farrell family puzzles.

She shook her head disapprovingly. Danny was tied in knots despite his glib tongue. And since he'd come back, so was everyone else in the family. Somebody was going to have to untie them. And Noele had not the slightest doubt who that someone would have to be.

After the programme Moms and Roger got on the telephone to congratulate the two smooth-talking participants. Noele trudged upstairs, feeling very worried. The phone was ringing as she entered her room, her personal telephone installed two years before so that her calls did not tie up the family phone. She picked up the receiver.

'That's it, kid. I warned you to lay off. You're not sending me to jail after all these years. And that includes your whole fucking family, blabbing the story all over television. You're going to be in the hospital before the next programme, you little cunt.'

The line went dead. Noele stood there with the phone in her hand, shaking with a terrible chill. Now she knew who the man was.

John

'If I hadn't seen it with my own eyes,' Danny said, shaking his head in dismay, 'I wouldn't have believed it.'

'The charismatics have become big since 1965,' John said. 'I don't especially go for it myself. But it doesn't seem to do anybody any harm, and a lot of people benefit from it.'

The two of them were walking back from the parish hall to the rectory. Snowflakes ricocheted off their faces. The false spring had vanished, and winter returned with a vengeance. Danny hung around the rectory now as he never had before, as did young men in their middle twenties occasionally, trying to recapture their teens. In the face of his piquant combination of wit and fragility, John lost all his resentments, indeed, wondered if he had ever truly resented his cousin.

'They call it baptism of the spirit?' Danny asked. 'And you mean you let them do that sort of thing around here?'

'You saw it, didn't you? The Dominican brother whips everybody into a frenzy and then one by one they all pass out. All eighty-five of them. One of the things you have to learn about the new church, Danny, is that a pastor lets the people do almost anything they want, short of heresy and public immorality – and it's not altogether clear what those are anymore.'

'So they all pass out, but nobody gets banged up when they slide to the floor. My Chinese friends would have understood it very well. . . .'

Rarely did Danny mention China. John did not want to press for an explanation of the similarity between slaying in the spirit and the enthusiastic public demonstrations of the People's Republic. 'Come on up to the rectory for a drink?'

'For coffee maybe. My rules say nothing but wine at meals.'

John brewed the coffee in his coffee maker.

'What were the reactions to our interview?' Danny asked as he blew on the coffee to cool it.

'The ratings soared, and the general manager of the channel was delighted. But I suppose you saw Larry Rieves this morning, suggesting it was unethical, since my brother was running for governor, to bring on a cousin who was allegedly a hero. Typical Rieves.'

'Yeah, I saw it,' Danny said grimly. 'I'd like to beat the shit out of the son of a bitch.'

'My sentiments exactly,' John agreed, noting that Danny's flashes of anger were infrequent but frightening.

'And your friends in the church who are giving you a hard time?'

John poured a second cup of coffee, wishing that he could trade it in for a martini. 'Edward Keegan was here today. He's the chancellor, the cardinal's number-one man. A big, tall, handsome guy, one of the brightest canon lawyers in the church. He's kept the cardinal in power for the last several years by arguing his case in Rome.'

'Sounds like the kind of man who would have done well in China too, especially during the Cultural Revolution.'

'The cardinal wants me to stop. In fact, this time it's an order, though not in writing. Too many Farrells in the news, and he thinks that it reflects badly on him.'

'On him?' Danny put his coffee cup on the end table next to his chair. 'How do the Farrells reflect badly on him?'

'We get public attention, and he doesn't. It was bad enough having to put up with me and Roger. Now that you make it three, he's genuinely threatened. And Keegan knows how to pull out all the stops: the personal wishes of the cardinal, orders from God's representative over me, esteem of my fellow priests – that sort of thing.'

'What bullshit!' Danny said contemptuously.

'Is it?' John sighed. 'When you've been raised in it, it has a powerful effect on you. Keegan is a sincere and dedicated man, according to his lights. When he tells me that I've lost the most important thing a priest can have, the esteem of his fellow priests, it shakes me. And when he says all my fellow priests think I'm on an ego trip and disgracing the priesthood and the church, I half believe it's true.'

'Is it true? Do you have any support at all? Are priests such finks' – Danny spit the word out contemptuously – 'that they actually think that way?'

John rubbed his hand across his forehead. 'No, not all of them, maybe not even most of them. But it's the ones who think that way who make the noise and call people in the parish to stir up trouble here. The pressure's going to mount again for me either to give up the programme or give up the parish.'

'Noele told me about the programme on which you were the target. Did that help?'

'I didn't hear a single word from any of the priests in the diocese: no letters, no phone calls, no comment from anyone at the funeral for an old priest I attended a week later. It was as though the interview had never happened. So far I haven't heard a word about the programme with you, either. The ratings were great, the mail and the phone calls were stupendous, and the priesthood is silent. Those who didn't like it are muttering behind my back and providing the cardinal and Keegan with more ammunition, and those who are on my side are not about to take the chance of speaking out.'

'Cowards?'

'No. Just practising the virtue that I have practised all my life as a priest up until now – prudence.'

'Fuck prudence,' Danny exploded. 'Roger walks on eggshells in his campaign and you're doing the same thing in the diocese. When are you two going to learn that if you want to do something in this world and you know you can do it well, you've got to fight for it.'

He was right, of course. Fuck prudence.

Danny left a few minutes later, walking down the rectory steps, his shoulders hunched over, to his Porsche, the one concession he had made to the fact that he had actually returned from the dead.

Back in his room John mixed himself a double martini and poured it all from the pitcher into a large glass. After Keegan's visit he had called Irene and begged that he might come and see her. Since Danny's return he had avoided her, jamming up his longings and his loneliness by a massive act of will. Keegan had broken not only his self-esteem, but also his willpower.

Irene said no, as he knew she would. But now Danny had fired him up again, just as Irene had done before Christmas. Danny had replaced Irene as his backbone.

A nice irony. All the old envy and jealousy were welling up again. The same emotions he had felt that summer when, after talking him into returning to the seminary, Danny had fallen for Irene himself.

Had he slept with her?

John's fist clenched and unclenched.

John hated Danny because Irene loved him. It was an absurd hatred. But his rage, while silent, was as enormous as Clancy's rage that night.

He emptied the martini glass.

Now the same conflict. And he was doomed to lose again.

Brigid

They were bidding on the construction of a huge office/shopping/condominium plaza on North Michigan Avenue. It was a big job, enough to keep the firm in excellent condition another year, regardless of interest rates. If they won the contract, she would certainly follow Burke's advice and retire. By then they would know what Danny intended to do.

Danny, Danny, how wonderful to have you back, even if you bring so much danger with you.

They had a good shot at the Michigan Avenue project. Only a few firms in the city were big enough to do it right, and Brigid was confident that her stern-eyed costing made Farrell & Sons the most competitive large-scale company in the city. It was not a clout or bribe situation; nothing like the old days, Brigid thought wearily.

She leaned over her desk, ball-point in hand, for one last searching examination, looking for enough fat to knock another million dollars off her bid.

Outside her office window construction vehicles that had not moved in several months were parked in neat rows, like mothballed Navy ships, their green and white paint shining dully in the faint February sunlight.

She had given so much of her time and energy to the firm. In retrospect, it was wasted time. The money she did not need; her sons were not interested in the inheritance. Danny, who had the most right to it, was still confused and, she thought, angry. God knows what would come of that. Burke's Mount Etna was waiting to explode.

She tried to concentrate on the column of figures. They blurred. She closed her eyes and opened them again. The figures went into focus, then blurred once more. The whole page turned black, and Brigid felt the yawning abyss reaching up, eager to swallow her.

Irene

She was working part-time in Roger's campaign headquarters at the Midland Hotel, stuffing envelopes, answering phones, typing lists – anything to take her mind off Danny.

She thought she might be invisible in the Midland Hotel offices among all the other volunteers. But she was the candidate's attractive wife and soon very much the centre of attention.

Mick Gerety and Angelo Spina were courtly and respectful – and delighted to have her around. Her interviews with the 'Life-style' writers from Illinois newspapers were good copy, and pictures of her appeared regularly in the papers.

'You take a great picture, Mrs Farrell,' Angelo said reverently.

'Is it dangerous for a candidate's wife to be too pretty?'

'No way,' he said fervently.

She knew that Mick and Angelo and Roger were still worried about the stolen file. And their worried expressions in the campaign office reminded her of what she was

trying to forget. It was Danny's mother who had been killed. So long ago. Almost unreal, like an old movie. How
would Dan react when the murder, if that's what it was,
became public? And Clancy's death? Was that murder, as
Brigid had said at Noele's party?

But Danny could not have . . .

She chased those thoughts out of her head. Only a few
weeks ago she thought she could love two men. Now she
couldn't love either of them. She had failed John. Oh,
God, how humiliated he had been when she refused to see
him after the chancellor's visit.

We would have made love, John, and I would have pretended you were Danny every minute.

With Roger, most in love with her precisely when he
feared that he would lose her, she was able to pretend.

And she no longer cared about his mistress at the University. Or about Maryjane Hennessey, the lovely TV journalist at whom Roger had been gazing hungrily all afternoon.

She is a sexy bitch. I kind of like her.

Maybe you need a couple of women, Roger. Who am I to
judge?

And Danny's anger at me is building up. Soon . . .
soon . . .

The private line in Roger's office rang. There was no one
there to answer it. Irene walked into the office.

'Noele? What? At Little Company? I'll find your father.
You and Danny are there already? We'll be right out.'

Brigid

Danny and Noele were the first to arrive. Danny sat on the
bed next to her, his arm thrown around her shoulders.
Noele held her hand as if she were determined never to let
it go.

'What sort of nonsense is this now, woman?' Danny said in his fake brogue. 'Wasn't it yourself that had a vacation in January, and now you're going to want one in early March, too? We'll have none of this misbehaving from you. Otherwise we'll have to hire a brand-new president for the firm. It won't do to be passing out in the office on winter afternoons.'

'I was dead, Danny. And I could feel them reaching up for me to drag me down into the pit.'

'I'll have none of that kind of talk,' Danny insisted. 'The doctors are saying there's nothing wrong with you at all. Your blood pressure is normal, your EKG is fine, you're a fit and healthy woman. You've been working a little bit too hard.'

'Maybe they missed me this time. But they'll get me someday, Danny. And they'll drag me down into the pit and keep me there for all eternity.'

'Stop that, Grams,' Noele said sternly. 'When you finally die, which is not going to be for a long time – not until you have great-grandchildren that are teenagers, anyhow – Jesus is going to meet you at the door of his cottage and say, "Come right on in, Bridie; I've been waiting for you. Sit down, now. I'll make you a pot of tea."'

Those wonderful, terrifying green eyes were glistening with tears. Brigid embraced both of them. Could Noele be right? Might the terrible things she had done to both of them be forgiven?

Then she looked at Danny.

What had been done to him was beyond forgiveness.

Burke

The house was hollow without her, a haunted tomb.

I'd always thought I'd die first.

The doctors say it's nothing serious. What do they know?

The hatred in Danny's eyes at her bedside was patent. He's planning something. I know it.

Even Noele had seen it, despite her adolescent crush on the man.

'You look totally unfriendly, Daniel Xavier,' she had said to him.

'Just worried about the woman, that's all.'

Smooth-talking bastard.

You never wanted me to have her. Well, I've had her for almost forty years. And I'm going to keep her, even if I have to kill you to do it.

Roger

His affair with Martha Clay was coming to an end. Yet the closer to its conclusion, the more ecstatic the pleasure. The two of them, knowing the end was near, were trying to drink the last possible ounce of delight from each other, savour the last taste of their fading love. He was harsher and more demanding of her, and the contortions of her marvellous little body in response were like an erotic, superbly choreographed modern dance in which he was a choreographer with total control over her movements. Their cries of pain and pleasure were as shrill and sharp as if they were two beasts locked in combat. And their moments of affection after lovemaking were poignantly bittersweet, a candy bar melting slowly in the mouth.

Roger was no longer worried by his young boy fantasies. They had become an integral part of his enjoyment. For he saw her as a young Danny, a forbidden fantasy that made her even more delicious. Oddly enough, he felt no sexual attraction toward the real Danny. He was merely a somewhat pathetic but always interesting friend.

He had stopped by Danny's house the night before and

found his cousin pounding fiercely on a secondhand Smith-Corona typewriter.

'Two hundred and fifty pages,' he said, and beamed exuberantly. 'When I get to seven hundred and fifty, I'll put an ending on and stop. Save the rest of the ideas for the next one!'

Roger had sunk into the broken sofa, which was the only other furniture in that part of the house besides the typewriter stand and chair. He had finally decided to tell Danny about the cloud that was hanging over his campaign. 'There's a nasty aspect of this election campaign that you ought to know about,' he began tentatively.

Dan kept his fingers on the typewriter keys. 'Fire away.'

And so he'd told him a vague story about the copies of the file taken by Joe Kramer from his office – materials about the probate of Bill Farrell's will – and about the phone calls from Rod Weaver threatening to publish the material. He avoided, as he always did, any reference to the death of Danny's mother.

Dan frowned thoughtfully. 'I suppose you're warning me because you think when the news breaks the press will be after me for comments. Okay, I'll tell you what I'll say to anyone who asks. "I don't give a damn what Uncle Clancy did. What is done is done, and he's paid for his sins." I'm not going to feel guilty about it and neither should you.'

The words had begun peacefully enough, but then were spit out in a machine-gun burst of anger. What did Danny mean? Was he saying that he felt no guilt for his own sin?

Roger went home and that night made passionate and violent love to Irene, forcing her out of her dreamy preoccupations. He knew that she would rather have Danny thrusting inside her. And that knowledge made her all the more satisfying.

For one deliriously perfect moment he was fucking both Irene and Danny the boy, the Danny who was forever lost.

Brigid

'I must say you look the picture of health.' Burke deposited his daily dozen roses on the bed stand and kissed her dutifully. 'You also smell nice and feel nice, so I suspect you're on the mend.'

'Stop the blabbering and tell me whether we've got the contract,' Brigid insisted.

'Of course we've got it, Bridie. Even without your shaving that extra million dollars off that put you in the hospital. The announcement will be made tomorrow, but I have my sources. And what do the doctors say about you?'

'They've had the head shrinkers in to talk to me, would you believe? So sure of it now there's nothing wrong with my poor worn-out old body. And are you certain we've got the contract?'

'Absolutely certain. Have you ever known me to be wrong about these things?'

'No, I haven't,' Brigid admitted grudgingly. 'Now I suppose you're going to tell me that since we have the contract and since clearly I've been overworking, I should take some time off and then retire.'

'I'm a reasonable man, Bridie. I'll give you until Easter, which is only a month away now. The primary election will be over, and you and I are leaving for a long, long time, even if I have to drag you all the way by your gorgeous red hair.'

'Sure, I'll come quietly enough. But what about Danny?'

Burke shook his head. 'I'll worry less about Danny when I get you away from him. I still don't trust the man. I think he's crazy. That glow in his eyes gets wilder every time I see him.'

'Sure, the poor lad is readjusting.'

'He's readjusting into an insane asylum if you ask me. Someday he'll explode, and we'll read in the papers he's climbed up on a tower with a high-powered rifle and shot fourteen people.'

'Do you think he might really do that, Burke?' She clutched impulsively at his hand.

'Bridie, dearest, I think your nephew and foster son is a ticking time bomb.'

Noele

The snow had melted off the Courts, and like hibernating animals, the boys of the parish had emerged on Saturday morning to play basketball, including Jaimie, who was old enough to know better. Noele would have driven right by the Courts, greeting the hoopsters with a faint beep from Flame if she hadn't noticed Daniel's silver Porsche parked on Ninety-third Street. She pulled up behind the Porsche, turned off the ignition, and watched. Danny was a little bit out of practice but surprisingly well able to take care of himself with the teenagers.

She got out of the car and sauntered over to the court just as the game ended, with Daniel sinking a twenty-foot jump shot to much applause from the real teenagers. 'Is there a new teenager in the Neighbourhood, Jaimie Burns?' she asked.

'Uh, a new kid with a pretty good jump shot, though he's kind of out of condition,' her lean, dreamy-eyed stalwart replied.

Cousin Daniel was sitting on the court resting his head against the basketball upright and breathing deeply. 'The new kid in town needs to get back into condition; that's all, MN.'

'What did you call me?'

He cocked a mischievous eye at her. 'MN. That's your name, isn't it?'

'Only for teenagers.'

'Well, you treat me like a retarded teenager. Besides, I think *MN* is neat.'

'That word went out of style *at least* ten years ago,' she said, and sniffed.

One of the boys bounced the basketball toward her. 'Can you still shoot, MN, or have you become too snooty to play with the rest of the guys.'

With as much haughty demeanour as she could muster, Noele doffed her white down jacket and sent a jump shot swishing through the rim.

'Let's see you do that, Daniel Xavier.'

'You're on, MN I'll play you twenty-one!'

Daniel *was* pretty good. He scored his first long shot and a short one after that. Then he hit on three more before it was Noele's turn. She was down thirteen to zip. And the male ruffians were cheering raucously for Daniel.

Noele decided it was time to give them all a lesson. She scored eighteen points in a row before missing a long shot, and then added a short, to be ahead nineteen to thirteen.

'Why don't you play on the varsity?' Daniel demanded as he bounced the ball from the edge of the free-throw circle.

'I find gymnastics a much more civilized sport,' she said airily.

The male monsters made their usual animal noises until Noele gave them her 'Noele look,' which usually reduced male monsters to silence.

Daniel missed his long shot and made the short. Nineteen to fourteen. Noele scored her long and then the short after. Twenty-two to fourteen. 'I win!' she exulted. 'I beat you, Daniel Xavier! I beat you!'

'No way. You have to win on a long,' he insisted.

'That's right, Noele Fair is fair,' Jaimie said.

'Whose side are you on?' Noele demanded.

She missed the shot. Then Danny made two shots and missed the third, leaving the score tied.

He bounced the ball to her. 'Next long shot wins, MN.'

Noele walked calmly to the edge of the free-throw circle holding the ball in one hand and smiling her most pleasant smile. Try to edge me before a shot, will he?

'Next long shot wins, Daniel Xavier!'

She swished the shot through without even looking at the basket.

There was more wild cheering from the monsters, a congratulatory hug and kiss from Daniel, and a not enthusiastic enough kiss from Jaimie Burns.

She decided to quit while she was ahead and walked to the car with slightly more exaggerated motions than normal. She assumed that the One who presided over the Courts, having provided her with a lovely ass, would not mind her swinging it when the situation warranted.

As she drove home, her down jacket tossed carelessly in the front seat of Flame, Noele was troubled by two things:

Number one: She was convinced that Daniel was still in love with her mother. She could see it in his eyes when he looked at her, an intense hunger that she saw sometimes in Jaimie's eye when they were alone. It was nice to be looked at that way, but when Jaimie wanted her, it was never with the devouring anger with which Daniel wanted Moms.

Number two disturbing thought: Noele realized she was half in love with Daniel.

There were two kinds of love. First of all there was love with boys like Jaimie Burns. You kissed and hugged and caressed and went to dances and parties and bought birthday and Christmas presents for them. And occasionally you were emotionally a Jaimie/Noele person together. Someday she would go to bed with such a boy more or less permanently and have children and grow old together.

The other kind of love was for rock stars and movie actors, basketball players and other distant idols. Daniel Xavier was not a boy like Jaimie.

But he wasn't a rock star, either.

John

He drank three martinis before he called the chancellor.

He had not seen Danny in a week. Apparently Danny was wrapped up in his novel. And he did not have the courage to call Irene. His backbone was gone.

And the latest issue of the newsletter of the Priest Association had another satire, this one by Terry Quirk, who, unlike Dads Fogarty, did have a finely honed, if vicious, wit.

Bitter and envious over his own unused talents, Quirk destroyed others. And this time he destroyed both Danny and John, making wild fun of their interview.

He tried to get Danny on the phone to read it to him, but there was no answer.

He did not have the fortitude to keep up his fight. Now was the time to put it all in the past.

'You can tell the cardinal that I'm going to discontinue the series. I'll inform the station when I tape this week's show that the next interview will be the last.'

'Your fellow priests will be very proud of you,' Keegan said smoothly. 'Eventually you will be accepted back into their ranks, just as though nothing ever happened.'

'I'm glad to hear that,' John said dully.

Irene

Noele had finally talked her into jogging. 'The cold weather is no excuse at all, Moms,' she'd insisted. 'They have running suits that are plenty warm. Besides, it's not that cold these days.'

For the first three times Irene ran, her body groaned and complained, muscles resenting the many years of disuse and bones protesting their unaccustomed responsibilities. And then she began to feel more in touch with her body, more in possession of herself.

This morning there was a hint of spring in the air. The temperature was in the high twenties, the sun was bright, and piles of snow along the curbs were melting as she trotted down Ninety-fourth Street.

She was conscious that a car was trailing her but chose to

ignore it. It was broad daylight, and there was nothing to fear. She glanced out of the corner of her eye and saw it was a silver Porsche. She kept right on running. The car drew up beside her and the driver rolled down the window. 'Good morning,' he said politely.

She stopped running and walked over to the car. 'You frightened me,' she protested.

Her body's instant reactions were not those of fear.

'And you overwhelmed me,' he said, his lips slightly parted with a smile.

'I thought you were beyond being affected by women,' she said.

'I thought so too.'

There was a pause while their eyes found each other's and then locked.

'Come home with me, Irene,' he said, half pleading, half ordering.

'I'm all hot and sweaty,' she said.

'That doesn't make any difference.'

They drove in silence to his house, like mourners on the way to the cemetery after a funeral Mass.

'Are you sure you want to come in?' he asked as he parked in the driveway at the top of the hill. His voice was tense, his fingers white on the wheel of the car.

He can't decide whether to love me or hate me.

'Am I still invited?'

'I'm losing my nerve, I guess.'

'You could take me back to my house.'

'That would be *gross*, as Noele would say, after waiting all these years.'

With some pride he showed her around the house, much more neatly maintained than she expected. Across the street was a small park and beyond that the grounds of a private school that used to be a military academy. From the front windows of the house, perched high on the top of the Ridge, eons ago the dunes on the shore of a prehistoric Lake Michigan, she saw the Sears Tower and the Hancock Centre, giant sentinels of the Chicago skyline. On the other side, at the foot of Danny's backyard, I-57 stretched out toward Memphis.

'Highest point in Cook County,' he said softly. 'Hills, curving streets, trees – hardly Chicago.'

His lips were thin, his eyes blank, anger fighting desire.

Irene undid the towel around her neck, took off her knit cap, and unzipped an inch or two of her running jacket while he made them a pot of tea in the kitchen. They sipped the tea quietly, his eyes devouring her and hers smiling back, revelling in his admiration.

'I am very hot sweaty,' she insisted.

'I don't think I'll notice.'

'A long time, Danny.'

'A long time, and only yesterday.'

He put down his teacup, took her hands, and lifted her to her feet. Their lips brushed gently, tentatively, as if exploring an old neighbourhood long unvisited.

'I shouldn't be doing this.' He tried to pull back, but her hands closed firmly on his.

'You have every right to do it, and so do I.'

'You look pretty in red,' he said, touching the zipper on her jacket. 'You always did.'

Hate me, Danny, or love me. I don't care which. But let's end the game.

'Noele picked it out for me. Just like she picked out your Notre Dame Windbreaker.'

'Noele takes charge of everything, doesn't she?'

The mention of Noele seemed to change Danny's mood. The tension ebbed from his face and in his eyes there flickered the swiftly moving ghosts of long-forgotten laughter.

Slowly he pulled down the zipper of her jacket. A sweet, passive lethargy oozed through Irene's veins.

I want to be naked for him again.

'That's because she's filled with enough love for the whole world.'

Irene had never thought of her persistent daughter quite in those terms.

Danny slid the jacket down her arms.

'Good heavens, woman, what sort of monstrous female garment is this?'

Irene laughed feeling as if she had been drinking champagne, not tea. 'It's a running bra. Noele insisted I wear it.

Here, let me get it off. Oh, Danny . . . you haven't forgotten anything, have you?'

His lips were deft and devastating.

'It surprises me how quickly everything comes back.'

There is anger in his eyes again. He still has not forgiven me.

He led her to the enclosed front porch, overlooking Mandrake Parkway and the Neighbourhood at the foot of the Ridge. A carefully made bed was shoved against the wall. 'I like to sleep with windows on three sides,' he said, drawing the thin drapes. 'Not that there's anyone on Mandrake Parkway to see us.'

Leisurely he finished undressing her and then held her arms out, so he could examine her, as though she were a work of art he was appraising. He had only begun the ritual and already she was light-headed with pleasure.

'I'm not graceful anymore, even when I have my clothes off,' she said sadly, beginning to feel awkward and shy in her nakedness.

'Quite the contrary, Irene. Now you're graceful all the time.'

Their first union was exploratory, a careful revisitation of old neighbourhoods. His eyes flashed several times with anger, but he was very gentle with her.

Their timing was off, and their pleasure, at most, only a promise. But so content was Irene that she slept peacefully afterward.

But suddenly her quiet, faceless dream became a nightmare. She was losing her breath. Someone was choking her.

Then she was awake and felt Danny's hand close on her windpipe.

Noele

In thick block letters she wrote down three words:

Florence
Clancy
Daniel
Three mysteries.

And then, oblivious to Ms Hounslow's *boring* lecture about the Third World, she thoughtfully added a fourth.

Noele

Ms Hounslow was a pretty woman, not too old, maybe twenty-six or so. And she was into feminism and protest and revolution, even though she was totally ladylike. Noele felt sorry for the people in the Third World, though she couldn't understand Ms Hounslow's arguments that they were poor because Americans were rich.

After the first name she wrote *Clancy or Burke*?

But she never argued with Ms Hounslow, because Ms Hounslow cried when students made fun of her. And then Noele had to force them to apologize.

After the second name she wrote *Daniel*? And then drew an angry line through it, leaving only the question mark.

Noele figured she would probably go into the Peace Corps or something like that after she graduated from college.

After the third name she wrote a large question mark.

Maybe with a husband, if she had one by then.

She crossed out her own name. No one had tried to kill her. The only mystery about her was who she was.

Then shock waves of terror raced through her nervous system, as if she had touched a live electrical wire.

'Is there something wrong, Mary Farrell?' Ms Hounslow looked scared.

'I'm, like, totally sick,' Noele cried, rushing for the door of the classroom.

She ran not to the john but to the chapel.

Brigid

She came into the office after chewing out a crane operator who had damaged an expensive piece of equipment.

Such outbursts made her feel young again, as if she were a girl back in Ireland.

It had been a hard, cruel life, yet somehow she remembered happiness there too.

Burke had not raised the question yet, but she knew it was coming. She must go back to Ireland, become Maeve for a week or so and make peace with the real Brigid and meet her children and grandchildren.

There was no reason to hate her, poor thing. And what would her grandchildren be like? Surely none like Noele.

So quick did forgiveness come.

Life was still hard in Ireland. The make-believe Brigid had had an easier time than the real one.

Life here was gentler, softer. And it so quickly turned sour.

Death – William Farrell, Martin, Florence. Poor, wonderful Florence. How hard it was to hate her, even though she married the man that Brigid wanted.

Then Clancy and Danny.

Only Danny wasn't dead. But there was so much fear around him, lurking like a black halo.

Nothing had worked out right. Except for Noele. And she had been so sceptical about that at first. Noele was the prize that made everything else worthwhile.

Then she was suddenly afraid. Automatically, not understanding why, she reached for her purse and clutched for the old rosary she had brought from Ireland almost forty-five years ago, her only possession. She did not know for what she was praying. But she prayed harder than she had ever prayed in her life.

Irene

'I'm sorry, Danny.' She would not resist her punishment. 'I betrayed you.'

Her words melted his anger. His grip relaxed, and kisses replaced his fingers on her throat.

'I'm a sick bastard, Renie. Forgive me. It won't happen ever again.' He pulled away from her, face twisted by remorse.

'Do whatever you want to me,' she said, extending her arm to him in a plea that he return to her.

His body quickly responded to her invitation. And his hands, strong and competent, on her breasts, down her belly, along her thighs, brought healing and grace and benediction. Then his lips on her breasts, drawing sweetness to drown his own pain.

Everything that was fear and terror inside of Irene melted, as if all the snows of winter had thawed at the same instant, and she was swept along by the rushing water, down country streams, into a giant river, over a roaring waterfall, and finally into a peaceful ocean on which she floated for an eternity of happiness.

Afterward she slept again and awakened to see Danny standing above her with a towel around his waist and a stack of typescript in his hand.

'I'll let your read this, if you let me read your stories.'

'I'm a lot more naked in my stories than I am here in your bed,' she said.

'Then I will really enjoy them,' he said, winking like a little boy who had found a copy of *Penthouse*.

He sat down on the bed next to her, placing the neat stack of typescript on the crowded bedstand. His thin shoulders slumped in quick dejection. He seemed so sad and defeated.

'What's the matter, Danny? Are you having second thoughts?'

'And third and fourth and fifth thoughts too. I shouldn't have let it happen, Renie.'

'Yes, you should, and I had something to do with it too, you know. I didn't exactly fight you off.'

'Ah, you always were a forward one.' He smiled wistfully, hiding behind his Irish accent. 'But the past can't be recaptured. And I'm terrified of the future.'

'Who isn't?' She shifted her position in the bed to see his eyes more clearly. Like the rest of his face, they seemed taut with terror. Unimaginable and undescribed suffering must still be locked up in his head, like pollution in a toxic waste dump. And it had been there even before he was shot down.

'Don't spoil this moment by worrying about the past or the future,' she pleaded.

The movement of her body brought something much softer and more tender into his eyes. He bent over her and began to kiss her again with infinite delicacy, as though she were made of fragile tissue paper that might be damaged if handled too roughly.

Later that morning he drove her home and waited in the car. She ran up to her office, took the red leather folder that contained her stories from the secret compartment of her desk, and ran back down the stairs and out to the car to shove the folder into his hands. He smiled, winked, and drove away.

Afterward, in the shower, she realized joyously that having given him the stories, there was nothing left of herself to reveal.

Noele

'You look totally edged, MN,' said Eileen Kelly as Noele joined them at their usual table in the school's noisy, smelly lunchroom. 'I looked for you in the john after class.'

'I was in chapel,' she said, putting her Tab and french fries on the table. 'I'm all right now.'

The waves of terror had stopped almost as soon as she had fallen to her knees at the altar rail, whether because they were going to stop anyway or because of Noele's prayers, she did not know and did not care.

Daniel. Of course, Daniel.

He was close to terrible evil.

A gross-out. She would tell him what she thought about it.

No, that would not be a wise idea.

It was all right now. For a little while, anyway.

But it might come back, whatever 'it' was.

Unless she solved the mysteries on the list she'd made in class.

There were no roses now. Only a heavy weight of obligation.

'I've never seen you look so pale,' Eileen Kelly chirped nervously.

'I'm worried about the Third World.' She laughed at her friend's concern.

Poor Eileen. I'd like to ask her for help.

But I have to do this alone.

Noele

'Were you as much in love with Moms as Jaimie Burns is in love with me?'

Daniel Xavier made a face, as though she had hit him over the head with a two-by-four. He swallowed his large mouthful of Redburger and came up for air.

'You are certainly candid, MN,' he said, wiping some of the coleslaw off his lips.

'Which doesn't answer my question,' she said briskly. 'And PLEASE sit up straight.'

He made a mostly unsuccessful effort to obey, but she was distracted by a group of extremely gross freshmen animals who had just come into Red's. Noele gave them her sternest Noele look and that quieted them for a few moments.

'Do you ever lose an argument, MN?' he asked, disposing of a trace of mustard from his fingers before she could admonish him to use a napkin.

She considered judiciously. 'SOMETIMES Moms thinks she wins, but she really doesn't.' She bit into her hamburger. 'Mostly in our family I win the arguments.'

'I'm sure,' he agreed with a wicked grin.

'Airhead,' she responded firmly.

She had drafted Danny to act as a chaperone at the High Club Friday night bash and he had, to tell the truth, performed rather well, despite the fact that he admitted that rock music was a change that took 'some time to adjust to.' He danced with the sophomore girls who asked him to, making Noele insanely jealous, even though she realized that cool chaperones did dance with those silly kids. He shagged away some boys who had too much beer and broke up a couple of fights between gross freshmen animals.

And he was wise enough to dance the last number with Noele. He was a good dancer.

Of course.

Then she spirited him away to Red's and hit him with her two-by-four.

'It was a different relationship. We were older but not so mature. It was an infatuation. You and Jaimie seem . . . well, much more stable than your mother and I.'

He smiled his charm smile, which still made Noele's heartbeat do strange things.

'You were going to marry her.' Noele jabbed her chili cheese dog at him.

'I . . .' He hesitated. 'I don't think that would have happened. It was a summer romance.'

'Which ended the night Uncle Clancy was pushed down the steps.'

Daniel did not bat an eye.

'Pushed or fell or whatever.'

'That had something to do with you falling out of love?'

'Not especially,' he replied smoothly. 'It was my going off to Asia that cooled things down. . . . Where is all this going, MN?'

'I think you ought to get married,' she said calmly. 'You enjoy women, even those JUVENILE sophomores. You should have, like, a permanent woman.'

'Marry your mother?' He choked, even though he didn't have any hamburger in his mouth.

'Don't be gross. She has a husband.'

Danny looked relieved. Too relieved, Noele thought.

'You mean any woman? I don't know, MN. If the right one comes along, maybe. I'm a pretty unstable person, not a good matrimonial risk.' He grinned cheerfully. 'And I have a lot of things to work out.'

'Like growing up,' she said. 'And sitting up straight.'

Guiltily he abandoned his slouch. 'Yes, ma'am.'

'Airhead.' She gave him her most devastating Noele look, a mixture of outrage and disgust.

Danny liked teen talk, was even trying to learn it himself, though he wasn't very good at it. Noele could turn it on and off at will, which was part of the secret.

'I keep trying.' He attempted to laugh it off.

'Not hard enough. And you don't care who was responsible for sabotaging your plane. And you don't care whether they might try again. That's obsessively self-destructive.'

A potent phrase she'd learned from Jaimie.

Danny bowed his head so that his chin rested on his fingertips.

'I'm a runner, MN, have been all my life. If you want to play shrink, you could say I'm running from responsibility for my mother's death. I am Joe Hero – that's teen talk from my era – in the short run, but not very good at loving or hating any longer than a week.'

Daniel looked so sad and so tired. The lines around his eyes were cool until you realized that they represented an eighteen-year bummer. He was very brave, and he never complained about what had happened to him. He covered it up wonderfully. Only occasionally, as now, did you realize how much unhappiness . . .

Noele's heart did several quick spins.

She reached out and touched his face in a spontaneous gesture of sympathy, the way she would pick up a crying baby.

He kissed her fingers.

'Those freshmen animals will think I am making a pass,' he laughed.

'Barf city,' Noele said, trying to regain her composure.

He didn't change his expression when I mentioned Uncle Clancy. And he almost swallowed the whole burger when I asked him about Moms. It's all too totally confusing.

Maybe he did kill Uncle Clancy. And maybe he didn't.

He still loves her, though.

Danny took her home and kissed her at the door.

It wasn't quite like a kiss from Jaimie Burns.

But it was still awesomely sweet.

You're totally falling in love with him, a voice in her brain told her. Really!

I don't care, she said, ordering the voice to mind its own business.

Roger

After he had found a parking place on University Avenue, a difficult task even at three o'clock in the afternoon, he strolled briskly down the street and into the concrete catacomb that housed Martha Clay's office. She had been away for the weekend, home for her mother's birthday.

He had good news to share. The administration had managed to mobilize its resources and make its decision. Martha would become an associate professor with tenure, a lifelong appointee at the University.

Almost as good as immortality, he thought ruefully.

It had been another bad day at campaign headquarters.

Rod Weaver had come to agonize with them, as though he and Mick Gerety were members of an advisory board whose input would weigh heavily in Weaver's decision to publish his copied files. Rodney was an over-age, over-weight swinger with bushy brown hair that did not quite successfully cover a growing bald spot, a bushy brown moustache, and a heavy, pasty face.

Roger had kept his temper carefully under control, much as he would with a highwayman pointing a pistol at him or a mugger with a knife at his throat. He let Rodney do the talking and nodded occasionally in what might have been interpreted as sympathy with the man's ethical agony.

'So you see what the problem is,' Rodney said for the fourth time. 'If you know what I mean, I have to balance the public's right to know with my obligation not to help a corrupt incompetent be, you know, re-elected.'

'I think,' Roger said, 'the governor is in so much trouble, Rod, that you could have evidence that would send me to jail for twenty years and I'd still beat him.'

Mick winced.

'Well, you know, there's still the moral problem of winning any extra votes for him.'

'You wouldn't look very good, would you, if you published those documents and the governor lost anyway,' Mick Gerety suggested.

'The point isn't, you know, what I'd look like.' Rodney shook his bushy head. 'The problem is, you know, what I ought to do.'

He knocked on Martha Clay's office in a rather brisk, businesslike way.

'Come in!'

'Wonderful news, Martha.' The words sprang from his lips as he burst into her office. 'The dean will notify you officially tomorrow that the president has approved your promotion to associate professor with tenure.'

And once more I'll be able to imagine you as Dan Farrell when we make love to celebrate.

Martha's response was underwhelming. 'That's very nice, Roger,' she said calmly.

Roger felt as if he had been struck with a huge wet blanket. 'Only very nice?'

'I certainly appreciate the vote of confidence.' She smiled sweetly. 'But I'm afraid I'll have to turn it down. You see, I saw Lloyd when I was home this week, and we decided it was time for a reconciliation. I'm returning to Boston next academic year, and the two of us will be commuting back and forth on the weekends the rest of this year. Lloyd is up for tenure at U. Mass. He thinks I can get a part-time teaching job either there or at Boston University or maybe even Boston College with the Jesuits.'

Raw animal anger exploded deep within Roger and raced through his body like an electric charge. He grabbed her shoulders in speechless fury and shook her like a rag doll.

'Beat me, if you want,' she sobbed as her teeth rattled, her nonchalance shattered by his rage. 'I deserve it.'

Roger's anger dissipated as quickly as it had erupted, a false alarm from a volcano. He enfolded her in his arms.

'That isn't my favourite feminist talking, is it?' he asked with a laugh.

'I feel so guilty.' She spoke through a mixture of laughter and tears. 'You've taught me how important love is and I realized how much I loved Lloyd and how cruel I had been to him. I couldn't believe he'd give me a second chance. But he did.'

She wiped her tears away, her tiny round face beaming with joy.

'I'm delighted for both of you,' Roger said, feeling as he imagined he would on the day of Noele's engagement.

'I knew you'd understand,' she said happily.

Oh, sure, Roger thought ruefully.

Still in shock, he stood in his bedroom looking slowly and carefully at the familiar objects – the television set on which Irene watched the second half of the *Today Show* while lying in bed, a habit of which he had once severely disapproved, the alarm clock that chimed discreetly to awaken him, an empty vase, the small clutter of tubes and jars on Irene's dressing table.

Who was the fool looking at him from the mirror above that dressing table?

A casual adulterer rejected by a woman he had thought he loved. And an unfaithful husband standing between his wife and the man she loved.

He knew what he had to do, the only thing he could do to restore his self-esteem and his sense of personal integrity. He would give Irene her freedom and perhaps through generosity to her and control of himself, he could recapture a few shreds of dignity.

Typical Catholic idealist doing penance, he thought, and grimaced at his image in the mirror.

But that doesn't mean I'm excused from penance.

He collected an armful of suits and jackets from the closet and carried them down the hall to the guest room. And then returned for toilet articles, shirts, socks, and underwear.

After supper, when Noele had gone up to her own room to do homework, he said to Irene, 'I've moved into the guest room for a while. I feel it's the only thing to do until matters are straightened out.'

Irene, who seemed especially pretty and especially preoccupied, nodded as if she barely heard him. 'I suppose so.'

Noele

She was driving home from school, early in the afternoon for her, and pondering what she would say in a letter she'd write before supper to Jaimie Burns. Notre Dame was only fifty cents a minute away by telephone after five o'clock, but as she told Jaimie, you say a lot of things in love letters that you wouldn't on the telephone.

She also had to do some more systematic thinking about Danny. No one in the family wanted to talk about him. She had the distinct impression they all thought he was a little bit crazy. All but Moms. It was hard to tell what she thought because she never said a word about Danny to anyone.

Was she still in love with him?

Is the Pope Catholic?

And that was bad for everybody, especially if he was still in love with her too. Noele felt a touch of jealousy, for which she severely reprimanded herself.

It was increasingly difficult for Noele to be objective about her cousin. It's a teenage crush, and I know it's a teenage crush. But I'm a teenager and we have crushes. And this is the worst one I've ever had.

She sighed. And what messed it up even more was that Noele knew, as surely as she knew that the sun came up in the morning and set in the evening, that she was the one who was going to have to resolve the Farrell family problem, settle down Daniel Xavier, and get all the Farrells back to the serious business of living their lives.

Including me, she sighed.

Tell me about it, Mary Noele.

She barely saw the van before it hit her. A huge monster, like a giant bull elephant on a rampage, smashed into Flame, turned him over, and extinguished all the lights in Noele's head.

DANCE
EIGHT

Ragtime

'Ragtime was an outgrowth of the minstrel show bands and music for dancing at pleasure houses. Ragtime was in great demand around the turn of the century. For many years it was performed in the music departments of the larger ten-cent stores.'

Roger

The phone rang, and Roger, his head slumped into his hands, heaved himself to his feet painfully and walked across the room to answer it. Who would be calling him this time of night? Some fool from the media, no doubt.

There was thick, heavy breathing on the other end of the line.

'Who is this?' Roger barked angrily.

'We warned the little cunt, and still you guys didn't stop. No more snooping, or the next time she's going to get hurt a lot worse.' The line clicked.

'Who is this? Who is this?' Roger shouted futilely at the lifeless phone.

He went upstairs to the second floor and down the corridor to Noele's room. She was sitting up in bed, with a bandage on her head and an enormous black eye, engaged in a profoundly serious argument with her mother and Danny.

'Roger, I'm telling Moms that I don't care whether Flame has been totaled. I want him back. Not a new red Chevette, but my old Flame. And I don't care whether it costs every bit as much as buying a new car, I still want him back.'

'I think the woman's delirious,' Danny said, and winked broadly.

'Daniel Xavier Farrell, I am not delirious. The doctor said I have a bump on my head, a black eye, and some contusions, whatever a contusion is. I don't even have a concussion. I'm not going to let some evil yukhead in a grey van take Flame from me.'

There were huge tears in her green eyes at the thought of losing Flame. How readily a seventeen-year-old could become a twelve-year-old, Roger thought. Flame was a four-wheeled doll. Once they're eighteen they no longer can go back to being little girls who play with dolls.

'We'll take good care of Flame, don't worry about that,' Roger said. 'But now I want to know, young woman, whether anybody's been threatening you lately.'

Noele looked anxiously from Roger to Danny to Irene and back. 'Well . . .' She dragged out the word.

'In God's name, why didn't you tell us?' he almost screamed at her.

'I didn't want you to worry.'

'Snowflake,' he said with exaggerated patience, 'I'm a candidate for governor. I have, as I'm sure you noticed, a beautiful wife and an equally beautiful daughter, both of whose pictures have been in the papers and on television. That can attract the attention of crazies. Did the man say who he was and what he wanted?'

'He said to stop asking questions about the past,' she said glumly.

Roger felt the colour drain from his face and his stomach tighten into an anxious knot. 'All right, young lady, I'm going to tell Lieutenant McNeally about those phone calls. Promise me that you will tell me if that man calls again. Do you understand?'

'Yes, Roger,' she said docilely.

'And that goes for you, too, Irene, and for you, Danny, and anybody else in the family who gets crazy phone calls.'

Roger went downstairs to his study, called Lieutenant McNeally, and mixed himself a stiff drink. The policeman, a freckle-faced, sandy-haired young Irishman, was at the door within fifteen minutes.

'It was a professional job, Governor,' he said, politely declining the drink Roger offered him. 'We have a description of the van from some bystanders and found it abandoned two hours later. It was stolen from an electrical contractor in Oak Lawn. The driver knew exactly how to smash into the car without banging her up too seriously.'

'Are you sure of that, Lieutenant?' Roger asked anxiously.

'Maybe it's just a coincidence, but I don't think so. This one has Mob written all over it. Have you done or said anything to offend our friends on the West Side?'

'Not that I know of. Is this the sort of routine warning they send to every candidate?'

'I've never heard of them doing it before.'

'How about threatening phone calls? My daughter just told me that she had received several. I answered one myself tonight. The man knew about the accident and said the next time it would be worse.'

'That does it, sir. It's the outfit. Someone must have a grudge against your family. We'll step up our protection of your family, Dr Farrell. But I think I should warn you that if somebody really wants your daughter dead, it will be damn difficult for us to prevent it.'

'My God,' Roger said in horror. 'Are we in a jungle, Lieutenant?'

'We're in America in 1982, sir, Anyone who wants to pay enough can have almost anyone else killed. You can't really protect anybody, not even the President of the United States.'

After the policeman left, Roger sank wearily into the easy chair by his fireplace. This was Rocco Marsallo's work. That may have been the Marshal's voice on the phone, worried that a murder committed thirty-eight years before might surface and send him to jail for what little remained of his life.

And it was not Noele's questions that were the threat anymore. The Marshal must know about Weaver's threat to publish the copied documents. It did not matter to him that the Farrells had no control over the *Chicago Informer*. His brain had been damaged by a life of vice. Torturing women amused him. And so he reacted to the threat of exposure the way he reacted to everything at this stage of his physical and mental deterioration – he went after the women of his enemies.

Evil that is irrational, Roger reflected to himself in his best professorial epigrammatic style, is no less dangerous because of its irrationality.

Burke

Flame had been delivered to him for treatment.

'There's a rattle in one of his rear wheels, Burkie,' Noele said. 'Could you see if you could fix him, please.'

Yes of course he would. Anything to take his mind off the Marshal.

His contacts in the Mob were sombre. That boy Rocco is crazy. Out of his mind. But his padrino is very good to him. Owes him for a big favour. A hit man's life would be worth nothing if he accepted a contract. He kills someone, then he's finished. Short of that, the council won't vote against him. Even for a future governor. Yeah, the padrino is that important. You kill him, it's another matter. Even the padrino would approve. But no contracts. Yeah, he probably will slip and kill someone. That's why the council is so patient. They know they'll put him down eventually. All right, but can't you control your own kids? Why is she messing around in Rocco's past?

I'm too old to kill him, Burke thought. So I tinker with cars. He wiped a thick layer of grease off his hands with an old rag. Part of the joy of repairing cars was wiping off the grease.

He had jacked up Flame and removed the left rear wheel. He examined it, and then crawled under the car to inspect the axle. Dangerous. But the jack was firm and the floor of the garage flat. He'd done it a hundred times before.

Lying under the car, he thought about the first Chevvy he worked on. A 1934 – cost 450 dollars. Probably better built than this one. And much better mileage.

Life looked simple and easy in those days. How had it all gone wrong? Maybe his mother had been right after all. Keep God's law and you'll stay out of trouble. Burke chuckled somewhat hollowly to himself. He had done neither.

Then he saw the sneakers next to the left rear wheel, a few inches from the jack – Danny's sneakers. A solid kick against the jack and Flame would fall on him, crushing out his life.

Danny was humming 'The Whistling Gypsy.'

So this is the way it ends. His life rushed before his eyes, as it always did in stories. So many regrets: Mother, father, wife, children. He'd let them all down. Even Bridie.

Damn it, man, get it over with.

One brown and white sneaker was now resting against the jack.

If I had to do it again, I'd still love her. And I'd still kill to protect her, if I could.

Don't prolong it, you bastard. I'm ready.

Danny stopped humming.

Now.

Another song: 'Roddy McCorley.'

Damn, I wish I had a cigar.

It's fair. I tried to kill you. I'm ready.

Only, dear God, end it.

Dear God. . . .

'Is it yourself under that vehicle?' Danny said.

'It is.' His voice was a rasp.

'Ah, 'tis a dangerous place to be, what with it suspended on the jack.'

'So I am told.' The smell of gasoline was teasing Burke's suddenly sensitive stomach.

'Have you found out what ails himself.'

'Bad axle work.'

'Auto repair isn't what it used to be in the old days, is it?'

Damn it, end it.

'It never was very good.'

'Sure, then, you should come out from under, so we can put the wheel back on. It's not safe, at all, at all.'

Burke eased himself out from under the Chevvy and stood up. Every muscle in his body ached from tension.

Danny was leaning nonchalantly against the wall of the garage, needing only a pipe in his mouth to complete his mask as an Irish countryman.

'I think I need a drink,' Burke murmured.

'In the middle of the morning?' Danny asked in mock surprise. 'That's no way to start the day. Still, I suppose it's all right, just this once. I may have a sip myself.'

A reprieve.

But for how long?

Brigid

'I tell you, Bridie, he was going to kill me. His foot was resting on the jack.'

They were driving to the Club for Saturday lunch, Burke's hands clutching the wheel of his Alfa, his fingernails still rimmed with traces of grease.

'But he didn't, did he?' she replied.

'You're pretty relaxed about it,' he grumbled.

'Well,' she said, trying to sound reasonable, 'you're still alive, aren't you? I think you're imagining things, what with that terrible man Marsallo on all our minds.'

She was deftly asking Burke what he had learned in his muffled phone conversation before they left for the club. She did not like to discuss Burke's connections with the Mob; her superstitions warned her that to mention them made them even more dangerous.

'Some of my friends talked to him. They think he's simmered down for the moment. He's been warned that if there is any more bloodshed his padrino may give up on him.'

'But if the papers publish the story?' She found fear clutching at her throat, like a blast of sub-zero cold when you emerge from a warm house on a winter day.

'That may set him off again. He's unpredictable as well as crazy. He could be watching the TV news some night when Roger is on it, think of those damn papers, and decide to do something to someone else who is close to Roger.'

'Irene?' Brigid gasped.

Burke drove into the nearly empty parking lot of the club.
'Or you.'

John

The faces in Kearney's Funeral Parlor rolled up and down,
as if they were bobbing in four-feet waves. John blinked
several times to clear his vision.

'It is beyond our comprehension why a man so young
and with so much promise of happiness ahead of him had to
go home in his early forties.'

Too much food, too much drink, too much smoking, too
many weekends in the office, too much strain.

'We are confident that we will meet him again, but our
confidence in the future does not alter our grief in the present. We weep as Jesus did at the death of his friend Lazarus
and as Mary did when the lifeless body of her son was
placed in her arms. We offer our sympathy as Jesus did to
the poor widow of Naim. We reaffirm our faith that Michael
Heggarty will rise again, just as that young man did.'

There were times when death seemed an easy way
out – Noele's life in jeopardy, the family history being passed around among reporters, Danny's return and his sup-
pressed rage, Irene as much in love with him as ever, his
own career at the mercy of a psychopathic cardinal.

'And we bow our heads in grief and pray God that time
will heal the wounds and give us all the strength to go on.'

The widow, looking all of her thirty-nine years, blew her
nose and nodded in vigorous agreement. Her oldest
daughter, a classmate of Noele's, embraced her mother protectively.

'For we know that, even though we are lost in the fog on
the side of a steep mountain, the summit is somewhere
above us radiant in the light of everlasting dawn.'

John shook hands with the widow, hugged her children, and joined his own family at the back of the red-carpeted funeral parlour.

'I liked the wake service,' Danny said. 'Chalk up one more for the new Church, and that was a very powerful little talk, Jackie. It meant a lot to the family.'

'Maybe you ought to be a priest, Danny,' Roger said jovially. 'You seem so interested in the church.'

Roger had no reason to be grinning. Too many things had gone wrong and worse might still happen.

'The only advantage I can see is the celibacy,' Danny replied. 'Sure, it would be wonderful to be free from temptations.'

'I have them occasionally.' John laughed, thinking of how lovely Irene looked in black.

They all laughed, all except Noele, who did not seem amused.

'Uncle Monsignor has his parish to love,' she said in her best mother superior tone. 'Some people are afraid to love anyone.'

'Do you think she means me?' Danny muttered in sotto voce.

'Really.' Noele sniffed disdainfully. She joined Julie Heggarty and hugged her as the rest of the Farrells walked through the lobby of the funeral parlour toward the snow-packed parking lot. Although it was a 'please omit flowers' wake, Kearney's still smelled of mums. The smell was probably sealed into the walls.

As he made his way carefully toward his car, John remembered another wake in an earlier Kearney's. His father was laid out in an open coffin, his head on a satin pillow that concealed the massive wound that had taken his life. Nothing had ever been the same since that night.

He climbed laboriously into his Buick and watched the others stumble across the parking lot, like drunken dancers after an all-night party. A dance of death, John told himself; like the characters at the end of a Bergman film. And if we can't stop that dance, some of us are going to end where Mike Heggarty is tonight.

Roger

Maryjane led him into Les Nomades and introduced him to Jovan, the proprietor.

'An honour to meet you, Governor,' he said, bowing over Roger's hand.

'Old-world charm.' Maryjane waved a casual hand. 'Bistro atmosphere, Parisian posters, and good food, without worrying about conventioneers.'

'My education has been neglected,' Roger said mildly.

He was sick with worry. The papers, Noele, Martha, Irene, Danny. He didn't need another love affair. But he was incapable of declining Maryjane's dinner invitation.

'The same rules tonight, Governor, at the risk of repeating myself.' The handsome, leggy blonde filled his glass with dry white wine. 'First, you're my guest, and I pay the bill. Second, it's deep background, not on the record. Third, no passes.'

'I wasn't planning any,' he protested, with singular lack of candor.

She raised her hand. 'No denials needed. I'm merely setting up the guidelines.' She pushed her long hair away from her tiny face. 'I happen to believe in marriage, and anyway, I couldn't compete with your resident sex goddess.'

'Irene?'

'If I were her and you fooled around, I'd cut off your balls.'

He tried to make his laugh disarming. She was serious. Too bad Irene wasn't that fiercely possessive. Then, in a quick, blinding insight, he realized that he had married Irene as a substitute for Danny.

'Do you object if I say something personal?' Maryjane's conversation seemed to be total free association.

'Not at all,' he said, realizing that the explosion of insight had not changed his facial expression in the slightest.

'I meet a lot of politicians in this business.' She looked

shyly at her wineglass. 'And you really are the class of the lot. I've never seen anyone so graceful under pressure.'

Roger was dumbfounded. The woman was not trying to seduce him. She meant what she said. He would never have thought of using the word 'graceful' of himself. Why would she see grace in him?

'I know what you're going through with that Rod Weaver stuff.' A faint flush coloured her face. 'You're really being quite brave, you know.'

No, I'm not. I'm a weakling and a coward. I have been both all my life. And you are a sweet kid, an appealing mixture of toughness and gentleness, of sophistication and naive virtue. You're my Snowflake in a couple of years.

'Did you read the copied documents?' he asked.

'A pile of shit,' she said briskly. 'Rod wanted me to promise to put him on TV with it. Don't worry, I certainly won't use it. My generation of reporters didn't grow up during Vietnam, so we have some ethical standards.'

'You believe in marriage, and you believe in privacy?' Regretfully he removed her from his sex object list. There must have been women like you around when I was younger, women who would have kept me on the path of virtue. His idiot romance with his cousin had blinded him to them.

And he comes back from the dead, and he's not the boy I thought I loved. Probably never was. And despite all my stupidity, I still think I'm qualified to be governor of this state.

'And I don't swear and I don't chase men and I don't drink much and I generally don't talk dirty, and I don't smoke. I only lie a little. But tell me more about Daniel Farrell. He really turned me on. How can anyone spend all that time in jail and still seem perfectly normal?'

'As normal as he ever was.' The girl's conversational whirl was making him dizzy. She would be very good in bed, if you could turn off the stream of chatter.

Chauvinist pig.

He saw Martha on his occasional forays back to the University. Crisp and correct in the corridors of the department, she greeted him as she would any other respected senior colleague, save for a glow of starry-eyed admiration in her eyes.

'You're the academic, so you know more about Freud than I do, but what does it mean to a kid to grow up knowing that his mother died to save his life? That's a heavy load to carry around.'

Roger never quite thought about it that way.

'Like having a ghost peering over your shoulder,' Maryjane said with a sympathetic little frown. 'Now, let's talk about state finance, Governor. Order the vegetable soup and the salmon mousse, and remember, it's on me.'

Flossie's ghost coming back for vengeance?

Ace

Another blizzard was on the way, so Ace McNamara rode the creaky, cantankerous Rock Island on his weekly pilgrimage to St Prax's, instead of risking his car in the streets of the Nineteenth Ward, a ward that was something less than loyal to the mayor and hence not likely to have a high priority for the city snow ploughs.

The Rock Island Line, once a proud name, no longer existed; and the Regional Transportation Authority, never a proud name, operated the trains with moderately benign neglect. But it would always be the Rock Island as it wended its weary way through the various Parks until it finally deigned to come down from its elevated roadway and, like a somewhat tipsy dowager, stagger into the Neighbourhood.

Ace was not the only naval officer on the train. 'Good to have you aboard, sir. Are you having a pleasant trip, sir?'

Ace briskly saluted the man in the ND jacket. 'Yes, sir.'

'At ease, Captain.' Dan gave a fair imitation of an admiral.

'Our officers' mess on this ship isn't very good, I'm afraid, sir.' Ace saluted again.

Dan stuck out his hand and grinned genially. 'Nice to see that one person from the Neighbourhood hasn't changed.'

'I was about to say the same thing.'

They both laughed.

'You were in Nam?' Danny said, now dead serious.

'Three times.'

'I think I may have lucked out on that one.'

'You'd be dead,' Ace said flatly. 'You're the kind of flyboy who would have gone back for that last run.'

'I guess so.'

'How does it feel to be back? Many surprises?'

'There aren't many surprises left when you come out of the fields one evening, dead tired as usual, and there's a geek from the Interior Ministry who says you have to take a plane ride with him. The next morning you're at the US Embassy being interviewed by American television.'

'But that's what it's about,' Ace said. 'Christmas is the surprise of light coming back. Easter the surprise of spring returning. Our faith is the ability to be open to surprises.'

'Ah, the poor church has changed so much.' Danny fled to the protection of his wonderful brogue. 'And here we have a pious and holy priest preaching paganism.'

'Catholicism is pagan symbols with a new overlay of meaning – like the blessing of the Easter water and the lighted candle: obviously a pagan intercourse ceremony converted to mean that on Easter Jesus consummated his marriage with his bride, the Church, and that we who are baptized are the fruits of this fertile union.'

'Saints protect us and preserve us.' Danny made a devout sign of the cross. 'Are you after saying that the Holy Easter candle is a phallic symbol?'

'What does it look like? And the water is a womb symbol.'

'Ritual intercourse.' Danny's eyes opened in mock dismay. 'On the main altar during solemn high mass with mother superior watching.'

'And the words are "May this candle fructify these waters."'

''Twas easier in the old days. . . . when the clergy didn't

go around suggesting that God was horny, Captain, sir.'
Dan shivered, perhaps from the cold, perhaps from fear of
the pursuing, love-crazed deity.

'At least I don't have to interpret the symbolism for the
likes of you,' Ace said. 'It's easy to see where your imagination is.'

'Terrible, terrible, terrible. And what comes out of the
union,' Danny said changing back to Chicago English, 'is a
surprise to all concerned.'

'As is usually the case.'

'It's not easy.' Danny shook his head sadly, the comic
replaced quickly by the troubled dreamer.

'Order out of disorder, cosmos out of chaos – it's not
supposed to be easy,' Ace replied. 'Creation or re-creation
never is.'

The Rock Island stopped at Eighty-third Street, blocking
traffic as it always did. The stations were designed by a
genius who arranged that every stop would block traffic.

Danny was thoughtful. 'That's what Noele said the
other day when she announced for the millionth time that
I am grossly immature: Resurrection is not supposed to be
easy.'

'Noele said that? Do you think she's right?'

Danny's head sank toward his chest. 'If I was certain
that she was right, my life might be a lot different in the
years ahead.'

'You'd keep on taking risks?'

'It was questions like that' – Danny took refuge again in
his brogue – 'that scared me away from you twenty years
ago.'

John

He had just come to his room in the rectory from a Wed-
nesday evening Lenten service in the church. It was the

associate's turn to take the service. But Jerry had pleaded in a last-minute phone call, with the noise of barroom conversation in the background, that he had run into a counselling case. So John Farrell took the service – scripture readings, hymn singing, and a homily about the Holy Spirit in the life of the church.

There were thirty or forty pious souls, a couple of devout teenagers, some older people who would have come if it was the rosary or benediction or the stations of the cross, or a sermon in Sanskrit, a few of the prayer group members, and some marriage encounter couples.

Danny, in the inevitable Notre Dame Windbreaker, had made himself at home in the pastor's parlour and was sipping a bottle of Coke the way he used to sip a bottle of beer in years gone by.

John was mildly annoyed. Danny had made the rectory his part-time hang out, wandering in and out almost as if he were a member of the staff. And to tell the truth, he was there more often, it seemed, than the associate pastor.

'Hell of a good sermon tonight, Jackie,' Danny said. 'Gave me a few ideas for the chapter I'm working on. From what I hear, most priests don't preach as well as you do. Must be the TV experience.' He grinned mischievously. 'And by the way, I hope you told that guy Keegan to go to hell?'

'No, I told him I would discontinue the programme week after next. It made him very happy. He said my fellow priests might eventually restore me to favour and I might be esteemed almost as much as I used to be. Wasn't that nice?'

'And you told them that at the station last week?' Dan's brow furrowed into a deep frown.

'No, I didn't; it was another great programme. Two professional football players from the Christian Athletes. The ratings will be sky high. I couldn't spoil their happiness at the station.'

'A priest paying attention to ratings and phone calls?' Danny asked, putting the empty Coke bottle on the coffee table.

'You're beginning to sound like Keegan. I'll tell them next week.'

The phone rang. It was, bizarrely enough, Ed Keegan.

'This is Monsignor Keegan, John,' he began formally, as though they had not been contemporaries at the seminary and called each other by first names for most of their lives. 'I've heard rumours that you really did not ask to be released from your contract at Channel Three.'

John felt irrationally angry. 'I'm going to talk about it to them next week.'

'The cardinal is most insistent, John. He's the representative of the Pope, the vicar of Christ. I am sure you wouldn't want to slip lower in the esteem of your fellow priests by resisting the cardinal's will any longer.'

'I'll talk to them next week.'

'Can you go down to see them tomorrow? It would contribute greatly to the cardinal's peace of mind.'

So pathetically eager to force the erring cleric back into line. 'You don't have to worry, Ed. I'll take care of it. You can assure the cardinal that I intend to be no further threat to his peace of mind.'

'I regret very much that I have to say this to you, John, but you give me no choice; if I don't hear within twenty-four hours that you have informed Channel Three you're withdrawing from your television programme, then I will at the cardinal's direction institute proceedings to have an administrator appointed in your place. You may continue as pastor and receive the salary of a pastor, so long as you say the required Masses, but your associate will become the de facto pastor of St Praxides.'

If Danny Farrell hadn't been there listening, his blue eyes shining with concern and support, John would have caved in.

'You crazy son of a bitch,' he exploded. 'Are you so much a creature of the institutional church that you'd turn the best parish in the city over to that creep because the cardinal resents someone else getting publicity? Don't you have any hormones left in your body?'

'The cardinal's will is the will of God,' Keegan said righteously.

'Go get him!' Danny whispered, leaping toward the telephone, loving every second of it.

'I know a little bit of canon law too, Ed. You're going to

have a hell of a hard time taking this parish away from me. And there are a couple of canon lawyers in the diocese who would dearly love to fight you. We can prolong this case until your psychopathic boss is gone and a new archbishop comes in who thinks it's a good thing to have priests on television. And of course you, you hypocritical bastard, will think the same thing.'

'You're defying the will of God, Monsignor?' Keegan said in outraged disbelief.

'Furthermore, you utterly misunderstand the temper of the people of this parish if you think they will accept as acting pastor a man who would rather associate with sixteen-year-old boys than sixteen-year-old girls. Finally, if you lift a finger against me, you or your psychopathic boss, you'll have a thousand angry adolescents around the cardinal's mansion tomorrow morning.'

'I'll have to consult his eminence about this,' said Keegan stiffly.

'You do that,' John said, slamming down the phone.

'Hot shit!' Danny embraced him. 'It's like the good old days, only you're crazier now than Roger and I ever were.'

'The word will be all over the archdiocese by tomorrow, Danny.' He stood up to walk to his liquor cabinet. 'And I'll be a pariah in the priesthood for the rest of my life.'

'That might just save your soul,' Danny said.

Irene

She and Danny sat across from each other at the Country Club, as nervous as two teenagers on their first date. It was an utterly safe place to meet; the eyes of two dozen people were there to watch them. Not that anyone would think it unusual that Danny and his cousin's wife would have an occasional meal together.

'What did you think?' Danny asked anxiously.

She had prepared her reaction very carefully, memorizing it word for word. 'I'm prejudiced, Danny, because I've known you for such a long time; but even allowing for that – and I think I'm objective enough to be able to do that – I think it's a great novel. It's got depth, power, and a wonderful story. I'm sure it will be a commercial success. Some of the critics will love it, and some will scream that you're a hack. But they'll all know that there is an important new writer to deal with. The people here at the Club and in the Neighbourhood, most of whom won't read it, will wish you'd stayed in China. And those few of us who will read it will celebrate the fact that you came from our parish.'

'Well, I guess I can heave my sigh of relief. You're the first one besides my agent and my editor to read it, and I don't trust agents or editors – well, not as much as I trust somebody like you.'

'And my stories?'

'I'll give it to you straight, Renie. They're not just very good. They are sensational. You're one of the best there is. They make me hesitate between pride that I know you and envy that I can't write nearly so well. But why have you kept such beautiful work secret for all these years?'

Her hand darted out to touch his fingers and then darted back very quickly. They were, after all, in the dining room of the Country Club.

'And you know what a worthless whore I am?' she said bitterly.

'I know that's the way you see yourself. But that's not the way a reader would see Lorraine. They would view her as a fragile flower at long last ready to bloom.'

'That's Lorraine, not me.' She felt the sting of tears in the back of her eyes.

'Yes, it is, but I won't argue. You'll find out for yourself in time. Let me send them to my agent. I know he can find a publisher.'

'I could never do that.'

'And I'm hardly the one to talk about bravery, am I?' he said sadly.

He drove her home after lunch, along streets slick with melting snow drifts.

'Come in,' she pleaded.

'I shouldn't.'

'Forget *shoulds* and *shouldn't*s for an hour.'

'No.'

She kissed him, her tongue jamming into his mouth and demanding his. 'Please.'

Whatever his hesitancies outside, he was not hesitant after she led him into the first-floor guest room. He undressed her slowly and leisurely, making each zipper and button and strap a delicate ceremony.

'One improvement over 1963 is that a man doesn't have to fight girdles,' he said.

'Noele treats them as historical improbabilities, like the Latin Mass.'

'Was she really born on Christmas Day?' he asked as he drew her hands to the buttons on his shirt.

'Really born on Christmas Day.' she replied softly.

'Would she approve of us?' he asked, slipping off her last wisp of clothing.

'I don't know. . . . Oh, Danny.'

'I didn't hurt you?'

'You won't leave me anything.'

'Clothes?' He was mystified.

'No protection at all.' She moaned as her body rebelled against all restraint.

'I've read your stories, Renie.' And his fingers and lips were everywhere.

Irene was now only pure sensation, soaring into the skies and dancing on the clouds.

'You're a wonderful lover, Danny,' she murmured sleepily afterward as they clung together on the sweaty and rumpled sheets, his head resting on her breasts.

The sun had broken through the clouds, and through the drawn shades bathed the room in soft, approving light when they awoke.

Peaceful and happy, she knelt next to him and he put his hands around her waist, fingers on the small of her back, thumbs on her belly. In this delightful position, she began to talk to him, pouring out everything that had happened since they had been separated. At first the stories were sad, but somehow they became comic and the two of them shook with laughter.

Then she was serious again.

'You've grown, Danny,' she said, as her hands touched his face. 'You are even more sensitive, more tender, and a better listener than you used to be. You make a woman feel that she is a woman and that she can tell you everything.'

'I try,' he said, a little puzzled.

'With other men I do the listening. With you I am able to talk.'

'And a good talker you are, too.' He winked, still mystified.

'But you're still not a friend,' she said. 'Friends not only listen, they talk. They share their hopes and their fears. You don't.'

Danny removed his hands from her body. She put them back.

'I'm getting too close to the real you again, like I did the last time,' she said without bitterness. 'And you're preparing to escape again.'

'I'm no good in the long run.' He sighed. 'You know that.'

She overpowered his lips with her own, holding him motionless with the force of her love. 'I won't let you leave me this time.'

Noele

The only after effects from the automobile accident were an occasional headache and the obligation to call someone every night to find a ride to school while Flame was going through the final phases of rehabilitation at the Chevrolet agency at Ninety-fifth and Kedzie, where Burkie had made ominous complaints.

Only two and a half weeks till Easter. Despite her

preoccupation with the Farrell mysteries, Noele had to prepare for the Holy Week Liturgy. She was busy selecting the music the folk group would sing at the end of the interlude between the Vigil services and the Mass on Holy Saturday, an interlude that she managed to pry away from Mr Creepy Crumb by a combination of charm and stubborness.

The phone rang. Even though her private number had been changed and there had been no threatening calls since the accident, she knew who it was before she answered. Again the thick, blue voice on the phone. 'McNeally and his fink cops aren't going to protect you. You're going to get fucked real good.'

Noele slammed down the phone and ran for help.

There was no one in the house.

She threw open the front door and collided with Danny, who was coming in with a stack of pictures of Roger to be hung in neighbours' front windows.

'I'm a precinct captain,' he said jovially. 'Hey, what's wrong?'

Noele clung to him desperately, sobbing with fear.

He held her tightly, gradually soothing her and exorcising the terror.

It was wonderful to be in his arms.

I love him so much.

John

The primary election in late March was a dry run for Roger's campaign organization. In fact, most of the voters cast ballots for Roger instead of George Washington Lincoln, a perennial Downstate Democratic candidate who wore Davy Crockett clothes, because their local Democratic organizations told them to vote for him, and there were enough organization Democrats in the state to turn out a half-million voters even if Roger had been running against no one. Hence his own personal organization had relatively little to do except admire the skill with which he read the text of his TV advertisements.

The victory celebration was something less than ecstatic in its enthusiasm. The Farrell staff found it hard to rejoice over one more defeat for Georgie Lincoln, especially since there was no evidence from the very modest turnout that Roger had ignited any prairie fire of voter enthusiasm, even though the polls showed him running well ahead of the governor.

But as Angelo Spina had put it, an orangutan would run well ahead of the governor.

The Illinois primary was cruelly early. More than seven months would intervene before the general election in the fall. The candidate and his staff must neither begin too early nor wait too long. In practice this meant no peace for the candidate or his family all summer.

Danny was standing next to Roger at the rear of the modest crowd in the grand ballroom of the Midland Hotel, awaiting the candidate's triumphant appearance. He continued to turn up at odd times and places, seemingly at loose ends save for his novel, which no one, as far as John knew, had ever seen. His dirty jeans, tattered sweat shirt, and the by now badly wrinkled Notre Dame Windbreaker had become part of the scenery. You almost forgot that this was a man who had been in a Chinese prison for eighteen years.

'I suppose the real reason for this celebration,' Danny said, 'is so the voters of Illinois can get a good look at Irene and Noele and decide if they want those two faces on the front covers of their newspapers for the next four years.'

'Very perceptive political observation,' John agreed.

There was a burst of applause, not exactly spontaneous, because one of the young staff members was leading it off camera. Mick Gerety appeared at the podium and announced, 'And now, ladies and gentlemen, the next governor of the great Prairie State of Illinois!'

The enthusiasm of the group was authentic enough, although perhaps motivated in part by the hope that they would find jobs in the new administration. The victorious candidate appeared with his black-haired wife and his red-haired daughter, both in white dresses that hinted at the coming of spring. There was something wrong between Roger and Irene. But that was not surprising, with Danny on the one hand insisting that he was not interested in turning back the clock, but on the other hand being very much a part of the Farrell family life and thus effectively activating all the old memories.

'This is an important first step,' Roger said after the cheers of his supporters died down. 'Both of those words are critical. What we have accomplished thus far in our campaign to bring a more compassionate and responsive government to the State of Illinois ought not to be minimized. We have proven that we can organize a mostly volunteer campaign to raise the issues and get out the vote and win decisively. But we have taken only first, cautious steps. While I appreciate the enthusiasm of your applause, I also accept it as your commitment to continue the attempt we have all begun. With God's help, and the help of my wife and daughter' – he smiled and raised his arms in both directions to draw his two women close to him – 'we will stay in this fight for the State of Illinois every single day from now until the fourth of November.'

'What's the state of your confrontation with the cardinal?' Danny asked as he fumbled with the zipper of his Windbreaker and turned to leave the ballroom.

'He backed down, as I thought he would. He's like running water. He follows the path of least resistance. If you stand up to him, he disappears. And Keegan is left holding the bag, but he's used to that.'

His temporary victory had brought back his hunger for Irene. Manhood restored.

'A good week for the Farrells.' Danny punched his arm.

'An important first step.' John Farrell grinned.

As he turned into the driveway at St Praxides, John hesitated. The big stained-glass window in the back of the church was not lighted, a stained-glass window depicting St Praxides marching toward the world with a large farm implement over her shoulder – Prax's ax, the parishioners called it.

John glanced at his watch. The light was turned off by a timer at eleven. It was only 10.45. He backed out of the driveway, and then carefully, because the streets were still slippery with two inches of March snow, drove the fifty yards to the entrance of the church. The massive and beautiful stained-glass windows had been smashed.

John jumped out of the car, opened the back door of the church, and dashed into the darkened nave. In the faint glow of the vestibule light he saw thousands of tiny pieces of coloured glass scattered on the pews and a dozen or so large bricks.

In the rectory, even before he called the police, his personal phone rang. An ugly laugh and then a harsh voice. 'That's not the only thing that's going to get broken, Monsignor. Unless your brother shuts that punk up.'

Irene

She encountered Danny in the lobby of the Midland after the victory celebration.

'Tomorrow morning at my place while you're jogging.'
His poor face looked so tired, his pale blue eyes so weary.

What did the election victory mean to him? Yet he seemed to be exultant over Roger's victory.

'Of course.'
'I can hardly wait.'
'Me too.'

Brigid

Despite Burke's wishes and the doctor's orders, she was the first one to arrive at the plant on the day after the primary. She promised Burke that she would leave before noon, but insisted there were a few 'minor matters' about the Streeterville Plaza job to which she must attend. In truth, she wanted to make sure that none of the wrong subcontractors was on the list of bidders.

She paid little attention to the yard as she drove in. It was only as she parked in front of the ramshackle office that she noticed that the cement mixer at the end of the yard was tilted crazily, as though it had been on an all-night binge. She backed up quickly, sliding on the new-fallen snow. The tyres of all the construction vehicles had been slashed, and the windows of a dozen or so had been smashed with bricks.

She stumbled into the office and reached for a phone to call Burke. It rang before she could touch it.

'Listen, you sweet-smelling shanty Irish whore,' said a deep and menacing voice. 'We're going to slash you up like those tires unless your favourite son shuts up that punk kid.'

Irene

She leaned over him, a sheet clutched at her chest in a senseless gesture of modesty.

He was asleep, his haunted face momentarily at peace. Poor, dear man, he had suffered so much.

Their relationship was changing. He had begun to share himself with her. He was still the competent, demanding lover who could turn her into a mass of seething and uncontrollable reactions, a blob of need and delight. In his arms and at the mercy of his skills, the eighteen years of separation were blotted out. The night at the lake seemed like the day before yesterday.

But then, his conquest complete, his passions spent, he would quickly become the injured little boy, sobbing his hurt against his mother's breasts – unnamed and undescribed, but terrible hurts.

And many of them older than China.

She smoothed his hair and kissed him gently.

A strange mixture of forceful lover and hurt child.

My child.

Oh, Danny, give me a son. Our son. I want to take care of both of you.

Roger

'I wish I'd known before that we were dealing with the Marshal.' McNeally shook his head in discouragement. 'That makes it a whole different ball game.'

Roger felt he had had no choice but to tell McNeally about the copied documents, documents that might make the demented mobster think he was threatened with jail. The officer's brown eyes had first widened in suprise, then narrowed in shrewd thoughtfulness.

'No wonder Marsallo is so upset. And when he's upset, he turns vicious. A couple of years ago he caught one of his juice men holding back. So he suspended the guy by his feet from pipes in the basement of his mansion in River Forest and beat him in the guts with a baseball bat until his entrails fell out and dangled on the floor. It took a long time for the guy to die.'

'And he still roams the streets of Chicago?'

'When he's not playing golf at Far Hills or wandering the streets of River Forest. It's one thing, Governor, to know that he did it, and another to get the evidence that makes it worthwhile even to bring him in. We've never been able to lay a glove on the Marshal.'

'A van demolished my daughter's automobile, a stained-glass window in my brother's church is smashed, vehicles at our family's plant are vandalized, threats are made against the physical safety of my mother and my wife and my daughter, and you tell me you can't lay a hand on Rocco Marsallo?'

'We're doing all we can, Governor. We'll put extra surveillance on your family and its property, and we'll try to keep an eye on the Marshal too. It's a lot harder than it used to be, with all the damn government regulation. I'll be candid, however, Governor. I could assign the whole Chicago police force to your protection, but if the Marshal wants you badly enough, he'll get you.'

'What would you suggest I do, Lieutenant?' Roger asked stiffly.

'I'd suggest that you persuade Weaver not to publish those papers and to tell everybody he's not going to publish them.' He tapped the pen on his notebook as he stood at the door of Roger's office at campaign headquarters. 'You might make a call to some of your political allies out on the West Side. They don't like the Marshal much. Maybe they can calm him down.

Half an hour later Roger made a call to the West Side to a contact Angelo Spina suggested. The man was friendly and sympathetic. It was a terrible thing that was happening. A real disgrace to the city, though, thank God, crazy Rocco didn't live in the city but lived in River Forest, which is 'a Republican place, Governor.'

'Do you think any of your friends or their friends could put a stop to this?' Roger asked anxiously.

'That depends.'

'On what?'

'Not on anything you can do, Governor,' said the West Side politician.

Roger then called Rodney Weaver to plead with him. But Weaver had made up his mind. He was going with the story the week after Easter. He was sorry about the threats and the vandalism but they could not divert him from his commitment to the public's right to know. Indeed, such criminal behaviour made it all the more imperative that the whole sorry mess get out into the open. 'A free and unfettered public opinion,' he thundered, 'deprives monsters like Marsallo of power.'

'Over the dead bodies of my mother, and my wife, and my daughter?' Roger asked icily.

'You should have thought about that before your family became involved with a man like Marsallo,' said Weaver, sounding like an old-fashioned Irish monsignor about to throw a couple out of the rectory as they were embarking on a religiously mixed marriage.

'You know those documents were copied without my permission, Rodney.'

'Frankly, I can live with that,' he said.

He should have withdrawn from the race as soon as he found his papers were missing. If he withdrew now, Weaver would still publish them and the Marshal might still take his vengeance.

As he was leaving his campaign headquarters there was a call from Angelo's contact on the West Side.

'I had my friends talk to some of their friends, Governor, and they are very sorry. But right now they can't do nothing about the crazy boy Rocco. Maybe later, if you know what I mean. But right now, they feel their hands are tied.'

'What might it take to untie the hands of your friends?'

'Well, Governor, that's a pretty tough question; you see, nobody likes this boy Rocco. They all think he's kind of crazy. You know, he didn't used to be that way; he comes from a very good family, good parents, good wife and kids, though they don't live with him much anymore. He's turned real mean the last few years, and the friends of my friends don't like that at all. Some one of these days he's going to kill somebody that he shouldn't kill. Then they'll have to do something about him.'

It was all quite clear: After somebody was killed, then the outfit would discreetly dispose of Marsallo. His coat still on, Roger sat down at the desk again. Oh, my God, which one will he kill?

A thought that had been lurking in one of the twisted side passages of the cavern of his preconscious finally forced itself to his attention. Suppose that he killed himself, leaving a letter blaming the Mob and in particular the Marshal. The council would have to take action. His death would be the Marshal's death warrant.

Roger had never in his life considered suicide; it was an admission of defeat that he could not tolerate.

Now self-destruction seemed to be a possible path of atonement. He did not drive the possibility out of his mind.

But how does one commit suicide?

Ace

'And all the time my poor child was in danger, Brigid was being threatened, and Saint Prax's windows broken, the only thing on my mind was screwing.'

There was no connection between the events. In or out of Danny's bed, Irene could not have prevented either the vandalism or the threats.

She knew that, of course. But Ace had learned in his years in the priesthood that women handled symbols differently from men. Irene was crying over the contrast between her pleasure and the danger to her family, not assuming responsibility for it.

And the story she had told him was easily the most astonishing tale he had ever heard. What the hell do I say now? I know, I duck.

'I won't touch the moral tangle, Renie; it's too much for me. I'll just say one thing: Your biggest flaw has always been not placing a high enough value on yourself.'

'You mean I give myself away cheaply?'

Her tears stopped.

Irene

St Patrick's Day was, as usual, cold, grey, and windy. The festivities of the day were enthusiastic but forced, like a May Day parade in Moscow. The faces of the young people in the parade and on the floats were pinched and red. The crowds on the sidewalk spent as much time blowing on their hands as clapping with them. The joviality of the politicians and their wives in the parade and on the reviewing stand was officially enforced, despite the shivering. The celebration no longer basked in the sunlight of Richard J.'s glowing Celtic charm. In the present administration, no one on the reviewing stand could be quite certain whether he was a confidant of the mayor or a member of the 'evil Cabal' to which her enemies were assigned with dizzying speed.

Roger, who considered the St Patrick's Day festivities to be grotesque, had strolled briskly in the first line of the parade along with the mayor, the county board chairman, whom the mayor had just dumped, two Polish congressmen, and one black ward committeeman. When he reached the reviewing stand, the cardinal, looking more than ever like a dissolute Renaissance despot – long white hair and hollow face to match his lean and hollow body – blithely congratulated him on his primary victory and on 'the great job your brother's doing on his television programme.'

Irene would have turned away and refused to speak to the man if Roger had not introduced her before she could escape. Noele, characteristically, was much more candid.

'If my uncle John is so good on television, Cardinal, why is Monsignor Keegan threatening to take the parish away from him unless he gives up the programme?'

The cardinal was unperturbed by her assault. 'Well, now, young lady, I can't always keep those chancery office people under control. I'll have to have a look-see myself, and if what you say is true, I'll certainly put a stop to it.'

'Tell me about it,' Noele had said, and sniffed.

Fortunately the cardinal did not understand teenage slang.

Irene shivered on the reviewing stand, smiled, and waved quite spontaneously at the passing marchers. The politicians and their wives on the stand were complaining about the profile of Roger that had appeared that day in *Fort Dearborn* magazine, a slick journal appealing to the limousine liberals of the lakefront Alps and the cocktail-party radicals of the suburbs, who sympathized with the poor and the oppressed so long as they stayed within the city limits. The magazine advertised such left-wing products as fifteen-hundred-dollar stereo sets, twenty-five-thousand-dollar Mercedes automobiles, and half-million-dollar condominiums.

Gery Jensen, the editor, had written the piece without bothering to interview Roger. He quoted one of 'Dr Farrell's distinguished colleagues' from the University as saying that it was 'probably a good thing for Roger to be elected to public office. He doesn't have much of a career ahead of him as a scholar. Mind you, he's clever, but not very profound.'

And the article observed that 'the professor's wife and daughter had faces of pretty, painted plaster of paris – two Barbie dolls, one middle-aged and one pubescent.'

'It's not true, Roger,' Noele protested. 'Moms only uses a little makeup around her eyes, and I don't wear any at all. I mean, my feelings aren't hurt, but why would he lie about us, especially when he hasn't ever seen either of us face to face?'

'Two answers, my dear,' Roger said. 'First of all, you have to sell magazines, and second, with his clientele you never lose any circulation by making fun of the Irish. None of us can afford vanity if we're going to be in public life, Snowflake. Besides, we have more serious, more deadly enemies out there than Gery Jensen.'

They made the rounds of boisterous cocktail parties and alcoholic receptions after the parade. Each successive appearance exposed the candidate and his family to a higher proportion of drunks, so that by the time they reached the Shamrock Festival, the South Side Irish classic

St Patrick's Day celebration, only a handful of participants were capable of even recognizing the 'next governor of the great State of Illinois.'

Irene drank a martini at each of the first four stops. A few months ago Roger would have discreetly warned her about that. But now, whatever the changes of chemistry that had occurred between them, he did not say a word. So she stopped after the fourth martini and managed to keep a steady walk and a pleasant face for the rest of the evening.

But at two o'clock in the morning Irene was wide awake. The alcohol had lost its effect in her bloodstream, and her head was clear. Roger was still in his self-imposed exile in the guest room.

Gery Jensen was perfectly correct, she thought. Even if she didn't wear layers of makeup, she was a middle-aged Barbie doll. All her life men had played with her: her father, then Danny, then Roger, and then for a few bittersweet weeks, John.

And now Danny again.

She had always responded, furnishing each of them the pleasures they demanded and enjoying their pleasure as though it were her own. In Danny's case she even provided him with the pleasure of her total candor. Never had she taken charge of herself or her own life. Father Ace was right. She gave herself away cheaply.

She sat up in bed and pounded the pillows angrily. 'Noele wouldn't put up with it,' she said aloud. 'Why should I!'

I am wide awake, I am perfectly sober, I am thinking clearly, I'm angry, angry at all of them and angry at myself. Who the hell is Dan Farrell to think he can keep me dangling on a string until he straightens out his emotional problems?

Feeling that she had crossed a decisive line, Irene bounced out of the bed, threw her mink coat on over her nightgown, shoved her feet into her boots, and rushed out into the hallway. She hesitated for a moment in front of Noele's door. The lights were still on in the Christmas child's room.

She and Noele had been squabbling more than usual lately. Noele surely knew that she and Roger were no longer sleeping together and was angry, not because she didn't understand the situation, but because she thought she did. And, whatever happened, Noele was certain to be affected. Innocently she had brought Danny Farrell back to life and would suffer the consequences like everyone else.

I've sacrificed myself for Noele, more than my Christmas child will ever know. It was time to stop the sacrificing.

She rushed by Noele's door, down the stairs, out of the house, and into the driveway. Chilled by the cold, she jumped into her Datsun and skidded three times on the way to Mandrake Parkway, the third time spinning in a complete circle. She was too angry to be frightened. She pounded the door furiously and leaned on the doorbell for several minutes before Danny, in his shorts and torn white terrycloth robe appeared to let her in. 'Glory be to God, Irene, what are you doing here at this hour of the night?'

She pushed into the house and slammed the door shut.

'I've come to tell you exactly what I think of you, you miserable son of a bitch. I'm sick and tired of being a prize dangling from the wall for men to take when they finally get around to deciding that I'll do until something better comes along. Who do you think you are that you can hide behind your stack of typescript and work through your silly sick psychotic problems while I wait patiently for an answer?'

'You're wonderful,' he murmured.

'And when your hormones become active enough that you want a woman, you pick me up off the streets, use me for an hour or so, and then dismiss me like a nice little whore who will keep herself on call in case you get horny again.'

'That's not true, but you're glorious.'

'And you don't care whether those criminals mutilate all of us – Brigid, Noele, and me.'

'That's not fair, Renie. What can I do?' A touch of fear and guilt. 'Please –'

'Please what? Take off my coat and go to bed with you because an angry woman turns you on? Then you can pretend that I'm your mother again. I'm not your mother, and I'm not a little girl. I'm an adult woman. Someday you might become an adult man, though I doubt it. But don't expect me to wait around till that happens.'

She stormed away from him, out into the cold night, and down the slippery steps to her car, praying to God that she wouldn't fall on her face. And as she pulled away she saw him standing in the panel of light at the door, rubbing his jaw in bemusement.

He's going to run away again. I don't care.

Fuck you, Danny Farrell.

Noele

'What were you and Maryjane Hennessey talking about yesterday?' Roger asked in his elaborately casual tone as he buttered his toast.

Moms was still in bed, like she always was at this hour, and Noele was trying to catch up on her trig while eating breakfast. She totally did not want to play Roger's inquisitive-father game.

'Colleges. I told her I was thinking of being a journalist.'

'You never told me that,' he said reproachfully.

'You never asked,' she replied, knowing that bitchiness always put him off in the morning.

She had told the truth, but not the whole truth. Maryjane was, like, real cool. And when she assured Noele it was all off the record they had a totally swift talk.

Her idea about Danny was really excellent. Why hadn't she thought of it?

Still feeling guilty because he didn't protect his mother.

A totally lame idea, but if a kid grows up being told his mother died to save his life, it figures that he'll feel guilty. Right?

It all fitted in somehow. No wonder Dan was afraid of

Moms . . . and of me, too.

But that doesn't tell me who killed Clancy.

And I can't mess with that or those retards will do something worse.

But I still have to find out.

Burke

His friend was on the phone again.

There had been a meeting of the council, he told Burke. The young men were angry. They didn't need a fight with a candidate for governor. But the padrino insisted that no one was to touch Rocco unless he killed someone. Then the padrino would strangle him with his own hands because he had brought disgrace.

The padrino is a man of honour.

Doubtless. But my family.

If you put him down, it's different. The padrino made that clear.

But I can't hire anyone to do it.

Silence.

And what if he hurts someone in my family, but doesn't kill them?

That would be a real disgrace.

Would the padrino change his mind then?

Too bad you couldn't keep that kid out of things that were not any of her business.

After the call Burke removed his father's gun from the safe. Old Redmond Kennedy had probably used it himself. Burke had hired others to do his killing for him.

His hand trembled as he tried to load the heavy weapon. In frustration he slammed his fist against the safe.

He was useless.

John

'Can I come in?' Ace asked.

'Sure. Pour yourself some Jameson's and sit down.'

John was drinking his second martini on the day after the St Patrick's lunacies, the Friday evening before Passion Sunday.

'I hear your associate has applied to the personnel board for a transfer.' The Ace poured himself half a tumbler of Jameson's, considered it critically, and then added several more ounces of the golden fluid.

'I'm not surprised. He and his allies missed their chance to take over here. So they'll probably try a shot at another parish.'

'MN scared the hell out of the old man at the parade. That young woman wouldn't hesitate to take on the Pope himself. That would be a fun fight to watch.' Ace downed a substantial portion of his Irish in pleasant contemplation of the big Pole and the little Irish chewing each other out.

John had so many more serious worries that he had almost forgotten about the cardinal. 'Did you know that Danny left town this morning?'

The Ace coughed, wasting some of his precious Jameson's. 'He did?'

'He called me from the airport and said he had to go to New York to see his publisher and might stay there, indefinitely. Sounded like something scared the hell out of him.'

'Oh.' The Ace sucked meditatively on the edge of his tumbler.

'Typical,' John muttered. 'When things get tough, Danny runs away.'

'Do you think he'll be back?'

'Oh, yes. He'll turn up again like a bad penny. He asked me to tell Brigid and Roger. My brother was out campaigning, so I told Irene.'

'And she said?'

'Nothing. Just thanked me for calling. She's still in love

with him, you know. Roger was a poor second choice. And as you yourself said, I was a substitute for Danny.'

'Sometimes I think that crazy bastard is a substitute for himself.'

John was astonished by the Ace's vehemence.

'You sound like you're angry at him.'

'I'd like to wring his, you should excuse the expression, fucking neck.'

James III

'Honestly, Jaimie, I can't imagine anything more gross. Daniel simply went to the airport, got on a plane, and flew to New York without packing any of his clothes and without saying good-bye to anyone but Uncle Monsignor. Isn't that geeky?'

Jaimie was inclined to agree that it was indeed geeky, although he was personally quite happy to have Danny out of town. He liked him but was wary of him as a rival.

He drove slowly, keeping a close eye on the unmarked police car that was following them. He did not know why it was so important but Dr Farrell said not to get too far ahead of the cops and Jaimie was not about to argue.

He and Noele had driven to Oak Lawn to see a movie called *Cat People*, which Noele wanted to see because she had heard that the cat people had green eyes like her own.

It was a weird film – strange, heavy mystical symbolism that Jaimie understood all too well. It frightened and intrigued him.

Noele kept up a running commentary through the film, as she usually did. 'Really, I think she looks gross without any clothes on. She looks much better on that poster with a cobra wrapped around her.'

'I think she looks pretty good either way.'

'I'm sure you would,' she complained.

'Not a bad flick,' he said tentatively on the way home.

'You like every movie in which the women take off their clothes.'

'It beats studying chemistry,' he agreed.

'I think the black panthers looked better than she did.'

'You were supposed to see a similarity between the panthers' sleek bodies and hers.'

'Really?' Noele was surprised. 'Gee, I wish I could see the things in flicks that you do.'

'I thought the redhead was especially sexy, but then I guess I like half-naked redheads.'

'Jaimie Burns! You are the most gross boy I have ever known!'

'Is it *most gross* or *grossest*?' Jaimie asked.

'Really!'

The signs were there for Jaimie to read. He'd better change the subject. 'Why did your cousin go to New York?'

'He said he had to see his publisher, but I think he's afraid of Moms. They were in love once, you know, probably still are. Moms isn't sleeping with Roger these days. Danny left so as not to come between them. Like Enoch Arden.'

'Enoch Arden?'

The police car had not made the stoplight at Western Avenue. Jaimie slowed down, but even after the light changed there was still no police car.

'You remember, it was a novel by Dickens.'

'No, I think it was by Tennyson.' Jaimie realized that he took a considerable risk correcting Noele, but he was never able to resist the temptation when he caught her in one of her rare mistakes.

'Well, whoever wrote it.'

'Actually it was a poem, and Enoch and the girl were married.'

'I didn't mean to be taken literally.'

Jaimie never had a chance to pursue his interpretation of the Tennyson poem. As they turned off Ninety-fifth Street into a dark and empty Jefferson Avenue, two cars emerged from driveways, one ahead and one behind them. Jaimie slammed his foot down on his brake as two men jumped out of the car in front and rushed to Jaimie's Chevvy, one at either window. Jaimie rolled down the window on his side of the car and only then noticed that they were both wearing ski masks.

The one on his side jammed a gun into Jaimie's throat. 'Not a word, punk, or I'll waste you and that slut. Get out of the car real quiet and peaceful.' Jaimie opened the door of the car prepared to deck his adversary the same way he would dispose of a wide receiver. He lowered his shoulder and smashed into the man's chin, sending him sprawling across the street.

Then he turned and tried to grab the shotgun away from another man who had appeared out of the darkness. He twisted the gun out of his hands and raised it like a club, swinging it towards the man's skull. But then something slammed against Jaimie's head. He felt himself falling into a deep pit. The last thing he heard as he crashed into the bottom of the pit was Noele's screams.

Later he tried desperately to climb out of the pool of darkness in which he had been struggling. He was in a car bumping down a rough road. His hands were tied, and there was a gag in his mouth. Somewhere in the far distance he heard Noele moaning and groaning. She too was gagged and through thick and blurry eyes, he saw a man's massive hand poking and jabbing at her bare flesh.

Then they dragged him into a house, either in the country or in a secluded section of the city. It was surrounded by trees, and there were no lights from nearby houses. He was pushed and shoved into the darkened house and then into a brilliantly lighted room.

One of the three men slapped him into consciousness. 'We're going to put on a little show for you tonight, punk, and we want you to see the whole thing from beginning to end. It's a preview of what's going to happen unless this slut's family does what we tell them.'

Then they made him watch while they tore off Noele's clothes and beat her. Then the three men took turns in raping her and sodomizing her.

DANCE
NINE

Dance Macabre

'Dance of death . . . depicts Death playing the violin and dancing in the graveyard at midnight. The music includes the Dies Irae from the Requiem Mass.'

Roger

Congressman Burns was screaming like a man being dragged into electroshock therapy. 'You're telling me, Lieutenant, that a young couple can be kidnapped and brutalized on the streets of this city and the Chicago police department can't do a thing about it, even when they know who's responsible?'

McNeally had been pushed too far. 'God damn it, Congressman, if I had my way we'd go out to River Forest, pick up those bastards, and castrate them. Don't blame us cops for what you congressmen and the Supreme Court have done. You know, I know, we all know, the Marshal is responsible, and that he and his thugs Dubuque Salerno and Little Tony Caputo are the guys who did it. But if I bring them in, their lawyers will have them out in four hours and the newspapers will have the whole story. We don't have a shred of evidence. They wore ski masks. Neither Noele nor your son can identify them.'

'Then they're free to do it again, as they threatened?'

'We can lock the girl up in protective custody someplace. We can take her to a new city and give her a new name, or we can send her to Europe. But if the Marshal wants her badly enough, he will still get her.'

'What the lieutenant is telling us,' Roger said with icy calm, 'is that civilization only works when citizens are either committed to stability or afraid of the consequences of instability. Marsallo is a throwback of a pre-civilized era, and those of us who are civilized aren't prepared to respond to him.'

The congressman slumped into a chair next to his wife and Irene, who was sitting erect, pale, and silent in the waiting lounge of Little Company of Mary Hospital. 'At least I persuaded Jim Wells to kill the newspaper story. I had to threaten the son of a bitch with all kinds of terrible harassment against his goddamned newspaper if he printed it. He kept babbling about "the public's right to know!"'

'I've heard that line,' Roger said ironically. Did the public have the right to know that a gubernatorial candidate now carried with him, wherever he went, a bottle of Valium tablets, obtained on the grounds that he needed to relax after an evening campaign address so that he could sleep, but secreted in his briefcase, in fact, so that the instrument of possible expiating sacrifice was readily available.

'We're putting a twenty-four-hour-a-day guard on both of them,' McNeally said, his eyes darting nervously at each of the four parents facing him. 'I understand your son will be released from the hospital in the morning, Congressman?'

'About noontime. Bumps and bruises and observation for internal injuries. But I don't think he's in any danger. He wasn't the target. Put the guards on Noele.'

The lieutenant nodded. 'The Marshal is not likely to do anything in the next few days. He'll know that we have a very close watch on him.'

'But there is nothing to prevent him from hiring someone else, is there, Lieutenant?' Irene spoke for the first time since she had emerged from Noele's room shaken and grim.

'I suppose not, but he seems to enjoy participating in these things himself. How's the girl, Mrs Farrell?'

'Sedated, hysterical, bruised and battered, humiliated, and ravished. How would you expect her to be, Lieutenant?'

'She'll pull through,' Roger said, hoping he was right. 'She's a strong young woman, and she'll bounce back.'

'If you were a woman you wouldn't be so confident,' Irene said stormily. 'She'll never be the same again, and we all know it.'

John

He was still at his prie-dieu as the early April morning sunlight streaked through the window. The days were getting longer – the triumph of day over night, life over death, Jesus over Satan. In half an hour or so the sun would begin to bathe the place on the Courts where the naked and brutalized body of his niece had been found a few hours before. Score one for darkness over light.

The Farrell family curse? He had never thought of that before. But if it was a curse, three generations of the family had brought it upon themselves. Now the fourth generation was suffering for it, perhaps irreparably. Dear God in heaven, please give her the strength . . . the strength to be herself again. Don't punish her for my sins – or Roger's or Brigid's or Clancy's.

At eight o'clock he would call Ace McNamara at his apartment near the University and tell him what had happened. If anyone could help Noele, it was the Ace.

But who could possibly help an innocent young woman who had been so savagely attacked?

Brigid

Rarely did Brigid attend weekday Mass. She was too embarrassed to appear in church except on Sunday. Himself would think she was turning soft, crawling back to Him in her old age. But this morning she came to St Praxides for her son's Mass. 'Please take me,' she begged the deity. 'If one of us has to die, let it be me. I'm an old woman, and I'm the one that deserves it. The woman is harmless and the child has never done anything wrong. She didn't deserve to be punished this way. If you want one of us, take me instead. I'm ready to die. I'm even ready to go into the pit, if that's where you want to send me. But let Noele live.'

After Mass she joined John in the sacristy, where he was removing the purple chasuble. 'We're being punished for our sins,' she wailed, nearly hysterical. 'That poor child is suffering for all the evil we've done.'

'God doesn't work that way, Mother.' John tried to be calm, patient, self-contained, though in one corner of his own soul his fears were the same as hers.

'A lot you know about God!' she screamed at him.

John put his arm around her, drawing her close, the way Danny would. She cried herself out of her anger and fear. He had never held her that way, not even the night his father died.

Dear God, why not?

'Have you heard anything from the hospital?' he asked softly.

'The woman called just before I came to church and said Noele was resting comfortably, whatever that means.' She wiped her eyes, once again the strong woman who could cope with every terror. 'They've probably filled her up with dope. Irene doesn't know when she'll be able to come home. Her problems are likely to be more psychological than physical, and may last a long time. That's what the doctors say, anyway. Though a lot they know. They're all men.'

'You sound like you think all men are rapists, Mother.'

'Sometimes I think they are. Did you talk to that psychologist priest fellow that she likes so much?'

'I did. He was horrified, of course. But he also said, and I quote, that we were out of our minds if we think Noele isn't going to recover.'

'A lot he knows,' she sneered.

'A lot he does know, Mother. More than all the rest of us.'

Irene

'That's right. Raped and sodomized repeatedly by three mobsters. . . . And they made Jaimie watch. . . . Hysterical. What else would you expect? . . . And then dumped her on the St Praxides basketball courts. Phone calls to everyone saying the next time they would do worse to her. . . .

'And the same treatment promised for me and Brigid. . . .

'No, the police can't do anything; they know who the men are, but they can't prove it. . . . They will have round-the-clock guards on her hospital room. But this man Marsallo has lots of money, and he can pay others to do what he wants. . . . I hope you're having a nice time in New York, darling.' She slammed the phone down, and huddled over it, wishing she could cry.

Noele

She felt pain and anger and shame and humiliation. She was abused, torn, debased, and discarded. And she was terribly, terribly afraid. They would come back for her again. They would do all those unbearable things to her yet another time – rip off her clothes, torment and torture her, taunt her with their obscene words, and then bury themselves in her body time after time until she thought she would die, wished she would die, begged God to let her die. Then they would kill her, slowly and horribly. No one could stop them. They were demons with unlimited power to hurt and to destroy.

And yet, although she was barely conscious and her mind had been dulled by drugs, Noele was not thinking only of herself.

Something had to be done about Jaimie. He would blame himself for what had happened, and it wasn't his fault at all.

She heard one of the stupid doctors say that there would be so much guilt and anger between her and Jaimie they would never be friends again. But in that small part of her consciousness where Noele was still in charge, she decided they would totally not take Jaimie away from her.

Something had to be done about Moms, too. Noele had pushed her away furiously when she had tried to embrace her, a mean, nasty thing to do – hurt Moms because she had been hurt.

And Roger, frantic, confused, powerless. Trying to explain the reason for what happened, he had spilled out the story that one of the men had been paid by Clancy to kill Danny's mother. Someone had documents that they'd copied from Roger's office to prove it.

Well, she and Jaimie had suspected that, even though she'd hoped that it had been Burke, because then Danny wouldn't have been the one to kill Clancy.

Noele began to slip into turbulent unconsciousness. She fought the darkness off.

So Danny's mother really had been killed, and that was why he killed Clancy. No, there was something wrong with that. There was too much medicine inside her to think why it was wrong, but it was still wrong. When she was better, she would sort it all out. But now she would give up for a while and let the darkness do what little healing it could.

Later in the day a young shrink came in the room and asked a lot of boring questions. She told him that, really, his questions were boring and she was sure he had better things to do on Saturday afternoon. Besides, she had her own personal psychologist who was coming to see her tomorrow.

'You've been through a very difficult experience, young woman,' the shrink said solemnly.

'Tell me about it,' Noele replied.

The yukky hospital smells made her want to throw up, hopefully over this geek.

The next day she was able to think more clearly and asked herself why someone who seemed so totally not into revenge would have killed even the man who murdered his mother. Daniel Xavier forgave people. And that was good. But he didn't seem to care, and that was bad. He had to learn that you could care and still forgive – like she cared about him and could still forgive him for not being here when she needed him.

Then she slept a little, still not able to separate in her haunted imagination what had happened to her and what had happened to all the others. In her dreams she was Clancy and Brigid, and Moms and Danny, and Roger and John, and Flossie. A lot of the time she was Flossie. Why?

At noon Father Ace looked in the doorway with a quizzical smile on his face. 'Ready for your personal psychologist, chaplain, confidant, and Ann Landers?'

She still hurt terribly and was frightened, but she managed to return his smile. 'How was the folk group this morning?'

'If that's the only thing on your mind, I suspect you're going to survive.' The Ace stood next to her bed, hands in his pockets, his eyes, as always, twinkling.

'Of course I'm going to survive,' she said tartly. 'There was this *boring* young psychiatrist who wanted me to fall apart yesterday afternoon, and I'm not going to fall apart for anybody. Do you hear that, Father Ace? I'm totally not going to fall apart.'

'There are going to be some tough times, MN,' he said softly.

'That goes with being a woman. We have to learn to live with being raped and things like that.'

'This is Passion Sunday, MN: suffering goes with being human.'

'Will I ever get over it, Father Ace?' She heard her voice catch and was angry at her own weakness. 'Will I ever be the little girl I was at the movie with Jaimie?'

'You'll never be the same, MN,' he said slowly. 'What happened will always be part of your life and your memory. Whether you'll come out of this experience a stronger and more mature woman is up to you.'

'I never lose fights, Father Ace.' She pounded the bed. 'Never. And I won't lose this one.'

'I'll bet on that, Noele.'

'It's all so *boring*.' She pounded the bed again.

'We grow up by learning to live with boring things.'

'Well, at least I don't have to worry anymore about being a virgin.'

'Virginity is not a physical matter, MN,' he said.

'Yes, it is,' she insisted. 'Well, partly, anyhow.'

'Not mostly,' he said, taking her hand in his, a big strong hand, bigger and stronger even than Jaimie's.

'Okay, not mostly. Now I'm going to cry, Father Ace. I'm not going to be hysterical, but I'm going to cry. Can you hold my hand very tightly while I cry and then go take care of Jaimie Burns? It's harder on him than it is on me.'

Before he left the room, Father Ace called Uncle Monsignor. 'Spread the word around the family. MN is okay. How do I know? She said so, that's how I know.'

And she and Father Ace laughed, as though they shared a great secret.

That evening she fiddled with her Passion Sunday supper, telling the nurse's aide who'd brought it that the food in the hospital was boring and then said yes, she would like a pill to help her sleep. She watched half an hour of television, called home to tell Moms not to come to the hospital because she wanted to sleep and that she loved her very much, and then closed her eyes.

Her sleep was deep and dark, like swimming in the lake at night with clouds over the moon and stars. But suddenly she was awake, confused, and terrified. Where was she? What had happened? Why was she so tense? Where was Moms? Then it all came back to her, the pain, the horror, the shame, the crude words, the evil, mocking laughter.

Someone was in the room, breathing heavily. Something jammed into her mouth so she couldn't scream. And a cruel hand squeezed her breasts, hurting her again. Something cold and hard against her skin, slicing into it.

'Just a little nick this time, cunt, a hint about what we're going to do to you when we have our next party.'

There was more blackness for a moment, and then Noele coughed the gag from her mouth and screamed hysterically. The light went on above her bed and Danny was enveloping her in his arms and swearing that no one would ever hurt her again.

Irene

'Permission to come aboard, sir.' Father McNamara saluted sharply.

'Permission granted, sir.' Dan saluted even more sharply.

'Glad to be aboard, sir.' The priest saluted again.

'Glad to have you aboard, Captain, sir.' And yet another salute from Dan.

'Glad to be aboard, Commander, sir.'

'Idiots.' She couldn't help but laugh. They were playing sailor and marine to get a laugh out of her, but also because they were both clowns.

In fact, Dan had been every inch a polished and competent Navy officer all night. He had soothed and reassured Noele even before Irene and Roger came to the hospital. With one of Dan's arms holding her protectively, she was quietly sleeping when they entered her room.

Then he had chewed out the truculent Lieutenant McNeally and called an elite private security firm to arrange for around-the-clock protection.

'To watch the cops,' he explained to Irene.

Then he organized a schedule of 'our own people' to 'watch the cops and the security guards' – Burke, Jaimie, John, Father Ace, the massive and brilliant DeWitt Carlisle.

He was in charge: charming with Brigid, gentle with Noele, reassuring with Roger, brisk and competent with the cops, and funny with her. Somehow he understood that only laughter could temporarily exorcise her demons. Or maybe he remembered that from the past.

Roger was sent on the way to a speech at a luncheon in

North Brook. 'Don't worry, Governor, she's in good hands, isn't she, Mr Carlisle, sir? And we must not let them think they have us worried. Give 'em hell in North Brook.'

One of the jokes that Danny arranged for her was that a massive young black like DeWitt had better be called 'sir.' Jaimie's roommate, whose father was a banker, as was his father before him, tried to talk jive with Danny, but he wasn't nearly as good at it. And although he had the disposition of a laid-back cherub, DeWitt did his best to play the part of a 'heavy' of whom Danny ought to be afraid.

Danny is so wonderful with young people. What a pity he doesn't have a son of his own. Or a daughter.

Jaimie kissed her on the forehead, a first, when he replaced DeWitt, and the large basketball player looked like he wanted to do the same but was too shy. So Irene, made bold and a little crazy by Danny's contagious wit, kissed him and murmured, 'Be cool, DeWitt.'

'They blush too,' Danny whispered outrageously in her ear. 'Would you drive me home for a few hours' sleep? We can leave Jaimie in charge.'

Danny Farrell, happy warrior, elegant commanding officer, tender protector of frightened women. How easy it is to love you.

But in the Datsun, he retired into silence.

Irene adjusted the windshield wiper. Rain again.

'That was very impressive, Dan.'

'Morale purposes,' he said, dismissing his show of competency. 'Whistling in the dark.'

'We needed it, all of us.'

'I'm good in the short run, Renie; you of all people know that. It's the long run that does me in.'

She didn't argue.

In front of his house he touched her cheek. 'Please, come in with me.'

Her longing to do just that burned like an acetylene torch.

'Only on my terms.'

Longing turned to pain as he raced through the rain to

the door of the house. But she did not cry. She would never again weep for Danny.

Not until tomorrow.

John

Danny and Jaimie stood in front of his desk in the rectory office like two gallowglasses, Irish mercenary soldiers who knew they were doomed to a life that would be short and dangerous, but also grimly determined to give at least as much as they got before they were snuffed out.

'You must be out of your mind,' John said. 'You'd never get away with something like that.'

Danny sat on one of the hard chairs next to John's desk and motioned to Jaimie to do the same. 'Let us worry about the prudence of it, John,' he said solemnly. 'It's theology we want from you. The cops tell us that the Marshal will strike again, and they are powerless to stop him, even if we beg, bribe, or browbeat Rod Weaver into tearing up those papers. It's now become a matter of principle with him. His reputation as a man who can torture anyone he wants is at stake. He might go after Irene or Brigid too.'

'I can't believe the police would give up that easily.'

'The Marshal's actions are a combination of Mob violence and psychopathic hatred, and no police force in the free world can protect anyone from that.' Jaimie spoke with terrifying softness.

The rectory phone rang. 'Monsignor Farrell. . . . Oh, yes, hi, Joe. . . . That's right. Our Easter Eve programme ought to be special. . . . No, the cardinal turned down our invitation. . . . Anglican bishop? Fine with me. He's a much better television presence than the cardinal anyway . . . A syndication contract? Fifteen markets, including New York and Los Angeles? . . . I'll have to think about that. Although it certainly is good news.'

'Congratulations,' Danny said. 'You're going to do it, of course.' It was an order and not a question. Danny's magic was as tough as Irene's.

'I'll have to decide about that later,' John said, dismissing the programme as unimportant. 'You want to know whether it's permissible to murder Rocco Marsallo?'

'No, Monsignor,' Jaimie Burns said quietly. 'We want to know about the theology of self-defence. If there were an invading army threatening the lives and the bodies of our women, wouldn't it be permissible to defend ourselves against them? If we were in a jungle and another tribe was attacking our village, if we were in a fort in the West and the Apaches had us surrounded, if the Vikings were storming a castle in medieval Ireland – under all those circumstances, wouldn't we have the right to defend ourselves?'

'Those were uncivilized societies,' John argued. 'We have police. We have a civil order. This is twentieth-century America, not medieval Ireland.'

'Did you notice what happened to your niece in our civilized, ordered, well-policed society?' Danny was dangerously calm. 'We're dependent on the Mob to defend us from its own crazies, and the best they can promise is revenge after someone is dead. Is that civilization, John? Hell, it was safer in China.'

'He who lives by the sword shall die by the sword,' John Farrell said, falling back on his scripture.

'The monks defended the monasteries and the sacred vessels in attacks by the barbarians,' Danny countered. 'Can we defend Noele?'

'You want revenge?'

'No, we don't, Monsignor,' Jaimie insisted. 'We want to protect Noele. Those men promised they would hurt her again. Neither Mr Farrell nor I feel we can let them do that.'

'I'm not an avenging-angel type,' Danny said. 'You ought to know that, John.'

The attack on Noele had transformed him, John thought, as if he had been driven to pull together the scattered pieces of his personality. He wore a neatly fitting blue suit, had combed his hair, and had polished his shoes. His words were forceful and carefully chosen. He was relaxed and self-possessed. The anger – and the fear – that had lurked in his eyes had disappeared.

'All right.' John sighed. 'The conditions in moral theology are quite clear. Self-defence of the lives and the physical well-being of one's family is licit when there is no other way to protect legitimate rights – so long as one practises blameless moderation.'

'And blameless moderation means?'

'It means you don't go any further than necessary to protect yourself or your family.'

'What does that mean concretely?' Danny's fists were clenched, his knuckles white.

'It means you don't use physical violence if moral constraints are enough and, if you do use physical violence, you only use the essential minimum.'

'What if the only way to protect your own life and the lives and bodies of your family is to kill?'

John rubbed his hands over his face. The theory was easy, the practise . . . 'Theologians have traditionally said that if someone is in the act of attacking you or those whom you are obliged to defend, and the only way you can defend them is by killing the attacker, then you may do so. This isn't just Catholic theory, Danny, it's traditional Western ethical philosophy.'

'You can kill them when you see them coming down the street with guns?'

'It suffices for you to know that they are prepared to strike and will do so shortly. To use your own terms, if you know the Apaches are going to attack you before tomorrow to kill you and carry off your wives and your daughters, you could attack their camp that night. Or you could ram the Viking ship as soon as it entered the estuary and not wait until the Vikings attacked your ring-fort.'

'That's all we wanted to know,' Dan said. 'We'll see you around, John.'

He and Jaimie rose and briskly left the office. John followed them quickly. 'You can't take the law into your own hands,' he said, trying to bar the door of the rectory.

'We're not doing anything with the law,' Danny said

confidently. 'Maybe we won't do anything at all. But I'm not going to let anybody hurt Noele again.'

John went back into the office and sat at his desk. He was trembling. He'd given all the right answers, but the solution was wrong.

Or was it?

He should call Joe about the Easter telecast. And the syndication. He'd almost forgotten about it. What difference did it make? Fifteen cities or five hundred – it was all worthless. All sham. To hell with it.

Instead he went over to the church to pray. Like he had never prayed before in his life.

Noele

'And so, Jaimie Burns, don't you dare turn space cadet on me because you feel guilty or because you saw them . . . do what they did. I don't care how many shrinks say we can never be friends again. I will totally not let that happen.'

'I promised I'd always protect you, and I didn't,' Jaimie said sadly.

She jabbed her finger at him.

'Don't talk like that. I won't stand for it.'

'We have to give it time, MN.'

'I know *that*. I'm just telling you what the outcome will be.'

Jaimie smiled. 'You're still overwhelming.'

'Of course,' she said, forcing herself to relax on the hospital pillow, and not feeling overwhelming at all.

At the door Jaimie turned and grinned at her.

'It was Tennyson.'

'Huh?'

'I was right and you were wrong. Tennyson wrote Enoch Arden, not Dickens.'

'Retard.' She threw the pillow at him and they both laughed a little.

That's better, she thought after he left. It would be a long time before the Noele/Jaimie person was back. But it would come back.

Maybe.

She thought about asking a nurse for something to help her sleep. But she was afraid of the dreams.

Ace

Irene wiped the tears off her face with a fragile tissue, investing even such a minor action with elegance and grace. Danny was working his magic on her, just as he had done long ago.

'He's the only one who seems to be keeping his head, Father,' she said. 'Crazy Danny acting like he has common sense.'

'You forget that he was a naval officer and probably better than most of them. An honours graduate from Annapolis who stood for racial justice long before it was fashionable. We could have used his intelligence and decisiveness in Nam.'

'He was a good officer, Father, because he could be good at anything. But I think he's too gentle for war.' A faint flush spread across her cheeks.

Ace wasn't so sure. In war the strong often turn and flee and the gentle fight to the bitter end to protect their own men, and sometimes survive precisely because they were gentle.

'Noele told me yesterday that I was as bad as Danny.'

'High praise.' Irene laughed. 'You two are the only ones who can make her smile. I'm not sure about Jaimie.'

'She'll be all right, Renie. . . .'

There was a police car parked outside. The Farrell family was trailed by police now whenever they left their homes.

'I worry a little about Danny. He seems so determined. I hope he doesn't do anything dangerous.'

'So the competent, determined Dan Farrell is as dangerous as the runaway Dan Farrell?' He laughed heartily.

She blushed deeply and looked away from him.

'He's acting at the hospital the way he acts in bed.'

'And that scares you to the core of your soul?'

'Can fear be sweet?' She looked away.

'You never did get over him, did you, Renie?'

'No,' she said, 'I never did. And I never will, but I won't sell myself cheap anymore, either. You persuaded me of that.'

'Only way to deal with him.'

'Right.'

But she walked slowly down the stairs of the rectory, like a widow who had just arranged for her husband's funeral.

As he watched her Datsun pull away, followed by the blue and white squad, Ace realized how helpless he too was. The Farrells did not need a psychologist or a Marine Corps chaplain. They needed an archangel.

DCI

'You can't get away with this sort of blackmail, Farrell,' the Director said without much conviction.

'Ah, but I can, Frank,' said the grinning leprechaun on the other side of the Director's coffee table, a seating arrangement used only when the Director was faced with a particularly intractable problem.

'I think he can, sir,' Radford agreed. 'Whatever he wants and as long as he wants it. The proverbial short hairs, if you know what I mean.'

'You'll never get away with it,' the Director insisted.

'Sure, isn't it a grand plan now?'

The Director was beginning to hate that phony brogue. And, God damn it, Farrell *had* designed an ingenious operation.

'What if you're caught?'

'I assume the Company will be praying that I'm not.'

'We would deny any connection.'

'Haven't I been through that with you folks once before?' Farrell grinned cheerfully.

'It's only logistical support, sir,' Radford said.

'God damn it, Radford, I believe you've been hypnotized by this bastard.'

'No, sir,' said his aide reproachfully. 'I just don't see that we have any alternatives.'

Charm, anger, and intelligence – the three layers of Farrell's personality. And the combination was impossible to resist.

'Our shrinks say that if you do this, you'll discharge all your anger from the, ah, China interlude.'

'A consummation devoutly to be desired by the Honourable Company, wouldn't you agree, Frank?'

'I think you'll be a millstone around our necks indefinitely.'

'Well, I won't run for Congress.' Danny smiled beatifically.

'I have no choice but to cooperate,' the Director said heavily. 'See to it, Radford.' And then, because he had daughters himself, he asked about Farrell's niece. 'How's the girl doing?'

'Our shrinks think she'll be all right.' There was no merriment on his comedian's face when he said it.

'Do you agree?'

'I think she's a very healthy kid, Frank. I intend to keep her that way.'

Roger

'I don't think this is a very good idea, Danny,' he said as his cousin dialed Rocco Marsallo's private phone number.

'Have to do it,' said Danny crisply. 'It wouldn't be fair not to warn him.'

'Warn him of what?'

'Rocco Marsallo?'

'Yeah.'

Roger was listening on an extension phone in his study. 'You're doing some bad things, Rocco boy.'

'Yeah?'

'You lay off those people, or you're going to find yourself dead.'

'Yeah?'

The Marshal seemed to think that was an amusing remark.

'A lot of us don't like what you're doing, Rocco Alfredo. Your friends aren't going to be able to keep the lid on us.'

'You don't scare me, punk. Me and my boys are just beginning to have fun.'

The line went dead.

'Well, he doesn't scare very easily, does he?'

'I don't know why you wanted to do that,' Roger said bitterly. 'It's like waving a red flag at a bull.'

'It may give him something to think about. His padrino must be under a lot of pressure.'

'I asked McNeally why he couldn't arrest Marsallo for Florence's murder. He says that there is no evidence that would make a case, only my speculations.'

'Did you pass that word on to Rocco Alfredo?' Danny's eyes narrowed.

'Some of my West Side contacts tried to talk to him. He doesn't believe it. We're dealing with a madman.'

'And there's nothing we can do?'

'Rodney Weaver has granted us an extension till the day after Easter. That means we still have almost two weeks. Maybe something will work out.' Roger was numb with fatigue and worry. Try as he might, he could not find a single ray of light in the darkness. 'We're going to send Noele and Irene to Ireland for Easter. The Irish police have promised full cooperation. Marsallo will have a hard time getting at them there.'

'And the IRA or some faction wouldn't dream of blowing up two American women in exchange for a couple of million dollars!'

'I know, Dan, I know.' Roger noticed that his hands were shaking again, as if he were a man twenty years older. 'I keep asking myself whether it would help if I withdrew from the race for personal reasons. Rod Weaver wouldn't attract much attention with his story if I were out of the limelight. He probably wouldn't even get his face on television.'

'It wouldn't do any good,' Danny said thoughtfully, 'would it? By now Weaver is just an excuse for the Marshal. Hang on for another week. Let's see what happens.'

'I know what's going to happen,' Roger said glumly. 'Someone is going to be killed.'

'Don't bet on it,' Danny said mysteriously.

At the fringes of his consciousness Roger was aware that Danny had been acting strangely for the last day or two. But he was so preoccupied with his own guilt and powerlessness that he had not found the time or energy to reflect on such odd behaviour as phoning the Marshal.

Roger walked to the door with his cousin. A pretty black woman patrol officer waited in the parlour; a squad car was parked in the driveway.

'How's the kid?'

'Up and down. Still groggy from sedation, still screaming at night, and still one tough, very self-controlled young woman during the day. The doctors and Father McNamara think that maybe she's too self-controlled.'

'The problem with us Farrells,' Dan said sombrely.

Dan winked at the woman cop, waved at the officers in the squad car parked in the driveway, turned up his raincoat collar, hunched his head between his shoulders, and walked briskly through the early April rainstorm to his Porsche.

Curtains of raindrops danced on the street in the lights of Danny's car. Then the Porsche slipped down the thick avenue of trees, around the corner into Ninety-first Street, and disappeared in the mists and darkness.

Noele

'Some crosses don't go away when you will them to go away, do they, MN?' said Father Ace.

'No, they don't,' she admitted ruefully.

Noele was back home in her own room, which she had promptly straightened up so that Moms wouldn't worry about it when visitors came. She had been looking over her family-history notes and charts when Father Ace came to visit her.

She quickly hid her *dossier* – another word she'd learned from Jaimie.

'Some people have to learn you must live with things for a while before they become okay again,' Father Ace continued.

'I guess.'

'Some people also have to learn that even though they are cute and smart and popular and maybe a little psychic, they please God the most by learning to live with suffering and tragedy.'

'I suppose.'

'You don't sound enthusiastic about your discovery of limitations, MN.'

She laughed. 'Someday I'll understand it all, Father.'

'In a little while, MN, it's going to be mostly all right, and then later on almost completely all right; but it's only going to be perfectly all right, probably, when you have a husband of your own.'

Father Ace never gave easy answers.

'How long will it take, Father Ace?' she asked, solemn again and even a little humble.

'The research says six months to six years, if ever.'

'You can forget the "if ever" bit.'

'For sure.'

'And the six-year bit too.'

'For sure.'

'Somewhere in between,' she said judiciously.

'For sure.'

'Tough little bitch, huh?'

'FOR SURE!'

She swung at him and he ducked, but not in time.

'Speaking of such things,' she said, brightening a bit, 'how's Jaimie Burns? I called him yesterday and pretended to be mad because he hadn't phoned me, and then after a while made him laugh. What do you think?'

'You like Jaimie Burns a lot?'

'Really, Father,' she said, and sniffed.

'He's a wonderful young man.'

'Tell me about it.'

'Wonderful enough to marry?'

'Maybe. Someday.'

Father Ace considered her very seriously. 'If you want to keep that possibility open, then you'll have to treat him very delicately for a while.'

'Which means?'

'Which means . . . well, keep on making him laugh a lot.'

'Is *that* all?' Noele felt greatly relieved. 'That's no great big deal.'

Then Moms came into the room and Father Ace began to kid her about her new short haircut, his usual way of paying women compliments. And, of course, he was trying to cheer her up. Noele realized that Father Ace not only liked Moms – which was easy enough for any man, even a priest, because Moms was so pretty – he also respected her.

'You're not going to Ireland?' he said when he was leaving.

'The decision isn't final,' said Moms, sounding very much like a mother.

'Yes, it is,' Noele said. 'I'm staying right here and learning how to shoot a twenty-two; that's *much* safer than going to Ireland.'

'What a bloodthirsty daughter you have, Mrs Farrell,' Father Ace said, kissing her on the forehead. Then he and Moms left her alone.

Noele was still having bad times, especially at night, when in her dreams three ugly demons out of the black pit of hell pursued her with fiery swords and caught her just as she woke up screaming. Each time that happened all the pain, the shame, the anger, and the fear erupted again and made her want to keep screaming.

Her classmates came to see her, having been told that she'd been in another auto accident. She worked in a desultory way at homework, trying to keep pace with what was happening in school. She bickered with Moms and fought with Roger and was moody with Eileen Kelly and Michele Carmody.

Why did it have to take a long time? Why couldn't you suffer all at once and get it over with?

She was still kind of half in love with Daniel and thought he looked especially cute in his neatly fitting suits and gorgeous ties. That would have to wait, however. What would not wait was the Farrell family mystery. Noele knew that she had to solve that one, even if people did laugh at her and call her the Jane Marple of Beverly Hills, because that was the only way any of the Farrells would ever be safe again.

She pulled the dossier out from underneath her pillow. Somewhere in all those notes there had to be an answer.

She looked around her room. Sophomore hop bid, pictures from the grammar school formal, Paul Newman and Robert De Niro, herself and Eileen Kelly on the catamaran. A whole corkboard full of pictures of Jaimie – in white tux, blue graduation hat and gown and, of course, blue and gold football uniform. Teenage room.

She turned on The Who very quietly. So the window didn't shake much.

Typical teenage rape victim. Well, I have better things to do than feel sorry for myself. She started once again to page carefully through her notes.

There were times when she thought she'd seen the solution. In the blink of an eye it was there and then gone. Maybe Daniel did kill Clancy, but there was a stubborn part of her personality that doubted that.

To begin with, there was something funny about Bill Farrell's will. Probably involving Burke and Grams. Was that when they started to love each other? Noele considered it. It was much more fun speculating on that than trying to catch up on the trigonometry lessons.

Yes, that was probably how it started. Someday Grams would have to tell her the whole story, just to get it off her chest.

Anyway, Clancy, who must have been *really* gross, had that terrible Marshal person kill Florence Farrell and tried to kill Danny, even though Grams and Burke did their best to stop them.

When Clancy died, the three boys inherited equal shares in the firm, though Grams controlled the shares as long as she lived. Then Danny died and his part of the firm was split between Roger and Monsignor John. And all of it someday was going to come to her.

Noele was drawing another chart. Funny how all the lines converged on her. Of course, with Danny coming back, some of the money and some of the stock in the firm would go to him.

Well, he ought to have it all. When she finally had her inheritance, she would give it all to him. That would end the trouble. She stared at her chart glumly, and then looked at herself in the mirror over her dressing table.

Really, you do look okay.

Back to the chart. Daniel might have pushed Clancy down the stairs because he was angry about the death of his mother. That was what Roger had told her, and Roger seemed to believe it was true. Brigid might have pushed him down the stairs because she hated him and she wanted to marry Burke – only Burke's wife was still alive and their affair was pretty torrid anyway.

Same thing for Burke. He was a very violent man, Noele thought, beneath his smooth smile and courtly manners. He could have done it in an outburst of temper. Maybe to protect Grams.

Noele jabbed her notes with an angry pen.

Gross city.

Clancy had probably pushed Grams around. And Grams had made Burkie put up with it. But had Roger and John known? That might have a lot to do with what happened. Roger or John might have shoved him down the stairs because he had goaded them to lose their tempers, something he often did when he was drunk, even though he was nice to his boys at other times, taking them to ball games and things like that.

They might have wanted the money too, but she really didn't believe that. Neither her uncle nor her father was very much interested in money, and Brigid was running the firm then, anyway.

Moms? There was something mysterious about Moms. Always had been. And Clancy had torn out after her family at the cocktail party before supper and violently objected to her marrying Danny. Moms wasn't the shoving type. On the other hand, if she were mad enough she might just do it, but Danny would have married her anyway, if he'd come back from China, so she didn't have to kill Clancy. Moms, if she killed anybody, would be much more likely to do it at the end of one of her long, gloomy moods than in an outburst of anger.

Why did Daniel go to China, or Japan, or wherever he'd been, if he loved Moms? Would he have really married her?

For a moment Noele thought she saw the solution; then it slipped away again.

She threw her pen on the desk in disgust.

Daniel Xavier Farrell was charming and funny and cool and cute. And scared. Was he that way as a young man?

It certainly seemed like he was the one who killed Clancy, probably not intending it. But it couldn't be that simple. There was still a piece of the puzzle missing.

She shoved aside her notes and her chart, then decided she'd better tear them up into little pieces and throw them down the toilet (not do something *dumb* like Roger). After she disposed of her documents, she came back and glared unhappily at the trig book.

Well, she'd call Jaimie Burns first.

But he wasn't home.

James III

Jaimie was waiting inside the door of the J. C. Penney store in a shopping plaza in Elmhurst. His own car, a battered old junk Plymouth, was in the shopping plaza across the way, where he'd been instructed to leave it.

Mr Farrell had called the night before and told him tersely where to be and when. Jaimie felt a little bit the way he did before a football game, maybe because he was leaning lazily against the door of the J. C. Penney the way people said he leaned against the locker-room wall before a game began, a picture of disinterested indifference.

While all the time great fierce fires were burning within him.

He was quite incapable of hating other human beings or wanting revenge. When he decked a wide receiver from another football team, his only goal was to protect the Notre Dame end zone. He had no ill feeling toward the other player, did not try to hurt him, and would have regretted it if he was hurt – though he figured the other player knew the risks he was taking when he went on the football field against the Fighting Irish and ventured into Jaimie's defensive zone.

He felt the same way on this lovely Friday morning in April. There was a job that had to be done, just as the Notre Dame end zone had to be defended. Jaimie had no more thought that they would fail than he ever thought that Notre Dame would lose a football game. Sometimes, however, Notre Dame did lose. And Jaimie Burns felt a touch of fear in the pit of his stomach. Then he thought of Noele and the great fierce bog fires burned again.

At precisely 10:30 a silver-grey Citation, indistinguishable from thousands of others in the Chicago area, arrived at the J. C. Penney door. The driver honked three times, briefly, like the call of a wild goose, and stopped a few yards beyond the door. Jaimie pulled his driving gloves out of the pocket of his battered old brown Windbreaker and walked casually around to the driver's door. Mr Farrell opened the door and then slid into the passenger's seat. He was dressed the same way he had told Jaimie to dress – old jeans, a white T-shirt, Adidas running shoes, and a Windbreaker that looked like every other Windbreaker in the world.

Jaimie drove the car, at Mr Farrell's instructions, back into Elmhurst and down a side street into a deserted alley behind a supermarket. 'You park your car in the shopping centre across the street?' Mr Farrell asked.

'Right.'

'We're going to have to change licence plates a couple of times. This set first.' He handed Jaimie a licence plate and a screwdriver.

'I want it done in a quarter of a minute. The screws are loose, and leave them that way.'

They scrambled out of the car, Mr Farrell to the front and Jaimie to the rear, quickly changed the licence plates, and jumped back in.

'These licence plates we hang on to, because when everything's over, we put them back on, right here.'

'When will someone notice this car's missing?' Jaimie asked as they drove out on the state highway and turned south.

'Not till the evening rush hour. And by then the police will have no trouble finding it in the parking lot here. Someday we'll have to thank the owners. I gave them a full tank of gas as rental.'

He laughed lightly, as though he were an experienced spy in a Le Carré novel.

'Where are we going, sir?' Jaimie asked, pretending for a moment that Mr Farrell really was George Smiley.

'We're joining our friends for a little game of golf at Far Hills. See the golf bag in the back seat?'

Inside his driving gloves Jaimie's hands were wet, something that had never happened before the kickoff at a Notre Dame game.

They drove on in silence till Mr Farrell instructed him to turn off the state road into a cross street. 'Turn right here, Jaimie,' he said at the gates of a large, old Catholic cemetery. 'We're going to visit a few graves.'

They parked the Citation on one of the back lanes and walked among the tombs to a grave site of a family named Finerty. Both the grandparents had been born in County Kerry in the 1860s and both were dead by 1905. It wasn't an easy life in those days, Jaimie decided.

They walked slowly back to the car while Mr Farrell glanced at his watch – a bit nervously, Jaimie thought. Then they drove to the far end of the cemetery, out another gate, and down an old asphalt road. They turned off that road into an even smaller gravel lane with trees on either side.

'This is where we hope the rain will wipe away the trails?' Jaimie asked.

'The only part we're leaving to luck and not much luck. The morning weather forecast said eighty percent chance of rain. Even if it doesn't rain, there will be no traces except ordinary Chevvy tyres, ordinary running shoes, and ordinary men whose appearance you wouldn't remember even if you happened to drive down this road and see them, which isn't very likely. Pull over to there, by the big oak tree.'

Jaimie did as he was told. As he stopped the car Mr Farrell reached into the backseat, zipped the cover off the old golf bag, and removed from among the clubs a couple of cylinders that he began to fit together.

'A Russian make, the best rifle in the world. They liked me so much on the commune that they made me one of the leaders in the local civil defence force, which was supposed to hassle the Ruskeys if they came over the border. They were so impressed with what I could do with a rifle that they even let me teach some of the young bucks of the commune how to operate it. If I'd stayed there long enough, I might have put together my own squad and started a revolution.'

'Then you haven't fired one in several months?'

Mr Farrell grinned cheerfully. 'You would mention that! Don't worry, it's a good weapon, and I'm only going to be shooting at close range. Take these glasses and see if you can pick out our friends.'

The binoculars were no bigger than opera glasses, but

had enormous power. Someone with good technology was assisting Mr Farrell.

'There are three men teeing off at the seventh hole. Two of them short and stocky. And the third one is tall, with a moustache.'

Mr Farrell took the glasses. 'The beer drinker is Dubuque Salerno. The fat guy in the blue pants is Little Tony Caputo. And the old guy in the white sweater is the Marshal himself. Are they the ones, Jaimie?'

'Not the slightest doubt,' Jaimie replied firmly.

'Perfect timing. We'll have our little encounter on the eighth green. You see where that is?'

'About a football field and a half away, on a side of a hill, and with no obstructions between us and them.'

'Good boy.' Fully assembled, the Russian rifle appeared deceptively simple – two rods, a stock, a scope on the top, a clip of ammunition. Mr Farrell jammed a few more clips into his jacket pocket. 'When they tee off up there for the eighth hole, I climb out of the car, hide between the car and the oak tree. When I'm finished, I climb back into the car, and we retrace our way to the cemetery and then back to the state highway into Elmhurst. At the stoplight after the town limits you take a right, then the seventh street to the left, then the third street to the right, then one block, then to the left down the alley. Got it?'

'Got it,' said Jaimie tersely. 'Perhaps I should turn the car around now.'

'Yes, that's a good idea.'

Jaimie backed up the Citation and turned it to face the direction in which they'd come, careful to leave no tracks on the muddy shoulder at either side of the road. The golf course was now on his left, on the driver's side of the car, and the cemetery was on his right. He raised the field glasses again. 'They're putting on the seventh green. Then they'll have to climb the hole to the eighth tee.'

'Okay.' Mr Farrell fastened another, shorter rod to the barrel of the Russian rifle – a silencer, Jaimie assumed.

If this were a movie, I'd think it was corny.

'Mr Farrell, why don't you climb into the backseat of the car, and then get out of the back door on my side? That way no one will see you getting out.'

'Jaimie, there are some people I know in Washington, well, in Virginia, who would like to get to know you. Okay. Here I go over the seat.'

Mr Farrell placed the Russian rifle in the backseat and then very clumsily climbed over into the back of the auto.

An old car turned down the road from the asphalt street behind the cemetery and raced by them at high speed.

'Teenagers, probably, Mr Farrell. Where there's one car, there's likely to be others. Don't take any chances.'

'We'll scrub it if we have to.'

'They're teeing off at eight,' Jaimie said, watching the golfers with his field glasses.

'It's protection we're looking for, Jaimie, not revenge.'

'Absolutely,' Jaimie replied. 'They're terrible golfers, Mr Farrell. Each one of them hit the ball into the pond. They're teeing off again.'

Mr Farrell ducked suddenly into the backseat. 'Here comes another one of your teenage friends. You think we've stumbled onto a drag race, Jaimie? Why the hell aren't they in school?'

'Spring vacation, sir.'

'Damn. . . . Hey, Jaimie, do me a favour and call me Dan. Our mutual friend will tell you I'm a teenager at heart.'

A second, and then a third, car raced down the road, spitting gravel in either direction. Unless one of these punks was like Jaimie himself, and hence very unusual, he would barely notice the silver-grey Citation at the side of the road next to the big oak tree. And almost certainly nobody would catch its licence plate. Moreover, since kids who drove 1975 Dodges did not read the newspapers, they probably would never know what happened in the Far Hills golf course on this Friday morning.

Yet another car raced by, but this one slower and more cautiously. A kid with some sense. And therefore danger-ous. 'I think that's the last one, Dan.'

'Do you think he noticed us?'

'I don't think so. He had his eyes glued on the road, eager to catch up with his buddies but afraid to drive as fast as they do.'

'Where are our friends?' Mr Farrell was a cool, collected Navy officer on the bridge of an aircraft carrier toward which the Zeros were diving.

'They're coming down the hill from the tee and walking around the pond. I think it's time,' Jaimie said. A faint breeze touched his face lightly. The smell of the coming rainstorm was already in the air.

Mr Farrell opened the back door of the car, rolled out, and closed the door, leaving it slightly ajar. Then he worked his way with his elbows and his knees through the dead leaves to the base of the oak tree. There were three rows of trees shielding him from the road, and he was completely invisible from the golf course.

Jaimie glanced quickly to his right. Through the trees to his left were the headstones of the cemetery. No one in sight.

He focused the glasses on the eighth green. The three men were on the fairway, fifty yards off the green, still protected by the trees that encircled them. Each of them dubbed his approach shot.

The last time you over-hit a lousy chip shot, Jaimie thought ironically.

As he watched them climb over the bunker and walk onto the green, Jaimie felt all of his muscles tense, as they did when the kicking team roared down the field, eleven men who wanted in the worst way to nail him to the turf.

Then he heard a click from where Dan Farrell lay on the ground. And one of the men threw his hands up into the air as his face disappeared. That was Dubuque, the man who had shoved the .22 into his throat.

He will never hurt Noele again.

Then another click, and the second man, Little Tony, doubled over, whirled around, and fell to the ground. He tried to stand up again and then, a fraction of a second after another click at the foot of the oak tree, he sprawled on the eighth green, twitched a few moments, and lay still.

The Marshal was running across the green toward the crest of the hill and safety. There were three rapid clicks from the base of the oak tree, and Rocco Marsallo staggered, his white sweater crimson with blood. Then he crumpled to the earth, rolled down the hill, and crashed into the pin that marked the eighth hole. The pin wavered and fell on top of him, the red of the flag dripping into the red of his blood.

Jaimie lowered the binoculars and watched Mr Farrell throw aside an ammunition clip. Jaimie almost shouted at him to pick it up, but recollecting what he should be doing, Mr Farrell salvaged the clip and shoved it into his pocket. Calmly and coolly he placed a second clip of ammunition on top of the Russian rifle. There was another rapid succession of clicks and the three bodies on the green jumped and shook as several more rounds of bullets burrowed into each one of them.

And once each of them had been a little baby, dearly loved by the mother who had suffered to bring them into the world.

Jaimie committed them to God's care, turned over the ignition key of the car, and, hardly noticing that Mr Farrell had slipped into the backseat and slammed the door shut, drove cautiously down the gravel road, like a sixteen-year-old trying to pass his driver's ed test.

Behind him Mr Farrell was retching silently.

'Don't worry, Jaimie,' he said, 'nothing coming up. I haven't eaten for twelve hours.'

Jaimie drove through the cemetery and out onto the state highway, observing the speed limit with infinite caution. He followed the signs to Elmhurst and, after making all the turns that Mr Farrell ordered, he pulled into another deserted alley.

'Here's where we change the licence plates, Mr Farrell,' he said tentatively.

'Okay, let's change them, Jaimie, and, God damn it, call me Dan.'

The licence plates were changed quickly. Mr Farrell was ashen, but perfectly self-possessed.

Jaimie drove down Washington and turned left into the Forest Preserve.

'No one in the parking lot, Mr Farrell, I mean Dan. No neckers on Friday morning.'

'Do teenagers neck these days?'

'Only when the girl wants to,' Jaimie replied.

They laughed louder and at greater length than they normally would have. But the tension eased.

'Some things don't change,' Mr Farrell said. 'Well, let's get this phase over with.'

They scrambled out of the car. Jaimie jammed the licence plates and the spent ammunition clips into the golf bag and threw the superb binoculars in after them. A pity. He zipped the bag up. 'You attach licence plates number three, Mr Farrell. No, not number one, number three. I'll throw this into the river. Then we'll drive back to Elmhurst and restore licence plates number one.'

The Desplanes River was running rapidly, the last of the snow on its banks melting. Jaimie leaned over the Forest Preserve bridge and very carefully dropped the golf bag into the river. It floated for a moment, then changed its colour and sank beneath the surface. 'Let them figure out how it got there, if they ever find it,' he said aloud, and then turned and walked calmly and confidently back to the parking lot, where he found Mr Farrell had finished changing the licence plates.

'Okay, we're on licence plate number three,' Mr Farrell said, 'which will be connected neither with the car's theft nor with what happened at the golf course. Now we'll ride back to our alley and put on licence plates number one, stuff licence plates number three under our jackets, park this car in front of J. C. Penney's, walk across the street, get into your car, and go back to the Neighbourhood.'

They went back to Elmhurst on Lake Street, careful to drive under the speed limit and avoid yellow lights. Then, in Jaimie's Plymouth, they drove down the Eisenhower – or the Congress, as Democrats still called it – to the Ryan and back to the Neighbourhood.

The operation had worked perfectly, except for the teenager in the last car.

'You must love her very much, Dan,' Jaimie said solemnly, at the top of Mandrake Parkway.

'Love who? You mean Noele? Oh, my God, Jaimie, you have it all wrong.'

Roger

He had played golf at the Club, his first decent exercise since the campaign started. And even though the second nine was rained out, Roger felt better for the exercise. It had cleared his mind and enabled him to make a decision he ought to have made long ago. He'd returned to his home on Jefferson Avenue resolute and determined.

Irene was typing something in her tiny office at the end of the upstairs hallway. He did not disturb her, but went immediately to his own study and began to compose a statement announcing his withdrawal from the gubernatorial race, citing threats on the lives of his family as the reason. That approach might take some of the sting out of Rod Weaver's story, and might even create enough of an uproar to force the Mob to take action against the Marshal.

Maybe I ought to withdraw from life, too.

The thought of self-destruction, a few weeks ago an absurd fantasy, was becoming more attractive every day. What was there left in his life?

Automatically he flipped on the television set to pick up the 4:30 local news, something he had never done before he had become a candidate. Maryjane Hennessey was informing the 4:30 viewers that a sudden rainstorm had ended Chicago's finest Friday since September, that Secretary Haig was in intensive negotiations with Chancellor Schmidt, and that three reputed members of the organized crime underworld had been shot to death at the Far Hills golf course.

It took a few moments for the implications of the third story to penetrate Roger's mind. He turned away from his typewriter and listened impatiently to the stumbling weather announcer and to a faintly bored correspondent trying to make sense of the latest Schmidt-Haig negotiations.

And then Maryjane again, a radiantly lovely combination of beauty, virtue and competence.

'Three reputed Chicago gangsters were killed by sniper

fire at Far Hills Country Club late this morning. The most prominent of the victims was Rocco Marsallo, also known as Robert Marshal and Rocco the Marshal.' Maryjane permitted herself only a tiny smile – even mobsters' deaths were not supposed to be funny. 'Marsallo, sixty-four, was reputed to have been a longtime power in vice and loan-shark activities of organized crime in Chicago. He was also alleged to be an enforcer, or "hit man," for organized crime in this area and was reported to be greatly feared because of his cruelty. Even though several brutal gangland slayings were attributed to him, he was never convicted of any of them. The other two victims were associates of Marsallo's known as Dubuque Salerno and Little Tony Caputo.

'The county sheriff's police said that the three men were killed by rifle fire. The weapon may have been of foreign manufacture, possibly Russian. Police sources believe that the killings were a professional gangland-style execution, although they admit that sniper fire is an unusual method for a gangland execution. The investigation continues, but there are no obvious suspects in the crime.'

As she talked, the camera followed three stretchers as they were carried from the rain-soaked golf course clubhouse to the sheriff's police ambulance, and then joined the investigation on the eighth green.

A handsome young county cop in a yellow rain slicker talked to a reporter who was protected by an umbrella. 'The subjects were shot by the alleged perpetrator from a very great distance,' he said in the computerlike tone cops think is a sign of the professional law enforcement specialist. 'The perpetrator's marksmanship was excellent. Two of the victims died almost instantly, and the third, Rocco Marsallo, alias Robert Marshal, died a few seconds later, while trying to run up the side of the green to safety. The alleged perpetrator fired several more rounds of ammunition into their lifeless bodies, presumably to make sure they were dead.'

'Will the rain hurt your search for clues, Sergeant?'

'All phases of the investigation are continuing,' said the cop grimly.

Roger turned off the television and ripped the half-typed sheet out of his typewriter, crumpled it, and tossed it in the wastebasket.

It was almost too good to be true. The council must have reversed itself and overruled the Marshal's padrino.

But since when did the outfit use Russian rifles?

John

Ace McNamara, back from pre-Easter confessions, poked his head into the pastor's study. 'I just heard it on the radio, John. Those three men that attacked Noele have been killed.'

'Are you sure?' John's hands were trembling.

'There wouldn't be three others guys named the Marshal, Dubuque, and Little Tony, would there?'

'Who did it?'

The Ace unbuttoned his cassock. 'The sheriff's police feel it was a professional, organized-crime hit job. The Lord works in strange ways. Are you coming down for supper?'

'In a few minutes. I have a phone call to make.'

'Monsignor Keegan, please. . . . Ed? John Farrell. I thought you might want to tell the cardinal, before he reads about it in the papers, that Channel Three is going to syndicate my interview programme. It will be small at first, only twenty or twenty-five markets. And, Ed, it doesn't take any more work for the programme to be on one channel or on fifty, so I'll still be able to handle my obligations here without any difficulty.'

Keegan muttered something about the canonical requirements for permission to engage in public entertainment.

'Anytime you want to make a fight out of it there's a few hundred teenagers dying for a chance to picket the cardinal.'

As he hung up the phone John thought that Irene would

be proud of him. And Danny too. They had both helped him. He was stupid to think of Danny as a rival. Life might begin again now for all of them.

Or maybe it wouldn't.

He was already late for supper. He stood up from the chair, hesitated for a second, then sat down and punched out an Evanston exchange.

'Father Fogarty, please. . . . Dads? This is Slick Farrell. . . . Hard feelings, Dads? Me? . . . Yeah, sure. I know. I'm doing a great job. . . . Well, Dads, when you're thinking of next month's character assassination, you might want to make the point that my ego trip is now going to be syndicated around the country, only thirty markets to begin with, a lot less than Phil Donahue. . . . What cities? Oh, Boston, New York, Los Angeles, San Francisco, Dallas, Houston. Nothing very big, Dads. . . . Sure, I know. Everybody in the diocese will be proud of me. Just like always.'

Tonight he had earned his martini.

Noele

Palm Sunday was a Rembrandt day, with clouds and sunlight, brightness and shadow, racing each other across the sky. Noele struggled out of bed at ten o'clock and turned on the radio to fortify herself with rock music for the rest of the day. The radio announced that there were tornado warnings for the South Side of Chicago.

'Gross.'

Even allowing for Father Ace's injunctions that some crosses had to be carried slowly, Noele was displeased with herself. She was not shaping up the way she ought to. Not only was she lagging behind in her homework, acting mean to her friends, bickering and bitching all the time with Moms; worst of all, she had abandoned the folk group on Palm Sunday because she was still afraid to go out of the house. She *had* to be better by Holy Thursday.

The dreams were not as bad as last week, and she didn't think that she woke up screaming as often in the middle of the night. But the demons were still after her. Now she was more afraid during the daytime, afraid even to go out of the house.

She turned her hi-fi up full blast and then jumped into the shower, leaving it nice and cold so she would wake up. *Actually* she didn't *look* violated anymore, just a few scratches here and there. It was all in her head now. But then she started to shiver and turned the shower up to warm. She kept shivering. The demons followed her even into the shower. She dressed in her prettiest lace under-wear – the kind that Moms said prostitutes used to wear twenty-five years ago – not that Moms didn't wear practi-cally the same thing. Then she put on her best white satin robe, went down to the kitchen, and poured herself a cup of coffee and a glass of grapefruit juice. If she were a real teenager, she'd drink Diet Pepsi instead of coffee.

She took the coffee and juice into the parlour, remem-bered that she hadn't turned off the stereo upstairs, and decided that it didn't matter anyway. She opened the Sun-day newspaper and thumbed through the papers till she found the story she knew would be there, a long feature article about the three 'crime syndicate' hoods who had been shot on Friday morning. She was sorry they were dead, just as she would be sorry anybody was dead. But she was not at all sorry that she didn't have to worry about them anymore. Still, the demons in her head didn't care much whether their real-life counterparts were alive or not.

She read the article through carefully a second time and a paragraph near the end caught her eye. A witness had reported seeing two men parked in a car on a road near the golf course at the time of the killing. But he could not iden-tify the men or the make of the car and did not note the lic-ence number. 'For all practical purposes,' the article said, 'it was one more gangland murder, more spectacular than most, but still destined to be just one of hundreds of unsolved crimes.'

Poor men, they never had much of a chance in life. Well, God would have to take care of them in his own way. Just so long as they weren't in the part of heaven she was in.

Daniel had promised to stop by sometime Sunday morning, and she hoped he would come before her parents got back from Mass. There were a couple of things she had to straighten out with him.

'Well, at least you wear a suit and tie to church on Sunday,' she greeted him when he came in the door.

'And at least you're out of bed on this Sunday morning.' He brushed her lips lightly as he always did and fingered her long, red hair. 'Looking quite happy and lovely, too.'

As usual, her knees became very weak. 'I'll bring you a cup of coffee. Do you want some bacon?'

'Yes, please,' he said humbly. 'Can I help?' He trailed her into the kitchen.

'Sit in the breakfast room,' she said, 'and don't distract me. I'll put some cinnamon rolls in the microwave, too.'

'May I read the paper?'

'Really!'

He came back from the living room with the paper and huddled over it.

'Did it feel good to kill those three men?' she asked as she put a dish with ten strips of bacon in front of him.

Daniel's hand froze in mid-flight toward the bacon strips.

'Don't bother denying it,' she said as his hand moved back from the bacon. 'When I was doing the term paper that started it all, I looked through your Annapolis yearbook. You were the best rifle shot in your class. And I suppose you learned how to use that Russian thing in China.'

Daniel loosened his tie and shoved the plate of bacon away. Noele filled his coffee cup.

'I was the second-in-command of their local civil defence militia. I taught the others how to operate Russian weapons, old Russian weapons.'

'And what did it feel like to actually kill someone with one of those weapons?'

She had to be pitiless, even though her heart ached for him.

Danny sipped his coffee before he replied. 'Terrible. I haven't been able to sleep a wink since then. Or eat much.'

'I'm sure Jaimie Burns's appetite hasn't been affected at all.'

'Did he tell you?' Danny rose halfway out of his chair.

'Really. The paper said two men. Who else but you two?'

Danny sank back into his chair and began to absently munch on a strip of bacon. 'We had to do it, Noele. He would have killed you, and maybe your mother and grandmother, too. In my mind I have a clear conscience. But my stomach isn't ready to agree yet.'

'I don't think you did *wrong*.' She relented a little bit. 'I was going to take gun lessons myself.'

'And assertiveness training?' He grinned crookedly at her.

In spite of herself, Noele laughed, the first good laugh she'd had in a long time.

'And you and Jaimie, er, persuaded Mr Weaver to return Roger's papers?'

Daniel's eyes flickered with interest and admiration. 'You don't miss much, do you, MN? Yeah, we made him an offer he couldn't refuse. He was impressed with what happens to people who refuse our offers.'

'And of course, if he had refused, you and Jaimie would have just meekly walked away, but he didn't know you two as well as I do.'

She laughed again. They both laughed together, as though they shared some great comic secret. But she must be serious. Now was her chance to ask the big question.

'Did it feel the way it did when you killed Clancy?'

Daniel was thunderstruck. 'Me – kill Clancy?'

'He told you at that cocktail party that he'd ordered the execution of your mother, and you came back and killed him.'

Daniel laughed. 'Look, MN, you didn't know Clancy. No one believed a tenth of what he said, especially when he was drunk.'

'But you had a fight that night. Why?'

'When Clancy was drunk he said and did crazy things.

He was terribly mad at me that night because I was interested in your mother, and her father had sought a grand jury indictment against the Farrells. He would have got over that as soon as he sobered up. Her parents would have been more of a problem, but they died right after I flamed out over Sinkiang.'

'And you fought about Moms?'

'He called her some terrible names. Then I lost my temper and called him some even worse ones. Then he said some things about my mother, and I took Irene's hand and ran away from them.'

'So you didn't believe that he was responsible for your mother's death?'

'Would it have brought her back to life?' he demanded.

'No, but you killed those men to protect me.'

Danny was annoyed with her. 'Only because you're still alive. If you were dead, I would have been brokenhearted.' He smiled quickly, if not very convincingly. 'The world wouldn't be the same without you. But what good would it do to kill them? If I could have kept my mother alive by killing Clancy I guess I would have killed him too.'

'You're still angry about her death, I can tell.'

He jammed his hands fiercely into his pockets and began to pace furiously around the kitchen.

'Sure, I am, and guilty about it, too. She died to save my life.'

'Sit down,' she told him. 'You make me nervous pacing around that way.'

He sat down.

'And I haven't killed Burke, have I? Even though he deprived me of eighteen years of my life. What else do I have to do to persuade you that I am not into revenge?'

'Burke?' she whispered.

'Sure, Burke. I guessed that before the plane crashed. I was furious about it till I got back here, and then I figured, why the hell even the score? It wouldn't give me back the eighteen years. Anyway, I suppose he thought he was protecting herself.'

'From what?'

Danny began buttering the cinnamon roll.

'Who knows? I never asked him. Why don't you find out? You're the one who asks all the questions.'

'Don't talk with food in your mouth,' she lectured him, ignoring his sarcasm. She began to nibble on the bacon herself. 'Aren't you afraid that he'll do it again?'

Danny waited till the food was out of his mouth. 'No way, José. Old Burkie has finally mellowed. He even kind of likes me.'

Burke was responsible for Danny's disappearance. Well, that made sense.

'He might have killed Clancy, then?'

'Ask him.' Danny was impatient again, out of the chair and pacing the breakfast room. 'All these questions are crazy, MN. What does it matter who killed Clancy?'

'Daniel Xavier, can't you see that murder is the key to everything?'

'No, I can't see it, Mary Noele, I can't see it at all. What makes you think it was a murder? Manslaughter at the most, and maybe only an accident. Now, for the love of heaven, MN, drop it. Will you, please?'

'I won't drop it. Here, drink some more coffee. And finish the bacon, too. You look starved. Anyway, I want to know who pushed Clancy down the stairs, and I won't stop until I find out. After that everything will work out. If you don't tell me, I'll find out some other way.'

Daniel's Paul Newman eyes glittered sharply. 'If I tell you, Noele, you might hate me.'

'Tell me anyway.'

Danny hesitated, then waved his hands in a gesture of futility. 'There's no stopping you. All right, I'll tell you. It was probably Roger.'

'Roger! I don't believe it.'

He sat down again and nibbled on the one remaining piece of bacon. 'See, I told you you wouldn't believe me.'

'Oh, I believe you. I mean, I believe you think you're telling the truth. But I'm astonished that you think it was Roger who pushed Clancy down the stairs.'

'I can't say for sure. Brigid sort of hinted to me that I shouldn't talk to the poor man – her words – about it. He certainly acted kind of odd towards me the next couple of days.'

She almost told him that Roger thought that it was he who had given the fatal shove.

'How can you prove that you didn't give your uncle the final shove?'

'Prove? Final shove? Noele, this isn't an Agatha Christie story.'

'I'm sure it isn't.'

Daniel forced himself to his feet, like a boxer who had been down for the count of nine and had lost his patience with his persecutor. 'Excuse me, MN, for violating your language rules, but *shit*. I don't want to talk about it anymore. If you need evidence, you can ask your mother. We were together until midnight that night. Then I went home to find Burke, Bridie, Roger, and the body.'

'Twelve o'clock!' exclaimed Noele.

'Burke, I suppose, put the fix in with the doctor and the cop so Roger wouldn't have to stand trial for manslaughter. I never could figure out why. No jury would have convicted him of anything. Poor Clancy was beating her with a cane, like he did when he was drunk. Roger pulled him off. They struggled, and that was that. I suppose Brigid wanted to keep it a secret to protect the family name. Ha, that's a joke, isn't it, Noele?'

Poor man, he had every right to be bitter, but Noele could not find a single word to say to him as he stormed out of the house.

Danny was innocent. But who. . . ? The key problem was still what it had been when she'd come out of Dr Keefe's office. Who was lying about the time of death, Grams, when she said it was early, or the doctor, who said it was late? Or maybe they were both lying.

Noele absently buttered a sweet roll for herself, raisin and cinnamon.

Or maybe they were both telling the truth.

She took a sip of coffee. It was cold and bitter, and then the roll slipped out of her hand.

Of course. Oh, dear God, how horrible for the poor person!

She had seen it all, as if she had been standing in a dark room momentarily illuminated by a flashbulb.

Then the room was dark again, and she had to think about what she had seen.

Roger and Moms came home from Mass, reporting cautiously that the folk group had done only fairly well without her. Absently she hugged Moms and said, 'That's a nice way of putting it.'

Then she hugged Moms again, to make up for some of the mean things she had said and done in the last two weeks.

Roger and Moms had to leave for a political luncheon on the North West Side. She assured them that she wasn't frightened anymore.

She spent most of the afternoon in the parlour, watching the changing lights and shadows as the tornado warnings continued. The wind whipped the still-naked tree branches, and the rain soaked the sidewalks, which dried quickly in the sunlight only to be soaked again.

She went upstairs to dress, put on a spring suit, and picked up her guitar. Too long since she'd used it. She went back to the parlour and strummed it, playing the chords for the Holy Week liturgies and humming the tunes softly.

Poor, silly, stupid people, she thought. None of them evil, except possibly Clancy, and he was crazy some of the time.

Now she had it in her power to free them from the swamp, give them all new lives, painful new lives, but new lives just the same.

Who was she to dare to do a thing like that? I'm only a nosy, bitchy, flaky teenager. What do I know about life? Maybe I ought to forget the whole thing.

Who do you think you are anyway, Mary Noele?

She sighed. It was St James's epistle, she remembered, that said the truth shall make you free, free to live again, only none of them – not Brigid or Burke or Moms or Roger or Monsignor John or Daniel Xavier – none of them wanted to be free. None of them wanted to live again.

She went back to her room, turned off the stereo, and removed The Who. She replaced them with her favourite singer, Mary O'Hara, the wonderful woman who had been a cloistered nun and came back into the world because she was convinced her vocation was to sing. Noele played the last band on the record – 'Lord of the Dance.'

'I am the dance which will never, never die.' And Noele could see the little Irish feet as children danced to the song.

Damn right, she murmured to herself, making up her mind.

She lifted the record off the player, fitted it carefully into its jacket, and turned off her stereo. Then she donned a yellow rain slicker and walked down the stairs and out of the house to the squad car in the driveway, where a pretty black patrol officer was reading some geek named Tolstoy.

'Officer Day, could you, like, take me out for a short ride in the patrol car?'

'Sure, honey.' She put the paperback book on the seat next to her. 'We both need the exercise.'

'I want to go to the Courts.'

Officer Day hesitated. She knew that Noele had been left at the Courts, tied and naked.

'No problem,' Noele insisted.

'Okay,' Officer Day said finally. 'If that's what you really want.'

'I want,' said Noele.

She remembered lying cold and hurt on the asphalt, unable to move or scream for help. But the Courts were still a kind of sacred place. After Easter she would come back and play basketball or volleyball. She would no more give up her Courts than she would give up her Flame or her Jaimie.

The rain had stopped, and the clouds were racing rapidly across the sky, the way humans raced through life. The naked trees seemed to be twisting toward heaven, begging God for the life and the covering and the beauty that spring would give them. And maybe even for the kids on whom the trees had looked down for so many years.

In the story Jesus told, the man who found a treasure buried in the field had to give up everything to buy the field and gain the treasure. He was forced to choose between the old and the new. Some of the members of her family would have to give up everything to choose a second chance. They wouldn't want to do that.

You must lose your life to find it. That's what this next week was about.

That includes you too, Mary Noele.

All right.

Noele Marie Brigid Farrell!

I said all right. All right?

All right.

Stop laughing at me. You're as bad as Moms.

All right.

Well! *You* can laugh at me if you want.

All RIGHT!

Then Noele saw a broad beam of sunlight move lazily down Jefferson Avenue, like a sophomore girl slouching home from the Ninety-fifth Street bus on a warm, Indian summer afternoon, daydreaming about a senior boy to whom she had never spoken a word in her life. Dark clouds moved ahead of the sun as though running from it, and Jefferson Avenue was bright all the way to Ninety-fifth Street.

Noele knew the demons from hell could still touch her, perhaps even hurt her. But they would never prevail against her. She heard in her memory Mary O'Hara's voice and imagined the little Irish kids dancing on the Courts with the Lord of the Dance.

'We can go home now,' she told Patrol Officer Day.

DANCE
TEN

Boogaloo

Start with my toes
you old Ghost
Spirit the soles of my shoes
And teach me a Pentecostal
Boogaloo
Sprain my ankles with dancing
Sandal around my feet
to roam with you in the rain
and feel at home in my footprints

Oh! look at me spinning,
Sprinkling, tonguing, teaching
Winsoming wondrous steps
lift me, how?
We'd better quit now,
to all dizzy down giggly
Stop – you're tickling
(My funnybone's fickle for you)

Stop – I'll drop
I'm dying, I'm flying

With your winding my feet and
legs and waist
Lassoed
Stop chasing fool – I'm racing from you

Don't catch me
Do!
I'll drown
Oh, drown me –. most
For I love you so
You old Ghost!

'Poem for Pentecost'
Nancy Gallagher McCready

Then down to hell I took my way
For my true love's deliverance
And rose again on the third day
Up to my true love and the dance

'My Dancing Day'
A Medieval Good Friday Carol

Roger

Good Friday dinner was a sombre event at Brigid's, another dogged tribute to the family customs begun by the determined Julie Farrell. Always whitefish and light dry white wine, though in Julie's day the Farrells could hardly have afforded Pouilly Fuissé. No potatoes, no dessert, no frivolous conversation.

Are we supposed to be waiting for the Lord's return? Roger wondered. Why would he come back to this crowd?

Brigid and Irene cleared away the fish plates. Noele solemnly poured the tea – no coffee on Good Friday at Brigid's – from the silver service in the middle of the table, and she replaced the teapot as if returning the ciborium to the altar after Communion. Then she seated herself next to Brigid at the head of the table.

'This is a good night to bury the family skeletons,' she said, her swamp-fire eyes scorching the room. 'If we're going to start living again, everyone has to sacrifice. And tonight truth is the sacrifice. We are all going to tell the truth for a change.'

The room was silent, as if someone had just died. It was absurd for a mere child to make such demands, and yet so great was the force of her determination that no one was able to speak or move. Noele had cast a spell that paralyzed them all.

'I have to get back to the rectory to rehearse for tomorrow's liturgy,' John said, glancing fretfully at his watch.

'I'm *sure* they need you, Uncle Monsignor. Well, you're

not leaving. First of all, Grams, you're going to tell us the truth about Great Grandfather William Farrell's will.'

Brigid was parchment pale.

'And if I don't?'

'Then I will.'

'Give me a cigarette, Burke.'

He lit it with trembling fingers, and Brigid took one long drag on the cigarette, nervously snuffed it out, and began to speak in a tone of voice appropriate for priests chanting the office of the dead. 'It all started when William and Blanche Farrell had twin sons. The second of them, Clarence, was her favourite, supposedly because his birth had been so easy, and Martin's so difficult. I know that sounds crazy, but that's the kind of woman she was. There had to be a good son and a bad son. Clancy could do no wrong and Marty could do no right. Bill wasn't much interested in raising the boys. He lived for the firm, I guess because it was an excuse to escape from Blanche and her crazy pieties. Oh, yes, she was as pious as they come. . . .

'Well, Marty grew up to be one of the finest human beings who ever walked the face of the earth. Everyone loved him – but his mother. And Clancy grew up to be a dull, harmless weakling, poor man – harmless, that is, unless he had a temper tantrum or was drunk or someone suggested that he wasn't much of a man. He flunked out of Loyola – Blanche wouldn't let him go to school away from home. Marty graduated with honours from Notre Dame, where he was in the Navy ROTC, and then into flight training. He married Flossie, God be good to the poor woman. About the time they were engaged, Bill found me working in a friend's kitchen and liked my spunk. He thought I would put some of it into his Clancy. Blanche hated me from the first day I came into the house.

'William wanted Marty to inherit the firm. But Marty told us all he would have no part of it. He was going to be a career Navy officer. That was one way to escape from Blanche's perpetual bitching. So William drew up a will leaving everything to Clancy. Marty went off to the war, and Clancy took over much of the firm's new work – defence plant construction. Bill insisted that I help because he was afraid Blanche's little boy would make a godawful mess of it.

'Which he did. And then he tried to bribe some government inspectors. I took the money to them, thinking I had to do what my husband told me. Then your father, Irene, got wind of it and would have indicted us if Bill hadn't had a word with Bob Jackson, who was attorney general then.

'Bill was so furious at Clancy that, without telling us, he had Parnell Kennedy, Burke's father, change the will, leaving every last cent to Marty, who was at sea on the *Hornet*. Bill died without warning three months later, the same week as Parnell, and then two months after that Marty died trying to return to the carrier in the battle of the Philippine Sea. Ran out of gas, they said, God rest him. So you see, Danny, every cent the Farrells have is rightfully yours.'

Danny's face was an expressionless mask. 'My father didn't want it,' he said coolly, and 'neither do I.'

'Bill probably would have calmed down and changed the will again, but he died too soon,' Brigid added with a helpless gesture of her hands. 'And that started everything.'

'When you found the will in your father's files, why did you tear it up, Burkie?' Noele shifted her searing eyes to the grim old man at the other end of the table.

'What right do you have to ask?' he demanded gruffly.

'The right of someone who has benefited from your dishonesty,' she replied sharply, a picture of affronted womanly justice as old as the race itself.

Burke shifted his position in the chair and toyed thoughtfully with a spoon. 'I agree with Bridie. Bill would have changed his mind if he had lived a little longer and calmed down. He knew that Martin would not touch the company. And while he liked Flossie, he wouldn't have wanted the firm to pass into the hands of the Careys, which is what would have happened. Besides, Noele, the Careys' auditors would have found out how Clancy did business. Conlon was still waiting in the wings with a grand jury. Clancy would have gone to jail. So would your grandmother. I tore up the will to protect her.'

'And then, when Danny's mother asked a few innocent questions, Clancy had her killed by that terrible man, Marsallo.'

Burke nodded, now no longer a warrior but a shrivelled old man. 'We tried to stop him. We didn't think he'd do it. I thought I had talked him out of it, but that pious old witch hated Floss even more than she hated Bridie.'

'And you were supposed to die too, Daniel, only your mother saved you at the last second, giving her life for yours.'

'I don't see what good all of this does MN,' Danny said sadly. 'We can't change the past.'

'We can change the present.'

'So Dad was telling the truth that night,' Roger interrupted. 'My God, Danny. . . .'

'I didn't believe him.' Danny said, burying his face in his hands as if he did not want his family to see his pain. 'Maybe because I didn't want to believe him. Anyway, what difference does it make?' Danny rose from the table and began to stride back and forth in the dining room. 'They're all dead. Drop it, MN. Let the dead bury their dead.'

'I won't let the dead bury the living,' she replied tartly. 'Go on, Roger, ask Daniel Xavier what you want to ask him.'

'But you killed Dad, didn't you, Danny? Didn't you push him down the stairs?' Roger felt like an actor in a play. How did Noele know what his lines would be?

'Certainly not,' Danny said impatiently. 'Why would I do that? Where did all this nonsense start about my killing Clancy? He wasn't worth killing.'

'Are you sure?' said Roger.

'Of course he's sure,' Irene said serenely, her face incredibly beautiful. 'I could have told you that if you had asked. After the cocktail party he dragged me out of the house and drove to Joliet and back, trying to calm down. I had never seen him so angry.'

'Because Clancy claimed to have killed his mother?' Roger asked, still confused.

'Course not, Roger.' Noele was impatient with his slowness. 'Because Grandpa Clancy had said terrible things to Moms. Daniel Xavier protects the living, not the dead.'

'This is all crazy.' Danny leaned on the table, his eyes beginning to burn with anger. 'Why would anyone think I killed Clancy?'

'Because you were supposed to be a hot-tempered, unstable young man. You had been thrown out of the Navy, for defending a black man. Wasn't that enough proof you were unstable? Killing Clancy in a temper tantrum was the kind of thing you might have done.'

'No, it wasn't,' he insisted. And then, shrugging at the foolishness of trying to convince them, he demanded, 'Who says I killed Clancy?'

The room was heavy with silence.

Finally Noele spoke. 'Grams,' she said softly, 'you lied to everybody, didn't you? And to make it believable, you even told Burke that Danny had threatened to come back and kill you, too.'

Burke came to life, leaped out of his chair, and hit Brigid in the face twice with the back of his hand. 'You murderous, lying whore!' he bellowed, the magnitude of her betrayal made even worse by the power of his wounded love.

Danny jumped across the room, twisting Burke's arm behind his back. 'Don't you ever do that again, you son of a bitch,' he shouted, 'or I'll do to you what I'm supposed to have done to Clancy.'

Danny released him. Burke slumped into a chair, his hands quivering like those of a palsy victim as they covered his face.

'So that's why Burke bribed someone to wreck your plane. He wasn't going to let you come back and kill Grams.'

'I figured that out in China. Who else would have had the connections? I even guessed that it had something to do with the firm.' Danny shrugged listlessly. 'So what?'

'You should have killed me when you had the chance,' Burke murmured.

'You *are* worth killing, Burke,' Danny conceded with a bitter grin. 'But I decided it wouldn't give me the eighteen years back.'

'Don't you want to know why Brigid lied?' Noele sounded like a mother superior in the pre-Vatican Council church reproving a guilty third-grade boy.

'No, not particularly,' Danny said, his lips pressed tightly together.

'Well, I'm not going to let you run away. Didn't Grams kind of hint to you Roger might have done it to protect her from another beating by Grandpa Clancy?'

'But, Mother, I couldn't have killed Dad.' Roger was so astonished, he could not manage to be outraged. 'I was playing gin rummy in the Country Club basement.'

'So now we know what actually happened,' Noele said sternly. 'Everyone was told that it was Danny because he was leaving the country and wouldn't be around to defend himself. And Danny was told that it was Roger, because he and Roger were best friends, and he wouldn't do anything to get Roger in trouble. Obviously it had to be somebody else.'

'All right, child, I'll confess,' Brigid said wearily. 'I killed him. I'm glad I did. I should have done it years before.'

'One more lie, Grams. Won't you ever learn to tell the truth? You wouldn't have had to cover up. There were marks on you from the beating. You could have argued self-defence if there'd been a trial. You were not protecting yourself, Grams, you were protecting somebody else, for whom even an involuntary manslaughter charge would have been a disaster, the end of everything important in life.'

'Who would that be?' Burke asked, sounding like a man who'd just come out of a coma.

'Someone who, when he was a young priest, always returned to the rectory before eleven o'clock at night, but someone Grams couldn't call at the rectory that night until twelve thirty because she knew he wasn't there.'

'I'd do it again, if I had to,' John said in a barely audible voice. 'He was beating Mother with a cane. I pulled him off her. Then he came at me with the cane. I yanked it out of his hands, and he started pounding me with his fists. I put up the cane to defend myself and pushed. He lost his balance. I reached out to grab him. I think I did, anyway. I wanted to. Maybe I didn't. He fought me off, lost his balance, tipped backward, and then . . . Oh, God, I don't know. . . . I was glad to see him tumble down the stairs. I wanted to sing with joy when I saw his head crack against the floor and the blood come pouring out. I hated the bastard. I wanted him dead.'

The room was as silent as a cemetery.

'No jury would have convicted you,' Burke said slowly.

'But he would have been finished in the priesthood,' Brigid said, 'sent off to a monastery or exiled to a poor mission country. It wasn't John's fault. I made him lie.'

'No, you didn't,' John insisted. 'I was happy to lie. The priesthood was the only thing that mattered. I was dumb enough to think I could cling to it by lying. I'm sorry, Danny.' John's hands were clenched on his knees, his head bowed over as if awaiting divine retribution. 'It seemed harmless: there wasn't going to be a police investigation. Burke took care of that. You would be away for a couple of years. When you came back we would straighten everything out.'

'Do you think it was, like, a mortal sin?' Noele's voice sliced through the heaviness of the room.

'Mortal sin? Diminished responsibility, self-defence? Telling Roger and Burke that it was Danny was a worse sin.' John extended his hands as if pleading for absolution he would never receive. 'If he'd been lying on the driveway and I hadn't seen him and I'd backed the car out and run over him, it wouldn't have been a mortal sin, and yet I would have been so happy to have killed him. I'm glad he's dead. That's sin enough. There has been no peace since then. Everything else in my life is a sham.'

'But, John.' Irene spoke for the first time since the beginning of the conversation. 'You weren't responsible. You stopped a man from beating your mother, maybe even from killing her. Of course you're happy he's dead. He was a monster. Just like we're happy those men who might have attacked Brigid and me and Noele again are dead. And if Danny isn't angry, ought you not forgive yourself?'

'I'm not angry, Jackie,' Danny said, tears in his eyes for his cousin's pain.

'Moms, like, you're the only one in the room who has any common sense.'

'He was my father,' John sobbed. 'He wasn't a monster all the time. I can never forgive myself.'

Brigid's head was buried in her hands, her body erect and frozen, like Lot's wife in the tundra, a shape of suffering woman never to be thawed. 'Maybe that's the trouble,' she said. 'We Farrells don't know how to forgive ourselves.'

'Then it's time we started,' said Irene crisply.

'Really!' Noele agreed.

I'm a minor character in this drama, Roger thought. I've lost my mistress, I've lost my wife, I've lost the image of the little boy I thought I loved. Maybe I've found myself. And my lost lovers have become my new friends. A little late to grow up, but not too late. Now I'd better make a friend out of my brother.

'It's all over, John.' Reassuringly, he gripped his brother's shoulder. 'We'll work it out. I'll help. It's going to be all right, now. Isn't that true, Danny? . . . Where's Danny?'

'He ran away a few moments ago, so quietly that no one noticed. Just like he did in 1963.' Noele sighed. 'Well, you can't make a man grow up who doesn't want to. We might as well go home now. I guess that's about everything.'

Not quite, Snowflake, Roger thought, some of his new-found and painfully won maturity slipping away. Not quite.

Burke

It was the first night since their marriage that they had not slept in the same bed. There was so much anger and hatred between them that they would never sleep in the same bed again.

They were both dead. Only the burial remained.

And yet they ate breakfast together; deprived of speech by their disgust and fury, but at the same table because even horror cannot wipe out the habits of a common life.

She wore a white linen robe, and her red hair hung over it loosely – even this morning a timeless beauty. But Burke no longer desired that beauty. Rather, he was repelled by it. It was her beauty for which he had tried to kill.

Somewhere deep inside him there was sorrow for her pain. She had suffered much and had done her best. But there was no truth in her. No truth and no trust. Not her fault perhaps. It was the way she was made, a greater monster than he was.

Then Danny appeared at the front door, came in the house, and, quite uninvited, sat at the table with them, bright and chipper as the morning sunlight streaming through the breakfast room windows.

'Sure,' he said in his fake brogue, 'it looks like neither of you had much sleep. Would you toast me some English muffins, woman of the house, and some bacon, too? I have to fly to New York, and I won't be doing it on any empty stomach.'

Brigid provided the muffins and the bacon. Burke filled his coffee cup again. Neither of them spoke.

'I'm glad we were after getting the air cleared last night,' Danny said cheerfully. 'Since I'm about to become a permanent part of the New York literary scene, I'll be at least confident that the firm will be in good hands.'

Burke broke his vow of silence. 'Is that all you can say?'

'Ah, sure, 'tis yourself that wants some great fucking denunciation, is it now?'

'It would be appropriate,' Burke agreed. 'We did damn you to almost two decades of prison in China.'

Danny dismissed it with a casual wave of his hand. 'Best thing in the world for me. Nothing like a stint in a beehive to straighten a man out.'

'You're daft,' said Brigid.

'That kind of forgiveness isn't possible,' Burke said dubiously.

Danny took Burke's hand and Brigid's in his own, and

placed them one on top of the other. Burke and Brigid tried to break away, but he stopped them. 'You're to make peace, and that's an order. Do you hear me, woman of the house?'

Bridie nodded, tears slipping down her cheeks.

'Good enough for you.' Danny kissed her lips tenderly, rose, and walked toward the back door of the house at the end of the breakfast room. 'And yourself?' He clasped his hand on the doorknob, his eyes, now ice blue, frozen on Burke.

'I hear.' Burke's voice was raw and weary.

Burke broke the silence as Danny was about to walk through the doorway. 'Forgiveness cannot be that easy.'

Danny turned around, held up a waggish finger, and winked like a mischievous leprechaun. 'If it isn't that easy, Burkie, it isn't forgiveness.'

He put his head back in the door with a parting shot. 'And you remember that, woman, when you go home to see your sister. Next week.'

After he had slipped away into the sunlight, Burke and Brigid remained motionless at the table, her hand on his, both of them too shy to face immediately the pain and the delight of beginning again.

Irene

It had been a long Good Friday night. She and Roger left the house on Glenwood Drive and drove around for two hours in the Seville, calmly and cordially discussing their problem. Roger was kind, sweet, and generous, making it all the more difficult for her. He knew what had to happen. His only regret was that so many years had been wasted, a waste for which he blamed himself completely, try as Irene might to insist that it was mostly her fault.

Roger was the only innocent. He was a man who had

suffered for what others had done, not courageously, perhaps, but at least uncomplainingly. Even to the end he did not complain. And now he was genuinely brave. Irene's regrets were as vast as a mountain range – heavy, implacable, insurmountable.

After her failure later that night to talk Danny out of his plan to flee to New York, Irene drove home at 2:30 in the morning, thinking with considerable irony that she had begun Good Friday with two men – three, counting John – and begun Holy Saturday with none.

The next morning Noele was furiously angry at her.

'Really, Mo-*ther*, I'm sure you and Roger can't continue like this. He is your husband; you're his wife. And it's not good for either of you to be sleeping in different bedrooms.'

'Did it ever occur to you, young woman, that my sex life is my business, not yours?' She drew her robe more tightly around her, as if to protect herself from the withering scorn of Noele's eyes.

'I think it's outrageous.' Noele was now becoming dramatic, as she often did in her fights with Irene as a prelude to storming out of the room in tears. 'Everyone else is ready to forgive and forget and to begin life again. And you're digging in your heels and living stubbornly in the past.'

Danny's rejection and Noele's harsh words combined to become a high wind fanning the prairie fire of Irene's anger, made worse by her guilt at not having protected her daughter from rape and not having helped her much after she'd been brutalized. 'You think you know so goddamned much, you smart-assed little bitch. Well, let me tell you, you don't understand anything. You have a lot of growing up to do before you give me advice on how to live my life. Now, get out of my room, and leave me alone. I'll work things out with Roger my way.'

Noele burst into tears. 'You don't have to be vile about it,' she sobbed dramatically. 'I merely want my mother and father to act like they're husband and wife.'

And then the words came, words that she tried to choke back before it was too late. 'You stupid little bitch. Roger isn't my husband,' she said, spitting out the poisonous words. 'And he isn't your father, either.'

Noele's tears stopped. She stood, a statue in jeans and a dark blue and red University of Arizona sweat shirt, frozen in the doorway of Irene's office. She watched the facial expressions on the statue begin to change as the little computer beneath the red ponytail worked away. *I never should have said it, never, never, never.*

She waited patiently, knowing that an outburst of anger and hatred would take place. *Will Noele hit me? She had every right to.*

I've lost all my men, and now I will lose my Christmas child.

'Shit,' said Noele, her own sternly enforced language code collapsing. And then in rapidly ascending tones, 'Shit, shit, oh, *shit!*'

'Don't use that kind of language, young woman,' Irene said faintly.

Then, astonishingly, Noele was on her lap, her arms wrapped tightly around her neck, her head against her mother's breasts.

'Oh, Moms, poor, poor wonderful Moms, you're the only good person in our whole family. And I bet you did it for me, too.'

How little you understand your own children.

'You even are our legitimate daughter, Noele,' Irene said absently, as though she were reciting facts from the history of medieval English monarchs to a mildly interested classroom. 'We were married the day after Easter, and you were born on Christmas Day, three weeks early.'

Noele would never know that they were both drunk and that they'd quarrelled, and that that particular night of love had been frustrating for the two of them. She was still a Christmas child, conceived in Easter week.

Noele lifted her head, her eyes round with shock. 'Well, *really*, I totally *assumed* that I was legitimate.'

Irene knew that she and Noele would continue to fight as mothers and daughters must always fight, but that henceforth they would be friends.

'We were married by a priest in California a week before

Daniel left for Japan. Then my father and mother were killed in an auto accident and left all the money to the other
kids. When I heard that Danny was dead, too. I went into
a depression, I thought I was too young to raise a child and
couldn't earn the money to support one, and that I'd
ruined my life – and I didn't want to ruin someone else's.
It was hard to give you up. You were such a cute
red-haired baggage even then.' She stroked her daughter's
hair. 'But I thought they would be able to take care of you
and I wouldn't.

'Then I met Roger in Berkeley, where I was typing, and
he was kind and sweet. I didn't tell him about you, but I
thought that after a while, some way, I might be able to get
you back. Then Roger became sick and we couldn't have
any children. And the people who were taking care of you
had terrible troubles. So we adopted you. Your grandmother thought that you were Roger's child. John didn't
know who your father was and never asked, or even suspected.'

'You never told any of them that Danny was' – she hesitated – 'my father?'

'I didn't know what they would do to you if they knew.
And I wanted to keep it my secret, a memory of him. It
seemed to be the only thing I had.'

'Of *course*, you should have kept it secret.' Noele was not
prepared to find any fault with her at all. 'Poor, dear, wonderful Moms.'

'I would have told you this long ago if I'd known that
you'd react the way you have.'

'I'm so glad that you were able to buy me back. I belong
with you and . . .' She straightened up and pondered for a
moment. Then with a dramatic sigh, she said, 'Well, at
least I won't have to choose between Danny and Jaimie. I
can love them both.'

'I hope so.' Irene tried not to laugh at her Christmas
child.

'That is a relief,' Noele said, the computer in her head
whirling again. 'And I won't have to worry about names
because I call both Danny and Roger by their first names.
Poor Roger, of course, he'll get all kinds of sympathy from

the voters for making a brave sacrifice because of faith and principles. Besides, he won't have any trouble finding himself another nice wife. Maryjane, maybe. She's cool. I'll have to be very good to him, though, so he knows I still love him.' She giggled. 'I'm the kind that needs two fathers anyway.'

'Noele, do you ever stop worrying about how to take care of other people long enough to worry about who's going to take care of you?'

Her daughter's surprise was genuine. 'Of course not, Moms, you'll take care of me. That's what mothers are for. . . . Now, what are we going to do about Daniel?'

'We are not going do anything about Daniel, young woman. The tissues are over there on the cabinet. Pass me some of them too. Daniel is going to New York to stay. He doesn't believe that the past can be re-created, and he doesn't want to spoil anything for anyone else.'

'Well, the nerve of him, how *totally obsessive* of him to do such a geeky thing. You just stop him, that's all.'

'I tried, Noele. I tried as hard as I ever did in my life. I threw myself at him the way I did the first time in Michigan, when I was only a year or two older than you. It didn't work. Daniel does not want to be a husband or a father. He does not want a family. He does not even want one child, much less a couple more.'

'Did he HUMILIATE you?'

Horrified teenage dramatics. Now I can enjoy them.

'No, darling. He did not humiliate me. Daniel couldn't humiliate anybody. He is too afraid of me to humiliate me. He merely wanted to run away from me as quickly as he could.'

Noele left her mother's lap and began to pace the floor, just as her father did when he was upset. How much she was like him. 'The nerve of him, the absolute nerve of him. You're right, Moms. You shouldn't run after him anymore. The son of a bitch isn't worth it.'

'Noele Marie Brigid Farrell, don't use such language!' Somehow Noele's anger was hysterically funny. She bit her lip trying not to laugh.

'If I'd known that he was going to act like such a child,' she fumed, 'I would have let him rot in China!'

Irene's laughter broke through her clenched teeth. Poor Danny had at last encountered his match.

'Mo-*ther*, it's not funny!'

'No, it's not, but you are!'

'Really!'

'He is your father, and my husband,' Irene said, permitting the words finally to cross her lips.

'I know. Is he worth it, Moms?'

'Sure he's worth it,' Irene said firmly. 'He's still magic, even if immature magic.'

'I'll bring him back, but then he's *your* problem.'

'As long as either of us lives, Noele, he'll be both our problems.'

'Really!' Noele said again, leaving Irene's office in a flurry, pulling off her sweat shirt as she went.

In a moment she was back in again, sweat shirt in hand. 'You're not pregnant, are you?'

Irene felt herself turn crimson. 'I certainly am not . . . and don't you dare suggest to him . . .'

'Just asking.'

Daniel Xavier

The sun of Holy Saturday morning smiled benignly through the great glass window across from the ticket counters at O'Hare International Airport. Danny was bemused by the crowds. A lot of people travelled at Easter. Two decades ago Christmas week was a vacation for many people. Now the Easter break was also time off. Nice work if you can get it.

What a spectacular show it had been last night. Noele by sheer willpower and intelligence and psychic sense had undone fifty years of sickness in the Farrell family, probably not permanently, but still enough to give Bridie and Burke, and Roger and poor John, who would weep himself back into happiness, a second chance on their lives.

He had considered stopping at the rectory, as he had at the house on Glenwood. But the Ace would take care of that. Roger and John needed a psychologist who had been a marine.

Irene?

She was not the woman about whom he had fantasized over Sinkiang just before the jet on the great blackbird had flamed out. She was more self-possessed, more intelligent, more poised, more sophisticated. She had grown up during the last eighteen years, and he had not.

She had become a tiny blur of pain in his memory during the years in prison. Then, as soon as he left for Beijing, he found himself longing for her the way an alcoholic yearns for sparkling champagne while wandering in a desert.

The few times they were together had not slaked his thirst at all.

But the bubbling wine was too rich for him.

She had wept last night, bitterly, angrily. She had accused him of turning his back on her, of walking away from his responsibilities. But leaving her was the best thing he could do – for her and for Roger and, of course, for Noele.

The moment he had set eyes on the Christmas child, he knew who and what she was. For one terrifying dizzy moment – like a man at the top of a tall building when the clouds are swept away – he was a little boy again. And the radiant, magic smile was his mother's.

No, it was not Florence Carey Farrell. Not quite, yet almost. He had composed himself quickly and covered up with blarney about Irish mythology.

And was happy and sad and proud and confused.

Irene knew that he knew. And readily admitted that Noele was indeed born on Christmas, conceived on their last night together. And somehow no one else knew, not even Noele.

I hung around the neighbourhood mostly because I wanted to know her better. And at least I saved her life, even if I couldn't save my mother's.

And then suddenly there she was, striding purposefully down the length of the ticket line with the Holy Saturday sunlight burning bright in her long red hair, piled high on her head like a flaming strawberry ice cream cone.

Oh, oh, thought Daniel Farrell. Now I'm in real trouble.

She was dressed not in her usual uniform of jeans and a sweat shirt or blouse, but in a V-neck suit whose colour could best be described as apricot, somehow matching the burnished flames of her hair and the crackling glow in her green eyes.

Easter dress.

She won't see me, he prayed.

Who the hell else is wearing a Notre Dame Windbreaker?

This dazzling young woman was, unaccountably, the fruit of his loins, a child of fire and water. As Irene would say, a red and green Christmas child. Part giggly teenager, part sophisticated woman of the world, part ancient Irish witch. And each one of her parts was almost impossible to resist. Noele, his ravaged daughter, now superbly triumphant. Violated and inviolable. Wounded and invulnerable. Battered and resilient, indestructible.

For a moment her hair turned from red to black, and he saw his mother. It was 1944 and he was a little boy.

Then the young woman was Noele again.

She saw him and changed her course like a battle cruiser in the Royal Navy seeking to sink the *Bismarck*. 'You are totally not flying to New York, you geek,' she announced.

'Airhead,' he replied.

'Nerd,' she said, continuing the litany.

'Flake.'

'Gelhead.'

'Retard.'

'Hodad.'

'That's a new one,' he said. 'What is it?'

They were both laughing, the way they did on the Courts or at Red's.

'Don't slouch; stand up straight,' she demanded, like a schoolteacher warning a little boy to put away his modelling clay.

Automatically he obeyed. 'What's a hodad?' he said, repeating his diversionary question.

'A way-out, lame retard, which is exactly what you are. You totally have to come home and provide me with little brothers.'

'Plural?'

'Moms has lots of childbearing years left. And besides, there are twins in our family.'

'I don't want to mess up anyone's life any more than I already have.'

I'm winning, he thought to himself. I'm facing her down. My emotions are still under control.

He barely heard the rest of her words, so fascinated was he by the colour of her hair, the dancing fire in her eyes, the glittering white rows of her teeth and her superlative gestures as she pointed first at the floor and then out of the windows of O'Hare to the general direction of the city of Chicago as she told what he *had* to do.

'It won't work, MN.' He pleaded his case, gesturing like the merchant who used to sell black-market goods in the commune. 'I've been dead too long. I can't come back to life, not that kind of life, anyway, I've tried – I really did try. You and Irene and everybody will be better off if I just slip quietly out of your life.'

The green fire in her eyes flared up as if someone had thrown gasoline on it. Her jaw muscles turned as hard as the cement of the airport walls.

She's going to lay down her high card now. What will it be?

He saw it coming. Just as long ago, at the crack of a bat, he had been able to see a line drive headed for deep left centre when he was playing the third-base line. He would begin to run as soon as the ball left the bat, knowing he would not be able to get there in time to catch it.

Oh, yes, he saw it coming and knew that his destiny was written on it.

'Daniel Xavier Farrell,' she began solemnly. 'Father . . .' Her voice wavered and tears formed in the bog fire. 'It's time you grew up and totally acted like an adult. You're magic, just like Moms says. She needs a magic husband and I need a magic . . .' Again the quivering lip and now the first tears spilling out of the swamp. 'A magic daddy.'

Done. Finished. Forever. The wandering days are over, boyo.

He linked arms with his Easter/Christmas mother/child and began to walk with her to the escalator, which would lead eventually to the parking lot of O'Hare International Airport and the rest of his life.

'Tell me about it.'

Daniel

Daniel and Irene stood toward the back of St Praxides church. Monsignor John Farrell had presided over the first half of the Easter Vigil liturgy, lighting the Easter fire, singing of Adam's happy fall, plunging the candle into life-giving water. Now the church was dimly lit, and the smell of extinguished candles and incense teased the nostrils with the memory of the dramatic blessing of the waters and renewal of baptismal promises.

All the Farrells had been reborn, one way or another.

John and Roger would need help. Noele had given him his marching orders on that subject during the drive home from O'Hare in the redoubtable Flame. They would have to wait till tomorrow. There was a greater challenge facing him before then.

He and Irene were still drifting in primal chaos, with little idea what the next step in their lives would be. It had not gone well that afternoon. He'd begun by unwisely saying that he had returned because Noele wanted little brothers.

Irene doubtless wanted little brothers for her too. But that was not a good line with which to start. They replayed their argument from the early morning hours, pouring out the anger and the frustration, the hurt and the pain, the betrayal and the disappointment of the last two decades.

Not even their hands had touched.

And then, exhausted by their fury, they sat silently staring at one another, looking for new ways to misunderstand
and injure.

'After three hours of shouting we're still in the same
room,' he said wearily.

And through the argument his desire for her had
increased. Fire yearning for water.

Irene was hunched over, her eyes fixed on the carpet.

She looked up and smiled wanly.

'We'll always be in the same room, Danny. From now on.
You know that. . . .' She rose from the couch. 'I'll make you
a cheese omelette. Then we'd better go to St Prax's for the
Easter Vigil. Noele will be furious if we're not there.'

'Woman of the house,' he yelled after her, 'put some ham
in my cheese omelette.'

He didn't hear her angry response exactly, since she was
already in the kitchen.

But she did serve him a cheese and ham omelette.

I should have asked for mushrooms, too.

In the brief interlude between the Liturgy of the Word (as
they called the Mass of the Catechumens these days) and
the Liturgy of the Eucharist (né Mass of the Faithful), the
folk group materialized quietly in the sanctuary, the young
women mature and self-possessed in dresses and high
heels, the young men not too awkward in suits and ties.

They were herded on tiptoe to the Easter candle by a
dazzling young woman in an apricot suit. The candle, with
1982 and the alpha and omega engraved on it, stood firm
and upright, its flame heralding the renewal of life with the
coming of spring.

A phallic symbol, if one was to take the Ace seriously.

Sure, what else was it?

I'm the candle and the water is next to me.

Champagne for breakfast every morning. Will I be bored
with it?

Not likely.

The folk group was ready, waiting their leader's signal.

He extended the tips of his fingers, searching for his
wife's fingers.

They were waiting for him.

'We're going to sing an Easter hymn about young men and young women.' Noele informed the congregation. 'It's called *O Filii et Filiae*, which is, like, Latin for teenagers. I'll sing a few of the stanzas in Latin in honour of old priests like the monsignor.' She giggled and the congregation laughed. 'And then we'll do it in English:

O filii et filiae
Rex caelestis rex Gloriae
Morte surrexit hodie
Alleluia!

Et mane prima sabbati
Ad ostium monumenti
Accesserunt discipuli
Alleluia!

Et Maria Magdalene
Et Jacobii et Salome
Venerunt corpus ungere
Alleluia!

In albis sedens Angelus
Praedixit mulieribus
In Galilaea est Dominus
Alleluia!

Discipulis astantibus
In medio stet Christus
Dicens pax vobis omnibus
Alleluia!

In hoc festo sanctissimo
Sic laus et jubilatio
Benedicamus Domino
Alleluia!

'Now everybody sing it in English,' Noele commanded the congregation.
Everyone did.

Ye sons and daughters, let us sing!
The King of heaven our glorious King,
From death today rose triumphing.
Alleluia!

That Easter Morn at break of day,
The faithful women went their way
To seek the tomb where Jesus lay
Alleluia!

An Angel clothed in white they see
Which sat and spoke unto the three
Your Lord has gone to Galilee
Alleluia!

That night the apostles met in fear
And Christ in their midst did appear
And said, My peace be with you here
Alleluia!

On this most holy day of days
To God your hearts and voices raise
In laud and jubilee and praise
Alleluia!

Personal Word

I was persuaded to add to several of my previous novels personal Afterwords in which I explained why a priest would write seemingly worldly stories.

These brief notes were supposed to prevent misinterpretation and distortion of the stories and to provide an answer to the mystified truth seeker who asked, with a puzzled frown, 'Why did you write that book?'

The Afterwords, however, turned out to be a waste of time. Those who were determined to misunderstand, misunderstood and misquoted them, just as they misquoted the books. I therefore conclude that those who for reasons of malice and/or ignorance will misinterpret this story will do so no matter how much I try to explain it.

But for those who may still be honestly confused, I suggest rereading Noele's brief homily before she leads the people of St Praxides in singing 'Lord of the Dance' and the conversation between John Farrell and Ace McNamara after that episode and finally the paragraphs at the end of Dance Nine, when Noele, in the sacred grove, sees the sun travelling down the street like a sophomore coming home from school.

If the image of Noele and the Church as correlatives, as sacraments of one another, is incomprehensible or offensive, I figuratively wave my blackthorn stick at the geeks and nerds and gelheads who react that way and say God Bless You!

REALLY!

And TOTALLY!